ICELANDIC HISTORIES & ROMANCES

For our parents and Dave

ICELANDIC HISTORIES & ROMANCES

Translated and Introduced by
RALPH O'CONNOR
Illustrated by Anne O'Connor

TEMPUS

First published 2002
Second edition with revisions 2006

Tempus Publishing Limited
The Mill, Brimscombe Port,
Stroud, Gloucestershire, GL5 2QG
www.tempus-publishing.com

British Library Cataloguing in Publication Data.
A catalogue record for this book is available from the British Library.

ISBN 0 7524 2894 2

Typesetting and origination by Tempus Publishing Limited
Printed and bound in Great Britain

Icelandic fonts designed by Carl Edlund Anderson

Contents

Preface

Readers are warned that the Introduction will spoil the story if read before the sagas. This applies in particular to the first-rate plot of *Mirmann's Saga*, with its unexpected twists and turns.

The printing of the first edition of this book was made possible by a gift to the University of Cambridge in memory of Dorothea Coke, Skjaeret, 1951. In this second edition, the texts of the translations and apparatus are largely the same as before, with a few minor revisions. Parts of the Introduction have, however, been more extensively revised to take account of the author's recent research into the concept of 'fiction' in the Middle Ages.

My translations owe much to the work done by the sagas' previous editors and translators. Some are no longer with us, but I wish to record my debt to the work of Sarah M. Anderson, Bjarni Vilhjálmsson, Terry Gunnell, Richard Harris, Jón Skaptason, Gwyn Jones, Anthony Maxwell, Phillip Pulsiano, the late Desmond Slay, Marvin Taylor and Þórhallur Vilmundarson. I also owe a particular debt to writings on Icelandic romance-sagas by Geraldine Barnes, Matthew Driscoll, Jürg Glauser, the late Hermann Pálsson, Marianne E. Kalinke, Torfi Tulinius and Gerd Wolfgang Weber.

I have received much help and kindness during the preparation of this book, and tried the patience of many. First of all, I am grateful to those long-suffering individuals, family and friends, who listened to sagas being read out and posed as trolls for the illustrations.

Any errors in this book are, of course, my own responsibility. However, for giving me their time and advice, and for help in various capacities, I would like to thank Aðalheiður Guðmundsdóttir, Anne Barton, Michael Chesnutt, Clémence O'Connor, Santanu Das, Clare Downham, Guðbjörn Sigurmundsson, Alaric Hall, Katie Hawks, Richard Kirby, James E. Knirk, Christopher Moule, Subha Mukherji, Anne O'Connor, Andy Orchard, Judy Quinn, Ragnheiður Mósesdóttir, Ian Robinson, Chris Sanders, Svanhildur Óskarsdóttir and Alistair Vining, as well as the editorial team at Tempus Publishing. I thank the staff of the Arnamagnæan Institute and Dictionary in Copenhagen for allowing me to spend an extremely stimulating three weeks there in September 2001, a trip made possible in part by a grant from Cambridge University's Scandinavian Studies Fund.

More general thanks are due to the Department of Anglo-Saxon, Norse and Celtic at Cambridge for the infectious enthusiasm and excellence of its teaching, and for maintaining a friendly, supportive and invigorating academic environment: this book grew out of interests sparked off and sustained by my teachers and friends in the Department. Special thanks, for help and support beyond the call of duty, must go to Harriet Truscott, Matthew Driscoll, Patricia Boulhosa, Paul Bibire and the late Desmond Slay. Finally, for keeping the whole project in perspective, I would like to thank the late Peggy Truscott.

Ralph O'Connor
Aberdeen
October 2005

Introduction

New worlds to the west

One of the most engrossing sub-plots in the history of mediaeval Europe must be the maritime explorations of the Norsemen in the late Iron Age, the so-called 'Viking Age'.[1] From the late eighth century onwards, new craft plied the western seas. Slender dragon-headed longships and sturdy cargo-carrying *knarrar* cruised the coasts and rivers, wreaking havoc but also bringing trade, settlers and rulers to areas as far-flung as Normandy, Dublin, Seville, Morocco, Kiev and Byzantium. The period takes its popular name from the notorious bands of Norse warriors who went *í víking* (raiding), extorting money from individuals and realms alike; but these represent only one aspect of an age characterized by large-scale migration – the last wave of the great Germanic migrations which had been changing the face of Europe since the fourth century AD. One of the most enduring achievements of this age of exploration and exploitation was the settlement of Iceland at the end of the ninth century, and the birth of that paradoxical creature, a nation without a ruler. Elsewhere in Europe, the arrival of Christianity strengthened and consolidated royal power, paving the way for feudalism; in Iceland such changes did not take place until nearly three centuries after the coming of the new faith. The old Germanic forms of government lived on and were adapted to a highly literate Christian culture. As Adam of Bremen put it in the eleventh century, 'They have no king, but only law.'[2]

No doubt the delay was partly due to Iceland's marginal position on the political map of Western Europe. Apart from a few Irish clerics (who had come seeking isolation in their own remarkably seaworthy craft), Iceland had been uninhabited when the first Norse settlers arrived, mainly from Norway, Ireland and the Hebrides: according to a much later account in Egil's Saga, 'you could shoot anything you wanted, for none of the animals were used to man and they just stood about quietly'.[3] For birds like the great auk, this was the beginning of the end. But Iceland had enjoyed a marginal existence long before humans arrived. Geologically, it is the product of tensions between two margins, straddling the Mid-Atlantic Ridge where the North American and Eurasian tectonic plates constantly strive to pull apart from each other. The resulting volcanic activity created the new island of Surtsey in 1963: massive quantities of lava erupted from the ridge on the sea bed, solidifying and lurching out of the surf. Similar forces had brought Iceland itself into being long after the last dinosaur had disappeared from the face of the earth. Along with the arctic climate, the violence of this young and unstable land has forced society to cling to the fertile margins. The interior is a wasteland of lava fields, glaciers and volcanic sand, fit only for outlaws, trolls and backpackers. The original settlers were, by dint of necessity, explorers: they had to map this virgin territory, stake out a human presence in the wilderness.

Some pushed further. That most ancient of isles, Greenland, enjoyed a mild enough climate for Icelanders to settle there late in the tenth century, though the voyage was extremely hazardous. Still further to the west, in arctic and subarctic Canada, lay the rocky wastes of *Helluland* (Slabland) and the forests of *Markland* (Forestland) which Greenlanders exploited for timber. Settlements were made further south in *Vínland* (Wineland), rich in natural resources and already inhabited by native Americans. The *Vínland* settlement did not last long, and the American lands soon passed into the realms of fantasy. The increasingly neglected Greenlanders lasted, their numbers steadily dwindling, until the fifteenth century, when they fell victim to the encroachment of drift ice and 'Americans' (i.e. the Inuit).[4]

By the thirteenth century the viking age itself had vanished: its distinctive lineaments had dissolved in the more politically-centralized Christian Europe of the new millennium. Bands of oath-bound thugs no longer crossed the North Atlantic in search of fame and fortune. The autonomous tribal and regional confederations which characterized early Germanic society were coalescing into larger and fewer administrative units, controlled by increasingly powerful individuals: in the mid-thirteenth century, even Iceland acknowledged a king. New lands were no longer sought out and exploited; the last wave of the Germanic migrations was over.

Exploring the past

Yet a different kind of exploration was already under way. For the educated Icelander, the past itself was a foreign country – or rather, several countries – whose dimensions, resources and curiosities were worth exploring, exploiting and recreating in a new genre of narrative literature known as the saga. This term needs defining: it is sometimes misunderstood to mean epic poetry, or used to mean a very long and often tedious series of events ('our gas bill saga'). In Icelandic, *saga* simply means 'story, narrative'; but in terms of mediaeval literary criticism, it is a form of historical narrative prose, in the vernacular rather than in Latin, and often incorporating passages of poetry. Sagas claimed – at least on one level – to record events which actually took place in the past.

This form developed on the Atlantic seaboard of mediaeval Europe, above all in Ireland (from *c*.700) and Iceland (from *c*.1150).[5] On each island the saga was the result of the fusion of (and tensions between) two cultures: native traditions of storytelling and history-recording, and the foreign tools of Latin literacy which had come with Christianity in the fifth and eleventh centuries respectively. The native traditions in each case were substantially different, giving Irish and Icelandic sagas their own distinct generic features; but both traditions were vigorous, since these far-flung Atlantic societies had never come under the homogenizing influence of Roman culture. The term 'saga', by the way, carries no necessary implication of length. Most are about the length of a short story, while some are only a few pages long; in terms of bulk, even the giants among them fall far short of the average Dickens novel or the latest J.K. Rowling. All the sagas included in this volume were written during the high point of mediaeval saga-writing, between the late thirteenth and mid-sixteenth centuries.

History-writing, however, did not begin with the sagas. The earliest surviving examples of Icelandic secular scholarship date from the twelfth century, and these writings are exceptionally mature and original. European models evidently provided a springboard, rather than a template, for a distinctively Icelandic practice of history-writing. Ari hinn fróði's *Book of Icelanders* (*Íslendingabók*, *c*.1122-33) is – if we can trust its seventeenth-century copyist – the oldest example of narrative prose in a Scandinavian language. It is a concise constitutional history of Iceland, and Ari is also said to have written an early version of the *Book of Settlements* (*Landnámabók*), a geographically-organized catalogue of genealogies of Icelandic settlers, heavily annotated with saga-like anecdotes and skaldic verses. It is tempting to see these anecdotes as the germs from which sagas about Icelandic settlers sprouted, but since the *Book of Settlements* only survives in much later reworkings, these particular anecdotes may well come from sagas rather than the other way around. Nevertheless, genealogy is an ancient and universal form of narrative organization, and the practice of hanging anecdotes from family trees would have helped these uprooted settlers in a new world to establish anew their cultural identity. Many such stories will have derived from oral tradition, passed down from the settlement period or later.[6]

A word should be said about the two major kinds of verse composed and preserved orally in viking-age Scandinavia: eddic and skaldic. Both were important repositories of historical lore, but neither was necessarily 'narrative'. Eddic 'lays', including the famous collection known as the Elder Edda (or Poetic Edda), represent a Scandinavian development of early Germanic heroic poetry. These 'lays' tell of the Norse gods and legendary heroes, relating their speeches in dramatic or didactic forms: they rarely tell the actual 'story' in which the encounter or soliloquy is set, since the story would already be known to the audience. When these lays came to be written down in or before the thirteenth century, the scribes added speech-prefixes ('Sigurd said .... Gudrun said ...') and prose paragraphs explaining the story. Several sagas about legendary heroes may have originated from kernels of this kind, with the verse remaining to provide dramatic focus. It later became a literary convention to have 'legendary' saga characters declaim eddic verse rather than skaldic when such a declamation was in order, as in *The Saga of Hjalmther and Olvir* (*Hjálmþés saga ok Ölvis*). An example is given in the Note on the Translations below (p.85).

Skaldic verse was a uniquely West Norse phenomenon: its affinities are more with Irish syllabic verse than with Germanic epic poetry. Rather than telling of legendary deeds and wisdom, these intricate eight-line stanzas usually tell of events in the viking age itself. They were allegedly either composed 'on the spot' to commemorate some event such as a battle or declaimed in the presence of the poet's patron (often a king). The latter practice lasted from the ninth century to the thirteenth, though after that skaldic verses continued to be composed in imitation of the 'genuine' article, in sagas set in that period. The verse given as an example in the Note on the Translations below (p.84) may well be one such later production. Icelandic writers considered this kind of verse to be a valuable historical source for the events it commemorates. But – as you can see if you turn to the example on p.84 – the art of skaldic poetry is musical and architectural rather than narrative. Its artistry lies in the densely-woven counterpoint of elaborate, often mythological, kennings for conventional objects such as 'ship' ('breeze-steed'). When the verse's content is unravelled from its form, the meaning is rarely any more historically specific than 'The man killed the other man' or 'The king sailed off'. So, when these haunting and often impenetrable verses came to be written down, whether singly or in long poems, the writer had to explain the event commemorated in a clear prose narrative, preserving the verse both as authentication and (in the sagas) as a dramatic moment at which the speaker's own emotions are suddenly laid bare. This double function can be seen in Helga's verses in *The Saga of Bard the Snowfell God* (*Bárðar saga Snjófellsáss*).[7] So, while we can never be sure, it is possible that several saga episodes originally sprang from the need to explain the stories behind these two kinds of poems.

The first sagas were apparently composed in the second half of the twelfth century: Icelandic (and Latin) histories of certain Norwegian kings, as well as some saints' lives (*heilagra manna sögur*). It is thought that the first sagas about tenth-century Icelanders, Orcadians, Faroe Islanders and Greenlanders were written in the late twelfth or early thirteenth century. Sagas soon constituted a branch of learning in their own right, developing the narrative element implicit in regnal lists and genealogies, and imposing literary forms on folktales. Like the earlier scholarship, sagas drew strength from Continental history-writing, but went very much their own way, particularly when it came to shaping and dramatizing their stories. Arguments have long raged over the relative importance of oral and literary sources to saga art, but one thing is certain: the sagas derive from a creative interplay between the two, and this applies as much to sagas composed in the nineteenth century as to those from the twelfth. Both kinds of information were used in differing proportions by different writers.

It is a truism that emigrants tend to guard their cultural traditions more jealously than those back at home. At any rate, most of the surviving literary sources for Norse mythology and legendary history were written by Icelanders, and other Scandinavian writers leaned heavily on their work. Among others the thirteenth-century Danish historian Saxo Grammaticus praised the Icelanders' unusual resourcefulness in gathering information and composing narratives about the past, and acknowledged that much of the material in his voluminous *History of the Danes* (*Gesta Danorum*) came from Icelandic sources.[8] So, whether we are dealing with oral or literary accounts of Icelandic settlers or Norse kings and heroes, it is clear that by the end of the twelfth century, narratives about the past were common currency in Iceland.

The saga vogue
By the end of the thirteenth century, when Iceland was safely under the Norwegian crown, the saga had acquired momentum as an independent branch of learning, now wholly vernacular and with its own generic conventions. Saga-authors drew freely on their total literary heritage, native and European. The great and the good in almost every sphere could become the subjects of sagas, original or translated: Biblical characters (e.g. Solomon) and saints (Mary of Egypt), kings (Clovis) and emperors (Alexios Komnenos), otherworldly beings (the Archangel Michael) and legendary heroes and heroines (the Volsung dynasty), native and foreign bishops (Gudmund the Good, Thomas à Becket), knights (of the Round Table) and of course the Scandinavian farmer-aristocracy, old and new. (Even the humble farm-worker Star-Oddi is one of the 'great' in being a famous scholar.) Taken as a whole, the sagas cover a vast

geographical range. Many Icelanders travelled widely as vikings, followers of foreign kings, or clerics in search of an education, and saga-writers reached out to Scandinavia, southern Europe, North America, Russia and the Holy Land. They peopled in their imaginations the more distant realms of Africa, India, Central Asia, Saracen-Land (*Serkland*), Blackland (*Bláland*), and the otherworldly regions of Giantland (*Risaland, Jötunheim*) in the Arctic, White Men's Land (*Hvítramannaland*) out beyond Ireland and the Land of the Ever-Living (*Ódáinsakr*) out beyond 'Uttermost India'. The real-life explorations made during the viking age were as nothing to their literary counterparts.

The identities of the saga-authors are rarely known; all the known authors were men, though the names of female poets and story-tellers survive. Some scholars have suggested female authorship for sagas which give prominence and narrative sympathy to their female characters, notably *The Laxdalers' Saga* (*Laxdæla saga*),[9] but the case remains unproven. Insight into the world of the opposite sex is not unheard-of for good writers, including mediaeval ones: *Troilus and Criseyde* was not written by a woman. Conversely, there is nothing in the psychologically-probing, male-centred narrative of *Egil's Saga* which specifically precludes female authorship. In any case, my use of the male pronoun to refer to saga-authors reflects convenience rather than conviction. These debates about the authors' identities and genders are not as important as they might seem to a modern reader: sagas differ from modern narrative forms in that they represent more the cumulative products of communities than the personal outpourings of individuals. They incorporate a multiplicity of male and female narrative voices, not merely that of the final 'author'.

The purpose of these narratives was that of much mediaeval European secular literature: to edify and to entertain their audiences, whether high-born or humble, native or foreign. History's chief function in the Middle Ages was to present moral examples for the instruction of posterity, but the saga-author also had to engage his listeners' attention. Almost all sagas were based, wholly or partly, on older material, both oral and written, belonging to a wide variety of oral and literary genres from Scandinavia and further south. These sources were employed with varying degrees of freedom. Epics, lays, skaldic stanzas, riddles, proverbs, folktales, genealogies, learned treatises, Classical histories, chronicles, the Bible, homilies (a form of sermon), *exempla* (moral fables), *fabliaux* (immoral fables), saints' lives, romances – all were grist to the saga-authors' mill. The tiny population of this inhospitable island (rarely more than 50,000 at any one time) displayed a literary fecundity that still beggars belief.

In itself, however, this surge of interest in historical writing was not unique to Icelanders. Iceland was a relative latecomer to that European-wide revival of learning, the so-called 'Twelfth-Century Renaissance' which extended into the thirteenth, fourteenth and fifteenth centuries and eventually led into the 'Renaissance' proper.[10] Further south, above all in France, the revival of learning was not confined to historical works in prose; it also spawned a new species of courtly narrative poem, the verse romance. In this kind of narrative, which often centred on the court of King Arthur, historical truth was pushed into the background: what was important here was the *sens* (inner meaning) produced by the author's skilful and self-conscious arrangement of his material. For this reason, romances – the direct ancestors of the novel – are usually regarded as a species of 'mediaeval fiction' as opposed to 'history'.[11]

We need to remember, however, that words like 'history' and 'fiction' have not always meant the same things. The mediaeval 'historian' was typically granted far more creative latitude than we would see fit today, resulting in writing we might prefer to label as 'fictional'. But in the Middle Ages, the concept of 'fiction' as we understand it occupied a very precarious position in moral terms, uncomfortably close to the notion of 'telling a lie'.[12] Romance-authors, even if they did make up their material, never admitted as much, but claimed to be using earlier, unnamed legends or 'accounts': in this sense they follow the methods of 'historians'. On the other hand, the stories they tell are usually set in a timeless and distinctly unrealistic fantasy-world. And even if 'fiction' may not be quite the right word, the romance form – by drawing attention so openly and explicitly to the author's personal role in creating the story's meaning – represented a serious step away from 'history' and towards 'fiction' as we know it.

Verse romances were soon entertaining the nobility of neighbouring kingdoms in England and Germany. In time, they were also written in prose, which blurred their boundaries with history-writing considerably; later still, French and Occitan romance-authors laid the foundations of the modern novel by subjecting romance conventions to outright parody.[13] Finally, in Cervantes's trail-blazing *Don Quixote* (1605-15), the realms of fact and fantasy – the historically-specific world of early modern Spain and the timeless world of chivalry – collided, with results that are at once hilarious and touching. Other novelists used techniques for writing about 'the real world' (letter-writing, eyewitness accounts) within a conventional romance framework. In this sense, novels – which are still called *romans* in French – blended romance with history.

As the title of this book suggests, something similar might be said of certain Icelandic sagas. In fact, most sagas composed after the mid-thirteenth century can be seen as simultaneously histories and romances – one element may predominate, but the other is rarely absent. Yet sagas arrived at this blend by a completely different route to that of the modern novel, and it is important to understand this before we read them – and certainly before we label them 'novels before their time'.

ICELANDIC SAGAS: HISTORIES OR ROMANCES?

Saga versus romance

The business of the saga-author was very different from that of a novelist, despite intriguing similarities between some of their products. Novels have their ultimate roots in the freely-constructed stories of romances and the invented case-studies of *exempla*; sagas have theirs in the dominant forms of history composition (oral and literary) in early Christian Iceland, namely folktales, genealogical lore and learned history-writing. Romance did influence saga-writing, but it never severed the saga from its roots: saga-authors experimented with the idea of prose fiction, as we shall see, but they did not overtly embrace it until they took up novel-writing in the eighteenth century. Three factors in particular differentiate the saga from the romance.

First, as we have just seen, many romances engage in a prolonged flirtation with fiction. The typical saga, on the other hand, *purports* to tell a true story, one that has (or might have) been told or written before, now re-edited and re-arranged for a new purpose, but not created. In Iceland, prose was the vehicle of factual report. Even the most fanciful of sagas were written in the light of this guiding historical principle. Like romance-authors, no saga-author admits to having 'lied' – made up a story – even where he almost certainly has; but, in sharp contrast to some romance-authors, saga-authors do not even admit to having tinkered with the story. This point is borne out by the changes which French verse romances underwent when translated into Icelandic prose. The process entailed a shift in genre as much as in language and style: the translator of Chrétien de Troyes's *Yvain* prefixes to the main story a summary of King Arthur's reign and his relative importance on the European cultural map, carefully anchoring the story of Yvain within a historical framework.[14] Other translators, schooled in the principle that history required geneal-ogy, felt bound to invent descendants for heroes who were childless in the French source. Even those sagas which experimented most self-consciously with romance techniques and fictionality, such as the highly entertaining *Ganger-Hrolf's Saga* (*Göngu-Hrólfs saga*, discussed below), resist easy categorization by interspersing nuggets of remarkably accurate geographical information within the unlikely story:

> England is considered to be the most productive country in Western Europe because all kinds of metal are cast there, and wheat and grapes grow there, and you can get every kind of cereal there. Also, more clothes are made and varieties of textiles woven there than in other places. London is its principal town, and then Canterbury; also there is Scarborough and Hastings .... [15]

And so on, for a whole page. This particular passage follows an extravagant and romantic description of the final triple wedding feast, and in a no less extravagant way it anchors the narrative to more safely 'factual' realms as it nears its end.

Second, the Icelanders had no need for (or understanding of) the complex philosophical-aesthetic apparatus of chivalry, courtly love and mysticism within which early romances operated. In the thirteenth century, French and Anglo-Norman romances were apparently translated for the self-consciously 'Europhile' royal court of Norway, but the main purpose seems to have been entertainment rather than chivalric education. [16] Even though the Icelandic aristocracy also liked to cultivate the trappings of knighthood (particularly after Iceland had become a Norwegian dependency), chivalric romances were valued in Iceland primarily for the stories they told. *Perceval*, Chrétien's richly symbolic and unfinished fable of spiritual awakening and the vanity of worldly heroism, was 'translated' (i.e. drastically cut) into an action-packed story of yet another burly knight from olden times. The Norse translator supplies an ending where Chrétien breaks off, completely ignoring the spiritual significance of the Grail and leaving the Fisher King unhealed, and in its place providing Perceval with a wife and a realm – a perfect resolution in the standard adventure-saga manner.[17] These stories, pruned of their foreign ideological trappings and transformed into 'history' to entertain and edify their northern audiences, might persuade us novel-readers that the originals have been somehow debased; but the process of translation across a cultural divide necessarily entails losing the original meaning and substituting a new one.

Third and most importantly, saga-authors were not 'authors' in the modern sense. The modern novelist (or, for that matter, historian) is an identifiable person uniquely responsible for the text: his or her name is either emblazoned on the front cover or conspicuous by its absence, and this author often maintains an ironic distance between himself or herself and the novel's narrator – a practice familiar from Chaucer's *Canterbury Tales* and a host of other mediaeval romances. In mediaeval Iceland, such authorial self-consciousness was largely restricted to poetry. Saga-authors saw themselves as the (usually) nameless conduits of a narrative tradition, however much freedom they may have exercised in their treatment of their material; and saga-author and third-person saga-narrator almost always seem identical. Even if a saga-author demonstrably invented the story, he never saw it as his personal property like a poem (or a novel). This attitude held out for a long time: the nineteenth-century Icelander Jón Hjaltalín composed several sagas, but never claimed them for his own.[18]

The difference between created poem and transmitted saga emerges in the terminology. A poem was *ort* ('wrought') from the raw material of language and metaphor, like an intricate clasp wrought from pure silver; a saga consisted of prefabricated narratives put together (*samsett*) and shaped anew (*samið*). Saga texts were rarely stable. Old stories and new were reworked and rewritten for new audiences, in a manuscript tradition that stretched right into the twentieth century – by which time saga-authors were using printed editions as well as earlier manuscripts as the bases for their retellings. Many sagas exist in what are known today as different 'recensions', where the story remains constant but the texts are different enough to warrant separate literary consideration. But the concept of recensions would have meant little to the saga–authors themselves, for whom every single text of a saga was a separate scribal 'performance'.[19] Nevertheless, some writers were more creative than others, and there were several levels of composition open to each new writer.

Most commonly, the writer might just 'edit' the narrative slightly – altering the wording here and there, adding or removing certain details, rearranging chapter divisions and incorporating the saga into a new manuscript alongside different sagas: such has been the case with the mediaeval texts of *Bard the Snowfell God*. This raises a serious question for the modern editor or translator, as it has done for the translations in this book. Should one attempt to assume a 'mediaeval' attitude towards these manuscript texts, treating each one separately – or may one treat some, or all, texts as close enough to each other to qualify (anachronistically) as a single 'recension'? The first option sounds superficially more 'true' to the original, but mediaeval attitudes cannot be assumed so lightly: a single scribal performance is *not* the same as a literary 'work'. Most modern editors have held to the other view in varying degrees, either striving for completeness or attempting to reconstruct a hypothetical 'original' text (these methodological issues are still hotly debated). In this book I have attempted to steer a middle course: I have followed a single manuscript text for each saga, but if it is fragmentary (as with the mediaeval texts of *Bard the Snowfell God* and *Mirmann's Saga*) I have supplied the missing parts with other texts judged by modern editors to belong to the same recension – always taking care to follow only one manuscript text at a time, rather than confusing matters by mixing and matching all the texts in question. This is not simply a matter of scholarly pedantry. Since the manuscripts (and sagas) involved span four centuries of literary activity, from the High Middle Ages to the Enlightenment, it seems important that the general reader should be aware of which manuscript's account he or she is 'looking at'.

To return to the saga-author: 'editorial' practice might extend to chopping a saga in two, as with one recension of *Bard the Snowfell God* in the seventeenth century. Writers might weld two narratives together or incorporate one into another, thus creating a new saga or making an old one longer: at the end of the fourteenth century, the compiler of the enormous *Book of Flatey* (*Flateyjarbók*) inserted *The Tale of Thorstein Shiver* (*Þorsteins þáttr skelks*) into his recension of *The Saga of King Olaf Tryggvason* (*Óláfs saga Tryggvasonar*) – itself already swollen by extra narratives like *Thidrandi's Tale* (*Þiðranda þáttr ok Þórhalls*), inserted by earlier compilers. A saga could be written without apparent reference to the form of any earlier recension, telling the same story but in different words: in the fourteenth and fifteenth centuries, several independent recensions of *Mirmann's Saga* were circulating. In such cases it is always possible that there was a common 'original version', but this is by no means certain (nor does it really matter).

It is vital for the reader to be aware of these compositional techniques in order to read and appreciate the sagas as literature. All these processes can be seen as 'authorial' in differing degrees, but to read a saga as if it were a novel is to treat the saga-author as if he had invented the whole thing, and to ignore the narrative strata beneath (and sometimes breaking) the surface of almost all surviving sagas. While it is justifiable from a modern perspective to direct most of our attention towards the 'saga-author' responsible for producing the recension at hand, a saga is the cumulative product of several creative minds across time. This is especially true of those sagas most often compared to novels. 'Realistic' masterpieces such as *The Saga of the Burning of Njal* (*Brennu-Njáls saga*) have often been celebrated as 'precursors of the novel', whose hard-headed realism and fresh, terse style allegedly set them apart from the main currents of mediaeval European narrative.[20] Part of the purpose of this book is to show by example that Icelandic sagas do not (and did not) have to be 'realistic' to be worth reading, and also that this much-loved freshness of style may be found in many a shamelessly unrealistic saga. And for all the 'novelistic' qualities of parts of *The Burning of Njal*, several important passages were clearly not composed in the saga-author's own head, but inserted by him from elsewhere (sometimes with alterations) – particularly at moments of crucial importance in the unfolding of the more otherworldly aspects of the drama. The skaldic verse which Gunnar sings in his grave, the lurid yet oddly detached account of the Battle of Clontarf, and the chant of the 'Fatal Sisters' – all these passages represent or contain earlier material incorporated whole-sale into the larger design by the saga-author, who has deliberately not resolved the minor inconsistencies of plot, mode and style they create.[21] This resembles the practice of a historian, quoting other sources to shed light on the main narrative. Yet the author of *The Burning of Njal* was more than a chronicler. These passages are made to jut out from the smooth surface of the saga, interrupting the flow of historical events and casting a weird, otherworldly light on the surrounding human drama to illuminate the troubled relationship between men and god(s). A 'novelistic' reading of this saga might condemn these discordances as momentary lapses of the author's taste and judgement, as also with similar instances in *Bard the Snowfell God*; but an understanding of the cumulative nature of saga art enables such passages to deepen the modern reader's experience of these unfamiliar, difficult masterpieces.

Finally, some of the people we call 'authors' of sagas may never have put quill to vellum at all. The great thirteenth-century chieftain Snorri Sturluson is the most famous of these, being the alleged 'author' of several sagas. He may indeed have physically written (or compiled and reworked) his recension of *Saint Olaf's Saga* (*Óláfs saga helga*), which would make him the narrator as well as the author; but he may have functioned simply as commissioner and overseer – a general editor – of a team of scholars. Several possibilities are implicit in his nephew's report concerning 'saga-books which Snorri had put together'.[22] To us, saga-authorship seems a maddeningly inclusive practice, dissolving the modern distinctions between commissioners, authors, editors, publishers and printers: the gulf between saga and novel is wide indeed.

The entertainment factor

Nevertheless, the novel's great ancestor – Continental romance – exerted a powerful influence on Icelandic narrative. Some scholars have cordoned off a large group of blatantly fictitious sagas and labelled them 'romances'. These sagas tell of events distant in time or in space (or both), and are often divided rather misleadingly into 'knights' sagas' (*riddarasögur*) and 'legendary sagas' (*fornaldarsögur*). *Hjalmther and Olvir* and *Mirmann's Saga* belong to this large group, as does the dream-narrative in *Star-Oddi's Dream* (*Stjörnu-Odda draumr*). Since sagas blend history and fiction, attempts to cordon off the one from the other are unsatisfactory – as witness *Bard the Snowfell God*, which is usually made to sit with its tail-end behind the cordon. But having glanced at some of the differences between sagas and romances, we must now examine one vital affinity between them: the aim to entertain.

Both romances and sagas reflect, in their different ways, an emancipation of written 'story' in Continental Europe from the twelfth century onwards. Formerly condemned by clerics as the deceptions of demons, secular stories came to be enjoyed more and more for their own sake.[23] The leisured classes – and a nascent bourgeoisie – were rapidly growing in France and neighbouring lands, and with them grew a demand for secular narrative to pass the time: romance-writing was one result. Since France set the cultural trends in high mediaeval Europe, their less wealthy neighbours also turned to writing down non-allegorical, entertaining narratives. Iceland

and Ireland already had traditions of secular storytelling, and in both islands saga-writing drew on this oral heritage as well as the new enthusiasm for writing such stories down for entertainment. As St Patrick's guardian angels reassure him in the twelfth-century Irish *Colloquy of the Ancients* (*Acallam na Senórach*), it is not sinful but delightful to hear tales about the pagan past, and to 'have these stories written down ... in refined language, so that the hearing of them will provide entertainment for the lords and commons of later times.'[24] Sagas might have moral or political lessons to teach, but a bored audience was unlikely to pay much attention.

The saga-writing tradition lasted in Iceland up to the early twentieth century, with many of its essential characteristics unchanged. Saga-entertainment also seems to have been a fairly continuous tradition. No detailed mediaeval references to saga-entertainment on Icelandic farms survive, but the information we do have tends to agree with the more detailed modern accounts. Silent reading is rarely referred to, but the (probably) mediaeval *Fljotsdalers' Saga* (*Fljótsdæla saga*) mentions an old man who sits up till dawn one night 'reading an ancient saga'.[25] More usually we hear of sagas being read aloud from manuscripts or from memory. Guests, like the one in *Star-Oddi's Dream*, were expected to amuse themselves and their hosts by telling sagas. Accounts from the eighteenth and nineteenth centuries reveal that in that period sagas were copied and read from manuscripts during the long, dark and tedious winter months. The British traveller Ebenezer Henderson, who visited Iceland in 1814-15, observed that some Icelanders earned a living during the winter as 'itinerating historians ... staying at different farms till they have exhausted their stock of literary knowledge'.[26] This was the time when trouble-free entertainment (*skemmtun*, '[time]-shortening') was most needed: there were plenty of other ways in which the young might choose to amuse themselves. According to the mediaeval author of *The Saga of Sigurd the Silent* (*Sigurðar saga þögla*), 'as long as people are enjoying the entertainment, they will not think of other, sinful things'.[27] Saga-entertainment could also be intellectually stimulating. Henderson comments:

> the [saga-]reader is frequently interrupted, either by the head, or by some of the more intelligent members of the family, who make remarks on various parts of the story, and propose questions ....[28]

One wonders whether the heckling was equally polite when foreign guests were not present, or indeed in the Middle Ages. Several mediaeval saga-narrators ask their audiences not to be too rowdy and not to criticize their story for seeming improbable, but to sit quietly and just listen.

One saga could serve several purposes, entertaining Norwegian monarch and Icelandic farmer alike, as a much-quoted passage from the thirteenth-century *Saga of Thorgils and Haflidi* (*Þorgils saga ok Haflíða*) suggests. The scene is a wedding feast in western Iceland in 1119:

> Hrolf from Skalmarnes told a story about Hrongvid the viking ... and the mound-breaking of Thrain the berserk and Hromund Gripsson, with many verses in it. This story was used to entertain King Sverrir and he declared that such lie-stories (*lygisögur*) were most amusing; men can, however, trace their genealogies to Hromund Gripsson. Hrolf himself had put this story together. Ingimund the priest told the story of Orm the Poet of Barra, including many verses and with a good *flokkr*, which Ingimund had made, at the end of the story. Nevertheless, many learned men regard this story as true.[29]

But this passage is more than a mere report of the wedding entertainments. Reading between the lines, we can glimpse some of the difficulties posed by the notion of narrative 'fiction' to this thirteenth-century Icelandic saga-author. He introduces his account by observing that many people 'are blind to the truth, and think what is fibbed to be true and what is true to be lied', yet the teasing comment attributed to Sverrir (himself a notorious self-inventor) suggests that the entertainment-value of fiction was not unknown at this time. But it is also clear that old habits died hard: for 'some people', the saga had a historical and genealogical function as well. Characteristically, the narrator does not tell us who he agrees with, Sverrir or the supposed descendants of Hromund: both audiences are simply presented responding to the saga in their own way. As for Ingimund, the narrator seems to wonder at 'learned men' thinking his saga of Orm a true story when many of the verses – its authentication – had been made up by Ingimund himself: his capacity for showing off is emphasized earlier in the chapter. But the matter is left deliberately obscure: the narrator distances himself from the entire saga-telling episode, preventing us from coming to a firm conclusion about the truth-value of what lies within.

Truth and fiction

This ambiguous attitude towards fiction was part and parcel of the saga-writing tradition. Nevertheless, saga-authors happily adapted and arranged their 'true' stories in such a way as to emphasize one character rather than another, or to highlight a moral theme or political concern. Such was the way in which historians worked throughout mediaeval Europe.[30] Indeed, many sagas seem to work on the principle that if a historical event could have happened in such a way as suited their own purposes, then it did. The compositional process, 'putting a saga together', merged seamlessly into what we would call outright invention, most obviously in those sagas whose purpose seems to have been pure entertainment. But, even at their most fanciful, sagas retained their roots in history-writing and communal tradition: outright 'lying' was unacceptable in prose, and to save face the saga-authors had to present their narratives as historically plausible. Mediaeval criteria for plausibility were very different to our own, and we might think saga audiences credulous;

in their own terms, however, they were perfectly capable of smelling a rat. Many sagas are manifestly implausible, dealing in extravagant otherworldly phenomena, unheard-of feats of swordsmanship and journeys across the known world being made in next to no time, and their authors resorted to elaborate devices to defend their stories from heckling sceptics.

Appeals could be made to known authorities – the extravagantly fictitious *Saga of William Purse* (*Vilhjálms saga sjóðs*) was apparently 'copied off a stone wall in Babylon the Great, and Master Homer [Humerus] put it together'[31] – or simply to an unnamed 'Master' to whom, it is implied, all complaints should be addressed. The reliability of oral tradition (the alleged source of many sagas set in Scandinavia) could be upheld. The improbable strength of the hero could be explained by the well-known fact that some men living just after the Flood were as large as giants, and have been degenerating ever since; so in former times, a greater man would have been perfectly able to kill many smaller men with a single swordstroke. The narrator might tactically attack his critics for their narrow-minded view of the bounds of possibility, or he might declare that nothing is impossible for God, or 'for the man whom fortune favours'. We are moving into the realm of last-ditch defences here. Several saga-narrators admit that their story has probably been exaggerated and corrupted during the process of transmission, but that such things do not matter, since something as trivial as entertainment is not worth fussing about. One recension of *Ganger-Hrolf's Saga* (*Göngu-Hrólfs saga*) begins with the warning that 'few things as unimportant as this are done perfectly', and ends by remarking that 'old poems and narratives have been offered more for transitory cheer than for eternal faith.'[32]

In this way the conservatism of the saga-writing tradition – dictating that a saga ought to tell a true story – forced more adventurous authors to look back with a critical eye on that tradition to see how to fit their new saga into it. In effect, they were forced to practise a form of literary criticism; so it is hardly surprising that a new and unfamiliar (and often cheeky) narratorial self-consciousness begins to emerge in the more fanciful sagas.[33] This self-conscious-ness appears most obviously where the narrator steps in to defend his saga from the unwelcome heckler by casting him as a pedantic spoilsport. At the end of *The Saga of Hrolf Gautreksson* (*Hrólfs saga Gautrekssonar*), the narrator enlarges on the damage that could be done by an enormous weapon to small men, ending as follows:

> everything in its way would be destroyed, even if the weapon failed to bite. It seems to me most fitting for someone to find fault [with the story] only if he is capable of improving on it; but whether it is true or not, may he enjoy it who can, and may the others find something more enjoyable to do.

> And here we end the saga of King Hrolf Gautreksson.[34]

The rational defence peters out, and the audience is simply invited to take it or leave it. Here the communal voice of the saga, which was apparently drawn from the 'memories' of 'learned people' rather than invented by the saga-author, gives way to the intrusion of the defensive first-person narrator ('it seems to me'), before returning abruptly to the communal 'we' to end the saga in the proper fashion. There is a strange irony in this, quite possibly deliberate. At the very point where the author is trying his hardest to dissociate the saga from pure fiction, a romance-like authorial persona emerges most distinctly.

Though the art of the saga-author is far less 'objective' than is often claimed, saga-authors were more reluctant to interrupt their own narratives with first-person commentary than other historians or romance-writers, unless the saga had a religious theme – in such cases the narration of a historical event is often interrupted by the narrator explaining its religious significance to his audience (as at the end of *Thidrandi's Tale*), reflecting the generic tug of the homily. In secular sagas such clear interruptions tend to suggest more the influence of Continental romance, and they are usually confined to the beginning or the end, allowing the main body of the saga to remain uninterrupted. The authorial *envoi* became something of a characteristic of the more improbable sagas, sometimes providing an excuse for the narrative equivalent of a two-fingered salute. *The Saga of Vilmund the Outsider* (*Vilmundar saga viðutan*) ends with its bumpkin hero safely ensconced within the aristocracy, after which the author puts his Icelandic audience in the position (literally) of the saga's humbler folk, the lusty kitchen-wench Oskubuska and her trollish lover:

> And so we end the saga of Vilmund the Outsider, with this final word from the writer: that he who read it out, and those who listened to it – and all those who are not so rich that they have to pay tax to our king – are to kiss Oskubuska's arse. Take for yourselves everything that went on when Kol Hump mounted her, and have whatever friendship you get from her. Goodbye.[35]

But even such a bold saga-author as this does not step out of his narrative until the end. The narrator of one version of *Ganger-Hrolf's Saga* had no such qualms. Immediately after one particularly improbable episode, in which a dwarf magically sticks the hero's severed feet back on, this narrator squares up to his audience:

> Now even if such things seem unbelievable to some people, everyone still has to report what he has seen or heard. It is also difficult to contradict what earlier learned folk have put together [*samsett*] .... There have also been some sages who said a great deal about some matters figuratively, such as Master Gautier in *Alexander's Saga* and the poet Homer in *The Trojans' Saga* .... No-one need put any more faith in such things than that – but let him enjoy it while he listens.[36]

The sagas mentioned here had been translated into Icelandic from Latin during the thirteenth century, and the author of this version of *Ganger-Hrolf* may have meant to overawe his audience with a display of learning. Perhaps his tongue was in his cheek: it is often suggested that such sudden interruptions may have functioned as signals for the more learned members of his audience to take the story with a pinch of salt – indeed, to laugh. But perhaps this is to read too much into it. It is just as likely that the narrator is trying to shut certain people up so that everyone (not just the learned) can enjoy a good laugh at Hrolf and his exploits without accusations of 'liar!' disrupting the convivial atmosphere of the saga-reading.[37]

The rollicking *Saga of Saul and Nikanor* (*Saulus saga ok Nikanors*) contains a scene so silly that the saga-author could not resist inter-rupting the narrative with further quips. The evil Duke Matthew has forced the heroine, Potentiana, to marry him, and he now thinks he has her beside him in the bridal bed:

> He turned to his bride, meaning to take her virginity …. But though the Duke was very mighty, she would not turn towards him. Rather, he had to grab her with both hands, and she seemed stiff to turn. And just when he expected to enjoy the pleasure and entertainment, he realized that this was no woman who lay beside him in the bed, but a figure made of clay. He now got very cross, shoving this clay woman off the bed at once so that she was completely smashed up into little bits.
>
> 'And I really do believe,' says he who has written the saga, 'that this bride must have had a dry and cold time in bed. And I'd call him a tried and tested ladies' man who could get such a woman with child.'[38]

Continental romance from Chrétien onwards is littered with this kind of comic (or not-so-comic) intrusion. Their occasional appear-ance in the generically conservative Icelandic sagas demonstrates the strength of the romance's influence on these authors. But such intrusions, hinting at the controlling presence of an individual author, are the exception rather than the rule – and in the Icelandic translated romances, they were ruthlessly cut. Even the tiniest flirtation with fiction did not belong in narrative prose.

Poetry was another matter: some romance conventions were whole-heartedly embraced in the development of a new Icelandic genre of rhyming narrative verse at the very height of the mediaeval saga-writing vogue. Between the fourteenth and twentieth centuries, a vast number of verse romances known as *rímur* ('rhymes') were composed. Unlike the sagas, and unlike the ballads from which they developed, *rímur* were wrought by individuals, many of whom (at least after 1550) became household names. On winter evenings they competed for attention with the sagas: they were enormously popular. Many sagas were themselves turned into *rímur*, some several times: just as French verse romance was turned into Icelandic pseudo-historical prose in the translated romances, so the more fanciful examples of Icelandic pseudo-historical prose were now turned into a sort of verse romance, full of narratorial asides. For their part, many *rímur* were turned back again into sagas from the sixteenth century onwards: the pseudo-historical 'matter' could pass back and forth between genres.[39] The *rímur*, a brand new genre, might be called the true representatives of romance in Iceland. Sagas, however, were rooted in ancient narrative habits and resisted the generic tug of romance. Their authors plundered plots and characters from romances (and, later, novels), but the result was always a saga.

Yet the pressure exerted by the romance tradition has helped to make the Icelandic sagas so engaging as *literature*, particularly today. It is often the romance elements in the sagas – their apparently 'fictional' qualities – to which we respond most readily, weaned as we are on novels and films, romance's modern descendants. Above all, it is this dimension of the sagas which gives us particular freedom in peering beneath their narrative surface to discover moral meanings, ironies, and purposeful ambiguities. Even though saga-authors were not 'authors' in the modern sense, the narratives they have left behind are the result of creative selection, manipulation, verbal play and rhetorical persuasion: they are as enjoyable as novels. And because they are also histories, compilations of lore handed down and reworked, they enshrine the views and purposes not of a single author, but of a range of past figures – all of them looking back, seeking to bring to life that which is lost. The result may be polyphonic or dissonant, but rarely monotonous.

THE ART OF THE SAGA-AUTHOR

The saga is a genre which fits ill with modern preconceptions of fiction versus history, orality versus literacy. As such it has its own distinctive narrative conventions, and some of these should be pointed out before we turn to the sagas translated in this book.

Many of these conventions relate to the sagas' oral origins, and to their primary purpose of being read aloud to audiences. The celebrated laconic prose style, carrying the bulk of a saga's third-person narrative, suits the pace required for reading aloud. The crystalline simplicity of *Thidrandi's Tale* exemplifies the so-called 'classical' saga style, but there are other ways of being laconic: compare the elegant rhetorical balance of *Mirmann's Saga* to the apparently artless vigour of *Bard the Snowfell God*, not to mention the irrepressible narrator of *Star-Oddi's Dream* who cannot resist telling the audience how wonderfully laconic he is being ('I'll cut a long story short'). A handful of extremely learned sagas seem designed more for other learned men to read silently or among themselves than for someone to read aloud to an audience, and these ones have no need for conciseness; but most supposedly 'florid' sagas are only relatively florid, indulging in the occasional elaborate description or long speech but rarely clogging the flow of the story.

Formulae and the principle of understatement
Sagas are formulaic on several levels, like many genres with oral functions and/or origins: they follow set patterns of plot structure, characterization, ethical theme and style. Individual sagas may diverge or break away from some of these patterns, but the corpus as a whole demonstrates remarkable consistency, so that when an expectation is subverted the effect can be striking. This formulaic tradition does not allow for the infinite variety of technique open to today's novelist. Rather, the paradigms of saga art function like the conventions of revenge tragedy in the early seventeenth century: they were open to a wide variety of expression within their own terms, and were themselves negotiable in the hands of a Webster or a Shakespeare.

Take the way in which sagas begin and end. Sagas never begin *in medias res*, and very rarely by introducing the main protagonist. They begin by introducing a high-status individual connected with the protagonist, usually setting that person in the relevant geographical (and often historical) context. So *Star-Oddi's Dream* begins by introducing Oddi's boss, the wealthy farmer who plays no part in the main story: 'There was a man named Thord, who lived at Muli in the north'. At the beginning of the second chapter, the saga-within-a-saga begins in precisely the same manner: 'There was a king named Hrodbjart, who ruled over Gotaland in the east.' If the individual in question was known to oral tradition, his father's name was often given, and sometimes a longer genealogy, providing the story with a narrative prehistory. A thumbnail character sketch might be added here. Other high-status individuals are then named and introduced in the same way before the story begins. This kind of introductory gambit may be repeated at a later point, when new characters come into the story. In a saga as dependent on genealogy as *Bard the Snowfell God*, the result can be daunting: introductory genealogies often include wives and descendants as well as ancestors, anchoring the story all the more firmly within the matrix of accepted tradition, confusing the reader still further by hanging anecdotes off these Heath Robinson-like frameworks. It is only on second reading that one comes to recognize who the primary characters are and which ones are included only for anchoring the story or setting up parallels: for an Icelandic audience, a mere name like 'Grettir' (mentioned in an anecdote attached to the introduction of a principal character's largely irrelevant neighbour) would conjure up that man's own tragic life-history and prompt the audience to make an intuitive connection with the present story. Part of the poignancy of *Bard the Snowfell God* derives from its unusual fondness for these unwieldy lists of names, many of them alluding to lost tales of vanished giants.

Sagas frequently end their story with a similar anchorage, listing the hero's descendants or stating that a noble line is descended from him. Then they usually sign off with 'here ends the saga of X', sometimes adding an authorial *envoi* at the very end which ostensibly defends the author's good intentions and/or the saga's reliability. The genealogical element is not universally present, but sometimes its absence may be pointed, as it is in two of the three full-length sagas here. *Bard the Snowfell God* is a saga about the disappearance of old ways and old races, and its reversal of the usual formula in the penultimate sentence is entirely fitting: 'There is no mention of Gest Bardarson having had any children.' This reversal lends an unexpected weight of finality to the entirely conventional final sentence: 'And here ends the saga of Bard the Snowfell God and his son Gest.' In *Mirmann's Saga*, the hero and heroine retire to a monastery and end their lives in pure living: the events of the saga have not suggested that families are much of a blessing. In his final sentence, this author distances his saga from the worldly honour attendant on a glorious lineage by invoking the language (in both senses) of the homily to bring honour to God instead: 'To that one and threefold God ... be honour and glory per omnia sæcula sæculorum, amen.' Only *Hjalmther and Olvir* conforms to type with genealogies, signing-off and *envoi* ('he who wrote it down and put it together both knew well and meant well').

The reader will discover many other formulaic conventions at work elsewhere in the sagas translated here. Plot developments are often introduced by phrases intended to signal the saga's oral, historical mode: 'It's said', 'The story goes', 'It is mentioned'. The interlace patterns which form the structural basis of most sagas, weaving different action-sequences together, give rise to stock expressions like 'The story now returns to X' or 'We must now take up the story elsewhere'. Opinions held by 'the people' almost always signify the narrator's own view: 'people criticized him for that' means 'he really should not have done that'. This last feature gives the saga an air of objectivity, since the narrator rarely tells us directly how to respond to an event; once we know the conventions, the narrator can wind us round his little finger with a few simple phrases. Characters are drawn by similar means: if someone is introduced as 'difficult' (like Hlegunn in *Star-Oddi's Dream*), we know they will cause no end of trouble. If a character reacts to a piece of news by 'saying little', he or she is deeply affected by it; if a character changes colour, he or she is immoderately upset.

The dominant narrative principle is one of understatement, which also characterizes most of the direct speech recorded in the sagas. Besides easing the flow of events, this principle also lends itself to irony and grim humour, in which the sagas excel: 'They asked where he was, and she said he had gone to invite monsters to the wedding.' Superlatives, on the other hand, should generally be treated with caution, as this example from *Hjalmther and Olvir* demonstrates: 'Hjalmther went to his seat and needed the space of two men, but Olvir needed that of three, for he was the largest of men. Hord was as large as both sworn brothers [Hjalmther and Olvir]; yet there was still enough room for them all where High-Stepper had been sitting.'

Heightened language: verses, dreams

The principle of understatement is suspended in the verses. They can give the audience an insight into the speaker's emotions, freezing the narrative and crystallizing a moment into poetic form. A particular event or character is momentarily raised into the universal, timeless realms of myth. The final stanza in *Bard the Snowfell God*, metaphorically transforming the Hjaltasons and Thorbjornssons into the 'Gods of old', is an especially clear example; Helga's second verse in the same saga gives her the pathos and grandeur of a universal figure in Germanic epic and elegy, the lamenting female, and the saga-author guides the audience towards seeing her as the tragic heroine of the Elder Edda, Gudrun Gjukadottir.[40] Dreams can work in a similar way in the sagas, drawing on a limited but colourful repertoire of mythological and animal imagery to transform the dreamer's particular situation into timeless images which invite interpretation. *Mirmann's Saga* contains several dreams in which the protagonists are represented as beasts of prey; the future history of Norway is revealed to *Bard the Snowfell God* in the growth of a marvellous tree near the beginning of his saga, and at the end of the saga Bard himself takes on a sinister (indeed demonic) mythic status when he appears in a dream to his son Gest. *Star-Oddi's Dream* takes the convention to new heights of ingenuity, transforming a district in twelfth-century Iceland into legendary Gotaland.

Historical setting

As histories, the sagas frequently make an effort to situate the events in a specific past time. Those set in heathen times have the opportunity of emphasizing the pastness of the past at burial scenes, as in *Thidrandi's Tale* and the dream-saga of *Star-Oddi's Dream*, in which people are buried according to a now-vanished custom. *Bard the Snowfell God*, obsessed with the idea of extinction, even infuses the vanished race of trolls with a kind of nostalgia: 'In those days the troll-woman Bag was alive'. *Mirmann's Saga* is aligned, less emotively, with the same historical distance: 'In those days all the people north of the Alps were heathen.' By contrast, *Hjalmther and Olvir* seems devoid of historical imagination, unless one counts the presence of vikings and sacrificial oxen as signs of times past.

Plot patterns

When saga plots are boiled down to synopses, they are often found to be based on a limited number of conventional narrative patterns, such as the hero's quest for a wife, the wronged man's quest for vengeance, the young man's quest for fame, fortune and a place in society, man's taming of nature, the consequences of a broken injunction, the sinner's quest for forgiveness, and the heathen's conversion to Christianity. However, few sagas are as simple as their synopses suggest: the interest (and the meaning) lies in what the author does with these narrative patterns.

A saga's plot tends to begin with the hero being placed in a difficult situation, which he must either resolve or escape from. The inexperienced King Geirvid (in *Star-Oddi's Dream*) is forced to take drastic action when robbers and, later, shield-maidens threaten his depleted realm, and the result is that his reign prospers. Hjalmther's father marries again, and his stepmother tries to seduce him: the outcome is that he is sent on a quest which simultaneously brings him honour and resolves the difficulties his stepmother has imposed on several other individuals. Thorstein Shiver needs to go to the lavatory and violates the king's express command not to go outside alone, landing him in a close encounter with a ghost. Thidrandi's death is the ultimate outcome of a similar violation, as well as of a hitherto unseen otherworldly conflict. Bard's exile from Norway and settlement in Iceland is prompted by two conventional motivations for viking-age emigrants: he avenges his father by killing those responsible, and he is unwilling to tolerate the tyranny of King Harald Fairhair. Mirmann's peregrinations are set in motion by a conflict with his parents over Christianity.

There are, moreover, many lesser plot-lines and narrative patterns being deployed or alluded to in most sagas, related or unrelated to the main plot: these elements impinge on, complicate and materially affect the main plot and its significance. Conventional narrative patterns may be used in unexpected ways, such as the 'lustful stepmother' pattern in *Mirmann's Saga* or the 'hero's land-cleansing' pattern in *Bard the Snowfell God*. Any one saga is a concatenation of narratives, some told in full, some left untold, but all linked in various ways to other stories outside the saga itself. When surveying the massive saga corpus as a whole, one gains the impression that the Icelanders had access to a common store of narratives whose threads were all more or less woven together in a rather chaotic fashion, and from which an author would cut sections of his choice, refashioning them as a single saga and choosing whether to tie up the dangling threads or to leave them suggestively loose. And it is the author who has arranged this narrative matter in such a way as to persuade his audience to make certain connections and guide them towards particular ethical judgements. For instance, a large number of apparently 'hero-centred' sagas deliberately complicate the straightforward story of a hero's career in order to raise questions about the nature of heroism.

Repetition and variation of conventional plot patterns is a particularly useful structural principle, setting up parallels between events and thus generating 'meaning' while never committing the narrative to a single interpretation. In *Mirmann's Saga*, for instance, Mirmann twice engages in battle with heathen adversaries and defeats them while invoking the Christian God in Latin, like a good crusader. Mirmann's third battle, against 'Earl Hirning', follows the established pattern up to the point at which he recites the Latin psalm – but this time he is defeated because his apparently heathen opponent is in the right this time. The parallels set up between the three events raise questions about the use of Christian rhetoric to justify brute force.

Much of the plot of *Bard the Snowfell God* is structured along two interwoven series of paralleled scenes: one series involves hospitality at someone's home, and in the other series a human encounters an otherworldly being in the wilderness. These two series merge in Gest Bardarson's final adventure, the climactic scene of the saga. Gest breaks into the undead King Raknar's grave-mound, which is 'both foul-smelling and freezing cold': this is a direct verbal echo of the site of Gest's previous adventure, an ogre's cave where he had come uninvited to a bogus 'wedding feast' and rescued his half-brothers from their comically horrid adversaries by dint of strength and luck. But now Raknar 'hospitably' allows Gest to strip him of his jewellery, then attacks him so fiercely that Gest's strength and luck are of no use and he is forced to call on his father Bard. Bard appears, but – contrary to all the expectations set up by the saga-author – even he is unable to help, and the ubiquitous missionary king Olaf Tryggvason has to make an appearance as a form of guardian angel. By subtly guiding the audience to make comparisons with earlier parallel scenes, the saga-author here invests Raknar with a terrible (and not at all comic) demonic power, and reveals that strength, luck and even pagan 'guardian-wights' can do nothing against such an adversary: only God's power can avail. It would doubtless have been easier to write a sermon; but the saga-author's literary method gets the message across with greater dramatic effectiveness, besides leaving the narrative wide open to further levels of interpretation.

Narrative worlds and modes

One of the most striking and important conventions of saga art remains to be described. This is the way in which sagas tend to move into different narrative modes when describing events in different regions or times. For instance, a story about tenth-century Icelandic farmers is likely to draw on a slightly different repertoire of narrative conventions than is a story about viking heroes in Europe – even if both stories are told in the same saga, and both involve the same protagonist. Saga plots arise from the daily life of the social group being depicted. As a viking warrior, the hero will naturally get involved in sea-battles, deeds of derring-do and male camaraderie, free from the constraints imposed by settled society; but once the same hero is transplanted to his farm in Iceland, these constraints apply and the plot will tend to turn on the more prosaic conflicts of daily life in a farming community. As a viking or a foreign king's retainer, the protagonist may win honour; as a farmer, he must struggle to retain it.

Many sagas set in Iceland play up the contrast between these two worlds: heroes return from adventures abroad, clad in honour and knightly finery, only to find that such status is hard to sustain in humdrum, claustrophobic Iceland. Prosaic conflicts about girls or grazing rights typically escalate into the sordid drama of blood-feud. Several saga-authors – some of them perhaps leading figures in Icelandic politics – were especially interested in the problem of upholding law, justice and individual honour in a kingless society without an executive authority. The weakening and eventual collapse of that problematic system in the mid-thirteenth-century may have encouraged saga-authors to look back at the origins of their society, and the resulting sagas are among the most celebrated works of mediaeval literature, besides (according to some) providing price-less social documentation about viking-age Iceland.[41]

But Iceland is only one of several 'narrative worlds' explored by the saga-authors.[42] The literary renown of sagas like *The Burning of Njal*, *Egil's Saga* and *The Laxdalers' Saga* has led to a loose usage of the term 'Icelandic saga' to mean only sagas set in viking-age (so-called 'saga-age') Iceland, as if none of the rest are real sagas. Among scholars, this relatively small group of texts has traditionally been assigned a literary genre all to itself, 'the Sagas of Icelanders' (*Íslendingasögur*), and it has been set apart from other saga 'genres' as the only one deserving the epithet 'classical' for its attention to historical fact, its relative lack of similarities to other European mediaeval narrative, and its laconic, 'novelistic' realism.[43] As we have already seen, however, a historical stance lies behind all the sagas; all represent something distinct from (yet related to) European forms; all are laconic in their different ways; and the relative realism of those set in Iceland has more to do with their subject-matter being close to the saga-authors in time and space than with a deliberate choice of genre. (This is a controversial area, and most of the items listed in the Further Reading section retain a more or less traditional saga classification.)[44]

The other 'genres' are traditionally held to have their own peculiar characteristics: 'knights' sagas' (*riddarasögur*), 'legendary sagas' (*fornaldarsögur*), 'contemporary sagas' (*samtíðarsögur*, set in twelfth- and thirteenth-century Iceland) and sagas of Norwegian kings (*konungasögur*) – not to mention all the other sagas which do not fit into these boxes. On examination, all the features held to define each 'genre' can either be found in many sagas belonging to other 'genres', or else are absent from several members of the 'genre' in question. These 'genres' are often arranged into an evolutionary parabola, plotting the saga's origins from chronicle-like beginnings (sagas of Norwegian kings) to romantic decline ('knights' sagas'), with the great 'Sagas of Icelanders' occupying the zenith between these two European-influenced forms.[45] This model also has its problems. Sagas about viking-age Icelanders, as well as the supposedly more 'romantic' sagas, continued to be reworked (and new ones put together) well into the nineteenth century, and some of the most celebrated 'classical' texts only survive in fifteenth-century fragments or seventeenth-century versions. The literary genre of the saga did not move steadily from chronicle to romance via a kind of historical novel. Between the twelfth and nineteenth centuries, many different sagas were put together and reworked: these blended the techniques of history and romance in different ways, depending on the needs and tastes of patrons and audiences and the education of the saga-authors. And while the novel in Iceland did develop in part from sagas and oral tales about Icelandic folk heroes at the end of the eighteenth century,[46] afterwards saga-writing and novel-writing continued as parallel but usually distinct practices.

Applying the traditional pigeonholes to the sagas translated in this book results in chaos. *Star-Oddi's Dream* is a 'legendary saga' framed within a 'contemporary saga'; *Hjalmther and Olvir* sits on the borderline between 'legendary sagas' and 'knights' sagas'; the extract from the *Book of Flatey* mixes a 'Saga of Icelanders' with ecclesiastical legends, all fitted within the saga of a Norwegian king; *Bard the Snowfell God* is part 'legendary saga', part 'Saga of Icelanders', with elements of saint-sagas' miracle-accounts; and *Mirmann's Saga* blends a 'knights' saga' with homiletic features. None of these sagas or tales is the product of a single authorial personality or a single historical period, so it is no surprise that they do not fit into the traditional boxes. If these are 'hybrids', then so – to differing degrees – are almost all sagas.

The saga corpus as a whole should not be visualized as a filing cabinet of separate genres. It is a single genre arising from the particular needs of Icelandic society, shaped by the opposing tugs of pre-existing oral and literary genres: folktale, genealogy, chronicle, saint's life, romance and so on. Within this multi-dimensional magnetic field each saga has its own coordinates, which may shift across time, moving from one generic position to another, depending on the purposes of a later saga-author (as may be seen in the different recensions of *The Saga of King Olaf Tryggvason*).[47] Subject-areas and purposes which are familiar to the rest of Europe inevitably move the saga in question much closer to a pre-existing European genre: so some sagas of Norwegian kings bear a strong resemblance to European royal chronicles, fused together into chronological compilations; and some Icelandic saints' lives are barely different from their Latin counterparts.

More significant in the present context is the fact that certain areas of subject-matter – early Iceland, legendary Gotaland – were so well-trodden in the saga literature that the narrative techniques felt to be appropriate for writing about these particular subjects hardened into conventional narrative modes.[48] It is not surprising that different representational techniques were felt to apply to different geographical and temporal areas, since the Icelanders would have had access to different kinds (and different amounts) of information about each area, requiring him to exert his creativity in different ways and to different degrees. Writing about legendary Scandinavia – the 'Matter of the North' – would naturally rely on folktales, eddic poetry and the back ends of genealogies. Writing about Hungarian knights – the 'Matter of the South' – would involve the saga-author in foreign learned works and the paraphernalia of Continental romance, and he might also transplant the folklore patterns and heroic postures of the 'Matter of the North' to the new backdrop. And when writing about his Icelandic ancestors, the saga-author might have access to a rich store of oral tradition relatively free from romantic overlay – hence the relative 'realism' of these sagas and their much-lauded concern with domestic politics.

Once established as part of the saga-writing tradition, these different modes could be used self-consciously. *Star-Oddi's Dream* is an unusually clear example, taking place in two narrative worlds: the protagonist is sent by the farmer on a fishing expedition in prosaic twelfth-century Iceland, but sent by the king to sail a longship against a trollish shieldmaiden in the legendary Gotaland of his dreams. Similar play could be made with the two kinds of 'matter' available to the authors of the relatively fantastic sagas set in the distant past. The 'Matter of the South' deals with refined knights, emperors, Saracens and fair princesses who know all about the properties of stones; the 'Matter of the North' is full of sea-kings, vikings, trolls and berserks. Many of these sagas move happily between the two worlds. Some relish the comic discrepancy: *The Saga of Samson the Fair* (*Samsons saga fagra*) sends an Arthurian knight up north where the manners are noticeably less refined, and *Hjalmther and Olvir* pits its bluff viking hero against a beautiful and eloquent Southern temptress, with hilarious results. The Swedish viking explorers in *Yngvar's Saga* penetrate into Asia, where they are puzzled by that most Southern of beasts, an elephant with a wooden tower on it. Their method of coping with the culture-clash is typically 'viking'. They lead it around for a while using the ropes and pulleys attached to it, but 'since they didn't know what kind of creature it was or what food it required, they speared it to death, then returned to their ships and rowed away.'[49]

All the same, most saga-authors paid little attention to such distinctions between North and South, gathering matter uncritically from learned treatises and oral tradition. The author of *William Purse* is more typical, packing in as much 'matter' as possible to colour his ripping yarn. Having come all the way from England to the Caucasus Mountains (via Saxony, Greece, Africa and Nineveh), William visits a moundful of troll-women – stereotypical denizens of the North – in the Caucasus mountains while riding on a kind of super-dromedary whose name proclaims its Latinate origins: 'its name was *katanansius*; it was long, thin and low-slung, with four-teen legs ... this animal could slink over every obstacle.'[50] The North–South opposition has dissolved: the *katanansius* is a mere gadget, and the trolls are merely enemies. Yet this artless eclecticism has a B-movie appeal of its own, and in Iceland until the twentieth century, *William Purse* was one of the two or three most popular of all the sagas.

Common themes

The texts translated in this volume cannot reflect the full range and variety of Icelandic saga-writing. Indeed, though *Thidrandi's Tale* is the only text commonly accorded 'classical' status, my selection does partly reflect the traditional bias towards sagas set in viking-age Iceland. Nevertheless, the selection is designed to blur the distinc-tions between the so-called 'genres'. Similar narrative practices are seen at work in widely different sagas, and common themes recur in different garb. For instance, the conflict between Christianity and heathenism – a topic that fascinated saga-authors – is central to the extract from *The Book of Flatey*, *Bard the Snowfell God* and *Mirmann's Saga*. It seems a natural enough interest, given the authors' clerical training. In this light, another common feature seems on the face of it more unexpected. With the exception of the *Book of Flatey* extracts, all these sagas display a lively interest in their female characters. Saga women tend to be strong, important and above all interesting characters, whether depicted negatively (Hlegunn in *Star-Oddi's Dream*, Brigida and Katrin in *Mirmann's Saga*, Luda and the troll-women in *Hjalmther and Olvir*, Prickles and other troll-women in *Bard the Snowfell God*) or positively (Cecilia in *Mirmann's Saga*, Hervor and Wolf-Ember and her sister in *Hjalmther and Olvir*, Groa and Helga in *Bard the Snowfell God*). These sagas have little time for the passive, pedestal-dwelling romance-heroine who does not contribute directly to the action: only Solrun (*Bard the Snowfell God*) and Princess Diana (*Hjalmther and Olvir*) veer towards this type. Mirmann the crusading hero is, in a sense, a minor player in 'his' saga, which is largely powered by the machinations of three strong women; much the same could be said of Hjalmther – that is, when he is not being told what to do by the swineherd.

The sagas' evident interest in women may or may not reflect the contribution of female story-tellers (or saga-authors) to the texts which survive today. It is, however, symptomatic of a general scepticism regarding the heroic or pseudo-heroic worlds through which the sagas' male protagonists move. Many a saga-hero is introduced as an uncomplicated paragon of all the known virtues, but the hero who bears out these expectations is a rare bird indeed – and a boring bird at that. All the sagas in this volume, and many others besides, glance searchingly or mischievously at the lineaments of 'old-style' heroism, whose ethics and efficacy are held up to edify and entertain the audience. This attitude is inseparable from the historical imagination of the saga-authors: all were variously engaged in exploring, exploiting and re-inventing a past which is now laid out before us in these marvellous and miscellaneous stories.

STAR-ODDI'S DREAM (*STJÖRNU-ODDA DRAUMR*)

The earliest surviving manuscripts of this unusually self-conscious saga date from the seventeenth century. The manuscript followed here, AM 555h 4to, was not written by a saga-author, creatively editing an earlier text. It was copied in 1686 by an Icelandic humanist scholar, Árni Magnússon. He claims to be copying the saga from a lost vellum book, or codex, known as *Vatnshyrna* (written 1391-5); from what we know of his procedure, it is likely to be more reliable than most. Assuming that the copy is accurate, *Star-Oddi's Dream* in its present form probably dates from the fourteenth century. The skaldic poem quoted at the end may be slightly older: parts of it have become corrupted during manuscript transmission.[51]

Star-Oddi himself was an Icelandic astronomer who lived in the first part of the twelfth century. His contribution to the scholarly renaissance of the time was (we are told) a set of tables showing the sun's midday latitude for each week of the year. For sailors, this kind of information was invaluable for westward journeys on the North Atlantic. It seems fitting, then, that Star-Oddi should be the character selected by the saga-author to undertake a journey in time and space, navigating the gulf between twelfth-century Iceland and legendary Gotaland. This journey takes place in a dream Oddi has while staying on Flatey in northern Iceland; and the mechanism by which he makes this journey within the dream is by listening to a saga. Oddi dreams that he is back at home, and that a guest arrives and starts telling a saga set in Gotaland. When a poet called Dagfinn is named in the guest's saga, we are told that Oddi imagines himself 'into' the Gotaland of the saga and 'becomes' Dagfinn.

It is a remarkable moment, unparalleled in Icelandic saga-narrative – the kind of trick one associates more with such novels as Flann O'Brien's *At Swim-Two-Birds*. The narrator has set up three concentric layers of narrative: his saga (Star-Oddi's Dream), told by himself; the dream itself, with Oddi as dreamer; and the saga within the dream, told by the guest. The boundary between the second and third layers now dissolves, so that Oddi not only becomes a character within the guest's saga, but he himself replaces the guest as 'creator' of the narrative. Oddi becomes at once protagonist and story-teller, so it is fitting that the character he assumes is that of the king's poet Dagfinn, whose chief function was to record the king's deeds for posterity – even though Star-Oddi is introduced to us initially as 'not a poet'. The two poems which Oddi/Dagfinn subsequently composes in his dream represent the innermost narrative layers of *Star-Oddi's Dream*. Yet we never 'hear' these poems recited by Dagfinn in their Gotaland context, since the saga-narrator himself relates them to us as *written* texts on the two occasions when Oddi/Dagfinn wakes up, and long after the events which the poems record. *Star-Oddi's Dream* itself ends with a defence of Oddi's honesty as reporter of his own dream, and the saga-author's parting shot to the audience is to apologize for the woodenness of the poems, which Oddi/Dagfinn had, after all, 'composed in his sleep' (in fact, the second poem is rather good). Every layer of the saga is infused with its narrator's own irrepressible loquacity, and his comments frequently undermine the principle of understatement on which saga art tends to be based: 'It seemed to people that he had been all but snatched out of Hel (which he had).' Such gestures to the audience are typical of this playful saga.

What is more, the world of Oddi's dream-saga appears to be inspired by, and literally mapped on to, the world of Oddi's daily life – as the saga's most recent editor, the place-name specialist Þórhallur Vilmundarson, has observed.[52] In the dream-saga, under orders from King Geirvid, Dagfinn sails to somewhere just off Temple Head, then out into Herringsound to wage war on the evil Hlegunn. This journey seems to be based on Oddi's own fishing journey which he made before falling asleep: under orders from Farmer Thord, he sailed out to Flatey. The route from his farm would have taken Oddi past a headland named Temple Head, and then out into the herring-rich Sound of Flatey. Two localities – one homely and prosaic, the other foreign, ancient and exotic – are thus mapped on to each other in the perception of the dreamer/narrator. The saga-author seems to go out of his way to emphasize the glamour of old Gotaland, its potential for adventure and romance, and its people's touching loyalty to their royal dynasty. Many of the motifs and narrative patterns typical of other sagas set in legendary Gotaland are used here – young man defeats berserks single-handed, trollish shield-maiden harries the realm, climactic sea-battle – but the effect of the saga-author's many self-conscious parenthetical intrusions (such as 'as you might expect') is to give this entertaining saga-within-a-saga and its allegedly 'wooden' verses an air of cliché, as if we have all heard this kind of story before.

This flavour is appropriate to its status as a dream-narrative, and here we have one possible explanation for the saga-author's unusual procedure. As already noted, dream narratives in sagas tend to raise the particular situation of the dreamer into the more general (and colourful) world of myth. Perhaps the author of *Star-Oddi's Dream* wanted to paint Oddi's home territory (Reykjardal) in legendary Gothic colours in order to make a veiled comment on the domestic politics of Oddi's own time. This is the line taken by Þórhallur Vilmundarson, and he draws some intriguing parallels which centre on the identification of King Geirvid of Gotaland with Oddi's boss, Farmer Thord of Muli, whose dynasty is glorified by the comparison. The battle of Herringsound is interpreted as an allegory of a chieftaincy dispute in early twelfth-century Reykjardal. Þórhallur's detective work is ingenious, but it would apply more to a hypothetical twelfth-century version of the saga than to the fourteenth-century *Star-Oddi's Dream* as we have it. A twelfth-century stratum may well underlie this text, but the fourteenth-century author's motives for preserving such an allegory remain unaccounted for – particularly since Iceland was subject to the king of Norway in the fourteenth century, and chieftaincies were now obsolete.

A more general reading of *Star-Oddi's Dream* might focus on the contrast brought out between the two narrative 'worlds'. Mapping the one on to the other makes the discord all the more apparent: the humdrum, parochial nature of Icelandic daily life emerges in comic clarity. Icelandic saga-authors frequently made wry self-deprecating remarks to this effect. The author of *Nitida's Saga*, another saga involving imaginary travel to distant lands, interrupts his description of a lavish banquet with the following apology: 'It is not easy to say, with an unlearned tongue, in the backwaters of the world … what joy there would have been in the middle of the world from such a courtly gathering.'[53] The elaborate narrative layering of *Star-Oddi's Dream*, and the way in which Oddi is made the author as well as the protagonist of his dream-saga, suggest that the saga-author is trying to create an ironic distance between himself and his narrator – a distance maintained by his own running commentary (in brackets) on the progress of the story and, finally, on the quality of the verses.

This ironic distance, more characteristic of Continental romance than of an Icelandic saga, hints at the potential fictionality of Oddi's imaginary Gotaland. We have already seen, in a passage quoted from *The Saga of Thorgils and Haflidi*, that mediaeval Icelanders were not all in agreement as to the historicity of sagas about legendary Scandinavian heroes: some people traced their ancestry back to Hromund Gripsson, but others called his saga (allegedly recited in 1119, during Star-Oddi's lifetime) an entertaining lie. The author of *Star-Oddi's Dream* defends Oddi's truthfulness in reporting the dream, but the fact remains that it was only a dream. This particular saga of legendary Gotaland is not historically reliable, but (like

many a 'lying dream' in mediaeval dream-theory) has been formed
by Oddi's own day-to-day concerns and experiences, as identified
by Þórhallur; the saga-author may be implying that much the same
might be said of other sagas.[54] One might even see Oddi as an
Icelandic Don Quixote, viewing his world through the rose-tinted
spectacles of legendary heroism. Yet his delusions, unlike the Don's,
are confined to his dreams – rendering them harmless and, above
all, entertaining.

THE SAGA OF HJALMTHER AND OLVIR
(HJÁLMÞÉS SAGA OK ÖLVIS)

Hjalmther and Olvir is a pure entertainment: its author dives into a
lurid heroic past, not so much to examine it as to romp around in
it. This saga is less self-consciously artful than *Star-Oddi's Dream*, but
casts a similarly irreverent eye on the heroic past.

   Hjalmther and Olvir is preserved in over thirty manuscripts from
the seventeenth century onwards. No two texts are exactly alike
– some have clearly been 'edited' with substantial cuts – and none
is likely to be a faithful copy of a mediaeval original. The saga probably reached something like its uncut present form in the fifteenth
century, and recent studies of the manuscripts of the closely-related
Bevers' Saga suggest that AM 109a III 8vo may be the closest seventeenth-century witness to the mediaeval saga. This is the text followed here. It is likely that there was an earlier mediaeval recension
of this saga, since a fourteenth- or fifteenth-century verse romance
called *Hjalmther's Rhymes* (*Hjálmþésrímur*) survives, preserving a different version of the story. Some of the verses in *Hjalmther and
Olvir* itself may also date back to before the fifteenth century: at
any rate, they have not travelled well, and some are impossible to
make sense of as they stand.[55] We may not be missing much: even
the uncorrupted verses are, in general, far more wooden than those

in *Star-Oddi's Dream* – though the exchange with the troll-women in chapter 8 has a certain rude liveliness.

The basic plot is fairly simple, yet not predictable: there are several surprises in store for the first-time reader. The widowed King Ingi of Mannheimar marries again: his bride – actually a troll – claims (and appears) to be a beautiful young Greek princess called Luda, recently escaped from Saracens. Luda soon shows herself to be a man-eater in both senses, and Ingi's son Hjalmther is suspicious of her. He and his sworn brother Olvir leave the kingdom and win fame and fortune. When they return to Mannheimar, Hjalmther's stepmother tries to seduce him. He spurns her violently, and her twofold revenge propels most of the rest of the plot. First, by means of a magic storm she sends him to her enormous brother; when that plan fails, she casts a spell on him so that he will know no peace of mind until he has seen Hervor, daughter of King Hunding. This perilous quest is undertaken by Hjalmther and Olvir, along with Luda's enormous slave Hord, who actually does most of the heroic deeds. In the end Hord reveals himself to be a snappily-dressed Arabian king (Hring) under another of the versatile Luda's spells (and a thick hairy cloak which he never removes), while two helpful female monsters from earlier in the saga are revealed to be his sisters under similar enchantments. The story of Hring and his family is related in a brief saga-within-a-saga at the end. Now that everyone is freed from their spells, they all live happily ever after: Hring's sisters marry Hjalmther and Olvir, Hring marries Hervor, and Luda dies in a rather perfunctory manner.

Let us not delude ourselves. This saga-author was no Homer, and strictly speaking, *Hjalmther and Olvir* is little more than the sum of its parts. Though certain themes run through the whole saga, the guiding organizational principle seems to be the stringing together of disparate episodes. Yet the saga is anything but tedious. If the author of *Star-Oddi's Dream* achieves humour by showing up his 'legendary saga' episodes as literary clichés, *Hjalmther and Olvir* transcends the conventional nature of such material by virtue of his obvious enjoyment in telling the story. Some of the episodes may be borrowed from other sagas, but most are drawn from the rich stock of North Atlantic folktale patterns and motifs, combined in new and entertaining forms.

For instance, most sagas about the legendary North reach their climax with a 'mother of all battles', normally at sea, between the heroes and the (usually more numerous) villains. *Star-Oddi's Dream* presents a typical example. In *Hjalmther and Olvir* the last battle is indeed at sea, but the viking ships and the two viking heroes play no active part until the very end. Most of the battle is fought by five people, all of whom have assumed animal forms (a magical practice known as *hamhleypa*, 'shape-leaping'). The villain, King Hunding, is transformed into a gigantic and vengeful walrus; a counter-attack is launched by Hring and Hervor, in the form of a whale and a dolphin respectively; and Hring's sisters come to their aid as vultures. It is a vivid and bizarre scene, not easily forgotten: the familiar 'mother of all battles' pattern and the 'shape-leaping' motif are combined and thus transformed into something more exciting. These deft recastings of traditional material made *Hjalmther and Olvir* extremely popular and fed back into the folklore: similar sea-battles between 'shape-leaping' characters appear in nineteenth-century Icelandic folktales.

It may seem odd that no translation of this popular and well-written saga should have been published before, but until recently scholars have been reluctant to study these supposedly 'late' and 'fictional' sagas, preferring those which appear to preserve a kernel of 'genuine' oral tradition. At root, this is a historian's attitude, but it exerts a powerful influence over literary critics as well. Lately, however, new avenues have opened. Sagas like *Hjalmther and Olvir* are now considered to be invaluable cultural artefacts, like the films of post-classical Hollywood to a student of modern culture: they reveal the normative values of the society in which they function. But this approach has a drawback: as with films, the hunt for predictable formulae and revealing stereotypes can, in the hands of an unsympathetic critic, completely obscure the sagas' individual qualities and make them appear far more boring – and far more normative – than they really are.[56]

Hjalmther and Olvir is a case in point. Superficially, it would appear to reinforce the feudal norms of fifteenth-century Icelandic society under a foreign king, with Hord's true nobility revealed, Hjalmther succeeding to his father's empire, and the feminine elements duly disempowered by means of execution (for the bad ones) and marriage (for the good ones). But the way the plot actually works in the telling tends to undermine these feudal norms. Along with many other sagas, *Hjalmther and Olvir* suggests that Icelanders refused to be overawed by royalty. The 'peerless hero' Hjalmther does not cut a very heroic figure for most of the saga. He is not even in charge of his own quest. Hord runs the show from the start, fighting the necessary monsters without Hjalmther's help (Hjalmther does at one point try to help Hord by furtively passing him a sword, but Hord never uses it) and marrying the object of the bridal quest. All this makes sense in retrospect: once we know Hord's true royal identity, his superiority to Hjalmther seems perfectly natural, but for most of the saga we have seen him as a swarthy slave outdoing the real heroes. The deep structure may reinforce heroic norms, but the story is staged so that we think Hjalmther is the true hero, and a rather ineffectual one at that. It is hard to take seriously a hero who allows himself to be turned (literally) into a chicken, even if only for a moment or two.

Hjalmther's heroism is further undermined by the way in which he is constantly the object of the attentions of powerful females, who want to help or harm him and/or enjoy his sexual favours. A quintessential viking, he thinks it 'worthless to yearn after a princess', but princesses and troll-women alike find much to admire in him. The first of these, Princess Diana, is entirely conventional, existing merely to increase Hjalmther's honour at an early stage in his career. After saving her from the heathen Prince Nudus, he departs from the conventional pattern by not marrying her, and when they part she gives him a magic tent and bursts into tears. But Hjalmther's later encounters with the opposite sex assume stranger forms.

The formidable Luda comes next: her magnificent 'seduction scene' in Chapter 6 is probably the saga's most memorable and artful scene.[57] This set-piece is carefully prepared for by Hjalmther's pointed absence at his father's second wedding, by the saga–author's pregnant comment at the end of Chapter 5, and by the laconic pillow-talk at the beginning of Chapter 6. Luda makes a graceful entry into Hjalmther's castle, unexpectedly walking straight through the locked door, and Hjalmther is all smiles at first – though his embarrassed men leave the hall one by one. With the Southern princess Diana, the viking Hjalmther had managed to play the romance-hero fairly well; but Luda's advances now prompt a dramatic culture-clash between North and South. First she asks him whether he likes the look of her, but he fails to take the hint, blandly responding, 'Yes, very nice.' So she launches into her seduction-speech, its florid and overflowing rhetoric highly reminiscent of the lustful stepmothers of Classical romance (as befits Luda's alleged origin) but also oddly clerical in feel ('the flesh is weak'). But her final sentence reveals her trollish nature: 'we can soon get rid of that old beggar so he doesn't get in our way.' All this Grecian verbiage bewilders our hero, who gives as Nordic a response as he can – 'Are you serious about this?' – before punching her on the nose. With admirable aplomb and a sinister 'We shall meet again', Luda sinks down into the ground, a traditional manoeuvre by which trolls escape from embarrassing situations.

Hjalmther's next close encounter comes in Chapter 7, where he has to kiss a *fingálkn* – a Jabberwock-like monster named Wolf-Ember – in order to win her sword and attain true heroic status. He is reluctant to submit to her desires: 'I don't want to kiss you …

I might get stuck to you.' But Wolf-Ember is the only female in the saga whose advances Hjalmther accepts, and later on he marries her. By then, of course, she has turned back into a beautiful princess, but we remember her as a rather forward *fingálkn*. The same goes for the other princess, Olvir's bride, whom we remember as the troll-woman Skinhood who turned the heroes into chickens to save them from Luda's brother. Even at the end, when the princesses introduce themselves to the sworn brothers, the audience is actively encouraged to remember the less glamorous aspects of their previous encounters: the kiss and the chickens are both mentioned in the princesses' verses.

The scene with Luda is echoed later on (Chapter 8) when Hjalmther meets Embers, a more obviously trollish troll-woman on some unidentified Nordic shore. Their exchange begins in a more Nordic manner, with a *flyting* (a ritualised exchange of insults in verse), but Embers soon lowers the tone with a proposal so indecent that many of the manuscripts replace the details after 'lose my virginity' with a tight-lipped 'etcetera'. Hjalmther does not even bother to reply and just chops off her hand, and in revenge most of his men are killed by Embers's sisters, one of whom (Sea-Giant) seems to him to pose a more formidable sexual threat than Embers. The ensuing verse-insults between the two sides turn largely on the troll-women's terrifying sexuality and their desire to eat the heroes for dinner. Luda belongs to a fancy Southern breed of troll, well trained in the liberal arts; these fjord-dwelling sisters are honest Northern trolls – more Northern than the heroes themselves, as Warbattle points out – and their dealings with men are more direct. The contrast between these two encounters is humorous, but taken together, they provide a wide spectrum of female predation in all its sophistication and bestiality.

Conventional misogyny doubtless lies at the heart of the narrative impulse to make aggressive women into predatory trolls (compare the man-eating Hlegunn in *Star-Oddi's Dream*); but let us not forget that these scenes, taken together, give an image of male heroism which is drastically at odds with that presented in Hjalmther and Olvir's initial adventures. More and more, Hjalmther is seen as a mere sex object; and when he and Olvir are not fighting off the ladies, they are being told what to do by them.

It seems incredible that *Hjalmther and Olvir's* seventeenth-century Swedish editors saw in it a glorious picture of the Swedish heroic age (Mannheimar being taken to mean 'Sweden').[58] Ultimately, this saga is not 'about' anything in particular: its aim is to entertain, and as such it succeeds brilliantly. Yet it is not without occasional seriousness: Hord's death, after the last battle has been won, comes as a genuine shock to the first-time reader as much as to the sworn brothers. The emotional disturbance causes them to behave most oddly (Hjalmther faints and suffers haemorrhages, and Olvir declares he would like to kill Hjalmther) but this behaviour is in no way ridiculous, and Hjalmther's artless memorial verse is strangely touching. No depths are plumbed – this is no *Pericles* – but both here and at the utterly conventional happy reunion, the seriousness somehow rings true. Whether these effects are crafted or accidental, this saga works.

EXTRACT FROM THE BOOK OF FLATEY (*FLATEYJARBÓK*)

The two tales which comprise this extract represent a different kind of narrative, blending ecclesiastical legends and folklore into finely-crafted miniature sagas. They are normally printed separately and treated (justifiably enough) as separate literary works. But since the earliest text of *Thorstein Shiver* is embedded within *The Book of Flatey's* recension of *The Longest Saga of King Olaf Tryggvason* (*Óláfs saga Tryggvasonar hinn mesta*, henceforth *Longest Saga*), it seemed worth translating it alongside the celebrated tale which accompanies and complements it there, *Thidrandi's Tale*.

The enormous and magnificent illuminated vellum codex *The Book of Flatey* (GkS 1005 fol.) was written by two priests, Jón Þórðarson and Magnús Þórhallsson, in northern Iceland between 1387 and 1394 for the wealthy farmer Jón Hákonarson, who may also have commissioned *Vatnshyrna* (containing *Star-Oddi's Dream*).[59] Along with some poems and annals, this codex consists mainly of sagas about Norwegian kings. The sagas of the two King Olafs, Olaf Tryggvason (995-1000) and Saint Olaf (Haraldsson, 1014-1030), are notable in this recension for their inclusion of a large number of narratives about Norway's tributary isles: Orkney, the Faroes, Greenland and, above all, Iceland. Pre-existing tales and sagas are woven into the stories of the missionary kings as separate 'strands' (*þættir*, also the word translated here as 'tale') which reveal the kings' temporal and spiritual influence on their subjects.

Icelanders had been composing sagas about Olaf Tryggvason since the twelfth century. His significance for Iceland approached that of a patron saint, and he was credited with effecting the conversion of Scandinavia to Christianity. For later Icelandic historians, this event became the crucial turning-point in their history, patterned after the Incarnation of Christ in the grand narrative of sacred history.[60] Scandinavian history was divided into two ages, pagan and Christian. Christians could look back over the boundary on their benighted past, and they could even learn Christian lessons from it (as from the Old Testament, prefiguring the New), but its 'pastness' was irrevocable – it could be wondered at, even longed for, but never recovered. Some of the greatest works of mediaeval northern literature are founded on this highly-charged boundary: the Old English *Beowulf*, the Middle Irish *Destruction of Da Derga's Hostel*, and the Icelandic *Burning of Njal*.[61] Conversion-narratives come with a built-in dramatic thrust: entertainment and religious edification support each other.

In the Scandinavian conversion-narrative, Olaf was seen as having generated, as it were, a tide of Christianity which flooded Norway and steadily spread out to the tributary isles, transforming their spiritual landscapes and forcing their pagan spirits to move further and further northwest, into the fantastic realms of the frozen North. In *Bard the Snowfell God*, Odin is found wandering north of the arctic Ocean of Mist, and the demonic Raknar still holds sway in the Slabland wastes. This 'tidal' process is emphasized by the contrast between the largely comic *Thorstein Shiver* and its sombre companion-piece *Thidrandi's Tale*: Olaf's Icelandic retainer is saved from a pagan ghost in Norway, but the new faith comes too late to save the more virtuous Thidrandi out in Iceland. Many other stories accumulated around Olaf's dealings with the the North Atlantic isle-dwellers, in which close encounters with pagan otherworlds constitute a running theme. The original *Longest Saga* (*c.*1300) was a massive compilation of Atlantic historical lore, the result of two centuries of accumulation. Jón Þórðarson reworked it for *The Book of Flatey*, adding tales like *Thorstein Shiver* to create the longest *Longest Saga*.

THE TALE OF THORSTEIN SHIVER (*ÞORSTEINS ÞÁTTR SKELKS*)

In this tale, as in *Star-Oddi's Dream*, two utterly distinct worlds are brought into contact in a mundane setting in the middle of the night. As in the *Dream*, the culture-clash is comical; but this is no dream. Desperate for the lavatory but unwilling to wake his companion, Thorstein breaks King Olaf's orders by going to the privy alone, where a real, flesh-and-blood pagan ghost crawls up out of the furthest hole. Thorstein is in mortal peril. He buys time and wakes King Olaf by asking the ghost all about pagan heroes in Hell and encouraging him to imitate their screams. Olaf has the church bell rung, and the ghost plunges back down the hole. Next day, Olaf cannot help but admire Thorstein's pluck: he gives him a nickname and a sword. His final reward, like that of many another Icelander, is to die heroically with his lord, fighting Olaf's pagan enemies at the Battle of Svold.

Besides *The Book of Flatey*, this (probably) fourteenth-century tale also appears in several later 'anthologies' of tales and sagas excerpted from that codex. It is an odd mixture of seriousness and broad comedy, ecclesiastical legend and *jeu d'esprit*. The ghost, Thorkel the Thin, represents Thorstein's pagan 'double': he was a retainer of Harald Wartooth, one of the greatest of all Scandinavian kings, whose life – like Olaf's – ended at a celebrated, almost apocalyptic battle. Thorkel fell with his lord at Brow Plains, just as Thorstein would at Svold. But Christianity has begun to impose a new perspective on the memories of ancient heroes, whose status is now uncertain. The old heroes still uphold heroic norms, with Sigurd and Starkad supplying stereotypically positive and negative poles; yet there is little difference between Sigurd's and Starkad's punishments. The enormity of eternal hellfire trivializes their heroic stature. Less well-defined pagans like Thorkel are already seen dissolving into demonization: Thorkel is identified by no fewer than four distinct terms, some more theologically specific than others (see Glossary under 'demon'). The tide of Olaf's new faith does not merely submerge the memories of pagan heroes, but pushes them down into Hell itself. Thorkel's final exit is that of a troll (compare Luda's exit in *Hjalmther and Olvir*, chapter 6), and in the next saga, *Bard the Snowfell God*, the interference of Christianity eventually turns a benevolent guardian spirit into a demonic figure.

But the encounter between man and ghost is, in the hands of this writer, a comic one. Thorstein allows himself to play stooge to Thorkel's terrible one-liners, which – though apparently revealing the true state of things down in Hell – are surely calculated to raise a laugh. When Thorkel 'puff[s] out his cheeks fearsomely', the effect is not so much terrifying as grotesque, like a cartoon. And as with most cartoons, we know that all will end well for the hero. The humour may stem from Hell's trivializing effect on pagan heroism;

yet the effect is not sardonic, but rather silly. A less glamorous setting than the lavatory could hardly have been devised. The dialogue is snappy, and Thorstein's stereotypically Icelandic 'stubborn pluck' is engagingly sketched, right up to his final conversation with Olaf.

It comes as no surprise, then, that one seventeenth-century manuscript of *Thorstein Shiver* (AM 164d fol.) couples it with the shamelessly entertaining adventure-tale *The Saga of Ref the Sly* (*Króka-Refs saga*). As for *The Book of Flatey*, it is tempting to see *Thorstein Shiver*, written (and possibly composed) by Jón Þórðarson himself, as his attempt to provide a little light relief before plunging into the icy depths with *Thidrandi's Tale*.

THIDRANDI'S TALE (*ÞIÐRANDA ÞÁTTR OK ÞÓRHALLS*)

Jón Þórðarson's version of this tale is little different to that in other *Longest Saga* texts. *Thidrandi's Tale* may date from any time before 1350, but probably not before 1300 in its present form. It is rarely found in manuscripts outside *The Longest Saga*. Once again, pagan and Christian worlds are brought into close contact after a feast, when the plucky young hero disregards a solemn order against going outside at night; but this tale is no *jeu d'esprit*. We have moved out from recently-Christianized Norway to soon-to-be-Christianized Iceland: Olaf's spiritual tide is on its way, and will arrive in the next strand in the saga (*Thangbrand Comes to Iceland and Preaches Christianity*). Indeed, one seventeenth-century scribe (in AM 116 8vo) dovetailed these two strands together as a single saga about Iceland's conversion. In *Thidrandi's Tale*, the ancient strife between the forces of light and darkness suddenly and mysteriously skims the surface of Icelandic history, with tragic results. Instead of a slightly ridiculous encounter with a cartoon-like demon, we are presented with a sombre vision of the last generation of pagans, still walking in darkness or, at best, half-light.

The prefatory matter to the tale has been excised by previous translators, but it is integral to the tale. Oddly enough, it breaks the *Longest Saga's* chronological flow of events, telling the seemingly irrelevant story (found also in the *Book of Settlements*) of how the noblest of the settlers, Hrollaug Rognvaldsson, came to Iceland in the days of Harald Fairhair. The author then traces Hrollaug's descendants down to Hall of Sida, then lists Hall's more illustrious descendants. Only then are we told 'About Thidrandi'. But the puzzle vanishes when we stop trying to see *Thidrandi's Tale* as a mere 'tale', and view it instead as a miniature saga centred on the family of Hall of Sida, Hrollaug's great-grandson. The opening genealogies anchor the story in Norwegian history, establishing Hall's noble ancestry and his descendants' laudable tendency to become bishops: the latter figures reflect back on Hall and remind the audience that Hall will be one of Thangbrand's first converts to the new faith, when the tide finally reaches Iceland in the next chapter.

This impending action of Hall's now brings the wrath of his pagan otherworldly guardians ('goddesses') down on the family they once looked after. Aware of their impending exile, the goddesses resolve to exact one final payment from Hall's household: his beloved son. They kill Thidrandi at the 'Winter Nights' feast, a time when families traditionally sacrificed to these goddesses. Hall has a bull named 'Prophet' for this purpose, though we never see it being slaughtered; instead, we are shown Thidrandi dying in the field. It is hard not to think of Abraham and Isaac – only here the situation is reversed, because the angelic bright riders arrive too late to save him.

Though narrated in an unusually laconic manner, Thidrandi's vision owes its content to European vision-literature.[62] The originality of *Thidrandi's Tale* lies in the way its author has staged the intersection of otherworldly and human spheres of activity. As befits their benighted state, the heathen protagonists remain in the dark as to what has really happened. Only the two characters named in the tale's title are vouchsafed any knowledge, and in their different ways they come closest to being Christians in spirit: Thidrandi behaves with a Christlike humility, while Thorhall is a prophet who glimpses a better faith coming on its way. Neither man is fully aware of the event's significance, because neither is quite Christian. Thidrandi has a vision of the goddesses, making him a kind of prophet, but he dies none the wiser. Thorhall never sees them, but has a dim foreboding that 'a prophet will be slain'; after Thidrandi's death he understands more clearly, but still hedges his explanation with admissions of ignorance and conditional phrasing. In this dark world the true meaning of events can only be revealed if the narrator himself steps in to explain – which he does, with such apparent clumsiness that some modern translators excise this crucial paragraph. (The stylistic contrast may be intentional, marking off this section as commentary outside the story.) The rest of Hall's household remain completely unaware of the otherworldly drama which has just played itself out on their doorstep. Despite Thidrandi having told them what happened, they persist in interpreting this as a merely human drama: 'inquiries were made about people's movements', as if this were simply a murder case. One twentieth-century scholar took a similar view, suggesting that the black-clad riders were really a kind of pagan Ku Klux Klan, lynching Thidrandi in revenge for his father's advocacy of Christianity.[63]

It is easy to see why this tale has been so widely praised: the author's mastery of stylistic register allows him to convey depths of meaning with the utmost economy. The darkness of heathen ignorance is counterpointed by the eerie distinctness of Thidrandi's vision, in which Thorhall's dim forebodings are given body. Thidrandi's experience is both visual and aural, giving this oddly stylized scene a sensory vividness which sets it apart from the rest of the tale. The wonder is laconically conveyed by Thidrandi's desire to go back inside and 'tell people about the sight'. And there is something affecting in the last image of Thidrandi alive: the saga-author somehow manages to suggest the nobility of pagan bravery at its best and most hopeless by closing this scene with the conventional formula 'He defended himself well and bravely.' With that the narrative cuts off, leaving Thidrandi to die unseen. When Hall and Thorhall go out to find him, something of the vision's chill beauty lingers on in the otherwise irrelevant detail 'There was moonlight and frost.'

Finally, Thidrandi's body is laid in a mound 'after the ancient custom of heathen folk.' No emotional reactions are portrayed: the narrator's reserve heightens our sense of detachment from this brief and sombre scene, which itself encapsulates the pastness of that past. Not merely a hero, but an age is being laid to rest. The new tide approaches, and after Hall's grief has driven him from his former home, Thorhall is at last vouchsafed his own vision. He sees all the land-wights packing their bags and moving out of the Icelandic landscape. The tone lightens, and Thorhall smiles. In a few months Hall will be accepting a new otherworldly guardian – the Archangel Michael.

THE SAGA OF BARD THE SNOWFELL GOD
(*BÁRÐAR SAGA SNJÓFELLSÁSS*)

In *Bard the Snowfell God*, these tensions between pagan past and Christian present are played out more expansively. But here they are dramatized from the opposite viewpoint, that of a 'guardian-wight' who once inhabited Snowfell's Ness. Bard is depicted as a pagan equivalent of the Archangel Michael, albeit one whose power has now faded from the landscape which preserves his memory.

Bard the Snowfell God was very popular: four fragmentary mediaeval texts survive from around the fifteenth century, and about thirty later texts (some of which split it into two sagas at chapter 9). It was also present, alongside *Star-Oddi's Dream*, in the lost codex *Vatnshyrna*

(1391-5). Humanist scholars like Arngrímur Jónsson used it in their historical works; it also fed back into folk tradition, spawning more placenames, and its characters were developed in later sagas like the second recension of *Armann's Saga*. No fewer than nine sets of post-mediaeval *Rhymes* (*rímur*) on Bard and/or his son were composed. The mediaeval fragments all represent slightly divergent texts, and in trying to follow a single textual tradition as closely as possible, only two of them are used here (see Note on the Translations). A single fourteenth-century saga lies behind these texts, but we do not know what it looked like and no attempt has been made to reconstruct it here. This saga reveals the work of a consummate literary craftsman and historian, and the following discussion does scant justice to its richness and subtlety, representing only one possible avenue of approach to this puzzling, fascinating text.

The first part of the saga follows patterns already established in sagas of Icelandic settlers. Bard may be descended from giants and trolls, but like many other noble Norsemen he finds himself unable to stay in Norway, and emigrates. His exploration of Snowfell's Ness, naming its landscape features, follows the usual settlement pattern (though in unusual detail). But Bard is not entirely human, and when his family is torn apart by loss and internal strife, he reacts by leaving human society and 'turning troll' in the Snowfell Glacier. Dramatically, this is the point at which the 'real' Bard emerges: we have not seen him utter a single word in direct speech until he bids his friends farewell, and apart from one verse this is the first speech in the whole saga. Bard lives in the glacier for the rest of the saga as a form of god or guardian angel, helping his friends when they call on him. The saga contains several miscellaneous stories about Bard saving people from evil sorcery. Many of these are similar to the miracles ascribed to saints (such as Hall of Sida's patron St Michael, the hero of another fourteenth-century saga), and this proximity hints at Bard's future fate. Though the saga ends just before Christianity reaches Iceland, we know – after the example of stories like *Thidrandi's Tale* – that Bard's days are numbered, and that Christian saints and angels will take over his role.

The problematic, painful nature of human contact with the otherworld becomes a central concern of this saga. For a start, the saga blurs the distinction between the two: the term 'supernatural' is deeply misleading, since magic and divinity are not *above* nature but part of it, and 'otherworld' falsely implies a similar separation. The saga-author shows a keen interest in the differences between the non-human races; my references here to 'otherworldly' and 'human' characters do not define their nature, but simply indicate their function in the scene in question. After Bard's disappearance, the saga is structured along two interwoven scene-types, both involving contact between otherworldly and human characters (as mentioned above, p.41). In the 'appearance' type, an otherworldly figure unexpectedly appears to a human in the wilderness (often in fog, rain or snow): Bard's 'miracles' take up the earlier occurrences of this scene-type, but similarly dramatic appearances are also made by other not-quite-human beings, both good and evil. Alternating (and eventually blending) with this scene-type are the 'hospitality' scenes, in which otherworldly and human characters mingle inside someone's home. These scenes begin as idyllic interludes from the harsh realities of the Icelandic winter, involving roaring fires and indoor pastimes (harp-playing, wrestling, love-making, feasting, skin-throwing), but they gradually take on a more sinister air, with games and feasts tending more towards carnage and cannibalism. The final such scene takes this tendency to a terrifying extreme: the aptly-named Gest enjoys the hospitality of death itself in Raknar's grave-mound, and a specifically Christian 'appearance' – depicted like a harrowing of Hel(l) – is required to save him.

Love-making is no mere pastime in this saga. We see Bard trying in vain to establish a male line and thus to preserve all he holds dear.[64] Like Jane Austen's Mr Bennet, Bard presides over a brood of eligible daughters who are slightly *déclassées* because of their unusual ancestry. Helga, the eldest, becomes the mistress of a married man and is brought back home by her father, only to pine away; Bard then marries his second daughter to an up-and-coming young man. Both unions are ardent but childless. Bard next seduces the daughter of Helga's seducer. The result is a son named Gest, who begins promisingly, taking up where his father left off and saving people from monsters. But Gest betrays his kin by accepting Christianity in a tight spot, and his father kills him, bringing his male line to a sudden end.

In Icelandic folklore, sexual union between an otherworldly being (usually an elf) and a human tends to end in tragedy and loss. Gest's death is characteristic, but the emotional pain of such liaisons is brought out most clearly by Helga's verses. Her beautiful and unique litany of longing for the landscapes of Snowfell's Ness is the first piece of direct speech in the saga, and it is somehow apt that such a speech should consist almost entirely of place names. Her second verse, though cast in a more conventional skaldic form, smoulders with passion denied. As Helga pines away and slips out of human society, so the web of metaphors turns on images of thinning out, presenting Skeggi as a 'jewel-scarcener' (generous dispenser of wealth), whose separation from Helga, the 'treasure' he used to clasp, causes her to 'wither' while her grief does not 'dwindle'. The tone recalls the heated verses of the Snowfell's Ness lovers Viglund and Ketilrid in *Viglund's Saga*, and of similar figures in *The Saga of Gunnlaug Serpent-Tongue* (*Gunnlaugs saga ormstungu*) and *The Saga of Helgi the Poet* (*Skáld-Helga saga*), all three of which are alluded to (in some form) by the author of *Bard the Snowfell God*. We glimpse only fragments of Helga's sad story, suggesting to some scholars that the saga-author was using an older 'Helga's Saga'. This fragmentary presentation seems, at any rate, to be intentional. Devastated by longing, Helga retreats into the stereotype of the 'lamenting female' (familiar from Old English poems like *The Wife's Lament*), even being mistaken for her legendary exemplar Gudrun Gjukadottir. At last she simply vanishes from the narrative, leaving only her verses and a string of place-names which trace her lonely wanderings in the desert wastes.

Yet for all the warmth with which Helga is portrayed, her father suffers the more grievous exile. He was born in Slabland, north of the Ocean of Mist, at a time when the forces of evil were shut out by the power of his father King Mist. Bard is forced to leave that land by the encroachment of ogres, and he takes up residence with a mountain-giant down in Norway. Forebodings about Christianity drive him away from there and to Halogaland: after avenging his father on the ogres he is unable to live on his home soil. The tyranny of King Harald Tanglehair drives him in turn to Iceland, where the combined pressures of grief and ancestral habit compel him to leave human society altogether and become a 'land-wight'. Finally, at the end of his saga even this refuge is threatened by the tide of Christianity spreading out from Norway. Where will Bard go next?

The saga does not tell us, but we can pick up hints from the way the legendary North has changed in the face of Christianity. When Gest comes to the regions his grandfather Mist once ruled, the landscape has been spiritually altered, and morally polarized, by the new faith. The tide has driven out the pagan spirits from southern parts, and the desert North is their (now wholly evil) refuge. The beginning of the saga had presented trolls, giants, ogres and so on as distinct races rather than mere embodiments of evil, calling them 'people who are not human'; but this new world has no room for shades of meaning. Hostile monsters are no longer ambivalent creatures that can be fought with weapons, like the ogres of Mist's day or the trolls of Iceland. They are all of a single stamp now – the demonic – and what they have lost in particularity they have gained in power to do harm. Faith in Christ is the only effective weapon against them. In stark contrast to the unsettling ambiguity of Thor's appearance to Ingjald of the Hill, a cartoon Odin wearing 'a blue-flecked hooded cape, buttoned all the way down to his feet' now quacks cod heathenism to Gest's men, and Jostein the priest does him in with a crucifix. The suspiciously minute visual detail, particularly in comparison to Thor, gives the impression that the real Odin has somehow been replaced by (or transformed into) a Satanic simulacrum dressed in the right costume and prating the appropriate falsehood like one of Hieronymus Bosch's grotesques. The effect is surely deliberate: the power of the Devil dwarfs and trivializes the old gods, as it does the old heroes in *Thorstein Shiver*. These encounters are framed as demonic 'temptations' rather than fights with monsters or struggles with ancient forces. Traditional heroism of the 'land-cleansing' variety is suddenly out of date.

Consequently, Bard is unable to help Gest when the latter calls on him in Raknar's grave-mound. King Raknar appears in this saga as the very incarnation of evil, but we only view him through the polarizing lens of the new faith. His past presents disturbing parallels with Bard and his family. Gest tells Olaf that according to his kins-men (i.e. Bard, who taught him), Raknar ruled over Slabland and other regions, then disappeared into a mound with his possessions. According to the probably fourteenth-century *Halfdan Eysteinsson's Saga*, Raknar cleared Slabland of giants.[65] Similar land-cleansing was later achieved by the giant/troll Mist in his prime, and Bard fol-lowed suit on Snowfell's Ness. But now, in the light of the new faith, Raknar the land-cleanser has become a demonic monster, sending out optical illusions to tempt Jostein and tricking Gest into staying longer than he ought with his glistering treasure. Perhaps something similar is happening to Bard at the end of the saga, when he kills his own son (as Raknar had killed his parents). This kin-killing was prepared for much earlier, when Bard killed his nephews and left his brother half-dead in his first troll-rage. But Bard does not put Gest's eyes out in a frenzy; he is angry, but calmly implacable in his revenge. The visual contrast between this vengeful spirit and the neophyte in his white baptismal gown is loaded with theological polarity: Gest is a martyr and will go to heaven, but his grim father is already halfway to Hell. There Bard's exile will be complete. The clerically-trained author may have been attempting to show the superstitious folk of Snowfell's Ness that there was no point in their calling on Bard (as they did, up to modern times), since his kind had been superseded by saints and angels; but far from preaching, the saga worries over this process of replacement, underlining the tragedy, not the triumphalism.

By the end of the saga, the new faith has still not reached Iceland, and while the pagan gods (the *Æsir*) may be reduced to cartoon characters in the demonic North, something of their old grandeur and mystery lingers on in Iceland. With Gest's quest and life at an end, his half-brothers (the Thorbjornssons) travel home. There they join forces with the brothers Hjaltason and defend the poet Odd of Breidafjord (who may have a connection with Raknar – see Glossary) in an extremely mundane-sounding lawsuit. At the Assembly, the Thorbjornssons and Hjaltasons look so magnificent that they are mistaken for the gods. The embedded verse records and embellishes this curious epiphany. In a saga full of charged moments of vision – appearances, vanishings and mistaken identifications – this last one is particularly haunting. As part of the saga's 'endgame', this epilogue situates the Thorbjornssons within a historical context before signing off, grafting them onto a pre-existing *Book of Settlements* anecdote (complete with verse) about the Hjaltasons. It ends by reporting that 'a great clan is descended from the Thorbjornssons, and so too from the Hjaltasons' and, in the same breath, that 'There is no men-tion of Gest Bardarson having had any children.' The extinction of Bard's semi-otherworldly race is counterpointed with the vigour and fecundity of these mere humans, who momentarily assume godlike stature because the future belongs to them. The gods themselves are about to become history, and Bard with them.

Several other parts of *Bard the Snowfell God* are grafted in from *The Book of Settlements*, giving the saga a stratified feel. These borrowings are often held up as evidence for the author's lack of artistic originality, but the example just discussed suggests otherwise. As in *The Burning of Njal* (discussed on p.24), these fragments break the surface of the narrative and affect its meaning. Moreover, Bard left no descendants: his memory did not survive in written settlement accounts, but in folktales and (according to the saga-author) in place names. In constructing a literary 'history of the trolls' (as Ármann Jakobsson has put it), the saga-author has had to graft this material on to anecdotes from *The Book of Settlements* and other genealogical material, to provide points of commonly-agreed historical anchorage. The genealogies are often very long, or are attached to characters of little importance to the narrative, suggesting to some readers that this author took no interest in shaping his material. To this reader, however, the humans' genealogies seem deliberately paraded by the narrative, contrasting with Bard's tragic failure to graft his line on to theirs – a contrast made explicit by the saga's final sentences, and hinted at in the irony of Bard teaching humans 'genealogical lore'. In the world of the saga, of course, these not-quite-human races were far from extinct – 'in those days the troll-woman Bag was alive' – and the 'hospitality' scenes at Eirik's farm (chapter 8) and Bag's cave (chapter 10) hint at a vibrant alternative society thriving in Iceland's caves and glaciers, where giants and men could mingle. Many of these characters are only names to us, but to the Icelanders these names – Surt of Hellisfitjar, Hallmund of Ball Glacier, Jora of Jora's Cliffs – would have conjured up further realms of narrative, whether in sagas like *Grettir's Saga* or in folklore. For many, even in modern times, these characters still haunted the landscapes named after them.

These landscapes perhaps represent the saga's deepest narrative strata. Much of the earlier part of the story may have been 'read out' from place-names on Snowfell's Ness. Such is Þórhallur Vilmundarson's thesis: for instance, he has considered 'Breeze Shingle' to have derived from the locality's windiness rather than from a person named Breeze, but by means of false etymology the saga-author or his source has built a personal narrative around it. Many other place-names can be similarly explained, some much more plausibly than others. Particularly intriguing is Þórhallur's explanation of the basic story of Bard settling on Snowfell's Ness and vanishing into the glacier. The word *barðr* means 'ridge, edge', and there are two such 'edges' either side of Shit Bay where Bard landed. This bay, depicted in the illustration on p.192, contains a ship-like rock formation now known as 'Bard's Ship', on top of which the likeness of a man's face can be made out (according to Þórhallur). If you stand on a certain slope between those two 'edges', you can look down at the suggestive rock formations in the bay, and over your shoulder you can see the Snowfell Glacier. Perhaps someone was inspired to tell or write the story by standing on that spot, drawing the name Bárðr by false etymology from the surrounding place-names connected to an 'edge' (*barð*). Around this kernel, according to Þórhallur, everything else grew.[66]

Whether that was the case or not, the author *Bard the Snowfell God* was fascinated – obsessed – by place-names. In his hands the tortured landscape of Snowfell's Ness does not simply represent a source of narrative, what Robert Kellogg calls 'a gigantic memory theatre'.[67] Over and above this, the landscape is fraught with emotional significance: it can be longed for, as Helga shows. With most sagas set in Iceland, landscape features named after saga characters allow the audience to make a mental connection between past and present: like a genealogy, they enshrine the memory of an ancestor and reveal the ancient connections of living blood-lines. These connections are broken in *Bard the Snowfell God*. Instead, this landscape harks back to a vanished race of elves and giants, no less mighty and no less extinct than the prehistoric monsters found living far below the Snowfell Glacier by the heroes of Jules Verne's *Journey to the Centre of the Earth*.

MIRMANN'S SAGA (*MÍRMANNS SAGA*)

With *Mirmann's Saga* we move at last outside the ambit of the legendary North and into the relatively refined, knightly world of the
South. This saga is usually bracketed alongside other 'knights' sagas',
alleged to be the most frivolous of the Icelandic saga 'genres', but
despite similarities of setting and a structural proximity to romance,
it sits uneasily in their company. Far from providing escapist entertainment, *Mirmann's Saga* is a serious moral tale. The humour is
often sardonic, and the outlook sceptical: the (almost certainly clerical) author cuts through the appearances of worldly conduct with
a surgeon's unflinching precision, and he does not like what he
finds. It is, nevertheless, an extremely rewarding saga. Because the
moral themes are so evident and the structure so transparent, the
novel-reader already has many of the tools required to enjoy and
interpret it.

Like most sagas, however, *Mirmann's Saga* was written and rewritten over the centuries. It used to be thought that it was a translation or adaptation from a Continental source, partly because of its
geographical accuracy, and perhaps also because it was thought too
good to be a home-grown 'knights' saga'. Forty-four manuscripts
survive, preserving six distinct recensions whose relationship is not
known. Thirty-four of these (only one of them mediaeval) contain
the text followed here, the A-recension (to follow Desmond Slay's
classification), probably first written in the fourteenth or fifteenth
century. The D-recension may date from the fourteenth century, and
there are two fifteenth-century manuscripts of the B-recension. Two
sets of *Mirmann's Rhymes* (*Mírmants rímur*) were also composed, and
the F-recension of the saga probably derives from one of these.[68]
All these texts tell the same story, but in markedly different ways: the
first *Mirmann's Saga* was probably written in the fourteenth century,
but we shall never know how it told the story. For the purposes of
this book, '*Mirmann's Saga*' means Recension A.

The saga's first sentence has never been deciphered – many manuscripts simply omit the illegible bit about Nero – but it places the story firmly within a synthetic chronology which brings together Saint Clement and the Emperor Nero from first-century Rome, the third-century missionary Saint Denys (see Glossary), and the fifth-century Merovingian king Clovis. Three crucial periods for western Christianity are thus conflated: respectively, its first flowering in Rome, its first appearance in France, and its official acceptance in France. A still later form of Christian expansionism is evoked later in the saga: Mirmann behaves as a kind of crusader, and the heresy he fights is always Islam. 'Mahomet' is worshipped not only in Spain, but also in Saxony and (apparently) England, and Clovis himself is said to have been Jewish before his conversion. The distortion may be intentional: by painting heathen Europe in 'Saracen' colours, the author fools his audience into expecting Mirmann to behave like the hero of an Icelandic crusader-romance like *Bæring's Saga*.

But Mirmann is a flawed hero, born of flawed parents: Hermann and Brigida are both uncompromisingly fierce individuals, and we are further led to expect trouble from their son by Hermann's ominous dream. Possibly in response to this warning, Brigida takes unusual pains to educate him in Classical learning, incidentally needling her husband for his lack of scholarly interests. Despite Mirmann's evident promise, his father Hermann has no love for him, thinking him self-willed and lacking in respect for the gods. This last aspect of Mirmann's character foreshadows his conversion to Christianity at the court of his foster-father Clovis. Hermann's dream is fulfilled when Mirmann comes back home and treats him to an elaborately learned lecture on sacred history. Tempers rise; their natural ferocity overcomes them, Hermann tries to kill his son, and Mirmann murders his father. Oddly enough, he never seems inordinately remorseful about this appalling deed: he comments to his men that it was only to be expected given his ancestry, and later on he tends to speak of it more as a misfortune to be borne than a crime requiring redress. His mother, however, takes a different view: not only has Mirmann killed her husband, but he has not even stayed behind to console her. Her fierce devotion towards her son turns to fierce hatred, and she tricks him into coming back with promises of conversion. Using natural magic (a worm or snake in his mead) she infects him with leprosy, then vanishes from the saga. Mirmann has seen the last of his dysfunctional family.

Back in France, however, he has also run into trouble with his adopted family: his beautiful young stepmother Katrin is constantly trying to seduce him. This lady belongs to the same stereotype as *Hjalmther and Olvir*'s Luda: the story of Clovis's second marriage initially follows the same pattern as Ingi's (and Ptolemy's), not to mention all the other North Atlantic stepmothers.[69] This pattern conventionally results in the hero spurning his stepmother, where-upon he is either falsely accused to his (foster-)father, or put under a spell which forces him to leave home. *Mirmann's Saga* sets up these expectations only to thwart them. In chapter 6, Mirmann does not accept Katrin's advances; but rather than overtly spurning her, he treats her love as if it were an honour from Clovis. Still more unex-pectedly, he tells Clovis what is going on. His ingenious method of defusing the situation bears out both the value of his liberal education and the chapter-heading advertising 'Mirmann's refine-ments, courtliness and chivalry' (the very qualities which attracted Katrin in the first place). A spell does indeed fall upon him, but at the hands not of his spurned stepmother, but of his own mother. And like Hjalmther, Mirmann has to leave home: when he returns to France a leper, Katrin cannot bear to be near him (as his mother had cruelly predicted).

Mirmann now assumes a disguise and embarks, pilgrim-like, upon a quest for healing which takes him south through Italy. Sicily – 'about as large as Iceland', the geographically-aware author informs us – is the most idealized realm in this saga. Here Mirmann is healed by Cecilia, the saga's true heroine (some manuscripts include her name in the saga's title). Far from being the passive object of a bridal quest, Cecilia is as active, determined and learned a lady as Brigida. Not only does she practice jousting and dress up as a man in her spare time; in her conversations with Mirmann she initiates and sustains a witty flirtatiousness which gives her some power over him while at the same time conveying genuine affection. Even in the serious matter of healing his leprosy, she makes sly remarks about his 'sweethearts in France'; and the healing itself is charged with a bizarre eroticism. After this act, involving snakes sliding in and out of mouths and bellies, Cecilia cannot resist asking him rather smugly, 'how many sweethearts do you have in France who would do such a thing for you?' – as if she had just performed an unconventional sexual act for his benefit. Appropriately, he is too exhausted to reply and just lies back on the bed.

Cecilia proceeds to worm the truth of his identity out of him, and the chess-playing scene (chapter 19) is a particularly fine example of laconic saga-dialogue at its best. Eventually he saves her from the unwelcome advances of a Saracen prince, her father makes him an earl, and they marry. Mirmann's quest for healing has won him a wife and a realm, and according to convention the saga should end here. But Mirmann is not as wise as his bride, and will not let sleeping plot-strands lie. He visits the ailing Clovis one last time, and here the 'lustful stepmother' subplot departs from convention yet again – for this time, Katrin succeeds not only in seducing Mirmann at last (using stories of Cecilia's unfaithfulness), but actually marries him. Interestingly, it is never made quite clear whether her true motive is lust rekindled, or fear for the safety of France after Clovis's death, or both. In any case, Mirmann commits the grievous sin of bigamy, besides his credulity and ingratitude towards Cecilia. She resolves to win him back by force. She travels north, disguised so convincingly as the heathen 'Earl Hirning' that one Saxon princess falls violently in love with her and has to be fobbed off with a story about an arranged marriage in Bulgaria.

By this time Mirmann's status as the crusader-hero of his saga has steadily grown: he has killed two Saracen rulers and demonstrated his knightly prowess in a tournament, after which the saga-author comments that 'there has never been a better knight in the Northern lands apart from Roland' (echoing an earlier claim that his sword was the equal of Roland's). This is high praise, and it is about to be put to the test. The hero of a crusader-romance typically clinches his position by defeating yet another Saracen army by the grace of God and marrying a Saracen princess. Mirmann now faces an apparently heathen army, led by its 'Earl': it is a situation he has seen, and triumphed in, twice before. He proceeds to behave in the customary manner, engaging in the usual pre-battle banter; but his opponent unexpectedly alludes to Mirmann's disobedience of God's law, besides cattily implying that Mirmann's power is directly dependent on his women. 'What need have you to name the god I worship?' asks Mirmann, wrong-footed as usual by his wife's superior wit. In the duel itself, he follows his custom of reciting psalm verses in mid-charge, but this tried and tested crusading strategy now fails him: God's grace is with 'Hirning'. Yet again Mirmann is completely in his wife's power: he suddenly loses all his strength and she unhorses him, captures him, and brings him home as booty, setting him on a mule. At last she removes her disguise and submits herself to him once again, and the happy ending comes round for the second time.

But even now the perfect felicity cannot last. No offspring are recorded, and twelve years later, at Cecilia's instigation, the pair retire to the celibate life of the cloister, where this world's tumult cannot touch them. Only by such means, it is implied, can they have a truly 'happy ending' to their lives. In any case, their renunciation is fully in keeping with the saga's sceptical attitude towards worldly glory and the moral and emotional quagmires awaiting those who pursue such a will-o'-the-wisp.

This scepticism cuts at several levels. First, old-fashioned, Northern-style heathen heroism is depicted as the triumph of brute force over intellect: Hermann, Bæring and Lucidarius are dinosaurs in an age of diplomacy. They bring their doom on themselves – though the author takes care not to make them into mere stereotypes, giving Lucidarius a certain nobility of demeanour and making Hermann into a complex, tortured character. Second, the underlying selfishness of human (especially courtly) behaviour is ruthlessly exposed. Some conventional pieties are explicitly laid open: the Saxon nobles show their devotion to their ruler's offspring 'to strengthen their own positions', and Mirmann's parents take pains with him 'for their own ... benefit'. More often, the author hints at such undercurrents, particularly in speeches involving formal, rhetorical balance.

Third, Mirmann's learning is shown to be an ambiguous gift for all concerned. Brigida provides him with the best possible education, and the result rebounds upon her and Hermann when Mirmann picks up Christianity along the way and becomes as ostentatiously learned in sacred history as he is in the failings of the female sex. His learning leads him astray in the end: his lengthy, hectoring sermon to his father has fatal results, and his reading about female fickleness makes him willing to believe that Cecilia has been unfaithful. His refinements helped him to outmanoeuvre Katrin the first time, but now that she brings a (faked) letter to prove her point, this student of the written word is taken in.

Fourth, this clerical author emphasizes the way in which the crusading ideal can be debased in practice. Mirmann's psalm-reciting tactics fail at the end: his prayers have become a mere magic ritual, rather than constituting true repentance. We have been led to believe that this will be a crusader's saga, but absolutely no authorial anxiety is shown towards the Saxons' persistence in heathenism, and the idealized Christian heroine parts from them with affection, having herself been happy to masquerade as an enemy of the faith. Questions of right and wrong are shown to rise above such matters.

Finally, woven into the saga is a chain of animal imagery, vividly embodying the brutality of this heroic world. It is chiefly sustained by the three dreams which predict three crucial events and raise them into mythic realms: Mirmann's conception, his fight with his father, and his defeat by Cecilia. Each time, the dreamer sees someone in his family as a fierce animal, attacking him: Mirmann becomes a snake to his father (making Brigida's revenge horribly appropriate), Hermann a bear to his son, and Cecilia a lion to her husband (though the Icelandic term *it óarga dýr*, 'the uneffeminate beast', highlights the dreamer's confusion at perceiving that this is a female lion). After killing his father, Mirmann calls his mother a 'she-wolf' and refers to himself as 'a wolf, not a hare'. Likewise, the sword he takes from his father comes from a den of wolves, and its name 'Wolfling' is another name for the doomed Norse dynasty of the Volsungs, some of whom turned into werewolves, and some of whom slaughtered their own children in the name of honour and revenge. The animal imagery provides a grim commentary on the superficial glamour and courtliness of Mirmann's world: no wonder he retires from it in the end.

In view of this bleak perspective, the final reconciliation between hero and heroine seems a remarkable achievement by the saga-author. As a plot element it is entirely conventional, and it would have been easy for this tough-minded author to make it a hollow, hackneyed moment. Instead, it is genuinely touching: as at the end of Shakespeare's *Winter's Tale*, the dramatic emphasis is upon the guilty husband's reaction, stunned by his wife's forgiveness and God's mercy. The scene is sketched with the minimum of detail: Cecilia's simple act of removing her helmet is made to speak volumes. The speeches themselves are formal, but somehow they ring true – the protagonists hardly know what to say. Mirmann is genuinely speech-less, and tries to remedy it by stating the obvious ('you must be Cecilia ... rather than Earl Hirning'). Cecilia keeps up the bravado as she removes her helmet, but after Mirmann has stammered out his response, the strain of pretending to be a man is finally too much for her to sustain: her first words as a woman, 'I don't want to hide from you any longer', reveal a touching emotional vulnerability of which, up to now, the audience has been unaware.

The sense of renewal is strengthened by the humour which always seems to creep in when these two meet: Mirmann comments that Earl Hirning 'is handsome, and his face looks like Princess Cecilia's.' 'I've often said so myself,' remarks Roger. Comedy is essential to a satisfying happy ending, bringing the miracle to earth. When Mirmann says 'I dearly want to stay with you now', we know that he means it, and that the 'very joyful reunion' is no mere courtly show: it has been hard won, and will not lightly be thrown away. But this is no fairytale: their delight in each other remains earthbound. By limiting it to twelve years, the author does not proclaim the vanity of earthly love; rather, he makes it seem the more precious and miraculous, briefly wrested from a world ruled by beasts of prey. It is a miracle they must let go of in the end.

Note on the Translations

These are not word-for-word 'decodings'; they are translations, rendering the texts' literary qualities as well as their linguistic forms. Icelandic is a rich and characterful language, and while I have tried to stay as close as possible to the literal sense, many idioms cannot be reproduced word-for-word without introducing a stiffness that is not present in the original. All translators have their own ways of steering between the Scylla of inaccuracy and the Charybdis of woodenness. For example, one common phrase translates literally as 'Now it is to be related that ...'; I have rendered it with the English idiom 'Now the story goes that ...'. The profusion of 'ands' in Icelandic sagas would tend to drive most Anglophone readers to distraction: several have been omitted here or turned into 'buts' – and so on.

VERSES

As far as possible I have tried to reproduce the sagas' fluctuations in tone – laconic, rhetorically elaborate, flippant, sententious – and some of these modes require greater artistic licence than others. This is the case above all with the embedded verses, cast in forms that simply do not cross the language barrier: it is sometimes difficult to believe that two different translations of the same stanza really represent the same original. These verses fall into two broad types, skaldic and eddic (see pp.13-14). In order to give the reader some idea of the procedure being followed in this book, here is an example of each type (showing the original alliteration in bold, and internal half-rhyme and full rhyme underlined) and a literal rendering of the sense.

The literal sense of this skaldic stanza from *Star-Oddi's Dream* must be read four lines at a time:

In trying to convey the sense (explaining concepts like 'wall' and 'sail-risky'), the translation loses the regular patterns of alliteration and rhyme and the strict six-syllable lines. On the other hand, in attempting to keep as much alliteration, internal rhyme, regular rhythm and consistent syllable-counts as possible, some less essential aspects of the sense have been altered slightly (the mast's top has become a yard-arm, some prepositions have changed):

Geirvid made good speed,
Glided from the seaweed
Out beyond the brine-garth –
The breeze-steed bit wind;
Headed then for Temple Head
Hardy men in gale-gusts,
Sail-wall stretching overhead
Hard against the yard-arm.

Unfamiliar kennings (such as 'breeze-steed' for 'ship') are explained in endnotes.

With its shorter lines and lack of internal rhyme, the typical eddic stanza is much less complex and less self-consciously artful, and accordingly harder to make into tolerable English verse. Most of the examples in this book are not very good in the original either. This stanza from *Star-Oddi's Dream* is one of the better ones:

Váru austr	There lived east	There lived east
á Jöruskógi	in Battlewood	In Battlewood
barmar tveir,	two brothers,	Brothers twain
böls um fylldir,	full of spite,	Brimful of spite;
ok til fjár	and for money	Treasure-thieves,
fyrða næmdu	they captured men	They pounced on men
við morðráð	with murder in their minds,	Many a time
mörgu sinni.	many a time.	By bloody schemes.

NAMES

The extent to which translators should or should not translate names has always been debatable. Whichever view one takes, consistency carries a heavy penalty: as with cats, the naming of trolls is a difficult matter. If one opts to translate them all, one ends up with a sizeable handful of names whose meaning is still unknown. If they are all left in Icelandic, as is increasingly the fashion today, only the initiated will understand their significance – and the meanings of names play a crucial role in many sagas. Leaving them all in Icelandic also tends to place nicknames and other special names in the same category as standard names, for someone who does not know the language. For instance, the name of the troll-woman *Þúfa* in *Bard the Snowfell God* is not known outside this saga, and has clearly been made up to explain the placename *Þúfubjörg*, which means literally 'rocks of the mound'. The personal name comes directly from the landscape-feature. Bard himself, on the other hand, bears a perfectly normal Icelandic name (*Bárðr*), but the uninitiated reader would have no way of telling that the transliterated Icelandic name 'Thufa' had a different status to 'Bard'. One could of course have one's cake and eat it by giving both Icelandic and English versions simultaneously, like this:

> Hjalmther now looked out to sea and saw nine troll-women ....These were their names: Hergunn (Warbattle) and Hremsa (Clutcher), Nal (Needle) and Nefja (Beak), Raun (Trouble) and Trana (Snout), Greip (Gripper) and Glyrna (Cat's-eye), and Margerd (Sea-Giant) was the ninth.

But this technique clogs up the narrative and makes a sharp and rattling troll-list look like a dictionary of etymology. Such names are *meant* to sound strange and grotesque: trolls do not usually have normal names. These are what Anne Barton has called 'speaking names', designed to tell us something imme-diately about the bearer's personal characteristics.[1] Just as it is appropriate for English readers of Grimm's fairytales to have names like 'Red Riding Hood' rendered in English, so I have translated speaking names.

My procedure generally follows the example of the Penguin Classics saga-translations by Hermann Pálsson and Magnus Magnusson, though I tend to leave slightly fewer names in the original Icelandic than they do. I have translated those names to whose meaning the saga-author seems to draw special attention. (Some readers may well baulk at a famous locality like Snæfellsnes being rendered as 'Snowfell's Ness', but in the context of *Bard the Snowfell God*, it is vital for readers to be constantly and directly aware of this name's weather-imagery, as well as of its reference to Bard's nature-wight grandfather Snow.) This principle applies to personal names as well as place-names: besides speaking names, I have also translated nicknames (e.g. *Skáld-Helgi* → 'Helgi the Poet'). The recognizably foreign (Continental) names in *Mirmann's Saga* are given in their standard English equivalents (e.g. *Gudifrey* → Godfrey). Most names, however, have not been translated at all. These are here transliterated following standard practice: accents are deleted, þ is represented by 'th', ð becomes 'd', and names are given in root forms (e.g. *Bergþórr* → 'Bergthor'). All this, of course, applies only to names within the sagas. The names of Icelandic writers, past and present, are given in the original spelling. The original Icelandic forms of all translated place-names are listed on p. 321-2. As for personal names, the original forms (spelt according to the edition consulted) may all be found in the 'Glossary of Characters and Terms' (pp.297-318) under the relevant name.

MANUSCRIPTS, EMENDATIONS, CHAPTER-TITLES

In view of the textual instability of the Icelandic sagas, as discussed earlier (pp.21-2), I have indicated which manuscript text is being followed at each point. A vertical line | indicates that a different manuscript is now being followed, and an endnote explains which one. The manuscripts for each saga are listed in the next section below. (Vertical lines appear only in the last two sagas; for the rest, a single text is followed in its entirety.)

Occasionally the text contains words or letters which simply make no sense, and which have to be either reproduced as such (as in the first sentence of *Mirmann's Saga*) or emended (as is the case elsewhere). Some words in the skaldic stanza from *Star-Oddi's Dream* quoted above are the result of this kind of minor textual tweaking by later editors. These editions are listed below. Not all editors suggest emendations, and where they do I have not always followed their suggestions: some supposedly 'corrupt' passages make sense to me. My translations do not indicate where emendations have been made, for fear of cluttering the text: readers interested in such matters will have to turn to the originals. The reader is however assured that only a few emendations have been made, mostly affecting only single letters or words, and this only where the text does not make sense and is obviously 'wrong'; they are not made in the cause of literary taste (with one exception – see the discussion of *Bard the Snowfell God* in the next section). Where possible, a related manuscript has been used to supply the gap.

Only *The Book of Flatey* and the first manuscript used for *Mirmann's Saga* contain chapter-titles. Such titles are useful for navigating the text, and where the text does not provide them I have made up my own after the example of the old Penguin Classics translations. These made-up titles, however, are enclosed in square brackets; original ones are not.

The division of a given saga into chapters has an important effect on its perceived structure. Many modern editions and translations, however, follow chapter-divisions arbitrarily imposed by the saga's early editors. This is a matter of convention and allows for convenient cross-referencing; but since the policy here is to represent the original texts as far as possible, 'editorial' chapter-divisions are disregarded in favour of those in the manuscript being followed.

Texts used for individual sagas

Apart from the stated exceptions, all the manuscripts mentioned here are in the Arnamagnæan Collection, housed in Reykjavik and Copenhagen.

Star-Oddi's Dream is translated in its entirety from AM 555h 4to, Árni Magnússon's 1686 copy of a late-fourteenth-century original from the lost codex *Vatnshyrna*. This codex also contained other dream-narratives and sagas about Icelanders. Some of the verses in the *drápa* are corrupt. My emendations generally follow those given by Þórhallur Vilmundarson in his edition: *Harðar saga*, ed. Þórhallur Vilmundarson and Bjarni Vilhjálmsson, Íslenzk fornrit 13 (Reykjavik, 1991). This and all other editions and translations follow a nineteenth-century chapter division that differs at two points from the manuscript. The saga has also been translated by Marvin Taylor in *The Complete Sagas of Icelanders* (see Further Reading).

Hjalmther and Olvir is translated in its entirety from the seventeenth-century manuscript AM 109a III 8vo, which – when it was whole – also contained sagas about knights, and translations from foreign romances. This text has never been edited, although extensive variants from it are provided in Richard Harris's (regrettably unpublished) edition of a different version of the saga: '*Hjálmþérs saga*: A Scientific Edition', PhD diss. University of Iowa (1970). This edition has here provided alternative readings for some corrupt passages in AM 109a III 8vo, particularly in the verses. Most of the verses are broadly eddic in form, but several of them are extremely irregular. Some have very long lines, or the wrong number of lines; some have internal rhymes like skaldic poetry; and some are almost ballad-like. This variety of tone and form is loosely reflected in the translation. Chapter-divisions here differ from published editions, which tend to split up the long chapter 11. No English translation has previously been published.

The late-fourteenth-century *Book of Flatey* (GkS 1005 fol.), mostly containing sagas about Norwegian kings, was most recently edited by Sigurður Nordal and others: *Flateyjarbók*, 4 vols (Akranes, 1944-5).The chapter-titles are original to this manuscript. *Thidrandi's Tale* has been translated into English many times, most recently by Terry Gunnell in *The Complete Sagas of Icelanders* (see Further Reading), but following a different manuscript: the complete *Book of Flatey* version is translated here for the first time. *Thorstein Shiver* was most recently translated into English by Anthony Maxwell, also in *The Complete Sagas of Icelanders*.

My choice of manuscripts for *Bard the Snowfell God* follows that of Jón Skaptason and Phillip Pulsiano in their edition: *Bárðar saga*, Garland Library of Medieval Literature A 8 (NewYork, 1984).The central section of my translation (pp.201-5, 206-32) uses two closely-related fragmentary fifteenth-century texts found in AM 162h fol. and AM 489 4to (the latter also contains sagas about Northern and Southern heroes, and adaptations of Continental romances). This translation's first seven-and-a-half chapters and its final half-chapter are taken from a mid-seventeenth-century collection of sagas about Icelanders,AM 158 fol.: according to the above editors, this contains the closest-related text to 162 and 489. My chapter-divisions reflect the manuscripts followed in each section. I have also referred to the edition by Bjarni Vilhjálmsson and Þórhallur Vilmundarson in *Harðar saga*, Íslenzk fornrit 13 (Reykjavik, 1991). *Bard the Snowfell God* was recently translated into English, following a nineteenth-century edition, by Sarah M. Anderson in *The Complete Sagas of Icelanders* (see Further Reading).These two works both use a different chapter-numbering to the version followed here.

Three of the verses in *Bard the Snowfell God* are in unusual forms. The first,'Blest would I be' (p.194), is more like a place-name rigmarole than anything else: its beautiful third and fourth lines were omitted from the text being followed (158), presumably to make it a regular eight-line verse, but – in shameless defiance of consistency – it was impossible to resist restoring these two lines here (following one of the less closely-related mediaeval fragments).The third verse,

'Row forth' (pp.199–200), is the earliest extant fishing-bank verse (later a common folksong form) and is in rhyming couplets; the fourth, 'Out alone he rowed' (p.201), is an eerie incantation with a refrain.

Mirmann's Saga is translated from four manuscripts preserving the A-recension, as laid out in the late Desmond Slay's critical edition: *Mírmanns saga*, Editiones Arnamagnæanæ A 17 (Copenhagen, 1997). The first ten and a half chapters (pp.235–61) follow a fifteenth-century manuscript in the Stockholm Royal Library, Sth Perg. 4:o nr 6, containing adaptations from foreign romances and sagas about knightly heroes. Most of the rest (pp.261, 261–92) is taken in turn from two seventeenth-century copies of the Stockholm manuscript, AM 181g fol. and AM 179 fol.. Slay printed these texts in full, and I have followed most of his suggested emendations. For the last section of the saga I have followed a related eighteenth-century manuscript, found in the composite multi-volume miscellany JS 634 4to (kept in the National Library of Iceland, Reykjavik), using Slay's printed variants. This is the first translation of *Mirmann's Saga* into any language.

GLOSSARY

Words marked with an asterisk★ are explained in the Glossary (they are only marked thus on their first appearance in the saga). The Glossary also contains brief entries on all the characters who contribute materially to the sagas' plots, even if only in a minor way. Of the characters who only appear in lists or genealogies, only those marked with asterisks are discussed in the Glossary.

Star-Oddi's Dream

There was a man named Thord, who lived at Muli in the north, in Reykjardal. There was a man named Oddi living there with him, the son of Helgi: he was called Star-Oddi. He was so skilled in calendar-calculation that in his day no-one in the whole of Iceland was a match for him; and he was knowledgeable in many other matters too. He was not a poet, nor did he know much poetry. This above all is said of his statements: people held it to be true that he never lied if he knew the truth, and in all things he was considered upright and the most trustworthy of men. He was poor, and not an especially good worker.

The story goes that an extraordinary thing happened to this man Oddi. He travelled out from his home to Flatey★ when his master Thord sent him on this journey to go fishing, and nothing else is mentioned except that the journey to the island went well. He stayed there and was looked after well – it's not mentioned who lived there. The story goes that in the evening, when people were going to bed, Oddi was treated well and made comfortable; and what with Oddi being travel-weary and comfortably settled, he fell asleep quickly, and at once he began to dream that he was back home at Muli. It seemed to him that a man had arrived to spend the night there, and it seemed to him that people were going to bed in the evening. The guest seemed to him to be asked for some entertainment, and he started to tell a saga. And it began like this.

2. [THE RULERS OF GOTALAND]

There was a king named Hrodbjart: he ruled over Gotaland* in the east. He was a married man: his wife was called Hildigunn. They had an only child, a son named Geirvid. He quickly grew to be handsome and intelligent and more mature than his contemporaries in every respect; but he was only a child when the saga begins.

The story goes that King Hrodbjart had appointed an earl named Hjorvard to govern a third of his kingdom. He was also married, and his wife was called Hjorgunn. They had an only child, a daughter: she was named Hlegunn. It's said of her that she was a difficult child, and became all the more overbearing as she grew older. It was also said that she did not wish to cultivate ladylike qualities in her behaviour. It was always her way to go about in armour and carry weapons; and if she had a disagreement with anyone, she made sure they were either severely wounded or killed as soon as she was annoyed.

What with this overbearing behaviour of hers, her father Earl Hjorvard felt that he couldn't put up with her disruptions, and he now told her plainly that he wouldn't let it go on like this.

He told her it wouldn't do unless her behaviour improved a little – 'otherwise, leave my court as soon as possible!'

And as soon as Hlegunn had heard this from her father's lips, that he wanted to make her leave his court, she made this reply: she declared she wouldn't be staying there, and then she asked her father to give her three longships, fully fitted out with both men and armour, and to prepare them as well as possible in every respect, with good troops so that she found them well manned; and if this matter was arranged as she'd just asked, then she said she'd be happy enough to leave forthwith. Earl Hjorvard was only too willing to grant this so that she would go away as soon as possible, for he thought (quite correctly) that great harm would come of her conduct.

He then had three longships fitted out as well as possible. And as soon as the troops were ready, Hlegunn the earl's daughter left the country with these troops, and later went on harrying expeditions and viking★ raids, and in this way won fame and fortune for herself. It is said that she never returned to the land as long as her father lived.

Meanwhile we must take up the story elsewhere. When King Hrodbjart's son Geirvid was eight, King Hrodbjart was taken ill; and there's not much of a story in it, for the upshot of the illness was that the king died. To all his closest friends and chosen companions, as to everyone else in the land, losing such a leader seemed a heavy loss (which it was). Afterwards a splendid feast was prepared, and all the most powerful men and the best leaders in the land were invited to it. What's more, everyone who wanted to attend the feast was also invited, both within the land and without, so that no-one should come uninvited. And after this feast had been held with the multitude of guests who had come to it, a toast was drunk to King Hrodbjart's memory with great reverence and respect, as befitted his rank and the honour which was due to him. And when the toast was over, the king was buried in a mound★ after ancient custom, as was usual among the nobility in those days.

3. [GEIRVID COMES OF AGE]

Now the story goes that after this great event which had befallen the land, all the wisest men and the king's closest friends saw fit to take another man as king and governor in place of such a leader as was lost. But so great had been the affection felt towards King Hrodbjart by all his countrymen while he was alive that the people wanted nothing else but to elect his son Geirvid for their king, and not to let the kingship pass out of his lineage. Although Geirvid was only young and seemed as yet little suited to governing a country at that time, all the people of the land were willing to take this risk under the supervision of his mother, the queen, since she was the wisest of women and capable in every respect.

But when this had been under way for a while, with such a young man as Geirvid being a ruler and governing many people, the government of the land soon grew weak (as might be expected). It also came about that his retinue grew smaller, because many of his retainers found themselves other occupations. Some went on viking raids; others went on trading journeys to various countries.

Now while this seemed a great setback, as was just recounted, many other troubles were brewing in this young king's realm. It's mentioned in the saga that two robbers were camped out in a forest called Battlewood. It was in this young king's realm. These vikings killed men for their money and were virtually berserks.★ One of them was named Garp, the other Gny. It's said that people never dared travel in small numbers. People were always going into the forest in large parties to search out the robbers and do away with them; but they were never found, even though a great many people were searching for them. So it went on until King Geirvid was twelve. And when he had reached this age, he was as great a man, in terms of height and strength, as many men who were fully developed in terms of age and ability, and almost like the men who were at the peak of their prowess in every respect.

On one occasion, when King Geirvid was sitting at table with all his retinue, he spoke up and said this: 'Now it is well known to you, all my people, that up to now I have only been young; so I have had little power, and for that reason I have provided the land with little governance. And I have often heard that said, as is to be expected. It can hardly be wondered at that up to now I have provided the land with little governance, because of my age. However, I am now old enough that it is time I put myself to the test and found out whether my rule is likely to ripen and prosper more than it has done, now that I have become a man of twelve – and there are many people of my age who are no more mature than me. Now I want to make known to all of you, my subjects and friends, that I mean to go and fight those berserks Garp and Gny, who are camped out in Battlewood and commit many outrages there. And I do not intend to come back as long as they remain alive. Either I shall overcome them, or they me.'

And when King Geirvid had said this, the first to reply to his speech was the queen his mother, along with all his best men; and all of them spoke almost with one voice and asked the king to travel in a large party to meet the highwaymen, and with a great deal of preparation, if he wanted to go.

King Geirvid replied, 'I had been thinking over this matter to myself for some time before I announced it, and it seems to me that even if I managed to defeat the berserks, I would not be able to win any renown in this expedition if I sought them out with a large and fully-armed host. And then it would be such a disgrace if they were not caught and I returned and left it like that – I'd have made a feeble job of it if that happened. Now I have decided to make this expedition against them with one other man, and fate will decide how the four of us part company. Fate willing, it may turn out that some honour will attend this expedition. I shall now venture on that course of action, however it may turn out. And the reason this matter has been laid before you now is that I now wish to know which man is the most eager to undertake this expedition with me. Now it is time for someone to wake up to it, whoever wants to take the chance. Let that man now answer my speech – since you should now know that for my part the matter is fully settled. I will make this journey, even if no-one volunteers to come with me and I have to go alone.'

But at this announcement of the king's, it's said that the queen herself was the first to speak against this expedition in every respect, and she said it had been planned with very little forethought (which it had), meddling with men of Hel,* namely the robbers, when so much was at stake, namely the king himself – for it seemed certain to everyone that in their encounter he would get the worst of it and perish at their hands, if it turned out as it would seem likely to, given the age of their king and the toughness of the berserks. All the king's friends spoke urgently against the expedition. They thought the king was done for if he went with only one other man.

The king replied that it was no use trying to dissuade him. And when everyone had grasped that the king wouldn't let himself be dissuaded, a man named Dagfinn volunteered and answered the king's speech. He was one of the king's retainers, and the king's poet.

'My lord,' he said, 'I know of no-one who has more honour to repay you for, in every respect, than I have. And the more danger you happen to be in, the more duty-bound I am never to part from you, if you are willing to accept my service and my company – and I am quite ready for this journey whenever you wish.'

4. [ROBBERS]

Now as soon as this man Dagfinn was named in the saga, the story goes that something very strange happened in Oddi's dream. Oddi himself thought that he was this man Dagfinn, whereas the guest – the man who was telling the saga – is now out of our saga and out of the dream; and then Oddi thought that he himself could see and perceive everything which came afterwards in the dream. So after this point the dream is to be told just as it seemed to appear to Oddi himself: he thought he was Dagfinn, and that he was getting ready for his journey with Geirvid the king.

And when they were ready, the two of them rode together with their weapons until they came to Battlewood, where they expected the robbers would be. The woods had grown in such a way that a wide road ran through the forest; and when they had come a long way into the forest, it is mentioned that a very high hill rose before them. It was steep on all sides. Then they went up the hill, wanting to look around from there and see if they could spot anything. There was a great deal of grit on this hill. From there they could see a long way. They were able to see two men walking. They were of great size, and they were making straight for the hill on which the king and Dagfinn were standing. These men were both well armed. And as soon as the king and Dagfinn saw these men, they felt certain that Garp and Gny had come.

Then Dagfinn said, 'My lord, I wish to make it known to you that I am not much used to fighting with weapons, and I do not feel very confident in my courage or fighting skills. Now I would like you to choose between two things: would you rather I attacked the berserks with you, or would you like me to watch your encounter from the hill so that I am able to tell the story to others?'

The king replied, 'If you are in two minds about this, then it seems clear to me that you should stay here on the hill and watch our encounter from here, and not come near our fight.'

Dagfinn took the advice the king had given: he stayed behind on the hill and didn't go near them, and that seemed very good advice to him. But the king himself went down the hill towards the brigands. It isn't possible to relate exactly how the blows went between them, and here I'll cut a long story short, for the story goes that in the end fate decided between them as follows: the king was granted life and luck, for he defeated both the berserks, and they perished from the great wounds the king had given them.

And after the robbers had fallen, the king and Dagfinn went on further along the road, and they came to a place where a small path led off the main road into the forest. They hadn't walked along this

small path for long before a very large clearing suddenly appeared in the woods, and there stood a house. The house was tall, firmly built, and firmly locked up, and the key was hidden in the door-frame. They unlocked the house and went inside. The house was well furnished and was almost full of all kinds of riches. They stayed there that night, and lacked neither good drink nor fine food there; and on the next day they set off for home, after burying the outlaws' corpses.

And when the king came home to his kingdom, he became famous far and wide in the land on account of his valorous feat and his glorious victory, and all the king's friends and kinsmen rejoiced when he came home with his noble victory. It seemed to people that he had been all but snatched out of Hel (which he had).

5. [PEACE IS RESTORED]

Now, after all these events, the king had an assembly★ convened, and a great crowd of people gathered there. And when this great crowd was all assembled, the king reported this great news; and it seemed to everyone a most glorious deed (which it was) that King Geirvid had beaten such champions single-handed. Then King Geirvid asked people to visit the house where the robbers had kept all that money, and he said each man should take the money he had lost. But they all gave up their money to the king, whatever each man had owned. They said it would be best seen to if he kept it, and they declared that he had fully earned it. The king then had the money fetched and took it into his possession.

After that, the king ordered construction work to begin, and people built a mound for the king to sit on. Then the king was seated on a throne which stood on the mound; and people exalted him in his rank all the more, and once again revered him and gave him honourable presents, as far as they had the means to do so.

It's mentioned that while Dagfinn the poet was there, it crossed his mind that no-one was more duty-bound than he to honour the king with a song. Then Dagfinn went up on the mound to the king, knelt before him, bowed to him, greeted him respectfully, told him he had composed a poem about the king, and asked him to listen to it. The king gladly agreed to do so. Then Dagfinn began to recite the poem: it was a *flokkr*.★

And when the poem was over, the king thanked him kindly, as did everyone else who was there, and they said it was well wrought, such as befitted their king's rank and worth. And when the king heard everyone expressing their approval and praising the poem so much, he wanted to respond himself and act magnanimously, and to give a princely reward: he wanted to give the poet a large gold ring which he wore on his arm.

But Dagfinn did not want to accept the ring and said he was very eager to have honour and respect from the king, but declared he did not need to accept money from him.

He said he lacked nothing as long as he kept him safe – 'but there are many others who look for wealth when looking to you.'

This pleased the king.

6. [HLEGUNN RETURNS]

The next thing to relate is that Hjorgunn, the wife of Earl Hjorvard, became dangerously ill, and there's no need to waste words on it: this sickness led to Hjorgunn's death. She was then honoured with a funeral feast, borne out and treated as was the custom for noble-women in ancient times. The earl felt the death of his queen to be a heavy loss (as was to be expected), and he grieved greatly over her, as did many other people.

Not long passed before his friends urged him to get himself another wife. He asked where they saw a match for him which would bring him honour. They reckoned he would do best to ask for the hand of Queen Hildigunn in marriage, and they predicted great advancement for him in that proposal if it were accepted. And when this had been suggested to the earl repeatedly, he came to see things the same way, for he was a wise man. Then he began his suit and asked for Queen Hildigunn to be his own wedded wife. At that time she was still a woman of no more than forty, and seemed a most distinguished match in every respect. And as for the discussion of this matter, the long and the short of it was that the queen ended up being married to Earl Hjorvard with the consent of the king, her son. Then a splendid feast was got up, and the wedding of Earl Hjorvard and Queen Hildigunn was celebrated with great pomp and with every honour. And when the feast was over, everyone went back to their homes. A great love soon blossomed between them, and their married life was happy; and it was not long before they had a daughter. She was named Hladreid.

It's said that the married life of the earl and the queen had not gone on for long after they had had Hladreid, before it came about that the earl was taken ill; and the upshot of this was that he died from that sickness. It was thought a heavy loss, because he had been a worthy ruler. After this event King Geirvid placed his own men over the realm the earl had ruled, and took possession of it himself. This news spread far and wide, as might be expected with the decease of such a ruler.

The news that her father was dead happened to reach Hlegunn, Earl Hjorvard's daughter, while she was on a raiding expedition, destroying some vikings. She reacted to the news by turning her entire army towards Gotaland and harrying there. And the result was that she conquered the whole realm which her father had ruled. Then she sent people before King Geirvid and asked them to tell him her message – that he should either grant her half the kingdom and half his authority to rule, or else get himself and his men ready and meet her with his army in a sound named Herringsound,★ and do battle with her there, and that would bring victory and triumph to whoever possessed the greater luck.

7. [PREPARATIONS FOR BATTLE]

We now take up the story at the point where the messengers Hlegunn had sent set off. They were shield-maidens.★ They went before the king and presented their message to him.

And when he had heard Hlegunn's ultimatum, he quickly made this reply: 'The less equal the alternatives, the easier it is to choose – I'd far rather fight with her than give up my kingdom in the face of her aggression.'

The messengers returned to Hlegunn and told her how matters stood, and she was extremely pleased with their journey's outcome.

Now the story goes that King Geirvid called up an army throughout his entire kingdom, and every man who could wield a shield or throw a spear had to go on this expedition. It should be mentioned that a promontory named Temple Head★ extended along one side of the sound, and all the king's troops had to assemble there by the promontory. And when King Geirvid was ready, the people conducted him on board ship.

Dagfinn the poet was there on the expedition with the king. But as they were going down to the ships, something happened which is worth mentioning, even though it might seem to be of little importance: Dagfinn's shoelace became loose. So he tied up the lace – and then he woke up and was now Oddi (as might be expected), not Dagfinn.

After these visions, Oddi walked outside and mused about the stars, since he had always been in the habit of observing during the night when the stars could be seen. Then he thought of the dream and remembered everything apart from the poem he'd dreamt he'd composed, save these verses written here.

8. [ODDI'S *FLOKKR*]

'There lived east
In Battlewood
Brothers twain
Brimful of spite;
Treasure-thieves,
They pounced on men
Many a time
By bloody schemes.

'But the hardy-
Hearted king,
Keen for glory,
Glutted wolves;
Battle-bold,
King Geirvid felled
Garp and Gny,
The brothers twain.

'Dealing fair,
Split the riches,
Hrodbjart's son
Praised his people,
Sons of fighters,
With the wealth
The wicked men
Had gathered in.

'Rings he gave,
The Gothic prince,
War-valiant,
To kin of men,

So his retainers
All received
Hawk-seat hangings
Made of silver.[1]

'Dagfinn now
In noble words
Must close his song,
His poem of praise.
Wisely wield
Land and glory,
Lordly king
Of Gothic folk!'

9. [THE BATTLE OF HERRINGSOUND]

And when Oddi had been outside for as long as he wanted, he went back to bed and immediately fell asleep; and he dreamt the same situation as before, from which he'd woken. Now it seemed to him that he had tied up his shoelace and was Dagfinn hurrying to the ships. It seemed to him in the dream that he was to be the captain of a ship. And when they were ready for the expedition, they sailed with the fleet until they came to the promontory, and all the king's army gathered there. Then they put out into the Herringsound. It's also said that the shield-maiden Hlegunn had arrived and was lying at anchor out there in the sound with her fleet; and she had an innumerable army ready for battle.

Then each side attacked the other. They clashed fiercely, and there was the bitterest of battles there. And both armies soon suffered heavy losses; but the battle had not gone on for long before the losses began to eat into the king's army and his ships became much emptier.

It's also mentioned that Hlegunn was not seen in the battle during the day, even though the king's men had made every effort to find her, and that seemed strange. And after this had been going on for the best part of the day, Dagfinn made a search using his skills,★ and then he saw Hlegunn. By then she had reached the king's ship, and a great change had now come over her. There appeared to him to be an enormous, trollish she-wolf's head upon her shoulders, and with it she was biting the heads off the king's men.

When Dagfinn saw this spectre, he left the ship he was steering – it lay far from the king's ship. Then he leapt from one ship to the next until he reached the king's ship, and when he came before the king, Dagfinn told him what was going on and what great monstrosities were afoot. Then Dagfinn pointed out to the king where Hlegunn was, so that he could see her. But the king could not see her because of her sorcery. All he saw was that his men were falling by the dozen. Dagfinn now told the king to look under his left hand, and he did so. And when he did this he saw Hlegunn. Then they both went aft to the sail together. Now the king charged forward with his sword drawn, and as soon as he came within striking distance of Hlegunn, he hewed at her with the sword. The blow fell on her neck and he swept off her head, and it fell overboard.

And when she had fallen, the king offered the people who had been following Hlegunn the choice of battling on against him or surrendering to him. They quickly chose to deliver themselves into the king's power. Afterwards, when King Geirvid left the battle, he placed the entire land under his control and set stewards over it, and in this way brought peace to the whole kingdom.

Then the king headed home, and a glorious feast was held in his honour. After that, an assembly was convened, and that assembly was very well attended. Then King Geirvid was enthroned anew, raised up on the same mound as before, and invested as king and governor over all Gotaland. One ruler after another then went up on the mound and paid honour and tribute to the king, each according to his power and means.

It occurred to Dagfinn the poet that no-one had more honour to repay the king for, in every respect, than he. He then went up on the mound and greeted the king well and courteously. The king accepted his greeting gladly. Dagfinn made it known to the king that he had now composed a further poem about him, and asked him to listen to it, and said he wanted to recite the poem now. The king replied that he would gladly listen to it. Dagfinn then began to recite the poem – it was a thirty-stanza *drápa*★ – which he dreamt he had composed.

And when the poem was over, the king thanked him very warmly, drew a thick gold ring from his arm and gave it to Dagfinn as a reward for his poetry. But Dagfinn did not want to accept the ring and said he had everything in abundance as long as he kept the king safe. But then King Geirvid made it clear to Dagfinn that he ought to do him more honour in every respect than anyone else in his kingdom. He offered to arrange a marriage for him, and said he would secure the hand of whichever woman close by in the land whom Dagfinn most wanted to marry.

Dagfinn was pleased with this offer (as could be expected, since the king was intending to do him so much honour), and he replied, 'If everything you've just spoken of is to be fulfilled on your part, then there's no concealing the fact that the choice of wife I would rather have also lies most of all in your own power to grant.'

The king said, 'Who is the woman you are speaking of?'

Dagfinn replied, 'It is Hladreid, your sister. She is the one woman I am most interested in winning – otherwise I do not think any marriage will be taking place.'

The king said that nothing should be denied to Dagfinn which he thought would increase his honour. Hladreid, the king's sister, was then of marriageable age even though she was very young, and she was the fairest and most beautiful of women, and most capable in all things. And as for the discussion of this matter, the long and the short of it was that Hladreid ended up being betrothed to Dagfinn the poet. Then celebrations were prepared, and a feast was held there, most magnificent in every way and with all the best trappings, for nothing was lacking that one could wish for. Also, all the best men in the land were present. Now their wedding was celebrated with the greatest honour and elegance. And when the feast was over, everyone who had come there went back to their homes. Between Dagfinn and Hladreid a great love soon blossomed, and their life together was very happy indeed.

But when Dagfinn's marriage had taken place in such a courtly fashion, as has just been related, the dream was over; and then he who was really Oddi woke up.

Oddi then mused on his dream and remembered the whole dream exactly, both the first part and the second part, and then he thought of the *drápa* he dreamt he'd recited later. He could remember no more of the poem than these eleven stanzas which are now written here, of which this is the beginning.

10. [ODDI'S *DRÁPA*]

> 'Geirvid made good speed,
> Glided through the seaweed
> Out beyond the brine-garth –
> The breeze-steed bit wind;
> Headed then for Temple Head
> Hardy men in gale-gusts,
> Sail-wall stretching overhead
> Hard against the yard-arm.[2]

> 'Swiftly slid the longship
> Over scowling billows;

Trusty heroes travelled
On their treasured wave-steeds;
I saw far-famed fighters
Go forth on this brave voyage –
Yet of all the Gothic men
Geirvid is their king.[3]

'Off Temple Head we held course,
Hardeners of Gondul,
In our royal ship-crowd –
The right way for the king's men –
Till shrewd ones, sure of winning,
Should hew the hostile war-crowd
In Herringsound, with spears,
And strike down the sword-trees.[4]

'Yet they waited, wary,
In their wave-borne stations,
Warriors who shattered
Shield-maidens' shimmer;
Men could see before them
Serried ranks of longships;
The helmsman's crew donned helmets,
Held back awhile from fighting.[5]

'Quick the king's men wakened
To the battle-bidding,
Where Hlegunn's ocean-horses
Hurried on in strength,
And, fierce and firm in spirit,
The prince's friends went forward –
Yet of all the Gothic men
Geirvid is their king.[6]

'Then the high-born ruler,
The blood-helmeted fighter,
With all his vigour whipped up
The storms of Hogni's sunset,
And war's red gleam was flung forth
From the furious fray;
Warriors went to battle,
The waves grew dark with gore.[7]

'Swords came swooping down there
When the soldiers battled,

Flocked together, fighting,
Gondul flying offshore;
Geirvid the spear-guardian
Speared men in that onslaught;
I saw the blood-oar bloodied,
Men's manes spurted lifeblood.[8]

'Warriors which the king steered
Went storming fiercely forward –
Fame follows many a monarch
When followed by such boar-lords;
I never knew a nobler band,
And none which battled better –
Yet of all the Gothic men
Geirvid is their king.

'Now I witnessed clearly
The cruel crimes of Hlegunn –
Bristling, with a wolf's head,
I saw her raging frenzy;
I saw her sharp-toothed troll-jaws
Chewing human charnel;
She made a fierce foray
With her snapping spear-gape.[9]

'I walked upon the wide waves,
One sea-ski to another,
Till with the helmsman's troop I trod
The gleaming mare of Gylfi,
Reported to the ruler
How ruthlessly the goddess
Of Ægir's gleam gave battle
And wrought the warriors' slaughter.[10]

'The king now saw it plainly:
Freya of the wave-star
Had upon her hawk-stem
The head of a heath-wolf's bride;
The far-famed, warlike ruler
Felled the flood-flame's goddess;
She fell from the sea-beam,
He showed her no mercy.'[11]

This is the end of the dream which Star-Oddi dreamt, according to what he himself has said. This vision may well seem extraordinary and unheard-of, but most people think it likely that he would have told only what seemed to appear to him in the dream – for Oddi was counted on as both learned and truthful. And no-one should be surprised if the poetry's rather wooden, since it was recited in his sleep.

The Saga of Hjalmther and Olvir

1. [KING INGI]

This saga begins with a famous king named Ingi. He was a celebrated man: in all his accomplishments he was greater, mightier, fairer and wiser, taller and stronger than anybody else in the world in his time. He sailed out on raids in the first part of his life, and conquered many kingdoms, and they paid him tribute. He ruled over Mannheimar,* which was the biggest and richest of all the countries.

The king had a celebrated queen named Marsibil. She was the daughter of King Margarus of Syria. She was gifted with all the womanly arts. A son was granted to them, named Hjalmther: he was handsome, big and strong, and skilled in all accomplishments. Even in his youth he was the ablest of men. The king had him instructed in all the arts that it was customary for young men to be taught.

There was a certain earl in King Ingi's realm named Herraud: he was acquainted with all the usual arts. He possessed more cunning and wisdom than anyone. He was the king's greatest friend, and was his sworn brother. He had a young and handsome son of his own, named Olvir. The earl taught him all the arts. He had thirty playmates, and rode daily into the forest to shoot animals and birds. Time passed until Olvir was fifteen. By then he was the tallest and strongest of men, and better than anyone else at chess, swimming and jousting.

One summer, King Ingi held a feast with all the pomp he could muster. The earl and his son were invited there, along with many other nobles, and it was the best of feasts.

One day, as the king and the earl sat at the drinking-tables, merry and cheerful, the king said, 'I would like you, brother, to foster my son.'

The earl told him to have his way. And at the end of the feast, the king gave the father and son good gifts. Hjalmther now went off with the earl. He learnt all the arts which Earl Herraud knew. It is said that Hjalmther and Olvir were fond of each other. The earl ordered Olvir to serve Hjalmther and yield to him in all things. Olvir did so.

And when three years had passed, the king sent for his son. Hjalmther went before the earl and said, 'I want to ask you to let Olvir come with me.'

The earl told Olvir to have his way. They did so. The earl himself went with them. The king had prepared a feast. He welcomed the earl and his son with great honour and kindness, and on the third day of the feast a tournament was announced on the fields which lay near the city. Many courtiers were gathered there. Hjalmther rode forth among them, laying his lance to both sides, throwing many knights to the ground, going like a bear into a drove of sheep; and there was no-one so hale or hearty, firm or fierce, that he dared fight against him. Olvir saw this, and he himself had already knocked many hardy knights off their horses. He now rode at Hjalmther as fast as he could, and each attacked the other – there was to be seen a brave charge on flight-swift horses as they laid into each other's shields with great force. This went on for a long time, until Hjalmther grew angry, pricked on his steed and rode at Olvir, driving his lance into the middle of his shield. But Olvir sat so steadily that the horse's back broke in two, and Olvir fell on his feet. Then they went back to the city, and everyone was happy.

Earl Herraud prepared to go home. He went up to Hjalmther and his son Olvir, and asked that one fate would befall them both – 'I want you two to become sworn brothers, so that your friendship will hold out.'

Hjalmther agreed to that; they then did so. Now the earl went home.

After that, Hjalmther had some construction work done: he built himself a beautiful castle out in the forest, and when it was finished he went inside with a hundred knights. He asked his men to lock the castle whenever he sat inside it.

A little later, the queen was taken ill and died. A grave-mound★ was raised and she was laid inside. This was a great sorrow for the king, and for everyone else. Hjalmther held a funeral feast in memory of his mother, and after the funeral he gave everyone good gifts. He usually stayed in the kingdom, but he rode into the forest to amuse himself.

The king had a throne set on his queen's mound: he sat there night and day, weighed down by grief and sorrow for the loss of his queen.

It came about one day, when the sun was shining beautifully and the king was musing on many things in his sorrow, that he saw his son coming with a large group of courtiers in splendid array.

Hjalmther went before his father, greeted him in a friendly manner and said, 'Must you sit here so long and pine for your queen? Such behaviour is unworthy of a king. I would rather make my way out of the kingdom, with your authority, and fetch you a new queen – and get her with spear and sword if she won't be fetched by other means.'

The king made no reply. Hjalmther stood for a long time in front of his father, then walked away, very angry.

A long time now passed, until early one day, when the sun was shining brightly, the king happened to look towards the sea. He saw a little boat coming in to land, quick as fire: it looked like gold. The king thought hard about this sight. There were two people on board. The king then wandered down to the shore, very worried and distracted, wondering how the world had grown so inconstant. He saw a man leave the boat: he was escorting a woman so amazingly attractive that the king thought he had never before seen anyone with such grace and nobility. All at once a great desire for her welled up inside him, and he greeted her in a friendly manner.

She accepted the king's greeting. The king asked her for her name and news.

'My name is Luda,' she said, 'and there is plenty of news to tell you, my lord. Lukratus, my own king, who ruled over the city of Boeotia, has been murdered in his own kingdom by the king of Serkland,* Nudus by name. He is taller and stronger than all men, and better endowed in every way than anyone in this part of the world. He has with him armies of every kind – black men★ and berserks,★ giants★ and trolls,★ dwarves★ and other sorcerers – so no human can withstand him and his vile host. They killed the king and took over the city. He wanted to force me to marry him, but I wouldn't have that. The next night I came secretly out of my bower with the slave who stands here, walking down to the shore and fleeing here into your kingdom, and I am now in your power and under your protection – but on condition that I be your own wife, not your mistress.'

The king said, 'Things have turned out very luckily here, because my queen died a little while ago, so the two of us might well do that. Let us go home to my hall.'

She agreed to this. Now they went home, and a wedding-feast was prepared at once, and it went ahead with all honour. Hjalmther was not at the wedding-feast.

Many people in the realm thought the lady high-handed and self-willed. Also, not long passed before a man disappeared every night, and many thought this odd.

As for the slave who had brought the queen there, she had him look after the swine. He was tall, and strong as a troll, though handsome-looking. So it went on like this in the kingdom for a long time.

2. [THE SWORN BROTHERS GO RAIDING]

One day, as the king was strolling outside, his son Hjalmther came up to him with his men and greeted his father in a friendly manner. The king accepted his greeting.

Hjalmther said, 'I have come to visit you for this reason, my lord: I want you to get me five ships with weapons and crew, well fitted out for battle. I want to travel abroad and win fame and fortune for myself. And I want all this to be ready within a month.'

'I will gladly do that, my dear son,' said the king, 'just as you wish.'

Now an assembly* was held, and a great multitude of people was invited to it. Then the king asked his son to pick as many men as he wanted, as well as ships and money. Hjalmther now did so, and picked an army of five hundred, all of them young people. And when this business was completed, Hjalmther stepped aboard with Olvir and all his men, and they sailed out into the ocean. Their fame and fortune prospered, for they cut down black men and berserks but let all peaceful people go in peace.

Late in the autumn they came to a certain island, and landed up a hidden creek. It was late in the evening. The island was wooded and surrounded by crags. Hjalmther and Olvir walked ashore, up into the woods and up a hill. From there they saw a great fleet of ships moored on the other side of the island – a very large, beautiful dragon-ship, and fifteen longships. There was a great tent on the shore, and there was a lot of smoke there.

Hjalmther said, 'Who can these men be, who behave so proudly? I want to pay them a visit and find out who they are.'

'Let's do that,' said Olvir.

Now they covered themselves all over with bark, took cudgels in their hands and stumbled on down to the tent. There was a lot of smoke. They sat down in the doorway. The others told them to get out of the doorway.

They said they couldn't do that because of the cold – 'but what's the name of the captain who has charge of this fleet?'

'You're joking,' said the others, 'or else you've been brought up so far away that you've never heard of our glorious master. His name is Koll, and his brother's name is Toki. In every accomplishment they are the greatest of the great. They have been on viking* raids, summer and winter, since they were twelve. Every creature is terrified of them: with their harrying they have subdued kings and earls, and their kingdoms. But now they have gone their separate ways for the summer: Toki has gone to England, and captain Koll has just arrived here. We've been in this harbour for a fortnight.'

'You tell a good story,' they said.

Then they went back to their ships and told their men everything they had learnt.

'Tonight,' said Hjalmther, 'we must make preparation and carry our goods ashore, and carry stones aboard, and tomorrow we'll give the vikings a good battering.'

They now did this. And when morning came, and the sun rose upon the ocean, they rowed at the ships and brought down a hard stony hailstorm on the vikings' ships. The vikings woke up to a bad dream. By then, the sworn brothers had won five ships from the vikings before they had put their armour on.

Koll now asked who was attacking them so boldly – 'you'll certainly find us getting in your way.'

Hjalmther identified himself. A bitter battle now began: Koll had a large, hard-bitten warband. Both sides attacked bravely, and countless men fell on both sides – though Koll's band lost more, for the sworn brothers felled them like saplings. However, not long had passed before Hjalmther and Olvir had lost their four ships and those on board. By now they had also killed every living soul on Koll's ships, except those who fled to him on his dragon-ship.

Olvir said: 'It would be best for us, brother, to see if we can reach Koll on his dragon-ship.'

'All right,' said Hjalmther.

And so they did. They got on board the dragon-ship, and so each man attacked the next. Another bitter struggle now began. One man after another fell dead, until Hjalmther and Koll came face to face. At once they hewed at each other very fiercely with sharp swords until the shields had been cut away from both of them. Hjalmther now thought to himself that this couldn't go on any longer, so he raised his sword and hewed at Koll's neck, and chopped his head off. Then he asked the survivors to swear allegiance to him. They agreed to that. They got a lot of booty there in gold and treasures.

Afterwards they headed out into the ocean and went home to Mannheimar, their fathers' realm. They sat in the castle over winter.

3. [MORE VIKINGS]

In the spring they went raiding: they now had ten ships and the dragon-ship *Koll's Gift*. They raided far and wide in the summer but won little wealth. When they were on their way home, they moored one evening in a hidden creek. They saw a large, beautiful dragon-ship sail into the creek along with thirty smaller ships. They sailed in to berth and cast anchors. These men behaved rather grandly. A man was standing by the sail on the dragon-ship, tall and nasty-looking, and he spoke this verse:

> 'Which rogues
> Rule these ships,
> Hard-bitten,
> Hapless ones?
> Your men's lives
> I will take,
> Split the riches
> With my men.'

Hjalmther heard, and said:

> 'I am Hjalmther –
> Who are you,
> Black-faced, on
> The sea-beast's prow?
> We will slay you,
> Take your hoard,

Loathsome liar,
Unless you fly.'

'My name is Toki,' he said. 'Are you the Hjalmther who killed my brother Koll last summer?'

'I am the very man,' said Hjalmther.

'It is well that we have met,' said Toki.

'I won't grumble at something you're so pleased about,' said Hjalmther.

'Truces shall stand until tomorrow,' said Toki.

Then they went to bed. And when there was enough light for a fight, they started the battle with stones and arrows, and when those ran out they took to their weapons and fought valiantly. There was no shortage of heavy blows, delivered one to another. The sworn brothers felt they had never met with such champions as these men were. One man after another fell. They fought all day until evening; then the peace-shield was lifted up. Three of the sworn brothers' ships remained, and four of Toki's ships.

So the night passed. And when morning came, they resumed battle. Toki attacked very boldly and struck to both sides. He was wielding a large, stout halberd, and within a short time he had killed thirty men. Olvir saw this and leapt aboard the dragon-ship with great fury and ferocity. He made sheer havoc around him and killed one man after another until he reached Toki, then hewed at his shield and split the shield clean through. Then Toki grasped his halberd in both hands and thrust it through Olvir's shield, skewering both his arms, heaved him up in the air, and flung him down on the deck so that he lay there senseless.

At that moment Hjalmther came and swung at Toki's arm and swept it off, and the halberd fell down. Toki now turned and leapt overboard, diving into the sea. At once Hjalmther leapt after him. Toki swam down hard and boldly, and Hjalmther gave chase vigorously until Toki grew tired. Then they drew together. Hjalmther immediately attacked him, and now they began to struggle bitterly and stayed under water for a long time, with each dragging the other down to the bottom, until Toki became exhausted from loss of blood and Hjalmther left him there, dead.

Then he swam back to his ships. His men were glad to see him, and he felt he had come back from Hel★ itself. Now Hjalmther bound up Olvir's wounds. There they got a great deal of rare and costly goods, gold and treasures. After a few days they headed homewards. Hjalmther steered the dragon-ship *Koll's Gift*, and Olvir steered *Toki's Gift*; and they sat in the castle over winter.

4. [PRINCESS DIANA]

When summer approached, they went out raiding and harried far and wide, and their fame and fortune prospered. As summer drew on, they came to a large country. There they saw beautiful cities, fair castles and a royal residence. Then the king sent some men down to the beach and invited them to his home for a splendid feast. They accepted this; the men returned and told the king. Preparations were then made on a grand scale.

The king had an extremely pretty daughter named Diana: she was familiar with all the liberal arts. And at the appointed time Hjalmther and Olvir walked towards the hall with two hundred men, leaving some by the ships. The king went to meet them with his handsome retinue and accompanied them into the hall. The king sat in his high seat, with Hjalmther and Olvir next to him. It was the best of feasts, and everyone was merry and jolly. And when evening drew on, people went to bed and slept all night long.

And in the morning, people got back to their drinking. The king was in the best of spirits, as was everyone in the hall, singing ballads and beautiful songs. The king sent for his daughter. She entered the hall with her ladies. The musicians played their harps, fiddles, lutes, psalteries and all kinds of musical instruments. Then the hall was all pomp and jollity.

Now the princess went before her father and greeted him affectionately, and greeted all the others seated further down. The princess was friendly and cheerful to everybody. Hjalmther and Olvir told the king much about their travels, and he praised their pluck a great deal. During the day Hjalmther and Princess Diana chatted away merrily, and the day passed like this until evening.

On the third day there was the handsomest of feasts, with all sorts of entertainment. Afterwards the tables were hung up. The king went out for a walk, and Hjalmther and Olvir went to the princess's bower. She gave them a friendly welcome and asked Hjalmther to play chess with her. This they did, while Olvir amused himself with the chambermaids: they were thirty all told. They went there every day.

Many days now passed, until one fine day, when the sun shone down on the city and the castle, they saw countless ships moving in from the ocean, quick as fire, and they moored in the harbour, carried their tents ashore, and set up camp. Now they saw a hundred men walking up from the beach towards the king. At this point Hjalmther and Olvir were near the king.

These men went before the king, and one of them spoke as follows: 'The prince of Serkland★ the Great, Nudus by name, sends to you, my lord, his greetings. He has been told that you have an attractive daughter, Diana by name: he wishes to marry her with honour and respect. But, if you do not wish to give him the princess's hand, he challenges you to battle on the third day of our truce. I would expect you then to lose, with little honour, both your realm and your daughter – and your life besides. It is not advisable for you to take this risk; rather, let him have what he wants.'

The king said, 'Tell your lord this: I will not give him my daughter. I will come to this field on the appointed day, with whatever army I can muster.'

The messengers then left and told the prince what had happened. The king now had the war-arrow despatched all around his kingdom and he summoned a great multitude of men. A countless host assembled. Preparations were now made by both sides.

5. [BATTLE WITH PRINCE NUDUS]

On the appointed day, both sides drew up their troops for battle, and then trumpets were sounded and both armies drew together, whooping and shouting. First, all kinds of missiles flew so fiercely that they made a great din: some were wounded from this, and some met their deaths. After that the king asked Hjalmther and Olvir to strike up a war-cry and so rush on them in a close fight with their swords drawn. The sworn brothers were on their horses, and with them a great troop of knights. Both had sharp spears in their hands, and now they struck up a war-cry, and so doing they pressed forward on them. There now began the fiercest of battles. And so fiercely did Hjalmther and Olvir advance on the prince's host that they gave way before them, and at this point many of Nudus's men were killed.

Nudus now saw that his army was retreating, and that many of his troops had fallen. Now he was filled with great fury, and called out to his men, and his berserks and black men, and told them to turn back against the king and his vile army, and ordered them not to be afraid. They now did so, and advanced hard with loud shouts and horrible noises. Then the berserk-fit came on them, hewing and thrusting, thrashing and bashing the king's troops on both sides and cutting right through the flanks. Many of the king's men now fled from them, terrified. Hjalmther and Olvir and their men saw that many of the king's men were fleeing and that some had been slain. They turned on this rabble and made a great charge against them, and it ended with them managing to kill all the prince's berserks and black men, and they drove back that vile flank.

Prince Nudus saw that his warriors had fallen like straw, and then he saw what Hjalmther and Olvir were doing. He now realized that he was about to put to the test fully. All the same, he was confident in his strength and good luck, so he pricked on his horse and furiously rode forth against Hjalmther. And when Hjalmther saw this mighty prince riding like a flying bird, he seemed to understand that Nudus wanted to meet him. So he quickly braced himself against him, fiercely shook his spear, then spurred on his horse and rode as hard as he could against Nudus. Each thrust into the other's shield, but they sat so steadily that neither man moved an inch in his saddle, but both their lances broke and the bits flew back over their heads. Now they took to their swords and struck at each other with great strength and alacrity. And because of the dreadful crashes coming from their swordstrokes, the horses beneath them became frantic, so that they could no longer get at each other. At this they jumped off their horses and gave them to their squires. Now they came together and fought so ferociously that you could see fragments of helmet and slices of shield in the air, and there seemed to be four swords in the air at once. Nobody thought they had ever seen a more valiant or outstanding duel, and they fought for so long that everyone thought it incredible they hadn't burst apart from sheer effort and exhaustion long before.

Hjalmther now became impatient that it had gone on for so long like this with no change between them. So he raised his sword with great strength and fury, and as Prince Nudus's shield had been all chopped up, he was not protected from his blows – so the blow came down on his helmet. It happened to be so forceful that it chopped him in half, body and mailcoat, right down to his waist. Then Nudus fell dead to the ground.

Everyone praised Hjalmther for the heroic deeds he had achieved in his attack, most of all the king himself. The entire army fled to their ships and sailed away, and the king and his men got a great deal of booty there.

Then all the host went back to the hall, and they were very merry and cheerful. Now there was the best of feasts, and nothing was spared that the body could wish for. And at the end of the feast, Hjalmther and Olvir went to the princess's bower. She gave them a friendly welcome and asked them to sit down. But Hjalmther said he wanted to set off for home.

She went outside, then came back and said, 'Here is a tent, Hjalmther, which I want to give to you. It has this property, that nothing can harm you when you are inside the tent. It is all woven with gold and set with precious stones.'

He thanked her affectionately for the gift and kissed her. She wept bitterly. Then Hjalmther went back to the ships, and the king was there before him. He gave the sworn brothers good gifts, and they confirmed their friendship and parted with affection. Then they stepped aboard and headed for home. They sat in their castle over winter.

But Hjalmther had not yet seen his stepmother.

6. [LUDA]

One morning, King Ingi and the queen were lying in their bed. She spoke: 'My lord,' she said, 'do you not have an heir?'

'On the contrary,' said the king.

'Why does he not stay at home beside you?' said the queen.

'He does not want to drink in our hall,' said the king, 'although he surpasses all men in skills and refinements.'

'I must,' said the queen, 'see this man.'

They ended their conversation.

One day, the lady ordered all her maids to go out into the forest and gather apples and berries for her. They did so. The queen walked into the forest, not stopping until she arrived at the castle, and she walked straight in through the locked door.

Hjalmther was sitting at table with his courtiers. He saw the woman walk in, and thought he recognized his stepmother from other men's tales. He immediately sprang up from the table, greeted her cordially and sat her on his knee. She accepted his greeting.

She was attractive to look at, gazing at him with a gentle expression while saying to him, 'My sweet son, why do you choose not to stay at home with your father? Surely it is more pleasant to be there than out here in the castle, far away from other people?'

Hjalmther said, 'That has more to do with my preferences than any ill-will.'

She said, 'Much has been said of your skills and refinements – and well-married the woman who won a man like you.'

He said that was not so. And as they chatted away, everyone left the castle, including Olvir.

Then the queen said, 'What impression do you have of me? Do you not think me womanly and graceful?'

'Yes, very nice,' said Hjalmther.

She said, 'Why should Fortune's wheel have turned this way for me? Better by far were you and I fit for each other, young and pure and well matched in potency. Listen, my delicious darling. I tell you truly, your father has not spoiled me, since he is a worn-out and feeble man, completely impotent, and no good at all in bed. But for me the flesh is weak, and I possess such potency in my womanly parts that it is a great loss to the world that so lusty a body should clasp so aged a man as your father and cannot blossom forth for the world's well-being. Well might we rather blend our two youthful bodies after our natural carnal desires, so that fair fruit might multiply from them – and we can soon get rid of that old beggar so he doesn't get in our way.'

Hjalmther spoke. 'Are you serious about this?' he said.

'Of course,' she said.

'I did think,' said Hjalmther, 'that you would be bad news, but never so shameful as I now know you are.'

He shoved her away from the table and punched her on the nose, so that the blood splashed all around her.

Luda said, 'We shall meet again.'

He said she would not find that pleasant. She sank down into the earth, just as she had come.

A little later, the men came into the hall. Hjalmther was so angry that he could talk to nobody.

Then Olvir went up to him and told him not to be angry. 'Has your stepmother caused this?'

Hjalmther said that was so.

One day Hjalmther wanted to go riding in the forest, and so it was done. And as they rode through the forest, they saw a large and beautiful deer. Now they rode after it, but it fled. They galloped after it until both their steeds had collapsed from exhaustion. Now they both sprinted on foot after the animal, but they soon became tired and threw off all their clothes apart from their shirts and linen breeches. Then a great mass of cloud advanced from the north-west, bringing rain and sleet. This went on until nightfall. Then came a hard frost with cold winds and snow. By then they had got on to a mountain slope.

Olvir said, 'It seems to me that it is getting cold, brother.'

Hjalmther told him not to speak words of fear. It was now well into the night. A little later the bad weather abated. They had now come to a big cave.

Olvir said, 'I am completely exhausted.'

Hjalmther said, 'We'll stop here.'

They went in under the overhanging rock. They saw a large giant sitting beside the glow of a fire. There was a lot of smoke in the cave. A creature was sitting by the fire and scratching the giant with wool-combs, and he was stretching out his head against it and contorting his face a great deal.

The giant said, 'Skinhood, go out and listen carefully. Do what I say and see if you notice anything new. It seems to me that those men are slow in coming – the ones my sister promised would arrive

this evening – because I want to go to bed soon. I've become rather fond of my beauty-sleep.'

She went out and saw the sworn brothers. She then passed her hands over them and asked them to turn into two chickens* and fly up into the cave. And they did. It was warm inside. A little later she came in.

The giant said, 'Did you see anything new, fosterling?'

'Far from it,' she said.

'Don't you trick me,' he said.

'I'll do as you say,' she said.

Then he lay down and snored vigorously.

Skinhood spoke to the chickens. 'Now turn back into men,' she said.

And they did.

Hjalmther said, 'We have to repay you for saving our lives.'

'What do you want to do now?' she said.

'Kill the giant,' he said, 'and so repay my stepmother for this errand, since she sent us here to him.'

'You're a brave man, Hjalmther,' she said.

Now they went further into the cave. A sword hung over the giant's bed, all worked with gold.

She said, 'No sword but that will bite into him.'

Hjalmther managed to get hold of the knob at the end of its hilt, and it slipped immediately from the scabbard.

Skinhood caught it and said, 'Lucky for us! Now I'll check whether he's asleep.'

Then she grabbed a great log and pounded on the bed.

She said, 'Hjalmther, I want you to climb up onto the frame and lay into him bravely.'

Then she leapt over the bed. Hjalmther now did so: he laid into the giant and jumped on the hilt-knob until it stuck in the bed.

The giant said, 'You've tricked me now, Skinhood.'

And he sprang up off the bed and made a clean sweep of the cave with his hands. A little later he died. Hjalmther took the sword and was pleased with it.

Skinhood said, 'You shall not have that sword, Hjalmther – Olvir must have it. But do not count yourself low in rank if you should see a better sword, because that one will surpass other swords as you surpass other princes.'

She gave them a lot of rare treasures and told them to call on her name if they should ever find themselves in need of a little help.

Then they went home, and everyone was pleased to see them.

7. [WOLF-EMBER]

In the spring they went out raiding again and slaughtered black men and berserks, and won a lot of booty in ships and garments, gold and silver. And in the autumn they headed homewards. They came to a certain large island late in the evening. It was thickly wooded. They pitched camp there on the shore and drew lots for the watch, and it fell to Hjalmther to keep watch.

And when they were asleep, he walked away from the camp and up a hill. He stood there for a long time and looked around him. Then he heard a great din with huge crashes in the forest, so that the oaks trembled and the branches shook. A little later, out of the forest came a great, stout *fingálkn*.★ It had a horse's tail and hooves, and a great mane; the eyes were white, the mouth large and the arms long. She held a sword so beautiful that he had never seen its like.

She came towards him, and he stood in her way. It now crossed his mind that he wasn't going to be left speechless.

He spoke a verse:

> 'Who's that girl,
> Elephant-tailed,
> Rushing, crashing
> In the night?
> You don't look
> Like other wifies,
> Wise one – where
> Are you from?'

She said:

> 'I am Wolf-Ember;
> Hear, O prince:
> Will you suffer
> Help from me?
> I suspect
> Soon enough
> You'll need well
> Your faithful friends.'

He said:

> 'You would frighten
> My fine heroes
> Though you came
> To offer help.
> Friend, you'll never
> Play us foul,
> Fierce-faced
> Fighting maid.'

She said, 'I would no more betray my friend than you would yours. But I can still help you, even if I do not come with you.'

He said, 'Do you own that sword you're holding?'

'Of course,' she said.

'Will you sell it to me?' he said.

'Of course not,' she said.

'You'll be wanting to give me the sword,' he said.

'Certainly not,' she said.

'Is there no way I can get it?' he said.

'I wouldn't say that, my lad,' she said. 'You must kiss me.'

A chant now came to her lips:

> 'Take Snarvendil,
> Victory's yours,
> Helmsman, if you
> Hold this sword.
> Kiss me now,
> One little squeeze,
> Dwarves' work then
> Will leave my hands.'[1]

'I don't want to kiss your snout,' said Hjalmther. 'I might get stuck to you.'

'You'll have to risk it,' she said. 'Please yourself.'

Now he turned away from her. But then he remembered what Skinhood had said. Then he turned back and spoke a verse:

> 'You can catch
> More quick than six
> That corpse-candle,
> Cruel-faced maid.
> Give the snake-fleeced
> Wound-flame here,
> I will kiss you,
> Come what may.'[2]

She said, 'Then you must fall upon my neck when I throw up the sword, and if it lands on you, it will be your death.'

She threw up the sword. At that moment Hjalmther fell upon her neck and kissed her, and she caught the sword behind his back.

Then she held out the sword to him and spoke a verse:

> 'Here's Snarvendil –
> Victory's yours,
> Heart-high hero,
> All your days;
> Victory, luck
> Will mark your life
> And follow you,
> Courageous prince.'

And she spoke another:

'Let not your rage
Do Olvir harm;
Be true to him
As he to you.
Let not your temper
Cause complaint;
Be true to friends
To win their trust.'

'There aren't any spells★ on the sword, are there?' he said.

'None at all,' she said, 'but I'll cast one now: that in the first battle you want to fight, the sword shall not bite; and at another time, you shall be unable to lift it at all. May glory and wealth attend you – and call on my name if you need a little help. Now you must go home.'

He said he would – 'but advise me on which man I should choose from my father's retinue in the summer.'

She said she would do that – 'though it might seem very unlikely that a young girl like me would know any advice, or that the greatest of princes would ask my advice – but you can be sure of this. You will be staying at home in the winter, and in the spring you must go before your father and ask him for troops. He will say he has few troops to spare. Ask him to give you one man: he will reserve Bjorn for himself. Then who will you choose?'

He said he wanted to have his father.

'You shan't have him,' she said. A chant now came to her lips:

'From the king's men
Choose the thrall
Who feeds swine swill;
Kings' retainers
Will not help
Should you slip.'

Then they parted.

Olvir woke up and saw that Hjalmther was missing. He got dressed, took his sword and left the tent. He saw Hjalmther coming, very angry. Hjalmther raised his sword, but it was so heavy that he fell down at his feet.

Olvir went up to him in a friendly manner, kissed him and said, 'So this is how your night-wandering goes, brother.'

Hjalmther said, 'Have my thanks, Wolf-Ember – it was good advice you gave me.'

On the next day they headed for home, and they sat in their castle over winter.

8. [THE QUEST BEGINS]

When spring came, Hjalmther prepared his fleet. He walked in before his father, asking him to give him some men. The king said he could not have any.

Hjalmther said, 'Give me a man from your retinue.'

'Have whoever you want, apart from Bjorn,' said the king.

Hjalmther went to the pigsty and saw a man lying there, large and tall and unusually strong-looking, in a fur cloak.

Hjalmther prodded him with the butt of his spear and said, 'Stand up, slave.'

The man lay there all the same. Hjalmther let him feel the spear-butt again.

Now he sat up and said, 'Surely this can't be what it seems – is this the prince?'

Hjalmther told him to stand up and come with him.

He said, 'I must place one condition on that: I want to have my own way in everything, and you yours in nothing.'

Hjalmther said, 'There is no way I can allow that. What is your name?'

He said, 'Please yourself. My name is Hord.'

Then Hjalmther went outside. He came to a bench, and standing by the bench he saw Wolf-Ember. Then he remembered what she had said.

And now he went back inside and said, 'Stand up, slave, and come with me, and you shall have your way in everything.'

'I'll go to the ships now,' said Hord, 'but you must meet your stepmother.'

Then Hjalmther went back to the hall. He saw his stepmother coming to meet him. She did not seem well-disposed towards him, and she now looked both hideous and misshapen, a thoroughly unpleasant sight.

She said, 'It is well that we have met, Hjalmther.'

He said he wouldn't grumble about it.

She said, 'Now I will repay you for the punch you gave me not long ago. I now lay this spell★ on you, that nowhere shall you know any peace of mind, day or night, until you set eyes upon Hervor Hundingsdottir, except on your ships or in your tent.'

Hjalmther said, 'You shall not lay any more spells on me, for your jaws shall gape open. It seems to me worthless to yearn after a princess. Down there by the harbour stand high cliffs: there you shall stand with one foot on each crag, and four of my father's slaves shall kindle a fire beneath you, and you shall live on nothing but what ravens bring you, until I come back.'

Then he went to his ships. The gangways were pulled in. He had five ships from that land, manned by a select crew. Then they set off.

At the first meal, Hjalmther asked Hord to sit beside him.

He said he wouldn't – 'I want to eat my food alone and sleep in your cabin.'

Hjalmther told him to have his way.

They travelled far and wide during the summer and won a lot of wealth for themselves, though they encountered high seas and great storms and the ships were damaged. But in the autumn they came to a large country. There was a great fjord and high mountains.

Hord said, 'We'll sleep here on the shore.'

Hjalmther spoke against it, but Hord said he wanted to have his way. So it was done: the tent was now carried ashore.

Hjalmther said, 'It will go badly for those on board ship.'

'No it won't,' said Hord.

He went aboard the ships and told the men to make merry. He gave them wine to drink, and gave treasure to each of them. They quickly became drunk. Hord took some food and ale and went ashore.

Hjalmther went out of the tent when they were asleep, and walked along the shore. A great high mountain rose from the shore. He saw, standing on the mountainside, a huge troll-woman. She had a gold-woven towel on her knees, and she was combing herself with a gold comb. Down below, on the shore, there was a spring: she was dipping her hand into it and washing her hair.

Hjalmther spoke a verse:

> 'Who's that monster
> Perching there,
> Peering at the prince?
> I've never known
> A thing so vile
> As you in all the world.'

She combed the hair from her eyes and became angry at his words, and said:

> 'You don't speak well to me –
> You'll be first, lad,
> Of your fighters
> Cooking in the cauldron.
> Watch the wise maid
> Dry her tresses
> With a golden towel.'

'An evil fate for that towel, to be rubbing your hair and getting close to your glittering cat's eyes,' said Hjalmther, and spoke a verse:

> 'Snarvendil
> Will get you first
> Before you put me
> In the pot;
> A hand you'll lose
> And loudly howl,
> Foul horse's cock,
> And so we'll part.'

She told him he was using a lot of disgracefully bad language – 'It would be more fitting for a manly man like you to behave in quite a different way to a nice young girl like me, rather than saying nasty things. You look a promising man to me. I'd be interested to try out a young man and lose my virginity, and have my belly-skin stretched – because it may well be that the grey beast I have between my legs is starting to yawn now and wants to be fondled.'

Then she dipped her hand into the spring. Hjalmther drew his sword and chopped off her hand at the wrist.

She let out a great screech, then looked at her stump and said, 'That's not much of a feat for this famous prince, to attack me by stealth. But it gladdens me that this deed will be avenged, and that will not be far off.'

She said:

> 'One thing cheers me,
> Fearless boar –
> You don't know
> What's in store,
> All my sisters
> Turn your men
> On the warships
> Into corpses.'[3]

Hjalmther now looked out to sea and saw nine troll-women so huge and evil-looking that he thought he'd never seen anything like them. They had torn apart all the ships, killed the men and carried all the goods ashore, and they had spared no efforts. They had heard everything Hjalmther and Embers had said. These were their names: Warbattle and Clutcher, Needle and Beak, Trouble and Snout, Gripper and Cat's-eye, and Sea-Giant was the ninth. She had a great humped back, and she carried it higher than her head. She had one eye, and that was in the middle of her forehead. She was not a nice-looking lady. She was walking in front of her sisters. She had a nose and claws of iron; two overgrown teeth stuck out from her chops, and her bottom lip hung down to her chest. Hjalmther realized she would be able to give a powerful kiss if her ability to manoeuvre her lip matched its size. The girls were scantily clad, their jaws gaped, and they wagged their heads.

Hjalmther now thought it would hardly do for him to leave matters like this. He ran down the mountain and went in front of the tent doors.

Then Warbattle spoke this verse:

> 'I trust my tools
> To talk to the king;
> Though we've learnt little,
> Glory beckons.
> We will hasten
> To their hall,
> Watch the king's man
> Cook in the cauldron.'

Then they made for the tent. Hjalmther thought he could not deal with them all. He spoke a verse:

> 'Wake up, Olvir,
> If you want women –
> You're so generous
> With your kissing.
> Sea-nymph's girls
> Are waiting for you;
> If you've courage,
> Come out here.'

Olvir said:

> 'What shall I say?
> Why wake me up,
> King, about women,
> Merry at midnight?
> Whatever chicks
> You find on the moors,
> You'll want them all –
> Worthless to me!'

Hord said, 'Let's get up now. Hjalmther seems to think this is serious.'
Warbattle said:

> 'I hold up my paws:
> Here, have a look
> At Warbattle's hands,
> My untrimmed claws.
> I'll tear up your cloak,
> Boar, if we meet,
> I won't stroke softly,
> King from the south.'

Hjalmther said:

> 'Come a bit closer
> Before dragging this king
> Into your cookpot –
> What a brave beast!
> Stretch out your iron paws
> If you trust in your strength,
> Braggart young woman –
> I'll stretch out my sword.'

At this they came out. Sea-Giant at once went for Olvir, but he fought back hard.

She spoke this verse:

> 'You don't fight fair, Olvir,
> You're not fit for girls –
> I can't get a grip
> On these great lords.
> Their sword-points are poisoned,
> Their prince in a rage,
> Their blades are all bloody –
> We're losing the fight.'

Hord was battling against seven sisters. They were very agile and each one of them carried a large broadsword, and they set upon Hord vigorously. But he defended himself well and bravely, and it came about at last that he killed them all, but by then he was exhausted.

Hjalmther was playing a very hard game with Warbattle: she had a fine shortsword in her hand, and defended herself superbly. He thought he had never been in greater peril because of her agility, for wherever he tried to strike her, the shortsword came immediately – until she grew tired. Then she became so wounded that she was gaping apart all over from the wounds.

She cried out loudly and said:

> 'Where are you, Sea-Giant,
> Mightiest of maids?
> Small glory you gain
> Against the king's gang.
> My back is half broken
> My shoulders are split –
> This troop is too tough,
> It's time we should run.'

They quickly took to their heels and both ran off as fast as they could. The girls took long strides, but Hord chased them to the foot of the mountain. Then Warbattle turned to fight him. He hewed at her and chopped her head off.

'The vilest of all men has killed you, my sister,' said Sea-Giant.

'It will soon be the same for you,' said Hord.

He slammed his sword into her and chopped her in half at the waist.

He now turned back. Hjalmther and Olvir had gone into the tent and were asleep. Hord walked down to the shore and gathered up the ships' timbers. From these he built a pretty little house where it would be of most use. He carried the food and ale and all their things into it. Then he went back.

The sworn brothers now got up and walked along the shore. Hjalmther saw a house up by the cliff.

He said, 'There is a house.'

Hord said, 'Won't Hervor be in there, for whom you are yearning?'

They went into the house. There was a bed, a table and chairs, tankards and a barrel as well. Hord gave them a drink. And then, when they were least on their guard, he went out and locked up the house.

Hjalmther spoke. 'Now you have betrayed me, Hord,' he said. 'It is bad to have a slave for your best friend.'

He tried to chop up the house, but the sword did not bite any more than if he had been hewing into stone. So they sat there quietly and consoled themselves.

9. [HORD TAKES CONTROL]

The story goes that Hord walked along the shore. He saw a large boulder in front of him on the foreshore, and got up onto it. Then he looked around him and saw a horrible giant approaching, up on the clifftop. He did not look very boyish, and Hord thought he had never seen his like before, what with his enormous proportions and huge head. He was holding a long staff with a two-edged spike sticking out of the end, four ells long. It reached down to the foreshore when he stood on the cliff.

The giant said, 'Where are the swaddling-babes who killed my girls? Come out now, if you dare, for that was the lowest of base deeds, seeing how young they were – the eldest was only twelve.'

'Here I am,' said Hord. 'I killed your daughters, and they were big for their years; but I want to ask for your support and protection.'

The giant said, 'Greetings, my friend, and welcome. Come up here.'

Hord said, 'There is no way I can do that. I've never been much good, although I have improved a little since I sailed out to sea with them this spring. Stretch your staff down to me instead, and I'll take hold of it.'

The giant said, 'I can do that easily, because the only ships that have come here are the ones I've driven my spike through, and hauled them ashore towards me. I'll stretch the staff down to you now.'

Hord grasped it as hard as he could. But while they had been chatting, he had tied himself down to the boulder with strong cables.

Now the giant tugged very hard.

Hord said, 'Pull harder and better, my friend — I'm not all that light.'

Now the giant became angry and drove the spike down into the rock. He now tugged on it so hard that he sank down into the clifftop right up to his belt. At that Hord was on the point of breaking in two.

The giant said, 'You are heavy, little one.'

'You're not trying,' said Hord.

At this, the giant now braced himself all the more, and he struggled with it until the boulder to which Hord had tied himself came loose. He lifted it up no less than six fathoms from the ground. At this point the spike slipped and the giant fell over backwards, and Hord came down with the boulder and lay senseless for a long time.

And when he came to, he said, 'You are very feeble, big one, and you can't do much if you can't get me up onto the cliff. Take my advice, and go down to the grassy slopes on the cliff-edge, then stretch out as far as possible.'

The giant let himself be fooled by this. He went down to the edge, stretched his neck out, and reached the staff down over the cliff. Hord then grabbed hold of the staff and pulled the giant off the cliff, and he broke all his bones.

Hord untied himself and ran at once up the cliff. He came to a large cave. Embers was standing in front of it, and she fell at his feet. He spared her life. He stayed there over the winter.

In the cave there was plenty of gold, silver and fine clothes which the giant had owned. And when spring approached, Hord took a valuable ring, a cloak, and a large purse full of gold. He put Embers in charge of the cave. She told him to call on her name if he ever needed any help.

Hord went back and unlocked the house. Hjalmther was pleased to see him. That winter Hjalmther had not thought about Hervor.[4] Hord had built a ship for them during the winter, and when spring came they put out to sea. The ship sailed as fast against the wind as before it.

In the autumn they came to a large country.

Hjalmther said, 'I want to go ashore here.'

Hord said they would. There they saw large, handsome halls.

Hjalmther said, 'These must be King Hunding's halls.'

'You are right,' said Hord.

They went up to the hall. It was made of stone. In another place they saw a house made of red gold.

Hjalmther said, 'This must be Hervor's tower.'

Hord said it must be. They walked below the tower. They saw sitting there such a beautiful maiden that they had never seen her like. Her hair was like gold, her face was as white and her skin as pure as a lily, her eyes as lovely as rubies, and her cheeks like a rose.

Hord went before her and spoke a verse:

> 'Lady, who are you,
> Fairest of women,
> Gentle of cheek
> And golden-haired?
> Not once have I seen
> Another such lady
> Of like courtly nature
> Throughout all the earth.'

She said:

'My name is Hervor
Daughter of Hunding;
If you chance to see
My stout-hearted sire,
With noble bearing
You must behave
If you would be
Worthy the king.'

And she also said:

'It goes as he wishes,
No man's more famous;
His men ply feats,
Feed flesh to ravens.
You'll sooner hang
High on the gallows
Than attend a fine feast –
Go no further!'

He said:

'Hord the high-minded
Asks only this:
Why try to terrify,
Hervor, with talk?
It were proper,
Purest of women,
Were you clear of counsel
To this cunning man.'

And Hord said to Hjalmther, 'Look, you have to show Hervor
how refined you are, and coax her.'

Hord gave him the treasures he had got from the cave and told him to give them to her. Hjalmther now gave her all these treasures, and this pleased her. She thanked him profusely and said she would help him.

She told him many things – how one or another thing was conducted with respect to her father, and about all the dangers they had to avoid there – 'for as soon as my father realizes that you have met me, he will be delighted to see you, since he comes to know everything through magical inspiration.'

And she said she would give him whatever advice she could. 'Now, soon you must go boldly before my father, and greet him graciously. He will give you a very good welcome and ask you about many things. You must answer everything wisely and well. He has a counsellor beside him, very tall and bad-tempered, whose name is High-Stepper. He is as tall as a giant and as strong as a troll. He knows all the king's plans. Getting to know High-Stepper is no more pleasant than looking at him, for he is as black as the earth, with a bald pate and glittering red eyes, vicious and deceitful.'

She spoke a verse:

> 'Go into the hall,
> Helmsman, and bow;
> Couteously greet
> The ambitious king.
> Don't let your fear
> Show on your face,
> Though in the hall
> Are tall, warlike men.'

'Ask the king for winter quarters, and he will give whatever answer he wishes. And when you have spoken as you please, go to the retainers' bench and do not be close-handed.'

She spoke a verse:

> 'Give wealth, warrior,
> If you think yourself worthy;
> Give gold to men,
> Behave with grace;
> But if a man swaggers
> At the gold-giver's side
> Show the wretch anger,
> Allot him disgrace.'[5]

Hjalmther now returned to his companions, then went to the hall and walked in. Hord stayed behind in the hall doorway when they went before the king.

Hjalmther spoke a verse:

> 'Hail to you, Hunding!
> Never have I
> Met a mightier man
> Throughout the whole world;
> You are held
> To be open-handed –
> Here I have come
> To visit the king.'

The king accepted his greeting and spoke a verse:

> 'Who's that man there
> From Mannheimar,
> Young in years,
> Visiting me?
> Young one, you've
> A snake's sharp eyes,
> But I can still
> Guard against guile.'

Hjalmther said:

> 'My name is Hjalmther –
> I'll not hurry my speech
> To the far-sighted king
> On my first night;
> I don't want to wait
> Here on the hall floor.
> Show me my seat –
> I'm King Ingi's son.'

The king said, 'I shall need to hear more first,' and he spoke a verse:

> 'Who is that wise one
> With helmet and armour,
> Strong, impressive,
> Standing beside you?
> Tell me fully
> Of your troop,
> Then I'll know
> Where they shall sit.'

Hjalmther spoke a verse:

> 'His name is Olvir,
> Never afraid
> Of fire, iron
> Or a war-march;
> Born like the best
> Of kings now alive,
> Better than princes,
> My sworn brother.'

'The man is well spoken of,' said the king, and he spoke a verse:

> 'Who is that ruffian
> In the door,
> Clutching still
> At his club?
> Stooped, hood down,
> He stares at the court –
> Just a blusterer
> If you ask me.'

Hjalmther spoke a verse:

> 'His name is Hord;
> Hardly refined,
> Seldom picks weapons,
> Won't take fine clothes;
> Likewise, he never
> Has any fear,
> A fierce fighter –
> I value him high.'

The king said:

> 'It hardly suits him
> To be with such men
> As glitter around me
> In gold-woven clothes;
> He'll sit further
> From my troop –
> My freedmen
> Will welcome him.'

'You shall not have your way there,' said Hjalmther. 'Either we all sit together, or not at all.'

'How extraordinary,' said the king.

Hjalmther asked the king for winter quarters.

The king said they could drink freely and have quarters, 'but for that you must perform a small feat: you are to fetch my calf's two horns. I want to drink from them on the eighth day of Yule – or else you shall lose your life.'

'That is a lot to manage,' said Hjalmther, 'but where am I to look for this calf?'

'You tell me,' said the king.

Hjalmther said, 'First, my lord, please direct us to our place.'

'It shall be done,' said the king, and he spoke this verse:

> 'At home you'll be hard
> If you try to take charge
> In front of us
> Within our halls;
> You have a sharp sword,
> A scabbard, chain-mail,
> A fine helmet too –
> Sit yourself down.'

Hjalmther spoke this verse:

> 'At home I was young
> But I commanded
> The host of men
> All as I liked;
> This state of affairs
> Seemed good enough
> To the wise king
> And noble men.'

The king turned to High-Stepper and said:

> 'Stand up, High-Stepper,
> Give the guests room,
> High-born men,
> Tired from travel;
> Princes like these
> I've never met –
> Those I have seen
> Have been more polite.'

High-Stepper turned to the king rather sullenly and said:

> 'You've never yet
> Ordered me
> To leave my seat;
> An evil fate
> Will harm the king;
> Hang them first
> From the gallows –
> They'll trick you,
> I know they will.'

The king turned to him very angrily and said:

> 'You're always vicious
> To my guests,
> Often sent them
> Down to Hel;
> Leave this bench,
> Ill-willed knight,
> Hard-eyed fighter,
> Or you'll be sorry.'

High-Stepper now stood up, went across the hall and sat down. Hjalmther went to his seat and needed the space of two men, but Olvir needed that of three, for he was the largest of men. Hord was as large as both sworn brothers; yet there was still enough room for them all where High-Stepper had been sitting.

A little later Hord took his purse full of gold. He gave with both hands, and when he had provided for everyone in the hall except High-Stepper, one gold ring remained. High-Stepper cast his eye on the ring. Hord saw this and offered it to him, and he reached out towards it. Hord had jammed a big stick into the ring, and he jerked this stick against High-Stepper's teeth. But High-Stepper could not see clearly, since the sun was shining through a window, and the stick hit High-Stepper so that he fell backwards with an almighty yell and banged his head very painfully. His benchmates laughed at him. He had cut his head badly, and he roared loudly.

At last, he who was in such straits recovered, rolled his eyes, groped about and said, 'I've been killed, lads.'

They told him to be quiet. At this Hord offered the ring to him again. This time he took the ring and kept it.

Hord said, 'It's usually the dog who gets the leftovers.'

High-Stepper's benchmates said that now the rascal had been deservedly tricked. Then the king appointed them a good loft-chamber to sleep in. The king asked Hjalmther about many things, and he answered everything well – for Hord had instructed him in many things, since he could say something about every country.

Hjalmther was always in Princess Hervor's bower, and he played chess with her. She was gifted with all the womanly arts. She also knew all about the stars and the properties of stones.

10. [A SACRED BULL]

One day, Hjalmther was sitting beside the princess and playing chess with her. Hervor asked Hjalmther what he had to do to earn his winter quarters. He said he had to find a certain calf.

'Where do you have to find it?' said Hervor.

'The king wouldn't give me any details,' he said.

'This is no calf,' she said, 'but rather an old ox, ninety years old. It eats sheep and kills men and horses, for it is more ferocious than any other animal. What's more, it has killed all the men who have gone after it and asked my father for winter quarters. It was, and still is, the greatest of sacred bulls,★ and it feeds mostly on human flesh. It has a piercing, powerful voice that no-one can stand. It lives in a strong, high enclosure in the middle of this country, and it cannot be set free because then it would destroy cities and castles and wreak havoc on men and livestock. All living creatures are terrified of that wretched ox.'

Then they ended their conversation, and Hjalmther went back to his loft and told his companions what the princess had said to him.

Winter now drew on towards Yule. Two nights before the first day of Yule, Hord got out of bed so that the sworn brothers did not notice. He took Olvir's shortsword, then went out and made for the woods, where there were wide roads.

He walked all night long until the roads branched out. He thought hard about his situation, wondering which way he should go. Then he walked along an old, well-trodden path through the dense forest, not stopping until he came out onto a wide and beautiful-looking promontory. Now he saw a high enclosure made of bricks. He walked up to it holding his club, twelve ells long, with great studs and a long spike sticking out of it. He could reach as high as the wall with it. He then walked along for a while underneath the wall. It was equally high on all sides. Now he saw this would hardly do,

so he took a rope, tied it to a large boulder and threw it over into the enclosure, and hauled himself up on to the wall.

The ox was lying there on the ground just inside the enclosure, and it had churned up the whole field. It was asleep, snoring and snuffling in an unpleasant manner, restless in its sleep. Hord felt sure he would fall in off the wall because of the bull's snorting, and he saw that it must have brought death to many. So he untied the stone and flung it down, and it landed on the ox's flank. It woke up with a great bellowing, springing up at once, and it rushed all over the place. Then it got wind of the man and leapt at the wall Hord was on. Now he could wait no longer, raised his spiked club and slammed it into the bull's skull so that all the spikes sank in. But at that the bull shook itself, jerked its head back and bellowed savagely, so that Hord dropped the club. It fell to the ground a long way off.

And the ox took a run at the wall, reached out at Hord with its tongue, and dragged him towards itself. Now he had no choice but to throw himself down flat between the ox's horns, and he clasped its neck. But the bull struggled hard and vigorously, leaping madly up and down the enclosure with fearful roars, stamping its feet and shaking its head. Hord knew that if he fell off, that would be the end of him.

It came about at last that the bull grew tired from all this exertion and loss of blood. Now it took a run at the wall with loud and horrible bellowings, and it got its front legs up on the wall. At that moment Hord thrust his shortsword in below the ox's shoulder so that it pierced its heart. The ox then struggled hard until it died. By then it had broken a big hole in the wall with its death-spasms.

Now Hord flayed the whole hide off the ox, and the horns came with the hide. Hord put it on his back, carried it home and threw it down before the loft door. The crash woke Hjalmther, and he sprang up.

Then Hord came in. Hjalmther was very glad to see him and greeted him cheerfully, but Hord was rather excited and told Hjalmther to come outside. He did so, and now he saw the hide.

Hord spoke. 'Now pick up the hide, Hjalmther,' he said, 'since you think you are so strong.'

Hjalmther now grasped the hide with all his strength, but he could not even move it from its place.

Hord said he needed to make more effort if he was to succeed. Hjalmther admitted that he had failed this, the greatest of trials.

'Then I will speak words,' said Hord, 'so that when you go before the king today and he sits at his table, you will take on the strength of both Olvir and myself, apart from what is in our little fingers; and you will be able to carry the hide in on the palms of your hands.'

It happened just as Hord had said. Hjalmther went before the king, and everyone in the hall was afraid of him. He flung the hide down on to the table before the king so hard that the table broke in two. Then he walked away, and both Hord and Olvir got their strength back. The king told High-Stepper to carry off the hide, and he took the horns himself. High-Stepper did so, and it was the worse for him – he walked with very bowed knees.

A new table was set up. Both sworn brothers now went into the hall, and there was the best of feasts. During Yule everyone drank from the horns.

II. [ESCAPE]

One day, the king asked Hjalmther whether he wanted to have any entertainment. He asked the king to decide.

'Tomorrow you shall wrestle with my boy,' said the king.

Hjalmther told him to please himself, and next morning the companions got up and went before the king. An incredibly large black man was now brought forward, as black and fat as an ox. He was hideous in every way.

The king said, 'Here comes the boy now, Hjalmther.'

Hord said, 'I shall wrestle with this lad, since we are of the same rank – we're both slaves.'

Hord did not take off his fur cloak. They now went for each other with powerful wrestling-holds and hard tugs that each gave the other, along with punches, kneeings, clawings and crushings. This went on all day. The king and those in the hall thought they had never seen such a tussle.

A low block stood in the hall. When the black man pulled Hord towards it, he fought back like a good wrestler and managed to get in an upper cut, and this took the black man by surprise. Hord now heaved him up on his shoulders and put a hold on him – not a particularly light one. Then he flung him down onto the block so hard that the black man's back broke and he screamed, not in a particularly pleasant manner. Then Hord kneed him in the belly, with vicious strangleholds, and crushed him to death. The king was very cross about this, but everyone else thanked Hord. The dead man was dragged away.

The king said, 'You have done me and my kingdom a great injury in killing this man, and for that, we two – or someone else I appoint – shall hold a tug-o'-war over the fire tomorrow, here in the hall.'

'You'll be wanting to decide that, my lord,' said Hord. 'It's all the same to me, whoever he may be.'

Early the next day people went to the hall, and a great fire was built there.

A little later the king came in and said, 'I choose High-Stepper to wrestle with you.'

Hord spoke. 'It is well that the two of us are to try out skin-pulling. Get ready for this, High-Stepper,' said Hord.

High-Stepper now took off all his clothes, but Hord did not remove his fur cloak. A very strong walrus-hide was placed in their hands. They got to grips with mighty great tugs, and the contest went both ways for them. They quickly pulled apart the walrus-hide between them.

The king had the ox-hide fetched, and it was brought to them. They now grasped it with all their strength, and there were such powerful tugs between them that each was alternately on the point of falling into the fire. High-Stepper was stronger, but Hord was luckier and more nimble.

The king said, 'It's not much of a wrestling-match, High-Stepper, if you let this baby fight you for so long without beating him.'

'It won't be long,' said High-Stepper, 'if I summon up my strength to the full.'

But while High-Stepper and the king were talking, Hjalmther took a broadsword and a shortsword and put them down at Hord's feet. Nobody saw this, for Hord's fur cloak hung forwards over them.

High-Stepper now took hold so powerfully that there seemed to be nothing for Hord to do now but tumble into the fire. Hord thought he had never been in such a brawl. The two of them struggled so hard that everyone in the hall thought it a great marvel and a wonder that they'd not collapsed from exhaustion or from what they suffered during their vigorous fighting and powerful grappling.

Then Hord said to High-Stepper, 'Now brace yourself – I am going to summon up my strength now, and you have not got long to live.'

'That I'll do,' said High-Stepper.

Now Hord set to with all his strength, pulled High-Stepper forward onto the fire and threw the ox-hide down on him, then he himself jumped on to his back. Then he went to his bench. The king ordered the man to be taken off the fire. High-Stepper was very burnt. The king was very angry, although he thought himself much to blame for it.

That evening the king went to bed early, and all the lights and fires in the city were put out. Hjalmther said he wanted to go to bed. Hord drew Snarvendil and the light gleamed from it like a lamp. Then they went into the loft and saw some new fittings over the bed. It was a beam with a sharp sword's blade in it. There was a thin cord at the end of the beam.

Hord said, 'We must not lie down. Whoever has contrived this intends a speedy death for us.'

So now they lay on the floor. The sworn brothers fell asleep quickly, and Hord snored loudly and pretended to be asleep. A little later he heard a man walk outside by the loft, take hold of the cord, and pull down the beam. The blade cut up all the bedclothes. Then planks were pulled out, and an enormous head poked through – but saw nothing in the bed. Then Hord chopped this man in two at the waist, and the two halves fell out. Now they lay down.

In the morning the king was told that High-Stepper had been killed by the very means he had prepared for Hjalmther. The king paid little attention to it.

The winter now passed. When there were three nights till summer, Hjalmther visited Hervor.

She said, 'Do you want to stay any longer here with my father?'

'No,' said Hjalmther.

She said, 'This evening you must go before him and thank him for the winter quarters, because he sleeps for three days and nights before summer and becomes aware of everything in and on the earth. Nothing can take him by surprise then. I want you to sail away early tomorrow, for he is not well-disposed towards you.'

He thanked her for all her good advice, and they ended their conversation.

And in the evening Hjalmther went before the king and thanked him for the winter quarters – 'I shall carry your fame and hospitality abroad to every land.'

The king said, 'This is the advice of my daughter Hervor. So now we are to part. I cannot do anything about that for the time being.'

The men now slept through the night. And early in the morning Hjalmther bade everyone farewell.

He asked Hervor to come with him, but she said she did not want to – 'because that would be the death of you. I would sooner lose my own life. My father spares no-one when he first wakes up, neither friend nor foe.'

Hjalmther bade her farewell, and she bade him farewell and wished him a safe journey and for all honour and glory to fall to his lot. At their parting she fell into a swoon.

And when Hjalmther and Olvir came to the ships, Hord said, 'I have not said goodbye to Hervor.'

He took a large rope of walrus-hide, went back and cast it around Hervor's tower, and so carried it right down to the ships and aboard his ship. The sworn brothers were on the other ship. Hjalmther asked what Hord was carrying.

'I am travelling with Hervor here,' he said, 'without the consent of her father, kinsmen or friends. She will come with me – she wants to see you quickly.'

'That was done wisely and bravely,' said Hjalmther. 'You have achieved more than the best of men.'

Hjalmther now leapt aboard the ship Hervor was on.

She stood up to meet him and spoke to him in a friendly manner. 'Have you not left yet, my friend?' she said.

'Not yet, dear princess,' he said. 'I would very much like you to come aboard my ship.'

'Gladly,' she said, 'but you have done my father a great injury by taking me away without his consent – though I would rather come with you than stay behind.'

Now a keen wind blew up. They put out to sea. But when they could no longer see land, the wind died down, and then they drifted at sea with the currents for four days. On the fifth day the ships were becalmed.

Hervor said, 'My father controls this weather, and that is why the ships are becalmed. He must have woken up now, and he will have dreamt not a little. He now knows all about your conduct and intentions, and that you have taken me away. You will have plenty of trials now for what you have done.'

A little later they saw a huge walrus coming at them with great splashings and revolting noises.

Hord said, 'There is the creature which I hate most, and I must not look at it. Now, brothers, you will be helped by a little bodily strength – but you must not speak my name while it is here, for then I would die.'

Then he lay down in the keel. They spread clothes over him. Then they saw a whale gliding out from beneath their ship, and it went for the walrus very fiercely and attacked it at once. They plunged around a great deal. A little later they saw gliding from beneath Hervor's ship a dolphin, elegant and handsome. It attacked the walrus at once. They were treating each other to great thrashings and fierce onslaughts. The whale and the dolphin soon became exhausted, for the walrus was heavier and very strong; so it threw

them off and they landed far out to sea. Hjalmther now felt sure this horrible creature would soon finish them off.

Then he said, 'When will I ever have more need of Skinhood and Wolf-Ember to come to our aid than now?'

As soon as he had said this, he saw two vultures flying. They had beaks and claws of iron. They perched on the walrus and pecked at it mercilessly, for they were tearing great gobbets from its nasty humped back. But it attacked fiercely in return. They tore and ripped at the walrus as much as they were able. Then the battle drew near the ships, and they were swamped by great waves. Hjalmther saw that all these creatures were giving way before the evil walrus.

He took his sword and said, 'I would rather lose you than not help these creatures.'

He flung the sword down into the walrus's skull. Olvir saw this and at once threw his shortsword, and that went into the walrus's other eye, like the first. At this the walrus became a little faint and did not know what to do. It rolled on either side, and snapped and tore whatever it could reach. The blood was running like streams down from the vultures, for they were gaping all over with wounds, as were the whale and the dolphin. It turned out at last that the walrus began to sink. Then they tore it to death, and it sank to the bottom. The vultures flew away completely exhausted, and the blood dripped from under each one of their feathers. They flew slowly and low.

Hjalmther went to where Hord lay and noticed that he was wet.

Hord said, 'Is the walrus dead now?'

Hjalmther said he was gone, 'and I have lost my sword with him, and Olvir his shortsword.'

'Here are both of them now,' said Hord, 'and that was quite a feat, for King Hunding has been put to death.'

They now thanked him for saving their lives, in that he had rescued them from the mortal danger they had come into.

Hord said, 'Go to Hervor, because soon she will need your help.'

Now Hjalmther leapt aboard her ship. She was lying senseless then, and was in a very bad way. Hjalmther then dripped wine on to her, and she quickly came round. Then a fair wind blew up and they hoisted sail. The ships were now free, and they sailed all summer.

And in the autumn they came to a large, splendid country. It had large towns, rich and fair pastures, large and beautiful forests, and all kinds of animals and birds. The sworn brothers thought they had never seen or heard tell of such a land. They asked Hord what land it was.

He said he did not know, 'but we must go ashore here.'

Hjalmther said he did not want to, but Hord said he would decide that. They put out their gangways and went ashore.

Hord said, 'Let's explore this country.'

Hjalmther said, 'Hervor must come with us, because I do not want to part from her.'

Hord said she must not – 'I want to have my way, and we shall not be going far.'

They walked all day, and in the evening they came to a pretty little house. Hord unlocked the house. There was a bed inside; there was some food and ale.

That evening, Hord talked more than usual and said, 'I felt strange when I came into this house.'

Now they lay down and slept soundly.

In the morning, when Hjalmther woke up, Hord was still lying there, and that was not usual with him. Hjalmther told Olvir he ought to sleep undisturbed.

The day now drew to a close. Hjalmther went up to Hord, took hold of him, and told him to wake up. Hjalmther realized he was dead and fell back on the bed, and blood trickled out from under each nail and from his nose. Olvir asked what the matter was with him.

For a long time Hjalmther was unable to make any reply. But at last he told him Hord was dead.

Olvir said, 'I know full well that if you were not my sworn brother you would soon die.'

Hjalmther spoke a verse:

> 'Let us bear on our backs
> The bold spear-thruster,
> Repay him his deeds,
> Not leave him behind;
> Let us not bury Hord
> Before we reach home,
> Let us dig him a grave
> By the walls of our hall.'

'Now choose, Olvir, whether you want to carry him, or his club and fur cloak.'

Olvir said he wanted to carry the club. Hjalmther now stripped him of his fur cloak. Underneath he was dressed in a scarlet tunic and had a silver belt around him, wound with gold lace.

Hjalmther said, 'You see now, Olvir, this was a finer prince than either of us, and not a slave, as we had long thought.'

Then he put Hord on his back: he found him light. They walked all day until evening, then came to another house and had a good rest there. They continued on their way for another day.

On the third day Olvir spoke up: 'I'm not carrying the cloak and club any longer, because I am utterly worn out by this burden. But it is even more remarkable that you have carried a dead man along with you for so long – this deed will live on as long as the world lasts.'

'You are speaking words of great fear,' said Hjalmther. 'Now give them both to me.'

Olvir did so. They walked on until evening and came to a third house. Hjalmther left Hord on his bed that evening. Hjalmther had not slept since Hord's death. He kept watch now as before, except that towards early morning, drowsiness overcame him.

When Hjalmther woke up, Hord was gone. He was no more pleased with this than with what had happened earlier.

Hjalmther said, 'I shall never be happy from this day on, until I have found Hord.'

Now they got up and went on their way until they came down on to a lovely plain. They saw a large town, very beautiful and carved all over; and the carvings were inlaid with gold and silver. It was handsomely walled with red stones and blue, golden and green, white and black. Its towers were high and fair, and tiled with gold.

They walked towards the hall and went in before the king. Olvir greeted him, but Hjalmther said nothing. The king accepted Olvir's greeting and ordered a chair to be fetched and set down before him, and they sat down. The sworn brothers saw that the hall was filled with worthy people. The king then invited them to be merry and cheerful after their exhausting journey. Hjalmther neither ate nor drank: he was now pale, now red as blood.

A little later the hall doors opened and thirty maidens came in there. Two of them were far superior, though the second was much more beautiful. Olvir thought he had never seen anyone with such grace and loveliness. Trumpets and all manner of musical instruments were played before them. There was now much merriment in that hall. The young ladies went before the king and greeted him affectionately, calling him their brother, and sat down.

Olvir saw that Hjalmther had gone very red, drawn Snarvendil from its scabbard and laid it down under his seat.

The king turned to Hjalmther and spoke a verse:

> 'Hjalmther, what's wrong?
> Your colour has changed,
> Your spirit is shaken,
> You're staring at me.'

Hjalmther responded and spoke half a verse:

> 'The brave man vanished,
> Hord left my troop;
> You look like him,
> So I've no mind to drink.'

The king became angry and spoke a verse:

> 'Your honour will suffer,
> Likening me
> To that vile slave,
> No great man,
> A coward in all
> But feeding pigs,
> A raven-black man
> In a carrion-shroud.'[6]

Hjalmther now wanted to seize his sword, but it was gone. Then Hjalmther said:

> 'Gone is Snarvendil,
> Fled its sheath,
> I cannot fight –
> Olvir's fault?
> I'd avenge Hord
> If I had it here,
> Redden my sword
> In men's blood.'

Then one of the maidens walked up to Olvir and said:

> 'You have a sword, Olvir –
> Rare are such blades –
> Gave death to a giant,
> Got from the cave;
> I changed the princes
> Into chickens;
> I saved your life,
> Now I look fairer.'

Olvir said, 'You are quite right, my lady,' and took the maiden and sat her on his knee.

A little later, the second young lady walked up to Hjalmther and said:

> 'You bought Snarvendil
> With a kiss –
> A small price,
> But enough;
> Be generous now

To get it back,
Fearless boar,
Fortunate one.'

Hjalmther pretended not to have heard, and said nothing as before. She went back to her seat.

When the king saw this, he leapt up from his seat and took a horn, poured wine into it, and went up to Hjalmther. He spoke this verse:

'Accept this horn –
Hord gives it you;
Rest your wrath,
Tomorrow we'll talk;
You have helped us,
We helped you –
Freed from our fetters,
Let us make merry.'

Then Hjalmther stood up to greet Hord, and each kissed the other. That was a joyful reunion. A merry banquet now began, and it was the beast of feasts.

12. [KING HRING'S SAGA]

One day during the feast, the king was sitting in his high seat with the sworn brothers beside him, and the princesses were on a seat before them. Everyone was happy, with fair words and kindness, joy and merriment, and all manner of entertainment. Hjalmther asked the prettiest of the maidens what her name was and who her parents were.

She said her name was Alfsol. 'My father, who ruled this land, is dead, and my brother, who has called himself Hord, took the kingdom after him. And his real name is Hring. My sister's name is Hildisif, and the name of this country is Arabia. My brother can tell you about our fates, our kin and our upbringing.'

Now they ended their conversation.

Then Hjalmther asked Hord to explain more clearly what she had told him. King Hring said he would gladly do that. Now all was silence and stillness in the hall.

The king began his story. 'First I want to make known to you that my father's name was Ptolemy, and he ruled this kingdom of Arabia. He had a very beautiful queen, and by her the king had us three children. So a long time passed, until our mother was taken ill and died. A mound was raised in her memory. The king pined greatly for his queen.

'The king had a faithful and trusty counsellor. One day he went before the king and said he wanted to seek out a queen for him, and the king agreed to it. The counsellor left, and came back in the autumn. The queen-to-be was with him on that journey. Her name was Luda.

'The wedding was held at once. Everyone liked this woman. But the three of us did not want to sit through the wedding. The feast went well. Not long passed before the queen seemed to them to become harsh, in both words and disposition, and with the worst witchcraft. She soon contrived my father's death, since she thought him old, while she was young and lusty.

'She wanted to have me then, but when I refused to consent to her hideous desires, she cast a spell on me so that I should appear like a slave, black and evil-looking, and that I should never be able to eat except off the floor, and never be freed from this spell unless some prince were to do this for me – to let me have my way in everything, and to carry me dead on his back for three days. Now you have done both these things. As a comfort, she also laid a spell on me so that I should be able to do whatever I wanted to achieve, that I should never become weak, and that I should overcome everything which might be put in my way.

'Upon my sister Alfsol she cast a spell so that she should turn into a *fingálkn* and never be freed from her spell unless some prince was willing to kiss her. Then my stepmother gave her Snarvendil: she had to hold it alternately in her mouth and her hands. And my sister Hildisif was made to look to all appearances like a troll-woman, and live with Luda's brother. He made his home in a large cave, and he was not to harm her in any way. She would never be freed from her spell until he was killed with the very sword which hung over his bed.

'Luda also did many more and far worse things, and after that she went abroad with me. That same woman is your stepmother. And so the saga of my life comes to an end.'

Hjalmther now thanked him for the good entertainment. Now everyone was happy. After this, Hjalmther spoke up and asked for Alfsol's hand in marriage. The king was very agreeable to that. Olvir also asked for Hildisif's hand, and this was granted.

Then Hjalmther and Olvir wanted to go home. Hring gave them twenty ships, and they did not stop until they arrived at Mannheimar.

And when Hjalmther looked up at his stepmother, she fell down into the flames.

His father was delighted to see him, and Hjalmther stayed there for some time, until he invited his father to his wedding, and the king accepted. They sailed to Arabia with a hundred ships, and when they arrived King Hring came to meet them, and led them to the hall with great honour and entertainment.

Now Hring took Hervor for his wife, and the weddings were held with splendid festivities. When they were over, everyone was given fine parting gifts, and each went to his home. King Hring, Hjalmther and Olvir confirmed their friendship, and each gave the other fine gifts. With that they parted.

Then Hjalmther sailed home to Mannheimar. He ruled that kingdom after his father. Olvir governed the lands his own father had ruled. King Hjalmther esteemed him in everything, and he was considered the most valiant of men.

King Hjalmther had two sons by his queen. The elder was named Ingi, and the younger Hlodvir. The king fought many battles after this, and he won all of them. Nobody was a match for him. Olvir supported him in all his adversities.

After Hjalmther, his son Ingi took over the realm. Hlodvir became a great viking: he bore Snarvendil after his father.

Olvir also had a son named Herraud. He used to go out raiding with Hlodvir. They became great champions, and many noble folk are descended from them. They conquered many kingdoms.

And here we end the saga of Hjalmther and Olvir, Hring and Hervor. And he who wrote it down and put it together both knew well and meant well.

Extract from the Book of Flatey

THE TALE OF THORSTEIN SHIVER

It is said that during the following summer King Olaf attended feasts in the east, around Vik and elsewhere further away. He feasted at a farm named Rein. He had a lot of men with him. Accompanying the king at that time was a man named Thorstein Thorkelsson. His father was the son of Asgeir Scatterbrain, the son of Audun Shaft.★ Thorstein was an Icelander, and he had come to the king the previous winter.

In the evening, while people sat at the drinking-tables, King Olaf said that none of his men were to go alone to the privy during the night, and that whoever needed to go was to take his neighbour with him, otherwise he would be disobeying him. The men drank heartily that evening; and when the drinking-tables were hung up, the men went to bed.

And in the middle of the night, Thorstein the Icelander woke up needing to go to the lavatory. But the man lying next to him was sleeping so soundly that Thorstein really did not want to wake

him. So he got up, slipped his shoes on, pulled on a heavy cloak and went out to the privy. The building was large enough for eleven people to sit on either side of it. He sat on the seat nearest the door. And when he had been sitting there for a few moments, he saw a demon★ climb up on to the furthest seat in, and sit down there.

Then Thorstein said, 'Who's there?'

The fiend★ replied, 'It's Thorkel the Thin, who fell on corpses with King Harald Wartooth.'★

'Where have you come from now?' said Thorstein.

He said he'd just arrived from hell.

'What can you tell me about that place?' asked Thorstein.

He replied, 'What do you want to hear about?'

'Who endures the torments of hell best?'

'None better,' replied the demon, 'than Sigurd the Dragon-slayer.'★

'What torment does he have?'

'He kindles the fiery furnace,' said the ghost.★

'That doesn't sound like much of a torment to me,' said Thorstein.

'Oh, but it is,' said the demon, 'He himself is the kindling.'

'That's quite something, then,' said Thorstein. 'And who endures his torments the worst there?'

The ghost replied, 'Starkad the Old★ endures them the worst, for he screams so much that it's a worse torment for us fiends than almost everything else. We never get any rest from his screaming.'

'What torment does he have,' said Thorstein, 'that he takes so badly, such a valiant man as he is said to have been?'

'He is in fire up to his ankles.'

'That doesn't sound like much to me,' said Thorstein, 'such a champion as he was.'

'Then you're not looking at it in the right way,' said the ghost, 'Only the soles of his feet are sticking up out of the flames.'

'That's quite something,' said Thorstein. 'Now give a scream the way he does.'

'All right,' said the demon. And he threw open his jaws and let out a great bellow, while Thorstein pulled the skirts of his cloak around his head.

He was quite stunned by that scream and said, 'Is that the loudest he screams?'

'Far from it,' said the ghost, 'for that's the scream of us paltry devils.'

'Scream like Starkad a little,' said Thorstein.

'Very well,' said the demon. And he began to scream again, so horribly that it seemed appalling to Thorstein that such a small fiend could bellow so loudly. Thorstein now did as before, wrapping his cloak around his head, but he was so badly affected by it that he blacked out and was unconscious.

Then the demon asked, 'Why are you so quiet now?'

When he came round, Thorstein replied, 'I'm quiet because I'm amazed at what a dreadful great voice you have inside you, as small a demon as you look to me. So was that Starkad's loudest scream?'

'Nowhere near it,' he said, 'that was rather his quietest scream.'

'Stop beating about the bush,' said Thorstein, 'and let me hear the loudest scream.'

The demon agreed to that. Thorstein now prepared himself for it: he folded the cloak, wound it like that around his head, and held it there with both hands. The ghost had moved closer to Thorstein by three seats with each scream, and now there were only three between them. The demon then puffed out his cheeks fearsomely, rolled his eyes, and began to bellow so loudly that it exceeded all measure for Thorstein.

At that moment the church bell rang out, and Thorstein fell unconscious on to the ground. The demon reacted to the ringing of the bell by plunging down into the earth, and the noise could be heard for a long time down in the ground. Thorstein recovered quickly. He got up, went back to bed and lay down.

In the morning the men got up. The king went to church and heard mass. After that, people went to table. The king was not in a terribly good mood.

He spoke up: 'Did anybody go alone to the privy last night?'

Then Thorstein stood up and knelt before the king, and admitted to having disobeyed his order.

The king replied, 'That was not such a serious offence against me, but you are proof of what people say about you Icelanders – that you are very self-willed. So did you notice anything?'

Thorstein then told the whole story of what had happened.

The king asked, 'Why did you think it would be of any use to you if he screamed?'

'I want to tell you that, my lord. Since you'd warned everyone against going out there alone and that demon turned up, I felt sure we wouldn't be leaving each other unharmed. But I thought you'd wake up, my lord, if he screamed, and I thought I would be saved if you found out about it.'

'And so it turned out,' said the king, 'that I woke up because of it, and I knew what was going on, so I had the bell rung because I knew nothing else could help you. But were you not afraid when the demon started screaming?'

Thorstein replied, 'I do not know the meaning of fear, my lord.'

'Was there no dread in your heart?' said the king.

'It wasn't quite that way,' said Thorstein, 'because at the last scream, a shiver nearly shot down my spine.'

The king replied, 'Now your name shall be made longer: you shall be called Thorstein Shiver from now on. And here is a sword I would like to give you for your name-fastening.'

Thorstein thanked him.

It is said that Thorstein was made one of King Olaf's retainers and stayed with him after that. And he fell on the *Long Serpent*★ alongside the king's other champions.

THE TALE OF THIDRANDI AND THORHALL

It is said that when Harald Fairhair★ became sole king over Norway, he took a bath and had Earl Rognvald of More★ cut his hair; then the earl gave him a nickname and called him Harald Fairhair. That was thought an appropriate name. Some men also say that the king gave Shetland and Orkney to the earl in return for the haircut. And when the earl spoke to his sons Hrolf and Hrollaug,★ they offered to go to Orkney for him, but he did not want that.

He said to Hrollaug, 'You cannot be Earl,[1] because you do not have a warlike disposition. I think your way lies out to Iceland.'

It came about, as the earl said, that Hrollaug went to Iceland. He was a great ruler and kept his friendship with King Harald, but never went back to Norway after that. King Harald sent Hrollaug a good sword, an ornamented horn and a gold ring worth five aurar. Afterwards Kol, the son of Hall of Sida,★ carried the sword.

Hrollaug is thought to have been the noblest of all the original settlers★ in the East Fjords. Hrollaug was the father of Ozur Wedgehill who married Gro, daughter of Thord the Bad-tempered. Their daughter was Thordis, the mother of Hall of Sida. Hall of Sida married Joreid, daughter of Thidrandi: their son was Thorstein, the father of Magnus, father of Einar, father of Bishop Magnus. The second son of Hall of Sida was Egil, father of Thorgerd, mother of Bishop Jon the Saint. Hall's son Thorvard was the father of Thorgerd, mother of Jorunn, mother of Hall the Priest, father of Gizur, father of Bishop Magnus. Ingveld, the daughter of Hall of Sida, was the mother of Thorny, mother of the priest Sæmund the Wise. Thorgerd, Hall's daughter, was the mother of Ingveld, mother of Ljot, father of Jarngerd, mother of Valgerd, mother of Bodvar, father of Gudny, mother of the Sturlusons.★

ABOUT THIDRANDI

There was a Norseman named Thorhall. He came to Iceland in the days of Earl Hakon.★ He took land at the mouth of Syrlæk, and lived at Horgsland. Thorhall was a learned man and had great powers of second sight, and he was called Thorhall Prophet. Thorhall was living at Horgsland at the same time that Hall of Sida was living at Hof in Alftafjord, and they were the best of friends. Hall stayed at Horgsland every summer when he came to the Assembly.★ Thorhall often followed invitations to stay in the east, and he stayed there for long periods.

Hall's eldest son was named Thidrandi. He was the handsomest and most promising of men. Hall loved him most of all his sons. Thidrandi went travelling between lands when he was old enough. He was extremely popular wherever he went, because he was the most accomplished of men, unassuming and friendly to all the people and to every living soul.

One summer, Hall invited his friend Thorhall to come east when he rode back from the Assembly. Thorhall went east a little later. Hall welcomed him, as he usually did, with much friendliness. Thorhall stayed there over the summer, and Hall said he should not go home until the autumn feast was over.

That summer, Thidrandi came out to Iceland, into Berufjord. He was then eighteen. He went home to his father. People continued to admire him, as so often before, and praised his accomplishments; but Thorhall Prophet always remained silent when people were praising him most.

Then Hall asked why this was – 'for what you say seems to me worth attending to.'

Thorhall replied, 'It is not that anything displeases me about him or you, or that I am any less aware than others of his promise and accomplishments. Rather, it is because many men praise him, and he has many qualities which deserve this, though he places little value on himself. It may be that his presence will not be enjoyed for long; and then you will have enough to look back on, remembering this son of yours, such a fine figure of a man, even though not everyone praises his accomplishments in front of you.'

And as summer drew on, Thorhall grew melancholy. Hall asked why this was.

He said, 'I have a bad feeling about this autumn feast, because I have a foreboding that a prophet will be slain at the feast.'

'I can explain that,' said the farmer.★ 'I have a twelve-year-old ox, which I call Prophet because it is wiser than all the other bulls, and it is to be slaughtered at the autumn feast. This need not make you melancholy, for I think this feast of mine, just like the others, will bring honour to you and to all my men.'

Thorhall replied, 'I did not feel this because I feared for my life. I have a foreboding of greater and stranger events, which I will not make known for the time being.'

Hall said, 'Well, there's nothing to stop the feast being put off.'

Thorhall replied, 'Saying that will do nothing, for what is fated must go forward.'

The feast was arranged for the Winter Nights.* Few of those invited came, for the wind was sharp and troublesome.

When people sat down to table in the evening, Thorhall said, 'I would like to ask people to take my advice: no-one should go outside tonight, for great harm will come of it if this is broken. Whatever happens by way of portent, take no notice, for it bodes ill if anyone answers.'

Hall told the people to follow Thorhall's words to the letter – 'because they never fail,' he said, 'and it's best to guard what's still good.'

Thidrandi was waiting on the guests. In this, as in other things, he was meek and unassuming. And when people were going to bed, Thidrandi set aside his bed for the guests while he cast himself down on the outer bench by the partition.

And when almost everyone was asleep, there was a summons at the door. Everybody behaved as if they had not noticed, and this happened three times.

Then Thidrandi sprang up and said, 'This is a disgrace, all these people pretending to be asleep. Some guests will have arrived.'

He picked up a sword and walked outside. He could see nobody. Then it crossed his mind that some of the guests would have ridden ahead to the farm, then ridden back to meet those who were riding more slowly. Now he walked under the wood-pile and heard the sound of riding from the north into the field. He saw nine women there, and they were all clad in black and held drawn swords. He also heard the sound of riding from the south into the field. Nine women were there too, all in light clothes and on white horses. Then Thidrandi tried to go back inside and tell people about the sight, but the black-clad women reached him first and attacked him. He defended himself well and bravely.

A long time later, Thorhall woke up and asked whether Thidrandi was awake, and he got no answer. Thorhall said then that they must have slept too long. Then they went outside. There was moonlight and frost. They found Thidrandi lying wounded, and he was carried inside. And when people spoke to him, he told them all that had happened to him. He died at dawn that same morning, and was laid in a mound★ after the ancient custom of heathen folk.

Later, inquiries were made about people's movements, but they knew of no-one likely to be enemies of Thidrandi. Hall asked Thorhall what this strange event could mean.

Thorhall replied, 'That I do not know, but I can make a guess that these women were none other than the fetches★ of your family. My guess is that soon there will be a change of faith here, and that a better faith will then come to this land. I think that those goddesses★ of yours, who have followed the present faith, foresaw the change of faith, and knew they would be abandoned by your family. Now, they could not bear to exact no tribute from you before they left, and they must have taken this man as their due. The better goddesses would have wanted to help him, but were unable to do so with things as they were.'

Now, as Thorhall said, this event and many similar things presaged this joyful time which came afterwards, when almighty God looked with merciful eyes upon this people who had settled Iceland. Through his messengers he freed the folk from their long thraldom to the Devil and then led his beloved sons to share in their everlasting inheritance, as he has promised to all those who wish to worship him with good works to confirm it. So too, and no less, did the enemy of all mankind show openly – in these events and in many others which have been told in tales – how unwilling he was to let loose his booty, that is, to divide up the people he had previously held captive throughout all time, chained with the heresy of his accursed graven images. With onslaughts like this he sharpened his savage wrath upon those in his power, when he knew his own

disgrace was approaching, and that fitting blow to him, his captivity.

But Hall took the death of his son Thidrandi so hard, he could not bear to live at Hof any longer. He moved house to Thvatta.

Once at Thvatta, Thorhall Prophet was staying there as Hall's guest. Hall was lying in a bed-closet and Thorhall in another bed, and there was a window in the bed-closet. And one morning, when both of them were awake, Thorhall smiled.

Hall said, 'Why are you smiling now?'

Thorhall replied, 'I'm smiling because many a hill is being opened and every creature, great and small, is packing its bundle and making this its moving-day.'*

And a little later, those things came about which must now be recounted.[2]

The Saga of Bard the Snowfell God

1. [GIANTS OF MIST AND SNOW]

There was a king named Mist:★ he ruled over the gulfs that stretch
north across Slabland★ and are now called the Ocean of Mist,★
named after King Mist. He was descended from giants'★ kin on
his father's side: they are a handsome race, larger than other people.
But his mother was descended from troll★ stock. So Mist took after
both sides of his family, for he was strong and handsome, and good-
tempered, so he was quite able to mingle with human beings; but
he took after his mother's kin in that he was both strong and hard-
working, but moody and harsh-tempered if anything displeased him.
He wanted to become sole ruler over the people of the North; and
so they gave him the name of king, for they felt he would provide
great protection against giants, trolls and evil wights.★ He was also
the greatest guardian-wight★ of all those who called on him. He
took the kingship at twelve.

He abducted Mjoll, the daughter of Snow the Old,★ from
Kvænland,★ and took her for his wife. She was the most beautiful of

women, and almost the tallest of all women who were human. And when they had been together for a year, Mjoll gave birth to a boy. The boy was sprinkled with water and given the name of Bard, for such had been the name of Mist's father, Bard the Giant. This boy was both tall and handsome-looking, and people thought they had never seen a better-looking lad. He looked remarkably like his mother, for she was so fair and white of skin that the whitest snow, which falls when the wind is still, took its name from her and is called *mjoll*.

A little later, a disagreement arose between King Mist and the ogres.* Mist did not want to endanger his son Bard in the strife there, so he took him south into Norway, to the mountains called Dovrefjell. A mountain-dweller* named Dofri ruled there. He welcomed Mist: they were the best of friends. Mist asked for his son to be fostered there, and Dofri accepted him. Bard was then ten.

Afterwards Dofri trained him in every kind of accomplishment, in genealogical lore and in battle-skills. It is by no means certain that he didn't learn sorcery and witchcraft, so that he became prescient and wise in many ways, for Dofri was well versed in these things. In those days, great and high-born men considered all these things to be arts, because at that time, in this northern part of the world, people had heard no tales told of the true God.

Dofri had a daughter named Flaumgerd. She was the tallest of women, and bold-looking, but not especially pretty. However, she was human on her mother's side; her mother was dead at that time. The three of them lived there together in the cave. Bard and Flaumgerd grew fond of each other, and Dofri did nothing to hinder it. And when Bard was thirteen, Dofri gave him his daughter Flaumgerd in marriage, and they stayed there with Dofri until Bard was eighteen.

Then, one night when Bard was lying in bed, he dreamt that a great tree seemed to be sprouting in his foster-father Dofri's fireplace. It branched out greatly up towards its crown. It grew so fast that it coiled up into the cave-roof and then out through the roof. Then it was so large that the buds seemed to him to be extending over the whole of Norway. But though all the branches were thick with blossom, on one of them was the fairest of flowers. One of the branches had the colour of gold.

Bard interpreted the dream as follows: someone of royal birth would come to Dofri in his cave and would grow up there, and this same man would become sole king over Norway. And that beautiful branch must signify a king descended from the ancestor who had grown up there, and that king would proclaim a faith different from the current one.

He was not particularly pleased about the dream. People consider it certain that the bright flower signified King Olaf Haraldsson.* After this dream, Bard and Flaumgerd moved away from Dofri. And a little later, Harald Halfdanarson* came and grew up there with Dofri the Giant. Afterwards Dofri supported him in becoming king over Norway, as is told in *The Saga of Harald, Dofri's Foster-son*.

2. [UNREST IN THE NORTH]

Bard went north to Halogaland* and settled there. He had three daughters by his wife Flaumgerd. The eldest was named Helga, the second Thordis, and the third Gudrun. But when Bard had lived in Halogaland for a year, his wife Flaumgerd died, and he felt it a heavy loss. Later, Bard asked to marry Herthrud, the daughter of the *hersir*★ Hrolf the Wealthy. By her he had six daughters. The first was named Ragnhild, the second Flaumgerd, then Thora, Thorhild, Geirrid and Mjoll.

The story now returns to the strife between King Mist and the ogres, which was gradually growing worse. They found him to be a very fierce foe. They then joined forces and made plans among themselves to do away with him. He who led them was named Hard-Worker. It happened one day that they came upon him in a stone boat. There were eighteen of them. They went for him and beat him with iron bars, and he defended himself with his oars; but in the end King Mist fell, and by then he had killed twelve of them. But Hard-Worker survived: six were left altogether. He then became their king there in the North.

Mjoll was married again to Redcloak the Strong, son of Svadi* the Giant from north of the Dovrefjell. They had a son named Thorkel. He was big and strong; he had dark hair and skin, and when he grew older he became the most overbearing of men.

A little later his mother Mjoll died, and Thorkel married Eygerd, daughter of Ulf of Halogaland. Eygerd's mother was Thora, daughter of Mjoll, daughter of An Bow-Bender.* Thorkel then moved to Halogaland and stayed near his brother Bard. They lived in the fjord of Salten in northern Halogaland.

A little later the brothers went north across the Ocean of Mist and burned Hard-Work the Strong in his house, and thirty ogres with him. After that, Bard dared not stay there. They then went back home to Salten and lived there until King Harald Tanglehair* took power in Norway. When he had accomplished that deed, Harald became so high and mighty that there was to be no-one with any power at all, between Raumelf in the south and Finnabu in the north, who did not pay tribute to him – neither those who burned the salt nor those who worked the land. And when Bard heard about this, he felt certain he would not escape this burden any more easily than anyone else had. Rather would he forsake kin and country than live under such tyranny as he'd heard the entire people was subjected to at that time. His first thought then was to seek out other lands.

3. [TO ICELAND]

There was a man named Bard, the son of Hoyanger-Bjorn, a Halogalander by birth. The namesakes entered into partnership and resolved to set out for Iceland, for there was said to be choice land there. Also, Bard Mist's-son had said his dreams had told him he would spend his life in Iceland. Each of them commanded his own ship, and each had at least nineteen men with them.

On board Bard's ship were his wife Herthrud and all his daughters. Apart from Bard, the most distinguished man there was Thorkel, son of Redcloak and brother of Bard Mist's-son. Also on board there was a great farmer★ named Skjold, a Halogalander by birth, and his wife Groa: they were very different in temperament. Also on board was a man named Breeze and his wife Mound: they were both very troll-like, difficult people and good for nothing. Two slave-women were on board, one named Nipper and the other Skin-Breeches; and a young lad named Thorkel who was called Skin-Beak. He was Bard's second cousin on his sister's side, and he had been brought up north of the Ocean of Mist where homespun cloth was hard to come by. The lad had been swathed in sealskins for warmth, and he had them for his swaddling-clothes: for that reason he was called Thorkel Skin-Beak. He was fully-grown at this point in the saga. He was a tall thin man, long-legged, long-armed and gangling, long-fingered and taper-fingered, long-faced and thin-faced, cheeks slung high on his cheekbones, teeth skewed and sticking out, pop-eyed and wide-mouthed, long-necked and large-headed, small of shoulder and stout of waist, his legs long and spindly. He was swift and skilful at everything he did, brisk and busy, and trusty in all things to those he served.

With Bard there was also a sailor named Thorir, an imposing man of enormous strength. He was the son of Knorr, son of Jokul, son of Bjorn the Hebridean. Also with Bard was Ingjald, son of Alfarin, son of Vali the brother of Holmkel, the father of Ketilrid, about whom Viglund★ composed most of his verses. Many other men were also on board Bard's ship, though they are not named here.

And when the namesakes were ready to set sail, they put out to sea and had a hard voyage. They were at sea for sixty days, and they came towards the land from the south, then held their course westwards. Then they saw a great mountain covered all over with glaciers. They called it Snowfell, and the headland they called Snowfell's Ness.

The namesakes parted off the headland there. Bard Hoyanger-Bjarnarson held his course west around the land, and then north; and he was out at sea for another sixty days. He came at last into the mouth of Skjalfandafljot: he claimed the whole of Bardardal from the streams Villikalfsborgara and Eyjardalsa upwards, and lived for a while at Lundarbrekka.

It seemed to him then that the wind from inland was better than the wind from the ocean, and from that he deduced that there would be better lands to the south of the highlands. So he sent his sons south in the spring, and they found horsetails and other vegetation. Then one of them went back while the other waited there. Bard Hoyanger-Bjarnarson then had a yoke made for every creature which could walk, and had each pull its provisions and his property. He travelled over Vonaskard: it is now named Bard's Path. After that, he claimed the Fljot district and settled at Gnupar, and after that he was called Gnupa-Bard.

He had many children. His son was Sigmund, father of Thorstein, who married Æsa, the daughter of Hrolf Redbeard. Their daughter was Thorunn who married Thorkel Leif, and their son was Thorgeir, the Chieftain★ of Ljosavatn. The second son of Bard and his wife was Thorstein, the father of Thorir who was at Fitjar with King Hakon, and who cut a slit in a hide and used it for protection (for that reason he was called Leatherneck). He married Freyleif, the daughter of Eyvind. Their sons were Havard of Fellsmuli; Hrolf of Myvatn; Ketil of Husavik; Vemund Fringe who married Halldora, daughter of Ketil the Black; Askel; and Hals. He lived at Helgastadir.

4. [SNOWFELL'S NESS]

Bard Mist's-son moored his ship in a lagoon on the south shore of the headland, and they called it Deep Lagoon. Bard went ashore there with his men, and when they came to a large jutting chasm they made sacrifices for their good fortune. This is now named Trollchurch. Then they beached their ship in a small bay. Those on board had gone and 'driven the elves* away' there in the lagoon, and that same excrement had washed ashore in this bay. Because of that it is named Shit Bay.

Then they set out to explore the island. When Bard came to a small promontory, Nipper the slave-woman asked Bard to give her the headland, and he did so. It is now called Nipperness. Then Bard found a large cave, and there they stayed for a while. They seemed to hear answers to everything they said there, for the 'dwarf-talk'* in the cave spoke back immediately. They called it Song Cave and held all their councils there, and that custom remained ever afterwards as long as Bard lived.

Later, Bard walked on until he came to a tarn. There he took off all his clothes and bathed in the tarn, and people now call it Bard's Pool. A short way off from there he built a large farm, named it Pool Edge, and lived there for some time. A man named Sigmund had travelled out with Farmer Bard: he was the son of Ketil Thistle who claimed Thistilfjord. His wife was named Hildigunn. They lived with Bard at Pool Edge.

Thorkel, Redcloak's son, claimed land for himself which is named Arnarstapi. Skjold lived at Trod; but his wife Groa took little pleasure in living with him because of her temperament, for she thought herself too good for him. So she went off into a jutting cave and cleared it by hewing at the rock so that it became a large cave, and she settled there with her belongings. She had no other home as long as Skjold lived, and it was called Groa's Cave. And after Skjold's death, Thorkel Skin-Beak asked to marry Groa. With the support

of his kinsman Bard, he married her, and after that they lived at Dogurdara.

Thorir Knarrarson looked after Bard's farm at Oxnakelda. Bard's slave-woman Skin-Breeches lived at a farm named Skin-Breeches' Brook. Ingjald went on round the promontory and, on Bard's advice, found himself some land at the place named Ingjald's Hill.

Breeze and Mound vanished from the ship on the first night, and they were not heard of for some time. In fact, they were up in the mountains, and both of them had turned troll there. As time passed, much mischief was caused by them, but people did not have the confidence to do anything about it because of their trollish nature. On one occasion, a whale washed ashore on Bard's land, and Breeze then behaved as was his custom: he went there at night to cut up the whale. When he had been cutting at the whale for a while, Bard arrived there. There was a mighty wrestling match between them. Then Breeze turned troll, so that Bard became the weaker one; but in the end it came about that Bard broke Breeze's back and buried him there in the shingle, and that is named Breeze Shingle. The next night he found Mound at the whale and killed her in the same way. This land-cleansing★ was considered most welcome.

5. [HELGA'S EXILE]

Thorkel, Redcloak's son, had two sons by his wife: one was named Solvi, and the other Redcloak after Thorkel's father. They grew up at Arnarstapi and were promising men. Bard's daughters grew up at Pool Edge and were tall and attractive. Helga was the eldest of them. Thorkel's sons and Bard's daughters used to play games together during the winter on the ice of the rivers there, which are named Children's Rivers. They played long and hard, putting all their energy into it. Thorkel's sons wanted to be in charge, for they were stronger; but Bard's daughters wouldn't let themselves be put down any more than they could help it.

One day they were at their games, and as usual there was rivalry between Redcloak and Helga. That day an ice-field lay offshore; there was a thick fog. They were playing their games then right down on the shore. Then Redcloak pushed Helga out to sea on an ice-floe; a strong wind was blowing out from the land. The ice-floe drifted out to the ice-field. Then Helga climbed up on to the ice-field. That same night, the ice drifted away from the land and out into the ocean. She went with the ice then, and it drifted so fast that within seven days she had arrived in Greenland on the ice.

At that time Eirik the Red,★ the son of Thorvald, son of Asvald, son of Oxen-Thorir, lived at Brattahlid. Eirik had married Thjodhild, the daughter of Jorund Atlason and Thorbjorg Boat-Breast and the stepdaughter of Thorbjorn of Haukadal. Their son was Leif the Lucky.★ Eirik had settled Greenland the year before. Helga now took winter lodgings with Eirik. There was a man lodging with Eirik named Skeggi, the son of Skin-Bjarni, son of Skutad-Skeggi. He was an Icelander and was called Skeggi of Midfjord because he lived at Reykir in Midfjord, although he often went on trading journeys.

Helga was the handsomest of women; but she was thought to have arrived there in an unheard-of way, and for that she was called a troll by some people. Besides, she was a man's equal in strength in whatever she did. She told the whole truth about her travels. Eirik recognized her lineage because he knew Bard, although Eirik had been young when Bard came to Iceland.

One day, Helga was standing outside, and she looked around her and spoke a verse:

> 'Blest would I be
> Could I but see
> Burfell and Bali,
> Both the Londrangar,
> Adalthegnsholar
> And Ondvertnes,
> Heidarkolla
> And Hreggnasi,
> The shingle of Dritvik
> At my fosterer's doors.'

All these place-names are on Snowfell's Ness.

Skeggi took Helga under his protection and she became his mistress. During the winter, trolls and evil wights came down into Eiriksfjord and did people a great deal of damage and harm: they destroyed ships and broke people's bones. There were three of them: a churl, a crone and their son. Skeggi made plans to do away with them: that went ahead only because Helga helped him do it and all but saved his life.

The following summer, Skeggi travelled to Norway and stayed there for two years. The summer after that, he went to Iceland with

Helga, home to his farm at Reykir. There is no mention of him and Helga having had any children together.

The story now returns to Bard's other daughters. They went home to Pool Edge, found their father, and told him how things had fared between his daughter Helga and Redcloak. At this Bard became very angry, sprang up and strode to Arnarstapi. He looked very dark with anger. Thorkel was not at home then: he had gone to the shore. The boys Redcloak and Solvi were outside: the one was twelve, the other nine. Bard then took them both, one under each arm, and walked off up the mountain with them. Struggling was of no use to them, for Bard was so strong he could have held them like that even if they were grown men.

When he got up on the mountain, he threw Redcloak into a ravine so deep and wide that he was already dead before he hit the bottom. That is now named Redcloak's Ravine. He walked on a little further with Solvi, up on to a high cliff. There he threw Solvi off so that he broke his neck and skull, and in that way he died. That is now named Solvi's Cliff. After that he went back to Arnarstapi, announced* the deaths of the brothers, and then went on his way home.

Now Thorkel came home and heard how his sons had lost their lives. He then turned and went after his brother; and when they met there were no greetings between them, but they went for each other at once, and nearly everything before them was torn up. It came about in the end that Thorkel fell, for Bard was the stronger of the two. Thorkel then lay there for a while after his fall, but Bard went home. Thorkel's leg had been broken in the brothers' struggle. Then Thorkel got up and limped home. Afterwards, his leg was bound up, and it mended very well. After that he was called Thorkel Bound-Leg.

As soon as he had recovered, he left Snowfell's Ness with all his possessions and went east to Hæng Thorkelsson.* Hæng's mother was Hrafnhild, the daughter of Ketil Trout.* He had claimed the whole of the Rang River Plains and lived at Nether Hof. On Hæng's advice, Thorkel claimed the land in the vicinity of Thrihyrning and settled there at the foot of the fell, on the south side. He is counted among the original settlers.* He was a great shape-shifter.* He had the following children there by his wife: Bork Blacktooth-Beard, the father of Starkad of Thrihyrning; Thorny, who married Orm Storolfsson;* and Dagny, the mother of Bessi.

6. [BARD AND HELGA VANISH]

Bard reacted to all this – the brothers' encounter and his daughter's disappearance – by growing taciturn and unapproachable, and people could not get anything out of him after that.

It is mentioned that Bard came one day to talk to his partner Sigmund and spoke as follows: 'I find,' he said, 'that because of my ancestry and my grief, it is no longer in my nature to deal with people, and so I must find myself some other course. But for your long and loyal service to me, I want to give you the land here at Pool Edge, and the farm which goes with it.'

Sigmund thanked him for the gift.

To Thorir Knarrarson, Bard gave the land at Oxnakelda. To Thorkel Skin-Beak he gave Dogurdara, and between them there was great friendship as well as kinship, which lasted a lifetime.

After this Bard disappeared with his entire household. People think he must have vanished into the glacier and settled in a large cave there; for it was more like his kin to live in large caves than in houses, as he had grown up with Dofri in the Dovrefjell. Also, in strength and size he was more like trolls than human beings; and so his name was lengthened and he was called Bard the Snowfell God, for people all but worshipped him there around the Ness, and they called on him as their god* in times of difficulty. Indeed, for many he turned out to be the greatest of guardian-wights.

Afterwards, Sigmund and Hildigunn lived at Pool Edge from Bard's disappearance until their deaths. Sigmund is buried there. He had three sons. One was Einar, who lived at Pool Edge: he married Unn, the daughter of Thorir, son of Aslak of Langadal. Hallveig was their daughter: Thorbjorn Vifilsson married her. The second son was named Breid. He married Gunnhild, the daughter of Aslak of Langadal. Their son was Thormod who married Helga, Onund's daughter and Hrafn the Poet's sister. Their daughter was Herthrud, who married Simon; their daughter was Gunnhild, who married Thorgils; their daughter was Valgerd, the mother of Finnbogi the Learned of Geirshlid. The third son was named Thorkel. He married Joreid, the daughter of Tind Hallkelsson.

After Sigmund's death, Hildigunn lived there with her son Einar. It was said that Hildigunn was skilled in sorcery, and she was accused of that by a man named Einar, known as Lagoon-Einar. He came to Pool Edge with six men and charged her with sorcery, but her son Einar was not at home. He came home just after Lagoon-Einar had left.

Hildigunn told him this news and presented him with a newly-made cloak.★

Einar took his shield and sword and a pack-horse, then rode after them. His horse collapsed from exhaustion on the rocks where Bard the Snowfell God had killed Breeze's wife Mound, and which are called the Mound Rocks. Einar managed to overtake them at the steep cliffs, and there they fought. Four of Lagoon-Einar's men fell, and his two slaves fled from him. The namesakes fought on.

Some say Einar Sigmundarson called on Bard for victory. Then Lagoon-Einar's trouser-belt snapped, and as he clutched at it Einar dealt him his death-blow. Einar Sigmundarson's slave, whose name was Hreidar, ran after Lagoon-Einar's slaves and saw from the Mound Rocks where they were running. He chased them and killed them both at a small bay: that is now called Slaves Bay. For that, Einar gave him his freedom and as much land as he could claim and fence in three days: its name is Hreidar's Enclosure, and he lived there after that.

Einar lived at Pool Edge until his old age, and he is buried a short way off from the grave-mound★ of his father Sigmund. Einar's mound is always green with grass, winter and summer.

Now, as was related earlier, Helga Bardardottir was living with Skeggi of Midfjord. And when Bard learned this, he went to fetch her and took her home with him, because Skeggi was already married. She knew no joy after parting with Skeggi; she was always yearning and pining after that.

One day, she spoke this verse:

> 'Soon shall I seek to leave.
> For him, the jewel-scarcener,
> Scarce dwindle my cares.
> A wretch must I wither;
> With a hot heart and wild
> Clasped I him who clasped treasure.
> No secret, my sorrow;
> I sit alone, spell out my woe.'[1]

Helga found no joy in living with her father. So she vanished away from there, and she hardly associated with any people, animals, or lodgings. She usually lived in caves and mounds★ then. From her comes the name of Helga's Hill in the Rocky Wastes; and many other place-names in Iceland are connected with her.

It was she – not Gudrun Gjukadottir,★ though some people may say so – who took winter lodgings with Thorodd and his son Skapti at Hjalli in Olfus. Helga was staying there in secret, and during the winter she would lie in the outermost bed in the hall, and she kept a curtain drawn before her. She used to play the harp every night, because she had as much trouble sleeping then as she had at other times. There was a Norwegian named Hrafn staying with the father and son. People would often talk about who this woman might be.

Hrafn was most suspicious about her, and one night he peered under the curtain. He saw Helga sitting upright in a nightshift. The woman looked pretty to him. He wanted to get into bed with her, but she would have none of it. They started to struggle, and it ended with Hrafn the Norwegian's right arm being broken.

A little later, Helga vanished away from there and travelled far and wide throughout Iceland, but found joy nowhere. She usually went in secret, always far away from people. She also stayed with her father on occasion.

7. [INGJALD GOES FISHING]

There was a troll-woman named Hood. She had her dwelling in Ennisfjall and was the greatest of shape-leapers,* evil in her dealings with both men and livestock. On one occasion she killed a great deal of livestock belonging to Ingjald of the Hill. And when he realized this, he set out to find her. She then fled, but he chased her up the mountain.

In those days there was a great deal of fishing off Snowfell's Ness, though no-one had keener fishermen than Ingjald of the Hill. He himself was the greatest of sea-heroes.

And as Hood drew away from him, she said: 'Now I will compensate you for the damage I've done to your livestock, and I will show you a fishing-bank where there's never any lack of fish if you look for them. And you need not break your habit of being alone in the boat, as is your custom.'

She then spoke a verse:

> 'Row forth past Fjordfell
> Out on the stirred-up swell
> If Grim's Bank you would see,
> Where glittering cod shall be.

There shall you lie offshore –
Frigg★ is loved by Thor.★
Snub-nosed fisherman, go,
Past Hrakhvamm's headland row.'

Then they parted. This was in the autumn.

The next day Ingjald rowed out, alone in his boat; and he rowed until he was a long way out from the mountain and the headland. It seemed to him rather further than he had thought. The weather was fair and mild that morning, and when he got out to the bank there were plenty of fish.

A little later, clouds appeared over Ennisfjall and soon covered the sky. Then a wind blew up with snow and frost. Then Ingjald saw a man in the boat, pulling in fish mightily. He had a red beard. Ingjald asked him his name, and he said his name was Grim.

Ingjald asked if he didn't want to head for the shore.

Grim said he was not ready – 'and you can wait until I've loaded up the boat.'

The weather grew steadily worse, getting so dark and stormy that one could not see from stem to stern. Ingjald had lost his hooks and all his tackle; the oars were also badly worn. He now felt sure he would not be able to reach land because of Hood's sorcery, and that all this must have been her doing. Then he called on Bard the Snowfell God to help him. Ingjald was fast growing cold, for the boat was taking in water rapidly and each wave froze as it came in. Ingjald was used to wearing a large fur cloak, and it was there in | the boat with him.[2] He took the fur cloak and pulled it over him for protection. Death now seemed to him more certain than life.

It happened around noon that day, back home at Ingjald's Hill, that someone came to the window of the main room at meal-time and said this in a deep voice:

> 'Out alone he rowed,
> Ingjald in his skin-cloak;
> Eighteen hooks he lost,
> Ingjald in his skin-cloak,
> And forty yards of line,
> Ingjald in his skin-cloak,
> And never returned,
> Ingjald in his skin-cloak.'

Everyone was startled at this. But people think it certain that Hood the troll-woman must have said this, for she believed – as she hoped – that Ingjald would never be coming back, just as she had planned it.

When Ingjald was at death's door, he saw a man rowing in a boat. He was wearing a grey cowl with a rope of walrus-hide around him. Ingjald thought he recognized his friend Bard.

He rowed swiftly up to Ingjald's boat and said, 'You're in a bad way, partner. It's a great wonder that a clever man like you should have let an evil wight like Hood trick you. Now get into the boat with me, if you want to see if you can steer, and I'll row.'

Ingjald did so. Grim had disappeared from the boat when Bard arrived: people think that must have been Thor.

Bard now began to row powerfully until he reached the shore. Bard took Ingjald home; he was exhausted, but regained his full health. Bard set off for his home.

8. [TROLLS' HOSPITALITY]

There was an evil wight named Cow of Turf River, also known as Skinhood. She lived at Hnausar. She did much harm, both in thefts and in murders. Thorir of Oxnakelda found her at his livestock one night. They went for each other at once and wrestled. Thorir soon found that she was the greatest of trolls. Their struggle was both hard and long, but it ended with him breaking her back and leaving her dead. And when he stood up, he spoke a verse:

> 'The Turf-Cow was a troll –
> As I'll tell, no trouble now.
> Warped, she walked the eastern shores,
> The hated one from Hnausar.
> I'd a mind to snap her spine
> This time, the brainless brute;
> The bold troll's lost her luck
> Now that I've bowed her neck.'

Many people said Bard must have helped Thorir in this matter as well, for all his friends used to call on him if they found themselves in danger.

Bard often used to wander around the country, and he turned up all over the place. He was usually dressed like this: he wore a grey cowl with a walrus-hide rope around him, holding a cleft staff with a long, stout spur on the tip. He would always use this when walking on glaciers.

It is mentioned that the brothers Bard and Thorkel met and made their peace fully. After that they had many dealings together, and they lived for a long time in Brynjudal, in a cave which has since been called Bard's Cave.

They also went to the games at Eirik's farm, Eiriksstadir by Skjaldbreid. Lagalf Little-Woman's-Son also went there from Siglunes in the north. They had wrestling matches, and Lagalf and Eirik were evenly matched, but Eirik had already beaten Thorkel Bound-Leg. Later, Bard and Eirik wrestled, and Eirik's arm was broken.

Lagalf had walked from his home to the games, and in the evening he walked home. On the way he wrestled with the herdsman of Hallbjorn of Silfrastadir, whose name was Whale:★ he was a shape-shifter. Whale fell, and his leg was broken. Lagalf carried him back to the farm and then went on his way. And as he was walking along Blonduhlid, he came to Frostastadir and went towards the house from the south, up to the window, and he saw into the house. The farmer was accusing his wife of taking meal from a mealbag hanging above them. He punched her in the face and she began to cry. Lagalf reached his axe in through the window and cut down the bag. It landed on the farmer's head, and he fell down senseless. Lagalf turned and continued on his way, and went home to Siglunes that evening; and he is now out of this saga. The farmer came to and thought the bag had fallen down by itself.

Some say that Orm Storolfsson had been at the games at Skjaldbreid, and that he wrestled with Bergthor of Black Fell, and that Orm had won. Also present was young Orm Forest-Nose.★ He wrestled with Thorir★ of Thorisdal, a valley in Geitland's Glacier:

Thorir had the better of it. Also present was Thoralf Skolmsson,★ who wrestled with Hallmund★ of Ball Glacier: they were evenly matched. However, Bard seemed to them to be the strongest. So these games ended without anything more to tell.

There was a man named Onund, who was called Broad-Beard. He was the son of Ulfar, son of Ulf of Fitjar, son of Thorir Stamper. He lived in upper Reykjardal on a farm named Breidabolsstad. He was married to Geirlaug, the daughter of Thormod of Akranes and sister of Bessi. Their daughter was named Thorodda. She was married to Torfi, the son of Valbrand, son of Valthjof, son of Orlyg of Esjuberg. Her dowry was half of Breidabolsstad, and so the farmland was divided in two. This Torfi killed twelve men of Kropp, and he figured most prominently in the killing of the Holm-Dwellers: the leaders there were Killer-Hord,★ Torfi's nephew, and Geir after whom the islet is named Geirsholm. Torfi was also at Hellisfitjar★ with Illugi the Black and Sturla the Chieftain.★ Eighteen of the Cave-Dwellers★ were killed there, and they burned Audun son of Smithkel in his house at Thorvardsstadir. Torfi's son was Thorkel of Skaney.

Onund's son was named Odd, a tall and promising man. No-one seemed more suited to leadership in those parts than Odd. When he was twelve, he made a journey out to Snowfell's Ness to buy stockfish, and when he returned he rode over the Rocky Wastes. Then Odd fell behind all his men, for he was seeing to his horse and taking his time about it. Then a thick fog came over, and as he drove his horse before him on the path, he saw a man coming down from the lava fields, holding a cleft staff. He turned towards Odd and greeted him by name. Odd accepted his greeting and asked him his name.

He said his name was Bard and that he had his home on the Ness – 'I have business with you. First, I want to befriend you and invite you to a Yule feast. And I would like it better if you agreed to make the journey.'

Odd replied, 'So be it, then, since you advise it.'

'You are doing the right thing,' said Bard, 'but I do not want you to tell anyone about this.'

Odd agreed to that, 'but I would like to know where I must attend this feast.'

'You must go,' said Bard, 'to Dogurdara, and have Thorkel Skin-Beak show you the right way to my home.'

Then they parted, and Odd went home and did not mention anything about this.

And in the winter, seven nights before Yule, Odd rode off alone, out to the Ness, and he did not stop until he arrived at Dogurdara. It was late in the evening; there were two nights till Yule. His horse was worn out, for it had had a hard journey with bad weather. Odd knocked on the door, but it was a long time before anyone came to the door.[3] |

But at last the door was opened halfway. A head poked out, quite revolting, peering out through the crack in the door. His eyes bulged and he tried to see what was out there. His face looked very narrow and ugly. And when he saw the man, he tried to shut the door again, but Odd jammed the shaft of his axe in the way, so that the door wouldn't shut. Next, Odd rammed the door so hard that it broke into bits. Then he walked into the house the same way as the other man had gone, all the way into the main room. It was bright and warm there. Thorkel was sitting on the cross-bench. He was very cheerful now and offered Odd lodgings. He stayed there overnight and was looked after well.

And on the next day Odd was on his feet early, and they got ready for the journey. The weather was cold and very frosty, with a clear sky overhead but gusts of snow near the mountains. Thorkel went on foot, while Odd rode. They set out for the mountain with Thorkel in front. And when they got on to the mountain, it grew very dark, with driving snow, and then the wind got up and the strongest of blizzards set in. They travelled on until Odd began to walk while Thorkel led the horse.

But when it was least expected, Thorkel vanished from view in the blizzard so that Odd had no idea what had become of him. It was windy and cold now, and the way was steep and slippery. He then wandered for a long time and had no idea where he was going.

Some time later Odd became aware that there was a man walking in the darkness, in a grey cowl and with a great cleft staff. He was digging the tip into the glacier. And when they met, Odd recognized Bard the Snowfell God. They greeted each other and exchanged news. Bard asked him to come with him. They had not walked long before they came into a large cave, and then into another cave which was bright within. Some women were sitting there, rather tall but presentable. Odd's wet clothes were then pulled off and he was treated with the best of hospitality.

He stayed there for Yule, comfortable in every way. There was no-one else there apart from those of Bard's household.

Odd liked Thordis the best of Bard's daughters, and with her he spoke most often. Bard soon noticed, but said nothing about it. Bard invited Odd to stay there for the winter, and he accepted. Then Bard took a great liking to Odd and taught him law that winter. After that, he was considered a more learned man than any other in the law.

When Bard realized that Thordis and Odd loved each other, he asked Odd if he wanted to marry Thordis.

Odd said, 'There's no hiding the fact that I have set my heart on her more than any other woman, and truth to tell, if you are willing to give her to me in marriage, I will not refuse.'

And so it was that Bard gave his daughter to Odd, and gave her rare treasures for her dowry. Bard was to visit Odd for the wedding, and bring the bride to him. Then they parted in friendship. Odd went home and prepared for the feast; and on the appointed day, Bard came to Tongue with the bride and ten others. Thorkel Bound-Leg was there with his brother, and his kinsman Orm the Strong.★ Thorkel Skin-Beak was also there with Bard, and Odd gave Thorkel a good welcome. Also present were Ingjald of the Hill, Bard's kinsman Thorir Knarrarson, Einar Sigmundarson of Pool Edge, and four other men whose names are not known. Many guests had arrived earlier: Odd's kinsman Torfi Valbrandsson, Illugi the Black, Geir the Wealthy from Geirshlid, and Arngrim★ the Chieftain from North Tongue. Odd's cousin Galti, Kjolvor's son, was also there, and many other people. Nothing worth telling happened at the feast. Afterwards everyone left for their homes.

There was much love between Odd and Thordis. They were together for three years; then Thordis died. They had no children. Odd felt it a heavy loss.

Later, Odd married Jorunn, the daughter of Helgi. Their sons were Thorvald, who led the burning of Blund-Ketil,★ and Thorodd, who married Jofrid, the daughter of Gunnar. Odd of Tongue's daughters were Thurid, who married Svarthofdi; Jofrid, who married Thorfinn,

Seal-Thorir's son; and Hungerd, who married Hallbjorn, the son of Odd of Kidjaberg. Kjolvor was Odd's aunt, the mother of Thorleif, mother of Thurid, mother of both Gunnhild – who married Kolli – and Glum, the father of Thorarin, father of Glum of Vatnsleysa.

9. [SKEGGI GAINS A GRANDSON]

The story now returns to Skeggi of Midfjord, who lived at Reykir in Midfjord. He had married a woman named Hallbera, the daughter of Grim. Their son was Eid, who later married Hafthora, the daughter of Thorberg Corn-Mouth and Olof Ship-Shield, Thord Gollnir's sister. They had another son named Koll, the father of Halldor, father of Thordis and Thorkatla, for whom Helgi the Poet* pined.

Skeggi had three daughters. One was named Hrodny: she married Thord Bellower.* The second was named Thorbjorg: she married Asbjorn the Wealthy, the son of Hord. Their daughter was Ingibjorg, who married Illugi the Black: their sons were Gunnlaug Serpent-Tongue,* Hermund, and Ketil. Skeggi's third daughter was named Thordis. She grew up at Reykir; she was the prettiest of women.

Thord Bellower, a great leader, lived at Hvamm in the Hvamm District.

Thorbjorn Oxen-Might* lived at Thoroddsstadir in Hrutafjord. He was son of Arnor Hairy-Nose, son of Thorodd who had claimed the land there. He killed Atli, Asmund's son, and Grettir* later avenged his brother and killed Thorbjorn. Thorodd Poem-Piece was Thorbjorn's brother.

Grenjud, the son of Hermund the Crooked, lived at Mel in Hrutafjord. He had a daughter named Thorgerd. Grenjud and Thorbjorg had a son named Thorbjorn, a most accomplished man.

It happened, one autumn at Reykir in Midfjord when Eid was thirteen, that there was a knock at the door late in the evening. Eid went to the door. A very tall man was standing outside, wearing a grey cowl and leaning on a cleft staff which he was holding. This man greeted the farmer's son by name, and Eid asked who he was.

He said his name was Gest.★ He asked whether Eid had any authority.

Eid said he had all the authority he wanted.

'Will you,' said Bard, 'provide me with lodgings for the winter?'

'I'm not sure about that,' said Eid.

'You don't make much of yourself, an up-and-coming man,' said Gest, 'if you won't undertake to give one man food for a few nights. I'll go away and spread your reputation wherever I go.'

Eid said, 'Why don't you stay here for the winter rather than take your leave in the middle of the night?'

Then Gest went inside with the farmer's son. The farmer asked where this man had come from, and Eid told him everything he had discussed with Gest. Skeggi did not think much of this, but he let Eid have his way. Gest stayed there that winter: he was really Bard the Snowfell God. Bard taught Eid law and genealogical lore. Eid became the most learned of all men in the law, and because of that he was called Law-Eid.

Thordis, Skeggi's daughter, was twelve at this time. Some people said Gest would be seducing her during the winter. When summer came, Gest went away and thanked Eid for his hospitality. And as the summer passed, Thordis began to thicken around the waist, and in the autumn she gave birth to a child in a shieling.★ It was a big and beautiful boy. She sprinkled the boy with water and said he would be named after his father; so he was called Gest.

On the next day, a woman came into the hut and offered to take the boy and foster him. Thordis let her do as she wished. A little later she vanished away with the boy. This was really Helga, Bard's daughter. Gest grew up with her for some time.

Skeggi showed Thordis little affection after this had happened. A few years later, Thorbjorn Grenjadarson asked for Thordis's hand, and she was married to him. Thorbjorn then established a farm at Tongue, beyond Melar. They were not long together before they had two sons: the elder was named Thord, the younger Thorvald. Both were promising men, though Thord excelled by far. Thorbjorn became a wealthy man in movable goods, having five hundred sheep in his keeping.

10. [A YULE FEAST IN BAG'S CAVES]

A man named Thorgils lived at Lækjarmot in Vididal, variously known as Thorgils Boomer★ or Thorgils the Wise; his son was Thorarin the Wise, Killer-Bardi's foster-father.

Audun Shaft★ lived at Audunarstadir at that time. He was old then, but he had been the greatest of men and a great warrior.

Thorbjorn, the farmer at Tongue, had many sources of income. He had a shieling out in the Hrutafjord valley, which he had manned early in the summer. Mistress Thordis was always at the shieling. At this time Thord was six and Thorvald five.

One evening Thordis was at the spring, washing her hair. Then Helga Bardardottir came to her with Gest, and he was twelve then.

She said, 'Here is your son, Thordis, and it's not certain he would have grown more if he'd stayed with you.'

Thordis then asked the woman who she was.

She said her name was Helga and that she was the daughter of Bard the Snowfell God – 'but Gest and I have travelled far and wide, for my home is not in one place. I also wish to tell you that Gest and I are brother and sister, and Bard is the father of us both.'

Thordis said, 'That's hardly likely.'

Helga did not linger there, but walked away at once.

Gest stayed behind with his mother, and he was both tall and handsome, for he was already as big as those who were in their twenties. Gest stayed at Tongue the following winter; and then his father Bard fetched him and took him home into the Snowfell Glacier. Bard had brought Thordis a handsome lady's outfit. Gest grew up with his father, who taught him all the skills he knew. Gest grew so strong that no-one then living was his equal.

In those days, the troll-woman Bag was alive and lived in Hound Cave, in the valley which has since been called Bag's Valley. Bag held a great Yule feast. She invited Bard the Snowfell God first of all, and with him went his son Gest and Thorkel Skin-Beak. Also invited were Gudrun, the widow of Knapp, and her son Kalf. Also invited were Surt★ from Hellisfitjar and Jora★ of Jora's Cliff. An ogre named Kolbjorn was invited there. He lived in a cave in Breiddalsbotnar – it is near the mouth of the Hrutafjord Valley, where the valley gets shallow in the west under Slettafell. With Kolbjorn came Gaper and Gulfspear, who made their home at High Gnup in Gnupsdal, and Glint and Tub from the Cliffs of Midfjord Ness. Gudlaug of Gudlaugshofdi was also there.

The seats in Hound Cave were arranged so that Gudrun, the widow of Knapp, sat on the inside at the middle of the cross-bench; on one side of her sat Jora Egilsdottir of Jora's Cliff, and on the other side sat Helga Bardardottir, and no-one else sat there. Bag served the guests. In the high-seat sat Bard the Snowfell God. Outwards from him sat Gudlaug from Gudlaugshofdi, and inwards from him sat Gest Bardarson, then Kalf and Thorkel Skin-Beak. Opposite Bard sat Surt of Fitjar. Inwards from him sat Kolbjorn of Breiddal, then Glint and Gulfspear; and outwards from him sat Gaper and Tub.

Then the tables were set up and a magnificent spread was laid out on them. The drinking there was completely out of control, so that everyone there got drunk. And when the meal was over, Bag and the ogres asked Bard what kind of entertainment he wanted: they said he should be in charge of that. Bard suggested they start a skin-throwing game.★

Then they stood up – Bard, Surt, Kolbjorn, Gudlaug and Gulfspear – and played a four-corner skin-throwing game. There was no small commotion then, but still it was obvious that Bard was the strongest, even though he was old. They had a big bear-pelt for a skin, and they'd rolled it up. Four of them threw it back and forth among themselves, while one person was 'out' and had to try and get it. It was not a good idea to get in the way of their shoves. Everyone stood up on the benches except Gest. He sat still in his place.

When it was Kolbjorn's turn to be 'out', he tried to get the hide off Bard and lunged at him all of a sudden. And when Gest saw that, he stuck out his foot in front of Kolbjorn so that the ogre fell right down on the rock so hard that he broke his nose. Blood streamed all over him. There was uproar, and a very violent struggle. Kolbjorn wanted to revenge himself on Gest.

Bard said it would not do for anyone to run amok in the halls of his friend Bag – 'where she has invited us out of friendship.'

Now it had to be as Bard wanted, although Kolbjorn took it badly that he could not have his revenge. It seemed then, as so often before, that all ogres were afraid of Bard.

In parting, when Gest went away, Bag gave him a dog named Snuffler. It was grey-faced. Of all dogs it was the best of companions because of its strength and intelligence. She said it was better in battle than four men. Then Bard went home, where he and Gest stayed for a while.

II. [KOLBJORN MAKES AN APPEARANCE]

Gust was the name of a shepherd of Thorbjorn, the farmer of Tongue. He herded sheep winter and summer; in all things he showed the utmost loyalty to the farmer. Gust was stout and swift-footed, but not strong.

Ten years after Gest had left Tongue, all the sheep which Thorbjorn had left in the shepherd Gust's care happened to disappear. He searched for three days on end without finding the sheep.

He then came home in the evening and said he would give up looking for the sheep – 'for I've searched for three days in all directions, and looked wherever I thought there was any likelihood that the sheep might be.'

The farmer gave him a severe reprimand and said the sheep must be nearby.

The next day, Thorbjorn rode to Reykir in Midfjord to see his father-in-law Skeggi. Skeggi gave him a warm welcome and asked the news.

Thorbjorn said he had no news to tell – 'except that my sheep have all vanished away, and they've been searched for now for three days on end, and nothing has turned up. I have come here because I'd like to have some good advice from you on how to proceed, and I'd like you to tell me what you think is most likely to have happened – for there's nothing very likely about the disappearance of these sheep.'

'I think I see,' said Skeggi, 'what must have become of your sheep. Some trolls have taken them and made them invisible. Nobody will succeed in getting them back except your sons, for this will be aimed at them. It may be that the trolls feel they have some cause for revenge, and that one of them has suffered a defeat at the hands of some neighbour of theirs, but cannot take revenge on him. My advice is that the brothers search.'

Thorbjorn rode back home after this and spoke with his sons about their looking for the sheep.

Thord said, 'My kinsman Skeggi must have suggested this, though it seems to me that whoever searches will be sent into the hands of trolls. But perhaps my kinsman Skeggi has seen something in this matter which will bring us honour in the doing. Of course we'll go.'

So early one morning the brothers set out for the mountains; but towards noon they had found nothing, although they had walked a long way.

Then Thord said, 'Now let's part company: you go up under Snowfell and search all the Tongues★ of Hvamm River, then take the high roads back over the mountains, and so to Svinaskard and Haukadalsskard, and from there go home. I mean to search the Hrutafjord Valley all the way inland. And if I do not come home tonight, then greet my father, mother, friends and family, for then it's likely I shall not be coming back.'

Then the brothers parted. Thorvald went all the way as described and came home in the evening, but he had not found any of the sheep.

But as for Thord, the story goes that after the brothers parted, he walked up the valley, meaning to search it up to the end. When he had been walking for a while, a dark fog came on, so thick that he could see nothing at all. But when it was least expected, he became aware that there was a man near him in the fog. Thord headed that way, and when he came near he saw that this was a woman. To Thord she looked pretty and well turned out, and of no more than medium height. But when he tried to reach her, she vanished from his sight so quickly that he could not see what had become of her in the fog.

After that, Thord wandered through the valley, but not for long before he heard a great din in the darkness, and suddenly he saw a man – if such be the right word for it. This man was huge and very gaunt. Bowed was his back and bent were his knees. He had a face so misshapen and loathsome that Thord thought he had never seen anything like it. His nose was broken in three places, and those were marked by great knots. From that it looked thrice-twisted, like the horns on old rams. In his hand he held a great iron staff.

When they met, this fiend★ greeted Thord by name. Thord accepted his greeting and in turn asked him what his name might be. He said his name was Kolbjorn and that he ruled over this valley. Thord asked if he happened to know anything about his father's sheep.

Kolbjorn said, 'I will not deny that I caused the disappearance of your father's sheep. Now it has turned out just as I would have chosen – he has asked you to do the searching. Have you seen anyone other than me since you left home?'

Thord said that yes, he had seen a woman, but he had not been able to talk to her – 'because she vanished from sight so fast.'

'That will have been,' said Kolbjorn, 'my daughter Solrun. Now this is my offer to you. Choose whichever you would prefer: either you lose your father's sheep and get back not a single head – for I am not especially fond of some of your kinsmen – or else we make a deal, and I marry my daughter Solrun to you, and the sheep will then be returned to you.'

Thord said, 'It will look to my kinsmen like a hasty bargain on my part, but such was my impression of this woman that it would not seem a great mismatch if she were married to a vigorous man.'

'This offer would not have been open to everyone,' said Kolbjorn, 'but I don't want to deny my daughter a good marriage.'

It was agreed that Kolbjorn promise his daughter Solrun to Thord, on condition that Thord attend the wedding in a fortnight at Kolbjorn's home. He said his home was in a cave in Brattagil.

Kolbjorn invited him to bring as many men with him as he liked – 'with the exception of Skeggi of Midfjord, his son Eid, Thord Bellower, Thorgils the Wise, Thorbjorn Oxen-Might, and least of all Audun Shaft of Vididal. I do not want you to invite ogres or mountain-dwellers, least of all Bard the Snowfell God and his companions.'

Thord agreed to this; and with that they parted. Kolbjorn accompanied Thord on his way; then they saw all the sheep, huddled up together in a small valley. Thord then herded them home with him to Tongue.

Everyone greeted him warmly and asked him for news; and he told what there was to tell and what had happened to him during his journey. Farmer Thorbjorn was much struck by all this, and said it was likely he had been bewitched by trolls.

Thord said it might turn out for the better – 'and I have no misgivings about this course of action.'

'I think it would be a better idea, kinsman,' said Thorbjorn, 'if you did not go to this wedding, and told no-one about it, and acted as though nothing had happened.'

Thord said little about it then. Time passed, until the appointed date came.

12. [THORD'S WEDDING FEAST]

Thord said to his brother Thorvald, 'Kinsman, will you come with me and attend my wedding?'

Thorvald said, 'I am afraid your doom is attending you if you want to deliver yourself into the hands of monsters.* But even if I knew beforehand that I would not be coming back, I would still rather go with you than stay at home, if you are bent on meeting Kolbjorn.'

They got ready for their journey and walked off up the Hrutafjord Valley until they found a large cave. They went inside, and it was foul-smelling and freezing cold there. And when they had been sitting there for a while, a tall man walked into the cave, and an amazingly large dog bounded in with him. They asked him his name.

He said he was a guest there. They said they were too.

'Are you Thord,' he said, 'come to attend your wedding?'

He said that was so.

'Would you like me,' said Gest, 'to be your guest and attend your feast with my dog?'

'My impression of you suggests,' said Thord, 'that you would be a great help to me whatever my need, so I'll agree to that.'

'Then stand up,' said Gest. 'You'll want to see your bride-to-be, and find out how honourably it's all set up.'

They walked further on into the cave until they reached an inner vault. There Thord saw Solrun sitting on a chair, and her hair was tied to the back of the chair. Her hands were bound; and there was food so close to her she could smell it, but she could reach no more of it than she could barely live on. She was as thin and starved as if she were skin draped over bones. Even so, Thord could see the woman was beautiful. He untied her. Thord fell deeply in love with her and kissed her tenderly.

She said, 'Hurry up and get away before Kolbjorn comes home.'

They asked where he was, and she said he had gone to invite monsters to the wedding. 'He has nothing else in mind but to kill both you brothers and to hold me here in the torment I suffered before.'

Thord asked whether she were Kolbjorn's daughter.

She said she was not his daughter, but that he had abducted her from Solarfjoll in Greenland – 'from my father Bard, by sorcery. He means to make me his slave and his mistress. But I have never yet given in to him, and so he has always treated me badly – but worse still since he promised me to you. He refuses to let any man marry me, whatever taunting promises he gives for it.'

Thord said he would lay down his life to get her away. Then they left her, and she stayed behind.

And when they had been in the cave for some time, they heard great thumps and loud yelling. Then Kolbjorn came in, and thirty ogres with him, and many other monsters. Thord and his companions went to meet Kolbjorn and his companions and greeted them. Kolbjorn was rather unwelcoming and in a bad mood, and he did not look on Gest with friendly eyes.

Then the tables were set up, and the seating was arranged. On one bench sat Gest, Thord and Thorvald; the dog Snuffler lay at their feet. On the middle of the other bench sat Gulfspear: he was Kolbjorn's best friend, and just like him in every bad way. Inwards from him sat Tub and Gaper, then Glint, and then each after the other, so that the cave was completely occupied on the side where they were. The bride did not come and take a seat.

Kolbjorn was serving. Now food was brought to Gulfspear and his benchmates. It was horsemeat and human flesh. They started to eat and tore the flesh from the bones like eagles and hunting bitches. Food quite edible for any man was brought to Thord and his companions. The drink there was strong and little spared.

Kolbjorn had a mother named Prickles. She was the greatest of trolls, though ancient by this time. Kolbjorn did not want her in their din and uproar; she stayed in an inner vault. But there was little that could take her by surprise because of her sorcery.

Now Kolbjorn's men began to drink with little restraint, and soon they all got as drunk as swine. They were not exactly whispering, and the cave resounded loudly with it all.

Kolbjorn went up to Thord and said, 'What would you like to do for sport or entertainment, kinsman-to-be? You must rule the affairs of this household.'

Gest said – for he was the quicker to reply – 'Have your men play whatever game they'd like best. Hold whichever you'd like, a bone-throwing contest or a wrestling match.'

Then Glint took a big knuckle-bone and threw it fairly hard, aiming at Thord's midriff.

Gest saw this and said, 'Let me see to the bone and this game, since I'm more used to it than you.'

And so he did, catching the bone in mid-air and throwing it back. It found its mark, hitting Glint's eye so hard that it popped out on to his cheek. Glint did not like this and howled like a wolf-cur. His sworn brother Tub saw this injury and at once grabbed the knuckle-bone and let it fly at Thorvald. Thord saw this, caught it and sent it back. The knuckle-bone hit Tub's cheekbone so hard that his jaw broke into pieces. Now there was great uproar in the cave.

Then Fright from Thambardal snatched up an amazingly large leg-bone and hurled it very powerfully, aiming it at Gest because he was sitting immediately opposite him. Gest caught it and didn't wait long before sending it back without mercy. The leg-bone hit Fright's arm and thigh with so much force that both of them were broken. The ogres now made more noise than can possibly be described, for it may well be said that their shrieks were more like the screaming of corpses than the cries of any living creature.

Then Kolbjorn said, 'Give up this game, for we shall all come to harm at Gest's hands. It was quite against my will that he was invited here.'

'That's how it goes,' said Gest.

Then they began to drink for the second time, until everyone started dropping off to sleep, each in his own seat, apart from Gulfspear and Gaper.

Kolbjorn said everyone should lie where he was, 'but you and Spear must come into my bed-chamber.'

And so they did. Gest told his companions they would have to make their beds somewhere else. They lay down; and when they were asleep, Gest got up, took his sword, walked back into the cave, and cut the head off each and every mountain-dweller in there. When he had finished this task, he walked on to see if he could find out where Kolbjorn and the others were lying. Then he found a door in the cave wall. It was so firmly locked that Gest felt sure they would wake up if he tampered with it.

Then he went into the cave where Solrun was. He asked her to stand up and come with him. She did so, but said she thought this would be the death of her, and of all the others too. They came to where the brothers were.

Gest now told them to get up as quickly as possible and get out of this cave, if possible before Kolbjorn woke up – 'Solrun is here.'

The brothers then got up and made their way down through the valley.

The story now returns to Prickles, Kolbjorn's mother. She woke up shortly after the others had left. Because of her trollish nature, she now realized immediately what the companions had done. Then she sprang up as if in perfect health. At once she charged so fiercely at the door behind which Kolbjorn was sleeping that the door splintered into several pieces. Kolbjorn woke up and asked who was making such a noise.

Prickles said it was she, and said, 'It would be a good idea not to lie around any longer, kinsman Kolbjorn, because Thord has gone, with Solrun and his companions. This is all Gest's doing. He has killed all your guests except these ones here. Now there's nothing else for it but to go after them and kill them all.'

Kolbjorn said, 'It's often been shown that your wisdom sets you apart from many others. Many's the time I would have come to grief if I'd not had your help. Now, mother, since you're ready, you go first and see if you can head them off. Take the high road over the ridges and catch them by surprise, and we'll take the low road through the valley. Then we'll be able to meet up with them.'

Then Prickles left, and Kolbjorn and his companions got themselves ready as fast as they could.

The others kept going until they realized they were being followed. Kolbjorn called out when he saw them, and told them to flee no further.

Solrun took fright at this and said, 'I knew this would happen! Now it's certain you will all be killed. Kolbjorn is such a troll that nothing can withstand him.'

Gest said, 'Fate will decide that. Now we must divide our forces. Thord shall take on his kinsman Kolbjorn. It is right that he should take on the hardest task, since he got us all into this mess. Thorvald shall take on Gaper, and I will fight with Gulfspear. We'll need all our strength this time. Snuffler, you take on the old woman. And Solrun shall watch our sport.'

And when Kolbjorn came, they all attacked each other and wrestled violently. Snuffler climbed up the cliff Prickles was under, and rolled large rocks on top of her. At this she grimaced nastily, and threw the stones back up. In the end Snuffler rolled a great boulder, and it landed on the old woman's back just as she was trying to pick up a stone, so that her spine snapped. She died from that.

Gest and Gulfspear went hard at each other; and in the end Gest caught him on the hip, hurling him up in the air with such force that he came down head first so hard that his skull smashed into smithereens. Shortly afterwards he was dead.

Then Gest went to where Thorvald was on the point of falling, and he chopped off both the legs from under Gaper, above the knees. Gaper then fell backwards.

Thord and Kolbjorn struggled long and hard; but in the end Thord fell. At that moment Gest came up, grabbed Kolbjorn by the hair, and shoved both knees into his back so hard that his neck was instantly dislocated. Then Gest pushed him off Thord. Thord got up and felt very stiff from Kolbjorn's handling. By then Thorvald had killed Gaper.

Gest said, 'Now it has come about, Solrun, that victory is ours, and you are freed from the trolls' clutches.'

'We have you to thank for that,' said Thord, 'and I would like you to choose your own reward.'

'I don't want to have money from you brothers. But if you think it worth a reward, then arrange a passage to Norway for me, for I am curious to see the king who rules there, about whom so much has been said.'

They said they would do that.

'But now I do not want to hide it from you,' said Gest, 'that I am your brother, born of the same mother. Here we must part for the time being. I'll come to the ship in the spring.'

Then Gest went on his way, and the brothers made their way home with Solrun to Tongue, and told the whole story of what had happened on their journey. And it seemed to most of those who heard it that Thord had had very good luck with it.

13. [KING RAKNAR]

There was a ship's captain named Kolbein, who had a ship at Bordeyri in Hrutafjord. The brothers rode there and secured a passage for Gest in the summer. They set out to sea as soon as the wind was favourable. There on the outgoing journey were Gest and his dog Snuffler, Thord and Solrun, and Thorvald. They had favourable winds, and came to land at Trondheim.

At that time Olaf Tryggvason* ruled over Norway. The brothers went to meet him with Solrun. They saluted the king and asked him for winter lodgings, and the king asked them if they would accept baptism. They were reluctant about that; but it came about in the end that they were baptized, and so was Solrun. They stayed with the king in good favour that winter. Gest stayed behind at the ship and lived in a hayrick-shaped tent. His dog stayed with him, but no people.

One day the king was in a good mood and said to Thord, 'Where did you pick up that pretty woman?'

'Out in Iceland,' said Thord.

'How old are you?'

Thord said, 'I am nineteen.'

The king said, 'You are a vigorous man. Where do you think you have been in most danger?'

'Out in Iceland,' said Thord, 'when I won this woman.'

'Who saved you?'

'His name is Gest,' said Thord.

'Did he come here?' said the king.

Thord said that was so – 'and now I would like to tell you what I want to ask of you. I want to become your retainer.'

'Then bring Gest to see me if you want to become my man.'

So Thord went to see Gest.

Gest was unwilling to do this and said, 'I am not keen to meet the king, for I'm told he's so overbearing that he wants to control everything, even what people believe in.'

At last it came about that Gest did go with Thord and went before the king. Gest greeted the king, and the king received him well.

Gest asked, 'What business do you have with me, my lord?'

The king said, 'The same as with others: that you should believe in the true God.'

Gest said, 'I'm of no mind to renounce the beliefs my kinsmen have held before me. I have a feeling that if I renounce this faith, I shall not live long.'

The king said, 'The life of men is in God's hands. And no man in my kingdom will be allowed to practice the heathen faith for long.'

Gest said, 'It seems likely to me, my lord, that your faith must be the better one; but I will not renounce my beliefs in the face of threats or force.'

'So be it,' said the king, 'for my impression of you suggests that you would rather lay down your creed on your own than under another man's force; and you are not altogether lacking in good luck. So stay and be welcome with us this winter.'

Gest thanked the king for his words and said he would accept the offer. Gest stayed with the king for a while, and it was not long before he was prime-signed.★

So time passed, and Yule came. On the evening before Yule, the king was sitting in his high-seat with all his retinue, each in his place.

The people were merry and cheerful because the king was in the best of spirits.

When the men had been drinking for a while, a man strode into the hall. He was tall and evil-looking, glaring and with restless eyes, black of beard and long of nose. This man wore a helmet on his head, was clad in a coat of mail, and was girt with a sword. A golden necklace he wore around his neck, and on his arm a thick gold ring. He strode into the hall and up to the king's high-seat. He greeted no-one. The sight of him filled everyone with awe. No-one spoke a single word to him.

And when he had stood before the king for some time, he said, 'Here I have come, and by this great man I have been offered nothing at all. I shall be more generous, for I am offering to present these treasures I am now wearing to that man who dares to take them from me – but there is no such man in here.'

Then he strode away, and there was a foul stench in the hall. At this a great dread came over everyone.

The king told everyone to sit still until the stench had dispersed, and they did as the king asked. But when people looked, it was found that many were lying as if half-dead and unconscious until the king himself came and recited over them. All the watchdogs were dead, except Fighter★ and Gest's dog Snuffler.

The king said, 'What do you think, Gest – who can that man be who came in here?'

Gest said, 'I have never seen him before, but I have been told by my kinsmen that there was once a king whose name was Raknar, and I think I recognized him from their tales. He ruled over Slabland and many other lands, and when he had ruled over them for a long time he had himself buried alive with eight hundred men, in his ship Slodinn.★ He murdered his father and mother, and many other folk. From other people's tales, I think his grave-mound★ is likely to be up north, in the wastes of Slabland.'

The king said, 'I think you are probably right. Now it is my request, Gest,' said the king, 'that you go and get these treasures.'

'One could call that a death sentence, my lord,' said Gest, 'but I will not refuse it, if you will prepare my journey according to what you know I shall need.'

The king said, 'I will put my mind to it so that your journey turns out well.'

Then Gest prepared himself. The king provided him with forty iron shoes: they were lined with down. At Gest's request, he also provided him with two magicians:* a man named Hook and a woman named Crook. Then he provided him with a priest named Jostein for a companion. He was a celebrated man and greatly valued by the king. Gest said he did not like him.

The king said, 'He will serve you best when your need is greatest.'

'Then why shouldn't he come along?' said Gest. 'You are often close to the mark – though one couldn't tell just by looking at this man that he would be of any use in great danger.'

The king gave Gest a shortsword and said it would bite if the need arose. He gave him a towel and asked him to wrap it around himself before going into the grave-mound.

The king gave Gest a candle and said it would light itself when held aloft – 'for it will be dark in Raknar's mound. But stay no longer than the candle lasts, and that will do the trick.'

The king provided Gest with three seasons' supply of provisions.

Then he sailed north along the coast, all the way past Halogaland and Finnmark* to the Ocean Gulfs.*

When they got north of the Ocean of Mist, a man came out from the shore and joined them in their travels. He said his name was Red-Moustache. He was one-eyed; he wore a blue-flecked hooded cape, buttoned all the way down to his feet. Jostein the priest did not like him. Red-Moustache preached heathendom and ancient magic to Gest's men and claimed it was best to sacrifice for their good fortune. One day, when Red-Moustache was preaching these empty beliefs to them, the priest became angry, grabbed a crucifix and hit Red-Moustache on the head with it. He plunged overboard and never came up again. Then they felt sure that had been Odin.★ Gest took little notice of the priest.

A little later they came to the wastes of Greenland. By then winter had arrived. They stayed there over the winter.

By some cliffs they saw two bars fastened to a cauldron full of gold. Gest sent Hook and Crook to fetch the bars and the cauldron. But when they came up to them and tried to take them, the earth gaped under their feet and swallowed them up, so that the ground closed over their heads. And when people looked, everything had disappeared – both cauldron and bars.

Every night that winter, Gest kept watch in the door of their hut. One night, a horrible bull came up to the hut, bellowing loudly and behaving threateningly. Gest attacked the bull and hewed at it with an axe. At that the bull shook itself, and the axe did not bite but broke. Then with both hands Gest seized the bull by its horns, and they wrestled violently. Gest found that his strength was no match for this devilish creature. Then it tried to force him against the wall of the hut and gore him there. At that moment Jostein the priest appeared and slammed the crucifix down on the bull's back. At that blow the bull plunged down into the ground so that no more harm came from it.

Nothing else worth telling happened.

14. [CROSSING THE DESERT WASTES]

They left that place in the spring, and each carried his own provisions. First they walked overland in a south-westerly direction; then they turned to cross that country. There were glaciers first, and then great stretches of burnt lava. They now put on the iron shoes which the king had given them; and when they had all put on their shoes except Jostein the priest, they walked out on to the lava field.

After they had been walking for a while, the priest became incapacitated. He was walking across the lava with bloody feet.

Gest said, 'Which of you lads will help this quill-pusher make it off the mountain?'

Nobody volunteered to do it, for they all thought they had enough to carry.

'It would be a good idea to help him,' said Gest, 'since the king spoke highly of him, and we had better not go against his advice. So come here, priest – get up on my pack and bring your belongings with you.'

The priest did so. Gest then walked in front, and he walked the fastest. They walked like that for three days.

And when the lava fields came to an end, they reached the sea. There was a large islet offshore. Leading out to the islet was a causeway, narrow and long. It was dry at low tide, and so it was when they arrived. Then they walked out to the islet, and there they saw a great mound.

Some say the mound stood to the north, off Slabland; but wherever it was, there were no settlements anywhere near it.

15. [A GUEST IN THE GRAVE-MOUND]

That day Gest had the mound broken open. By evening they had broken a hole in the mound with the priest's help. But in the morning it had closed up as before. On the second day they broke into it again, but in the morning it was as before.

Then the priest wanted to keep watch at the opening. He sat there all night, and he had holy water and the crucifix with him. When midnight came, he saw Raknar, magnificently clad.

He asked the priest to come with him and said he would make his journey worthwhile – 'and here is a ring I would like to give you, and a necklace.'

The priest made no reply but sat still as before.

Many extraordinary things then appeared to him to make him go away instead. He thought he saw his kinsmen and friends there, and even King Olaf with his retinue, asking him to come with them. He also saw Gest and his companions getting ready and preparing to leave, and they were calling to Jostein the priest to come with them and hurry away. The priest paid no attention; and whatever wonders he saw, and however savagely these fiends behaved, they never came near the priest because of the holy water he was sprinkling.

Towards dawn, all these wonders vanished. Then Gest and his men came to the mound. As far as they could see, the priest had suffered no ill effects. Then they lowered Gest into the mound, with the priest and the others holding the rope.

It was fifty fathoms down to the floor of the mound. Gest had wrapped the king's towel around him and girded himself with the shortsword. He was holding the candle, and it lit up as soon as he reached the bottom. Gest now looked around the mound. He saw the ship Slodinn, and five hundred men within. That ship had been so large that it could not be manned by fewer men. It was said to be as large as the ship Gnodin, which Asmund★ had commanded.

Gest then boarded the ship. He saw that the men had all been about to stand up when the candlelight shone on them, but then they were unable to move, and they rolled their eyes and snorted through their noses. Gest chopped off all their heads with his shortsword, and it bit as if cutting water. He pillaged all the trappings from the dragon-ship and had them hauled up.

After that he looked for Raknar. He found a passage leading down into the earth. There he saw Raknar sitting on a throne. He was utterly horrible to behold. It was foul-smelling and freezing cold there. There was a chest under his feet, full of coins. On his neck he wore a splendid necklace, and a thick gold ring on his arm. He was clad in a coat of mail, had a helmet on his head, and a sword in his hand.

Gest walked up to Raknar and greeted him with the respect due to a king; and Raknar bowed to him in return.

Gest said, 'You are both famous and, in my opinion, most glorious to look upon. I have come a long way to visit you. You will now let me have a fine reward for my journey, and give me the fine treasures which you own. I shall then proclaim your generosity far and wide.'

Then Raknar bent his helmeted head towards him. Gest took the helmet, and next Gest took the mailcoat off him; and Raknar was most amenable. He took all of Raknar's treasures except the sword, for when Gest reached towards it, Raknar sprang up and lunged at him. Gest now found him neither old nor stiff. By then the king's candle had burnt all the way down. Raknar was in such a troll-rage that Gest was completely taken by surprise. It now seemed to Gest that he saw certain death approaching. Also all the men who were in the ship stood up. That was enough for Gest. He called on his father Bard.

And soon Bard appeared – but he was unable to do anything. The dead ones handled him so roughly that he could not get anywhere near.

Now Gest vowed to the one who had fashioned heaven and earth that he would accept the faith King Olaf proclaimed if he got out of the grave-mound alive. Gest pressed King Olaf hard to help him, if he were able to do more than he himself could.

After that, Gest saw King Olaf coming into the grave with a great light. At that sight Raknar was so startled that all his strength drained from him. Then Gest went for him so fiercely, with King Olaf's help, that Raknar fell backwards. Gest then hewed the head from Raknar and laid it by his buttocks. All the dead ones had sat down at the appearance of King Olaf, each in his place. With this task accomplished, King Olaf vanished from Gest's sight.

16. [ESCAPE]

Now the story returns to those who were up on top of the mound. While all these wonders were taking place, as has just been related, they all reacted by losing their wits, apart from the priest. He never left the rope. And when Gest tied himself to the rope, the priest hauled him up with all the treasures and welcomed him: he felt he had pulled him out of Hel.* They went up to the men, where they were fighting amongst themselves, and the priest splashed water over them. At once they came to their senses.

They prepared to leave. The earth almost seemed to be shaking under their feet. The sea, too, surged right over the causeway with such a great crashing of surf that it all but swamped the whole islet.

Snuffler had never left the mound while Gest had been inside. Now they were not sure where they should be looking for the causeway. Gest sent Snuffler out into the surf. The dog dived at once into the surf where it expected to find the causeway; but it could not withstand the powers of Raknar, and the dog drowned there in the waves. Gest felt it a very heavy loss.

Jostein the priest then took the lead, holding a crucifix in one hand and water in the other, which he sprinkled. Then the sea split, so that they could walk dry-shod to the mainland.

They travelled back all the way they had come. Gest presented the king with all the treasures and told him everything that had happened. The king then asked him to accept baptism. Gest said he had vowed to do so in Raknar's grave-mound. And so it was done.

The night after Gest was baptized, he dreamt that his father Bard came to him and said, 'A poor deed you have done – abandoning your beliefs, which your forefathers have held, and letting yourself be forced to change your faith because of your feebleness of character – and for that you shall lose both your eyes.'

Bard now seized Gest's eyes somewhat roughly, and then vanished. After this, when Gest woke up, he had such a fierce pain in his eyes that on the very same day they burst out. Then Gest died in his baptismal clothes. The king felt it a very heavy loss.

The following summer Thord, Thorvald | and Solrun made ready to go to Iceland.[4] They beached their ship at Bordeyri in Hrutafjord, then went home to their father. They were considered the greatest of people.

Thord lived at Tongue after his father's death. Thorvald married Herdis, the daughter of Ospak of Ospaksstadir, and lived at Hella in Helludal.

Their father Thorbjorn was cousin to Hjalti Thordarson, who had claimed Hjaltadal. Hjalti's sons★ were also named Thord and Thorvald: they held the largest funeral feast which has ever been held in Iceland, in memory of their father. There were twelve hundred guests. Odd of Breidafjord★ recited a drápa★ there which he had composed about Hjalti.

Before that, Glum Geirason had begun legal proceedings against Odd at the Thorskafjord Assembly,★ concerning the misappropriation of a ewe's milk. Then the Hjaltason brothers came south by ship to Steingrimsfjord. The Thorbjornsson brothers came out from Hrutafjord to meet them there. Together they all strode south over the fells, the way that is now called the Hjaltadal Road.

And when they arrived at the Assembly, they were so magnificently turned out that people thought the gods★ themselves had come. Then this was recited:

> 'Aught else none thought of those,
> The men of iron, acquainted
> With war, but that the glorious
> Gods of old were treading there,
> When, beneath their skull-prows scored
> With fishes of the sward,
> To Thorskafjord Assembly
> Hard Hjalti's sons strode.'[5]

They defended the lawsuit on Odd's behalf, with the support of the brothers from Hrutafjord. Then both parties went back to their homes, and they parted, the best of friends ever afterwards. A great clan is descended from the Thorbjornssons, and so too from the Hjaltasons.

There is no mention of Gest Bardarson having had any children. And here ends the saga of Bard the Snowfell God and his son Gest.

Mirmann's Saga

1. HERE BEGINS THE SAGA OF EARL MIRMANN

In the days of Pope Clement★ ... Nero was then ... Rome ...[1] there was a celebrated king in France, whose name was Clovis. He was one of the wisest rulers in heathen times. He was married to an earl's daughter whose name was Hirena. She was of Hungarian descent. In those days everyone north of the Alps was heathen.

At this time there was a powerful earl in Saxony,★ Hermann by name. He was a forceful man. Most of the time he had his seat in a city named Mainz. And though another man bore the name of king, it was the earl who made the decisions in every important matter and governed the land. Under him no thief or plunderer could thrive in the land; and he made all good men so faithful to him, with gifts and fine words, that they all wanted to live and die where he was. And it was a very great shame that he was not a Christian.

The earl was a married man, and since he himself was widely renowned, he had seen to the matter with honour. He had a wife named Brigida, daughter of King Jading of Hungary. She was young when she came to the earl; and she was so handsome that no-one saw any flaw in her features. Her knowledge was such that everything other women did seemed like children's games compared with what she did. As for the wise words and worldly wisdom which she had learnt from heathen books, the best scholars could not stand up to her. She defeated kings and scholars with her eloquence if they crossed words with her. But, as they say, few are without fault. Her nature was such that she grew fierce and domineering, so that all important issues had to be resolved in accordance with her wishes. And if noblemen spoke against her – barons, earls or knights – then they soon lost limbs or property thanks to her, or else lost their lives altogether. Likewise, if noblemen owned any treasures which she wanted to have, and they did not send them to her as soon as she demanded them, then they didn't have to wait long for something unpleasant that they would feel to the depths of their being.

She and the earl had been together for six years; but they had no children, which seemed to them a great pity because they had plenty of property and other joys of this world.

2. MIRMANN'S BIRTH

Now the story goes that one night, when they were lying in their bed, she told the earl that she was with child, and said things looked rather promising for them having some offspring.

The earl was silent for a long time.

She asked why this was – 'I thought this would be joyful news for you, because we have both longed for this for a long time.'

The earl then replied, 'If this birth brings joy, well and good. But a strange thing recently appeared to me in a dream, and I was silent because of that.'

She asked what he had dreamt.

'I dreamt,' he said, 'that you had a snake in your shirt, and it seemed to me amazingly large and savage. And when I tried to grab it and pull it away from you, it bit me so hard that I had no strength against it.'

And she replied, 'This dream seems pretty insignificant to me. Do you remember, when we were playing our games in the summer, you scratched yourself on the knife I was carrying in my shirt? This has no more point to it.'

The earl said, 'You are not short of words or determination. But however much you smooth this over with your tongue, I would rather that half the realm I rule in Saxony had sunk into the earth, and that I had not had this dream.'

Now this subject was dropped for the time being.

And soon the time came when the queen went into labour and gave birth to a son. That was a great joy for all the earl's friends, who were most keen to support him and strengthen their own positions of trust in the country. This boy was sprinkled with water and given the name Mirmann. There is no need to describe at length the great honour in which this boy was brought up, being the only child of such a couple. First they themselves, together with everyone else, rich and poor, took great pains with this young man for their own perpetual glory and benefit. The renown of the earl – indeed, of both of them – increased and drew strength from this birth. The people all served the earl for love and goodwill; but they served Queen Brigida out of fear, because those who went against her wishes soon came to grief.

This lad Mirmann soon resembled his mother in form and fairness. When he was seven, he was no smaller or weaker than those of twelve. Also, when he was still young he played roughly against the other boys. The earl scolded him a great deal for this and told him to use his strength to bring honour to himself, not disgrace to others. But his mother Brigida did nothing about it except to laugh a little when she saw him knocking them about. The earl sometimes said to her that she would weep one day for what she now laughed at.

'I don't think I'll ever weep,' she said, 'just because my son is more powerful than the sons of churls.'

And when Mirmann was eight, his mother had him taught Latin letters, and he soon became as quick and determined in that branch of learning as a grown man would be. Then she set before him some Latin books she owned, containing many arts, the first of which is called *grammatica*, and many other ancient books.

She now spoke to her son in these words: 'Now I have shown you some books. I have learnt nearly all of these, and I know that if you don't want to be a coward or a disgrace to the family, then you'll want at least to master what a woman can manage. Now, because you are the son of the man whom I know to be the greatest ruler west of the Ægean – and some say your mother isn't just a pretty face either – then if you turn out badly, people will call it a great misfortune that such a failure should be descended from valiant men, and they will say it would have been much better if you had never come into the world. Difficulties may also fall to your lot: then it would be better for you to know what to do about them for yourself than for you to have to look to the wisdom of other men – and it isn't certain that you'd get any of that unless you crouched beneath their beards, earning rebukes and disgrace. And then I would have brought you up for no good.'

Mirmann sat and listened to her speech, and said little in reply, though he was greatly affected by it. Then she had a teacher sent for, whom she knew to be the best in that land, and had him taught many Latin books. He understood it very well.

It went on like this for about five years, and he was now a lad of thirteen. Then his teacher was taken ill. Mirmann took it badly, and his mother took it worse.

Now she asked the earl how they should proceed with the lad – 'he has now been studying for some time, but it seems to me there is still a lot to be learned.'

The earl made this reply: 'Our kinsmen have been no worse than other men, and they didn't get through all the books in the world, or learn all the arts men have dreamt up. And if he has to learn all that, it seems to me that you will probably have to try other lands besides this one in which we were born. All the same, I'm not counting on him managing to learn everything. Now where do you want him to go first?'

She replied, 'It wouldn't seem bad to me if my son were a little more learned than you, for whenever good scholars speak wise words I hear you going quiet, and I think that adds little to your status. I have decided where he shall go. The king of France, Clovis by name, is a trusted friend of ours. There is a teacher with him whom I know to be the best in the Northern lands. He will also be able to learn many kinds of arts there.'

The earl said, 'You're giving this man labour enough, and there seems to me to be a danger that it will hardly help. But I would gladly have him go away and never come back.'

She became angry at his words, and asked why he spoke so harshly about their only child, who was rather a fine man and promised well. And there the discussion was dropped for the time being.

3. BRIGIDA'S MESSAGE

Now Queen Brigida sent people with letters to King Clovis, in which she asked for the lad to be fostered; and for the sake of the friendship that King Clovis had with the earl, he granted this gladly, and the messengers returned with that news. But Mirmann's mother had him stay at home over the winter, and had him taught riding, chess and such pastimes. It is said that there were not many in the earl's company who could stay in the saddle against Mirmann, and he was fourteen then. So it was with the other skills he tried, that no-one stood up to him.

There was one thing in his behaviour which seemed very unsatisfactory to his mother Brigida, and also to others: when people went to sacrifice to the gods they believed in, Mirmann found himself some other entertainment and never went there.

And when people asked why he did not want to honour the gods in whom his father and the other wise men in the land believed, then he answered in this way: 'I've thought about it, and I don't see or understand why you set your heart on doing that, because whenever I go there it stands and stares with its eyes, and says nothing. I see it entertaining no-one with persuasive words, and it gives treasures to no-one. It seems more likely to me that it just steals food from those who creep and crawl to worship it. And I know for certain that if I had my own way, I'd find some other way to manage my wealth than bringing it here and getting nothing in return but mockery and nonsense.'

And the knights who heard this said, 'You won't want to do that once you are able to think it over.'

But Mirmann replied, 'I don't think we would become better friends from that. I think, if I had my father's power, not many days would pass before I'd smashed up every last splinter in them, so that it wouldn't thrive in the land.'

His words seemed astonishing to everyone, but they dared not do much about it. His father the earl did not talk about it, whether it seemed to him good or bad, and he acted as though he did not know whether Mirmann were his son or not.

But when the noblemen asked the earl, he made this reply: 'It does not appear to me that his behaviour is very helpful towards us who live in this land.'

4. MIRMANN GOES TO KING CLOVIS

Now it was summer, and the weather improved. Queen Brigida got her son ready for the expedition and provided him with four men who would stay behind with him, supplying them extremely well with horses and armour. Now the day arrived when Mirmann the earl's son was ready for his journey, but the earl arranged matters so that

Mirmann did not meet him before he rode away. But his mother rode with him all day and gave him much advice; and then they parted.

They rode up along the Rhine to Basel, then to Avenches, and from there into France, and they heard that King Clovis was in Rheims. They headed that way and arrived there; the king was told who had arrived, and at once he sent for the lad and gave a warm welcome to him and all his company. It is not reported how long the knights stayed who had accompanied him there, but the four mentioned earlier stayed behind with him.

The king also did the following: he secured for Mirmann the best teacher in Paris, to teach him all the skills in which he seemed to be lacking. King Clovis had Mirmann sit in the high-seat beside him, and honoured him well. Mirmann also took pains to serve the king, so much so that he could not have done more even if he had been set to it. And he was so rich, both from what he had brought from home and from what his mother sent him, that he had more than enough of it. And he made this use of it: he gave with both hands. As a result he became so popular that everyone would sit and stand just as he wished.

King Clovis was a wise and celebrated ruler. He was of the Jewish faith, loved God, and did not deal in sacrifices like the Saxons or Spaniards to the west. He was now getting on in years.

The next thing to be told is that King Clovis's queen was taken ill and died. King Clovis felt it a heavy loss, and they had no children living. Some time now passed.

Then the king's earls and barons spoke to him with these words: 'We have been thinking over the needs of our country, and it seems to us that there is nothing else for you to do but seek out a wife. Since the people have a great love for you, everyone would be willing to put themselves out to support that course of action, for their comfort and for the government of the land after your day.'

The king made this reply: 'I don't have much of a mind to try that business again, for I am now growing old. It is hard to manage a young woman, since – the age gap being great – I don't know for sure that we'll find one who has both the nature and the wisdom to moderate her inclinations in every way so that no mockery falls on me or her. Indeed, it is not certain that if we did try it, we would end up with a son who would be fully suited to sit in my throne after my day. Now I can see another quicker and better plan, if it could go ahead.'

They asked what it was.

The king said, 'Give the kingdom to my foster-son Mirmann after my day, if he will accept it and if you are willing to serve him, for I know nobody so well suited. And I could have had no son to whom I would rather grant this gift.'

They replied, 'That would be making good provision, if he is willing.'

The king said, 'I want you to discuss this matter with him.'

They did so.

Mirmann was silent for a long time, and then made this reply: 'I am very grateful for the king's kindness, which he has shown to me ever since I came to him. Now he has added on still more kindness. However, he has not thought through the consequences of this case. It seems to me that the king may still rule his land well and for a long time, and it is not certain which of the two of us will live longer, though he may be bent with age. If he lives the longer, then this hope will be gone. The king also has many noble kinsmen in the land, any one of whom would be well suited to take the realm after him; and I know it would be a cause for envy if I took the realm you all owned. Now, my advice is rather that the king seek out a wife, and see if that turns out well for him and his friends.'

They reported Mirmann's answer to the king.

Things went on like this for a while: they often reminded the king of it, and he always responded in the same way – 'so where do you want to send me for a woman?'

They replied, 'We have certainly thought about that. King Æthelred of England has a young and beautiful daughter.'

The king said, 'You have mentioned that she is young and beautiful, but you have not followed it by saying she is wise and true.'

They replied, 'We assumed that must follow, since her father is a wise king and a good ruler.'

'Yes,' said the king, 'I would take a risk on that, if she were like him. But if she is like her mother, I would never want her to come to France.'

And Mirmann was present at their conversation, but he did not contribute to it. The king asked why he was so silent regarding his need.

He made this reply: 'I don't think I, a young and ignorant man, am able to discuss this matter, since wise old men are sitting here. But it looks to me as though you probably won't find a woman who is both young and likely to conceive, but also tried and tested in wisdom and constancy. For it can be found in ancient books that few things are harder to govern than a woman's disposition, because it sometimes grows too harsh, sometimes too weak. If it is too harsh, you may find it easier to wear down marble than to manage to moderate it; likewise, if it is too weak and not constant, then nothing can be done at the right moment even if the wisest of men is making the arrangements. I think those women are very rare who do not have these faults but can be ruled with moderation. But as they say, "you have to shoot at a bird before you'll get one" – and somehow you will need to try out whatever luck you or your friends bring to this business.'

And the king made this reply: 'You have spoken well, my son, and wisely; and I will do just as you have advised me, though it seems to me that it will have its problems.'

5. KING CLOVIS MARRIES KATRIN

Now this was resolved, and two earls were readied for this journey, as well as the barons and knights who were best suited for it, as the king planned. Their journey was prepared magnificently in every way. Then they rode from Rheims west to Paris, and from there to Saint-Denis and Compiègne, and so north to Dover. They heard the king was in London, and they headed that way. Then they sent word to the king that they wanted to discuss the King of France's business with him as soon as he thought it an appropriate time.

And at the appointed time they announced their business and reported the words and wish of the king, and also the plan of all the wisest men in the land. King Æthelred gave them a courteous and friendly answer, and asked them to wait seven nights for the decision he would give on this matter. They now did so. The king brought up this matter before his earls and counsellors, and reported the purpose and wish of King Clovis. And everyone there was of one accord, agreeing that this plan would appear to hold out promise for binding his kin together with King Clovis, and for making an alliance between the two kings for support if either land should come into difficulties. Then the king also expressed his wish to go along with it. He talked about this plan with his daughter Katrin: she responded positively to this matter, and mentioned in what she said that the man was old, but that she dared not go against her father's will at all.

This business ended up like this: they betrothed the princess to King Clovis, both according to law and to the land's customs, and they set a time when they would come for her. Now they went on their way and did not break their journey until they came to King Clovis in France. They told him about their journey.

At this he grew silent, though he thanked them for their trouble.

So now it drew on to the time which had been set for it. King Clovis prepared the journey of the men who were to go and meet the princess. The king assigned to that journey a company of men both noble and numerous. And when they were ready, they rode on their way and went to meet King Æthelred. He greeted them especially well and gave them a fair feast, at which they told the king

they were eager to go home. He said they would have their way. Princess Katrin's departure was then prepared with great honour and with royal treasures. Her father also gave her plenty of good advice and sound suggestions before they parted; but it is not certain that she benefited from all of it.

Now they went on their way out of the city, came into France, and arrived at Rheims. King Clovis was there before them with all the most important people in the land. And he himself and all the others welcomed Princess Katrin especially well, as one would expect. There was a splendid feast there when King Clovis held his wedding, and it went on for seven days. Afterwards the people for whom this had been intended went back, and the women and men who were to serve the princess stayed behind in good favour.

6. ABOUT MIRMANN'S REFINEMENTS, COURTLINESS AND CHIVALRY

It is said of the princess that she was the fairest of women, soft in speech, and so generous with money that she gave gold and silver with both hands, and as a result became popular among the folk of the land. On the other hand, sooner than might be expected she took to thinking about Mirmann the earl's son's good looks and prowess – which, as has already been told, he had more of than other men. He had a fair face, as befitted a great man, and in every refinement and courtly grace, as well as learning, his equal could not be found. Moreover, there was no knight in all France or Saxony who could keep his seat in the saddle when riding against this lad, if they chose to joust against him; so too with the lesser accomplishments, that there was no need for anyone to compete with him.

Now all this made an immoderate impression on Queen Katrin, and it's said you could count the time in weeks rather than months in which she shifted her thoughts, her desire and her love – but not rightly, for she turned it all towards the earl's son. And so she set down the one she was meant to take up, that is, the king. She had enough art to hide this and dissemble before the people. But she was quite open before Mirmann himself, for whenever the king was not nearby she gave him many messages about fine clothes, feasts and other entertainment. She had contrived these snares for unseemly catches; but Mirmann acted as though he did not want to know about her love, but valued all her gentleness and affection as if it were from the king. But she made no less effort to entrap him, even though she saw that he avoided it. She wasn't able to have her way, because he valued the kindness he received from the king more than her shallowness. And he spoke to the king about how friendly he was finding the queen.

'Yes, my son,' said the king, 'well should you accept from her all that it is well for her to give.'

But he spoke no more about it, for he saw that Mirmann was steadfast and discerning. Yet he knew exactly what was going on, for it was not easy to deceive a wise king about such things, though he did not want to have much to do with it.

It went on like this for some time.

7. KING CLOVIS AND MIRMANN ACCEPT THE TRUE FAITH

At that time Saint Denys★ came into France under the patronage of Pope Clement. Since King Clovis himself was a man of virtue, and saw and heard true signs of almighty God and his saints, and of this man, the blessed bishop who had come there, he then accepted baptism and the true faith along with everyone else in his country, both rich and poor. And Mirmann the earl's son accepted the faith, and baptism, at the persuasions of King Clovis his foster-father. But those who did not want to submit to the faith fled from the land. Some went westwards to Spain. An earl named Bæring ruled there; he was widely known for his valour in battles and single combats. But some went under the protection of Hermann in Saxony. These two were thought to be very much alike in their boldness.

But when Earl Hermann and Queen Brigida were told the news that their son Mirmann had accepted Christianity, they became furiously angry and upset, and at once sent men to France with letters. They gave King Clovis the letters.

These words were written there:

To King Clovis of France, Earl Hermann and Queen Brigida send the greetings of our gods.

We have received news we hardly wish to believe, that you have cast down those laws you ought rightly to have kept, and which your kinsmen cherished. It seems to us a great loss that such a wise man should fall into such great heresy as to forsake our gods, from whom we have had all our help. Now, since you intend to keep on with this heresy, send home that family disgrace who has turned out so badly while staying there with you. You may make yourself a laughing-stock, but don't bring up other people's children in this heresy. You shall also know this for certain: all the enmity I can muster up and bring to you and your realm's disgrace will be your lot, unless you abandon these outrageous things you have taken up.

When King Clovis had read the letter, he had his foster-son Mirmann summoned, gave him the letter and asked him to read it.

When he had read it through, he said this: 'Yes,' he said, 'the way this matter has developed, I expected just such a message from them. I know for certain that what we have resolved on here in France does not please them at all. From there we can expect great difficulties from now on, rather than friendship.'

King Clovis replied, 'My son, you are surely right. But it is a heavy blow to me, losing the friendship of such a man. I would like the two of us to find some plan for it which could end up with us agreeing over Christianity.'

'What is that plan?' said Mirmann.

The king replied, 'We gather the wisest men in France, and they go to the earl and recount to him what God's apostles and the popes teach people, and the miracles God has worked.'

Mirmann said, 'I know you have seen the earl, and both of them, but you don't know them. Their dispositions are much too hard for them to be brought away from their heathendom. You could try, but you will not achieve much.'

'I do want to try,' said the king.

This was done. Men went and met the earl, and they greeted him well and nobly. But the earl received their greeting coldly. They stayed there that night. On the next day they went before the earl and the queen, and spoke the messages which the king had told them to.

And the earl was silent for a long time, then replied: 'I have heard that the men of Rome have deceived King Clovis. It seems bad to me that they have fooled such a good ruler, and with such great effect that he has lost the favour of our gods, and of his many friends who would have laid down their lives to help him in his need. And because he is the first in the Northern lands to have submitted to these monstrosities, we Saxons, Spaniards and Englishmen will march against him, and then he will find out whether that Christ he now believes in stands up for him. And as he has broken our friendship with so much foolishness, tell him this: only someone who has greater power could be worse to him than I will, with all the men I can muster to bring grief to King Clovis and all his people.'

Then they got ready for their homeward journey.

And when they were ready, Queen Brigida had them summoned to her and said, 'You won't be achieving much in your errand. But last night I spoke to the earl on this matter, and I am convinced that if his son Mirmann comes to meet him and speaks to him, then there is more hope that his disposition might be softened. Tell King Clovis, either that will help, or nothing will.'

Now they parted, and they went to meet King Clovis and reported the earl's speech and that of Queen Brigida. And Mirmann was nearby and remarked that things had gone rather as he had warned.

8. MIRMANN IS SENT BY THE KING

So time drew on, until the king summoned Mirmann and said, 'It seems bad to me that your father takes so badly that message I had him sent last time. It is a great blow to me if I must expect enmity from him rather than friendship. I would like the two of us to try what your mother advised – that you go and visit him, if he would rather listen to your words than those of others. Besides, I know no-one better able to speak about God himself and his great wonders than you, my son. You are not short of eloquence or wisdom.'

Mirmann said, 'I would be duty-bound to give them wholesome advice, and to go wherever you wish to send me. But in this case, I am afraid that for our labour we may not get anything back which we could rejoice in – though you must decide. But I go very reluctantly, and I have a foreboding about it.'

The king asked how many men he wanted to have with him. Mirmann said he should give him a hundred knights, the most valiant in France – 'for I know something dangerous will happen on this expedition.'

And the king asked where that attack would be coming from, but Mirmann did not want to talk about it any more for the time being.

Mirmann the earl's son now prepared for his expedition, and the best knights in France were picked for travelling with him. They were all ready to follow him, and they were all clad in chain-mail along with their horses, and had gilded helmets. When they were ready they rode out of Rheims, and the gleam from their weapons could be seen from afar. They rode to Avenches, and to where the German kingdom borders with France. There Mirmann the earl's son asked his knights to keep a good watch on themselves, and said he knew they would soon be put to the test in some way. They now did so, and were ready for battle both night and day.

They journeyed onward and rode along the Rhine until they came to Mainz. And at once the earl was told who had arrived, and he appeared very upset. But Mirmann's mother Brigida gathered a great crowd of men and women and went to the lodgings where her son Mirmann was staying. She welcomed him in a very friendly manner, and asked him to go and visit his father. Mirmann now went with his mother and many of his men before the earl and greeted him.

The earl looked at him and made no reply.

Mirmann spoke. 'My lord,' he said, 'I would like to tell you a message from the King of France, when you have leisure for it and are willing to hear me.'

The earl replied, 'I shan't sacrifice any time for that, since I have no interest in it.'

And the earl became so upset that he did not speak to anyone that day.

Now Mirmann saw that the earl was unbending and would not speak to him. Then he had to decide whether he should go home leaving things as they stood, or attempt to speak to him; and he felt it would be ridiculous to tell the King of France that he had not had the courage to speak to his own father. And during the night he dreamt that a large and fierce bear came towards him, and rushed at him and bit him. At that moment he awoke, and he told the dream to his knights and asked them to put on their armour and have their horses readied.

Then he called on his mother, and said that now he wanted to try for a meeting with the earl – 'and I want you, mother, to be near our discussion, and have the wisest men in the city summoned to it.'

She did so – 'but you must speak cautiously, my son, for he will not take kindly to your words. And you would be hearing many hard words for your heresy from me as well, if I were not treating you like this for love's sake. Still, I'll say little about it now, though it does not please me.'

9. MIRMANN SPEAKS TO HIS FATHER

After this they went to the earl. He was there in his temple beside his god Mahomet.* Mirmann had summoned fifteen knights from his retinue: they were all wearing mailcoats. He himself was wearing a good mailcoat, with a sword in his hand and a helmet under his cloak. He asked all the rest of his knights to wait outside by the temple with their horses ready.

Then they went into the temple, and Mirmann sat down near the earl with his mother Brigida. Now the earl owned a sword which was named Wolfling,* and there was an old story that the sword had been near a den of wolves: one wolf had dragged a corpse into the den, and that man had been girt with this sword. Because of that it was named Wolfling, and along with Durendal, Roland's* sword, no better sword has ever existed. The earl had this weapon in his hand wherever he went. And now he had drawn it up to the middle and held it bent across his knee; and he was sitting like that, completely prepared.

Mirmann the earl's son began his speech like this: 'King Clovis sent me here, my lord earl, to visit you for the sake of friend-ship and affection. You have found him to be your best friend, and such he wishes to remain. I know you have heard that King Clovis has accepted Christianity and abandoned the heresy of idolatry, at the instigation of the Pope and those other rulers who proclaim Christianity. He and many others find that they have been persever-ing in evil and worshipping pieces of wood and stones, which have no power but what the Devil gives them. And now, since he has been reliably informed about the God who rules and governs everything, he wants to worship him as well as he can. And he sent word to you, my lord, with much entreaty – along with his earls and barons and all the best men in the land – that you should agree with him about the faith, since he knows that if the two of you follow the same course, you will bring about much good throughout Christendom. Now look to your need, and give up the evil ways you have cherished for too long; and don't be offended that a young man is giving you this advice, since no-one is too old to learn well. I am duty-bound to improve your affairs, if somehow I am able to do so. Now I hope to hear those good answers from you which would benefit you for ever, bring joy to King Clovis, and peace to our lands.'

The earl was silent for a long time, and then said, 'You said rightly enough that I think you too young to give me advice, even if you were not laying before me such evil advice as you are now – telling me to abandon Mahomet, my god, who has given me victory and health and many other things, and that I must change this to worship a dead man who couldn't save his own life, but who is called a god. Now don't come here before your kinsmen with these suggestions if you don't want to suffer for it, but ride home to France with your heresy and be glad for it that you've got away without being thrashed.'

'Yes,' said Mirmann, 'it seems well enough to me that I have not been thrashed, and there are only a few who would get away with thrashing me. But what you were saying about Mahomet, that he has given you health – that is pure nonsense. Many men know that there was a man who travelled with our Lord named Nicholas Athemas.* And after the Lord allowed himself to be punished for the redemption of all mankind, and rose up to heaven in his glory, this Athemas went to France. A little later he performed illusions with the power of the Devil, and claimed to be a god, and in this way led the wretched people astray so that they believed in him. That evil heresy has spread so widely that almost the whole world has been fooled by it. But you must know that he cannot give health to anyone. The Devil deceives you like this: he throws on you sorrows and diseases and evil, but when you call on this evil man's graven image the Devil leaves off punishing you, and then it seems to you as if this thing, which is both blind and deaf, has power. But the man you are worshipping lies tormented in hell, and so will all those who worship him.'

And the earl replied in great anger, 'You need not dishonour our god, because your faith seems to me no better, believing in that man who allowed himself to be killed and dishonoured. And what can you say about this – why did he suffer shame back then, if you claim that he rules everything?'

Mirmann said, 'You surely can't be so ignorant that you don't know whom men are descended from.'

The earl replied, 'We know that men are descended from Adam.'

'And who,' said Mirmann, 'do you think fashioned Adam?'

The earl said, 'We have heard that God the Ancient fashioned him.'

Mirmann said, 'It is a pity you are not so wise on the other matter as on this. You know for certain that this same God fashioned all Creation: sky and earth, men and angels. And when he had fashioned the angels, one of them – the most splendid one – set about raising an envious host against him. And when God saw his mischief he threw him out of the kingdom of heaven, and he turned into a black devil, along with all those who had followed him. He is the one you are worshipping, you heathen people! And when God saw the loss which had come about from that, he fashioned Adam and Eve and set them in the bliss of Paradise, and meant their kin to fill that part of the kingdom of heaven which the angels had lost. But they were so unfortunate that the Devil deceived them, and they broke God's commandment and were thrust out from their bliss and into the sorrows of this world. Now, since Adam had committed the most grievous sin in the whole world, then that man who was better than the whole world was needed to set it right. God sent his son from the heights of the kingdom of heaven after that fleeing wretch, so that he would overcome that fierce viking,★ the Devil, who had brought him into this dungeon. And because the angels could not free mankind from its torments, God's son took on full humanity for the redemption of men. And this you shall know for certain: this was all one God, he who fashioned Adam.

'He also taught Noah how to build the ark, and gave life to him and his sons; and he led Moses over the Red Sea, and cast down King Pharaoh when he tried to pursue them. He gave strength to King David when he killed the giant Goliath. He gave life to the prophet Daniel when he was thrown into a pit with seven lions. God worked these miracles before his incarnation. But when he was here in the world he raised Lazarus from death, who had lain for four days in the grave, and he made wine from water at a wedding feast, and at one meal fed five thousand people from five loaves of bread and two fishes. God worked many other miracles. But in that guise, when he was a man, he suffered death without deserving it and freed the dead from the torments of hell, and he overcame the Devil who had deceived Adam, and he opened up the kingdom of heaven. Then he rose from the dead and ascended into heaven. He gave his apostles the authority and power to work miracles, such as happened in Rome when Simon the Evil★ opposed the apostle Peter and performed an illusion so that he flew in the air with the Devil's power. Peter then asked God to cast down his heresy, and Simon fell down and broke into four pieces; and so his life came to an end. It happened likewise when Zaroes and Arphaxat★ opposed two of God's apostles, Simon and Judas. They sentenced them to death along with other heretics, but God punished Zaroes and Arphaxat with fire, and so their lives came to an end. And though I mention only a few of the miracles God worked both before and after his passion, they are both many and great.

'So you can see clearly – if you are willing to – that you ought to give up this heresy to which you are clinging. And then things may flourish so that you enjoy worldly prosperity, but also eternal bliss, if you turn to this God who rules everything and grants all goodness. But if you want to keep to these bad ways until your dying day, the Devil will reward you for your worship like all the rest, with eternal torments and evil – for he has nothing else to give but that which is evil.'

When Mirmann had said this, and much besides, the lords and barons replied that he had spoken with great truthfulness.

10. HERE MIRMANN KILLS THE EARL

But the earl was in a great rage, and felt overwhelmed by the lad's words.

Then he became angry and said, 'If any man of mine follows this man's words, he shall lose life and limb. As for you, Mirmann, go away and do not come to Saxony on this kind of errand again. If you do, I'll give you the mount* the worst of thieves gets, and you shall ride on it.'

Mirmann replied, 'Many men promise better gifts to their sons. And I am happy enough to ride home to France. But if I come back, most of the churls will think there are guests enough when I come by. And if I get my hands on those stinking gods you clutch at, I'll smash up every last splinter in them and use them for firewood.'

And the earl's disposition grew no more favourable at this exchange of strong arguments, and he sprang up, drew his sword, and hewed at his son. But Mirmann had already seen the earl's frenzy and had put his helmet on his head, and the blow came on the helmet, slammed down on the gorget★ and cut it in two, so that the sword stuck in the bone of the gorget. And the knights leapt up and tried to calm him down, but nobody looked to the lad. And in this case it was not good to goad a bad temper, for Mirmann had been badly provoked and had drawn his sword before they noticed. He dealt the earl his deathblow in their arms.

Now he laid hold of Wolfling and said, 'I think no-one can be more duty-bound to carry you than I, Wolfling, since the earl must give you up.'

And now he went out to his retinue, got on his horse and at once rode out of the city. The young knights who loved him most accompanied him out of the city and lamented his deed, that he had not had more patience with his father's hot temper.

But Mirmann replied, 'Why did he have to attack me with such cruelty? He himself was fierce, and he married the woman whom I know to be the greatest she-wolf in the Northern lands – so he must have known he would sire a wolf, not a hare.'

Although Mirmann spoke these words so that they would long be remembered, he understood his crime and ill luck, and he rode home forthwith.

There is no need to describe the grief which was felt in Saxony after this event, having lost the earl whom they had loved as much as themselves, and this young man, too, who had seemed to promise so very well, if only he had not been cursed by such ill luck. Nearly everyone in the land seemed as if half-dead.

Let us now leave the queen and her people to their mourning.

11. ABOUT EARL BÆRING AND MIRMANN

We now pick up the story at the point at which Mirmann came home into France. He did not want to tell King Clovis this news himself.

He soon heard about it, however, and he summoned Mirmann and said, 'This ill luck which has befallen you seems bad to me, and I myself am to blame for the earl attacking you without cause – though you didn't stand for it when you were badly provoked. Now you will think you have lost your patrimony in this mishap, and so you must take whatever lands and moveable goods you want here. Take heart, and hope for God's help.'

Mirmann thanked him for his words and said, 'It seems to me that mine is the worst of crimes, for it is so unheard-of that people will think no-one as witless as me can have come into the world, since I didn't have more self-control in this matter. But I certainly want to follow your advice and throw off this heaviness from myself, even though I think it was very wrong.'

Now Mirmann stayed with the king in good favour. And then King Clovis's spies came east from Spain and reported that Earl Bæring was gathering an invincible army and meant to attack King Clovis and win France with the sword. When King Clovis heard this news, he called the earls, barons and other nobles to him and sought their advice. And they all gave him the same advice: he should gather his army, march against Earl Bæring and do battle with him, and this business would be settled as it might and as God willed.

This was now done: the king gathered his army from France and Flanders, and they went westwards to a city named Gisors, pitched their tents there, then waited two nights for Earl Bæring. Then he came from the west with a great heathen host and pitched camp on the other side of the valley. The next day, as soon as it was light, Earl Bæring rode out and called to the nearest men, and said he wanted to speak to King Clovis. King Clovis was now told this, and he had his horses readied and rode to speak to the earl. Mirmann the earl's son rode with him, and there were twelve men on each side. Truces were set for three nights.

Now each side rode to meet the other.

And as soon as he could hear them, Earl Bæring called out and said: 'I've heard, King Clovis, that you've picked up heresy from the men of Rome. It seems bad to me that you, who think yourself such a good ruler, have been so monstrously fooled that this unheard-of thing has come upon you – and, what's more, that you're dragging this traitor behind you who has killed his father, our best friend, whom I thought no less of than my father or brother. My chief mission here in France is to avenge him. You have two choices: either you shall deliver this evil man into my power, or I shall drive you out of France or take your life outright, if our god Mahomet wishes to help us.'

And King Clovis replied, 'This I have not deserved, that you lay waste my land. And as for what you demand, that I give up Mirmann my foster-son, you shan't get that from me, for I'd rather be left lying here on this plain with honour than give him up shamefully.'

Earl Bæring said, 'Which of these men with us here is the one who has done this deed? Show him to me, because I want to speak to him. I'm told he's quite a peacock.'

Mirmann was standing nearby and said, 'Here is the man you ask after. What do you want to say to me?'

Earl Bæring said, 'If you are in any way fit company for other knights, then come tomorrow at sunrise and ride in single combat against me. And I suspect that something quite different will stroke your cheek here than when you're kissing Queen Katrin in her orchard. I certainly shan't leave France before you're paid back for the treachery of killing your father, my best friend.'

Mirmann replied, 'I don't think you are wrong to blame what was badly done. I killed that man, and that would have been against the order of nature had fortune been smiling on us. I will defend that deed neither with weapons nor with words, but I lay it before the merciful judgement of almighty God, whom I wish to worship. As for your calling me to single combat, I know I am ill-matched in age and experience against a berserk⋆ like you. But since I am very guilty, and need God to redeem my body if he lets me live, I shall certainly come to meet you.'

Earl Bæring was very glad, and both sides rode back to their camps. King Clovis said to Mirmann, 'You have been rash in this decision, for it is widely known that no-one is bolder than this man. And you are only a child and not used to fighting, and it seems bad to me that you did not seek my advice.'

Mirmann said, 'The way things are, my life seems to me good for nothing, and either things will improve for me or I don't want to live at all.'

Now that night passed, and King Clovis was very anxious, as were all the host. To everyone, this man seemed as good as dead. At dawn the next day, King Clovis and Mirmann got up and read their canonical hours, and then they had three masses sung: a *de Spiritu sancto*, a *de sancta Maria* and a *de omnibus sanctis*. Afterwards Mirmann put on his armour and girded himself with the sword Wolfling. King Clovis put on his armour, as did all the host, and rode with Mirmann to the battlefield. Earl Bæring had arrived there, and with him eighteen thousand knights and another great multitude from Spain. It was horrible to hear their din and the rattling of their weapons.

And as soon as Bæring saw Mirmann, he called in a loud voice, 'Are you resolved, Mirmann, to cross swords with me?'

Mirmann replied, 'If God wills as I do, then put it to the test when the sun appears in the south-east.'

Then Earl Bæring said, 'In what do you trust, young lad, that you dare fight against me? Leave off this nonsense and heresy and turn to Mahomet. Then come with me, and I will make you a great man in my kingdom and so help you on in life.'

Mirmann replied, 'I am neither old nor used to battles. But I trust in the power of almighty God who strengthened David, a young lad who only a short time before had been looking after his father's sheep, but after that killed a giant named Goliath and became king over Israel. And when you, Bæring, offer me glory and worldly honour, I realize that fear and trembling have come over you. That wicked Mahomet can do nothing to help you, and you'll win no victory today.'

Earl Bæring became very angry at his words. He was sitting on a horse named Marmori: there has never been a better horse north of the Ægean. Now he spurred his horse on and rode at Mirmann – he was sitting on a horse which he called Bevard, which his mother had been sent from Hungary. It was big and strong.

He then rode against Earl Bæring and sang this verse which David had composed in his psalter: *Deus iudex iustus fortis et paciens numquid irascetur per singulos dies.* This is translated as follows: 'Hear, O God, righteous judge, strong and patient; do not be angry with us throughout every one of our days.'

Now they met, and Earl Bæring laid into Mirmann's shield with his spear, and it pierced his shield and mailcoat and went | under his arm, but then God saved him and it did not enter his body.[2] Then Mirmann aimed at the earl with his spear, but the shaft broke in two.

The earl was glad and quick-tongued and said, 'I guessed you wouldn't be sure of yourself, and it went as I thought it would – that you wouldn't prevail against me,' – and he raised his spear and meant to put it through him.

Mirmann said, 'Don't smile too soon – we've hardly parted yet,' – then he grasped Wolfling and hewed at the earl, and the sword struck his helmet first, then slid down on to the gorget and cut it in two, taking the arm off with the shoulder; and it all fell together on to the ground.[3] |

The earl grew faint from loss of blood, then stepped down from his horse and said, 'You are an evil god, Mahomet, and no-one should believe in you.'

'You've learnt that too late,' said Mirmann, and then he hewed at him so that his head and torso flew apart.

Afterwards Mirmann got up on the horse Bæring had owned, and his squires took Bevard. And when the heathen saw the earl fall, they fled in terror and all those who could ran away. King Clovis and Mirmann the earl's son pursued the fleeing host for a day, and killed many hundreds of knights. Afterwards they turned back home to France. They had earned themselves great wealth and fame, and they thanked almighty God for these spoils and this victory. Mirmann the earl's son was also much heartened from his grief, for he saw that God still wanted to accept his service, even though he was sinful.

12. [BRIGIDA SENDS FOR MIRMANN]

Now not long passed before King Clovis gave Mirmann the title of earl and a third of all France. And when he had accepted this gift, he came to be a man of great distinction. He was kind to poor people and comforted them with compassion, and he was generous to noblemen. In this way several years now passed.

The next thing that happened was that messengers came from Saxony to Earl Mirmann and brought him a letter. He recognized his mother's seal on it.

This was written in the letter:

To Earl Mirmann, Brigida sends greetings from the god you believe in, and likewise from herself.

It seems extraordinary to me that you do not wish to come and visit me when I have suffered so much grief. If you wanted to cheer me with your words, then I would cast away my troubles. I also realize now, since you overcame Earl Bæring, that the god we believe in is worth little, and I want to give up this heresy and go away to France with you if this people does not wish to accept Christianity and confess your faith. And as for everything I have collected together, it shall be made ready for taking away, and it will be carried to France with me.

And for this reason she now asked him to make haste and visit her.

Mirmann was glad about this message, although he suspected that not everything would be as she said. He showed the letter to King Clovis. The king was delighted about it and urged him to proceed.

The earl replied that this would be a good thing if some good came of it, but that 'we shall find the truth to be otherwise.'

But since the king believed her words and encouraged Earl Mirmann, he grew eager to try. He now prepared his journey and rode to Saxony, and did not stop until he arrived at Mainz. And when Queen Brigida learnt this, she went to meet him and welcomed him especially well. She wished him a happy homecoming and led him into his father's hall, and set him in the high-seat. She showed much friendliness, and so did Mirmann in return; and on that day a splendid feast took place there.

The day and night now passed; and on the next day, when Mirmann had dressed, his mother was called to him. He asked what she wanted to do, and asked that the words written to him should be upheld.

She replied, 'My son, I would like you to stay here in the land for some time – to know your kinsmen again, and the people of the land, and know that they would yield to your words. But if that is to no avail, then I want to come with you as I have said.'

The earl replied, 'That does not seem advisable to me, because I know you want to keep me back here so that I become reconciled to your heathendom – but that does nothing to persuade me. Rather, take my advice now and get ready for your journey, mother, and give up your evil plan, and I shall honour you in every way.'

When she saw that he was steadfast and would not listen to her advice, she turned her speech to the effect that she wished to uphold everything she had promised him. And now she showed him her property and the treasures that they would be carrying off with them, and that day everything was made ready.

The next day, when it was light, the earl asked if she had spoken for all the property they owned.

'Yes,' she said, 'I have shown you everything apart from your drinking vessels, and we shall now go there.'

Then she led him into a stone house. It was built down into the ground, and there was beer and wine inside. There was another room up above, with no door into it except a hole in its floor, and a trapdoor lay across it. There were steps beneath the hole, leading into the cellar. When they came into the cellar, the earl looked around him and saw a goblet standing there, and it looked as though something were fermenting inside the goblet. The earl asked why that was.

'I had a little mead brewed,' she said. 'It does you good to drink before meals.'

The knights accompanying the earl said they wanted to drink. A lad from Hungary was with her. She then spoke to him in a way they could not understand. Then she went up the steps, took a bowl out of the loft-chamber, and handed it to the lad. She was standing on the steps leading up to the hole. The lad poured some into the bowl and she wished Earl Mirmann good health. He made the sign of the holy cross over his eyes, and then drank. At once it was as if cold water had been spilt over him.

He realized at once that there had been witchcraft in the drink, and said, 'Now this is no motherly drink you have given me, and may God divide us! I would have gone with you to the kingdom of heaven and eternal joy, but you have given me sickness and earthly shame.'

She replied, 'You deserved this from me. You ruined all my happiness when you killed the earl, my husband, and dealt so shamefully

with your father, and you wouldn't comfort me by staying with your kinsmen here and making us all some redress for it. It is better now, for I have avenged the earl, and done so with neither sword nor spear. And it cheers me that Queen Katrin in France will take little pleasure in gazing at you, or you at her.'

After that she herself walked up into the loft-chamber and let the trapdoor slam behind her, and mother and son parted there with great bitterness.

Now Earl Mirmann went outside. He got on to his horse, as did all his men, and they rode home to France. And as each day went by, he felt more sickness on his body, for the flesh swelled up and grew black. He had caught the disease which is called *lepra* in Latin, and in our language, 'leprosy'. But his eyes were as fair as they had been before, and he realized that this had been brought about when he had made the sign of the holy cross over his eyes before he drank. And his eyes never became damaged.

13. [THE LEPER]

They now came home to Rheims, and it came about that the king
both saw and heard this news. He took it so badly that he hardly
cared to look after the land or any other things. He had those
doctors sent for whom he knew to be the best, and he hoped they
would be able to help him in some way. But whatever was done,
his illness always grew worse. King Clovis wanted him to continue
sitting in the high-seat beside him, even though his illness had
become horrible.

One day it happened, when they sat at the table, that the queen
said to the king, 'Your behaviour is strange – wanting to have such
a sick man as close to you as the earl is. Even though you feel much
affection for him, you ought to think of yourself so that you don't
do yourself any harm.'

The king said, 'You are not saying what I would have expected.
I noticed that not so long ago you did not think the earl too close
to you. But since he needs your friendship much more than mine
in his sickness, let him now enjoy some benefit from the fact that
you loved him greatly when he was well.'

And she could think of nothing to say in reply, but it made her
go as red as blood. And the earl heard what they said, but they did
not realize it.

14. [TO ITALY]

Now some days passed before Earl Mirmann spoke to King
Clovis.

'My lord,' he said, 'you have shown me great kindness since I
came to France, and may God reward you for it. But even though
your goodwill towards me may be unchanged, you will end up with
nothing from our living together except yet more sorrow. So I want

to go away now, foster-father, and live for as long as God wills it where no-one knows me. And while I remain here I shall stay in a separate chamber.'

The king wanted him to stay in the high-seat beside him, but Mirmann said it was not right that the queen should catch a disease because of that. Now it was done as he wished, and the king had a splendid chamber prepared for him, with many treasures. Earl Mirmann now went inside, along with two young men whom he trusted well, named Godfrey and Roger. Nobody visited them except the king. He often spent time talking to Mirmann.

Now some time passed in this way.

On one occasion Mirmann said to the king, 'Now you must report that my sickness is particularly grievous, and after a delay of seven nights you must report my death, and so make a coffin. And I want you to arrange my funeral as honourably as possible in every way. I am doing this so that people here in France will grieve more for my death, and so pray for my soul more fervently than if they heard about it from other lands.'

Now the king did as Mirmann wished. He had a coffin made, and after that he prepared it himself, and then this funeral was arranged with the utmost honour. But Mirmann was in hiding with those two lads. And there is no need to say any more about the grief which was felt in France – but the news brought tears and grief for this man, the noble Earl Mirmann.

Three nights passed before Mirmann was conveyed out of the city with the two lads named earlier. The king himself prepared his journey by night, and so he rode away from the city. He was riding the horse Marmora and had his sword Wolfling. The lads also had good horses. They had plenty of money with them in gold and silver. The king himself accompanied them out of the city.

Now they always rode by night, and slept in hiding during the day. They travelled south to the Alps in this way so that no-one would recognize them.

Then they arrived in Lombardy, and now they rode during the day. And when people asked who that sick man was, he gave his name as Justin, and said he had been the king's champion in France. Now they travelled to Rome, and from there went out to Apulia, and they did not break their journey until they came to Salerno. There they found themselves lodgings with an excellent man, and stayed the night there.

In the morning, when mass was over, Justin asked where in the city were the doctors who afforded most help to people.

The householder replied that there was an old man there named Martin – 'and I expect he'll give you sound advice.'

And Justin went to him and asked what advice he could give him for his illness.

Martin looked at him and said, 'It is bad, my son, that you should have this disease, such a handsome man as you have been; but it looks to me as though you have succumbed to witchcraft, and I do not know any doctor who would be able to cure you. But there is one piece of advice which I want to give you. Cecilia is the name of the king's daughter in Sicily: she is young, but the greatest of doctors, and nobody can match her. She has the gift of God in her healing. I do not know anywhere where you have any hope of help, by the grace of God, except there; and I think you would do well to try it.'

Now they parted, and Mirmann went down to the shore and there secured for himself a passage across the sound.

Sicily is about as large as Iceland. At that time King William lived in the city of Valerina,* which is the chief city in that land and a very long way from the sea. Lady Cecilia was so beautiful and perfectly formed that her equal could not be found. She had also learnt all kinds of skills which adorn a lady; but one skill she had which was a rare habit among women. She had taken pains to learn jousting like men. Not many knew this, however, because she used to practise in the forest in men's clothes, in the confidence of few people. And she did this because God, who foresees all things, knew that she would need it in the end.

15. [PRINCESS CECILIA]

Now to return to Justin's journey: he went on up to the city, and his sickness had now worsened so much that he was unable to walk and could hardly sit on horseback. Now they came into the city and found themselves good lodgings with a householder, and they stayed there overnight.

Now Justin asked at which church the princess attended mass. The householder directed them, and they went there, and Mirmann sat down. When they had been sitting for a little while they saw the princess on her way, for a great crowd of women and men went with her, and a multitude of musicians went before her with harps, fiddles and stringed instruments of every kind. When the princess had almost reached the church, Mirmann was sitting just inside the church door. And then she stopped.

Then Mirmann said, 'My lady, Princess Cecilia, I have heard that almighty God has given you the power and understanding to heal. Now I call on you in that God's name, and I beg you to see if he will let my body receive some help at your hands.'

And she looked towards him, and said, 'Since you have such great cause in your request, I dare not deny you whatever God wishes to do for your case.'

Then she spoke to a man and asked Mirmann to follow him into a house which she had appointed. They now arrived, and several men were there, all of them sick, and everyone present a nobleman's son. Now they stayed there for a while. And then Princess Cecilia came to them, and she was given a good welcome there, as might be expected.

At once she went over to where Justin was, sat down beside him and asked him this question: 'What is your name, good man, and where are you from?'

He replied, 'My name is Justin. My father is English by descent, and he has been at the court of the King of France, and his occupation is to look after the King of France's best horses. I was there too, and served my father.'

'I see,' she said, 'that the King of France has splendid men, if his grooms are men like you seem to have been.'

'I am sure, my lady,' he said, 'that you have read in books that the way it is in the world, people tend to look fairer in northern lands than here in the south, under the sun.'

'I know,' she said, 'that it is so. And what was the news in France when you left?'

'There was no other news except that Earl Mirmann died shortly before we left home.'

'We had heard,' she said, 'that he had been bewitched, and it was a hard lot for such a valiant man and a good knight that such ill luck should have befallen him.'

Now she examined his symptoms, as doctors usually do, and then she said, 'It appears to me that you have been the victim of witchcraft, and that will have been in a drink. From that, this evil power has quickened in your belly, more like a snake than a worm, and it is swelling up and aggravating your whole body. It will not be easy to get it out of the lair it has now, unless other lodgings are offered to it – but what pleasure would you grant to the person who did such a thing?'

He replied, 'I know that no-one would do such a thing.'

Now he stayed there, and then she had a drink prepared for him according to her directions. And when it was made up, she herself went with him into a small room, along with one lad, her servant.

Then she herself took the drink, offered it to him and said, 'So shall it be, Justin, as I have told you – this creature will not move from where it is now unless it is offered other lodgings to move into. Now, as soon as you have swallowed the drink, we must place our mouths together. I expect that this evil creature will then slide up into your throat and out into my mouth. Then, catch with your teeth the part which you have, and I'll take care of the part I have. And now, may it go according to the will of my Lord.'

Now he took the drink, and drank; and sooner than expected he felt the evil creature slide into his throat and lie there for a while. And she spoke some words to the creature and conjured it then, in the name of the Lord Jesus Christ the crucified, to come further. And then they placed their mouths together.

This evil creature had to obey her words and the will of God, and so slid into her mouth. He bit into the tail and she did the same with the head, and she had hold of a knife and cut the snake in two between them. At once she took both halves and threw them into the fire.

Then she said, 'What do you think, Justin – how many sweethearts do you have in France who would do such a thing for you?'

But at that point he was so exhausted he could say nothing in reply. She now had him rubbed with herbs named *balsamus*, and after that his flesh grew smoother day by day.

16. [MIRMANN BECOMES A KNIGHT]

The next thing to tell of is that one day, Princess Cecilia went to visit Justin in his lodgings, had him summoned to her, and spoke.

'How is your strength now, Justin?' she said.

'Now, thanks to God and to you, princess, I am as well as when I was in the best of health.'

The princess replied, 'Then it seems to me that things are going well for you. What do you want to do with yourself now, Justin?'

He replied, 'Wouldn't it be most likely that I'd go home to France and stay there with my father? For there I am short of neither food nor clothing.'

She said, 'I don't think you should hurry away from us so soon. Rather, I will ask my father to dub you a knight. Stay here with us these twelve months, for an army is expected to come against my father, and it would be manly of you to be of whatever assistance you can to us.'

Justin asked where this army was expected to come from.

She replied, 'There is a king named Lucidarius who rules over a country named Danubium.* He is heathen, and fierce in battles. This king has given my father two choices: either to give me to him, or else fight him. But I would rather die than give up my faith and live amongst heathen folk.'

And when Justin heard this, he was eager to stay, and Justin was now made a knight of King William; and everyone admired his beauty, not least the women. But he kept quiet about his abilities, and spoke little about most things; and in this way the winter now passed.

17. [A TOURNAMENT]

Now the story goes that some knights had arranged a tournament among themselves: those from Rome* in the north versus those of

Sicily and Apulia. Now King William's knights prepared themselves. Justin went to Princess Cecilia and spoke:

'I am curious, my lady,' he said, 'to see this tournament, and I would like you to ask your father to let me go.'

She replied, 'If you have any faith in your knightly prowess, then I can ask him that; but if not, you'd better stay at home, for I don't know who would redeem you if you were captured.'

'I'll be prudent, and look for the lightest men, and see if I can find some weakling whom I can unhorse.'

'Do what you think fit,' she said, 'but I'm not encouraging you.'

And now he had a stout pole made for himself in such a way that it didn't seem likely to be a tilting-lance. Then people asked what that pole might be. Roger replied that they would be carrying hay on it for their horses.

Now they assembled near a city in Apulia named Capua, and a great multitude of knights and other folk now arrived from Rome. There was an earl over the Romans named Placidus: he was the best knight in Rome. He did not ride in tournaments unless those on the opposing side allowed it. It was their rule that if one knight unhorsed another, then the one who had been unhorsed had to redeem himself with money. Nobody had the right to make a claim there, whatever kind of injury he might receive.

Now Justin watched silently to see which of the noblest Romans he could spot, and he asked them to tell him their names. He was sitting on his horse Marmori. A knight named Florentius now came forward. He was from a city named Frascati. He was a great man, and wealthy. As soon as Justin saw him, he rode across to him and swung his pole against his side, so that the horse's feet went up and the knight's head went down. Now Justin's squires sprang towards Florentius, caught him and his horse, and led them to the tents. Then, when Justin rode against a knight named Almakus, they attacked each other very hard and broke their lances. He was from a city named

Sutri, which Northmen call Sutaraborg. Next he knocked down a knight named Valternir: he was from a city named Acquapendente, which Northmen call Hangandiborg. And after that he rode away from the games and hid until they showed him whom he should unhorse. Now although no more than these three are named, he knocked down fifteen knights there who were thought to be the best and noblest of the Romans; and they all went back with him to his tents.

And in the evening, when the Romans came to their tents, it was very quiet in their company, and it seemed to them that they had suffered much disgrace during the day. Earl Placidus asked why this was, but they were hardly in agreement. Some said one man had knocked all of them down; but others said that was not so.

Earl Placidus replied, 'I shall find out the truth about it before tomorrow evening comes.'

And on the next morning, both companies rode to the games and fought very hard. Now a knight named Peter came forward: he was the best knight in the earl's company. As soon as Justin saw him, he swung his lance under his arm, so that his feet went up over his head. Then he unhorsed a man named Marcus. And after that, Justin took to changing his clothes and horses, and then many people thought that these were different men. So that day came to an end, and Justin had unhorsed and captured twenty knights, all of whom were great rulers.

This disgrace did not please Earl Placidus, and he now had them asked if they would allow him to ride in the games. Some people spoke against it.

Justin said, 'Why shouldn't the earl be allowed to ride in the games? Since you have captured many knights from him and left only a few behind, it doesn't matter if he should win some knights from you and so make the numbers even – and in any case, it's no bad thing that each should have his due.'

So it ended up with the earl being allowed to ride in the games. Now they got ready for the games.

And when the earl came forward, he called to them and said, 'If one of you has knocked down most of my knights, then I appeal to his good faith that he should come back and ride against me, if he dares.'

Justin said, 'Here is the knight for whom you ask.'

'Yes, yes,' said the earl. 'What is your name and kin?'

He replied, 'My name is Justin, and I was born and bred in a city named Salestra in Bulgaria.'

The earl said, 'Now prepare yourself. I want to find out how good a knight you are.'

Justin replied, 'I am ready whenever you wish.'

He now spurred on his horse Marmora and swung the lance forward into the saddle-bow, splitting it in two, and in so doing struck the earl's thigh, heaving him up out of the saddle so that he landed in the field a long way off. Justin's squires at once captured the earl. But the earl's knights had plotted to avenge him, and a hundred knights rode forth and laid into him as well as they were able, some aiming at his shield, some at the horse under him. But Justin sat so steadily that he did not even tremble – nor was that surprising, for there has never been a better knight in the Northern lands apart from Roland, the nephew of Emperor Charlemagne.* And so that day ended for them with Justin having won fifteen knights from them, and the earl besides. By then he had won fifty knights.

With the men of Rome were two scholars who had studied in France. When the people marvelled at his strength and skill in riding, they gave this retort.

'You need not be surprised at this, because we know who that man is,' they said. 'That's Earl Mirmann.'

But the people laughed at them a great deal, then said that theirs was a bad lot – 'if dead men can defeat us,' – and then made so much fun of them that they were relieved when the people quietened down.

18. [CECILIA BECOMES SUSPICIOUS]

Justin now went home, along with the host which went with him. News now spread of how the games had turned out for them. And when Justin had stayed at home for a while, the princess came into his room and said,

'Your father was an extremely good groom, teaching you to ride so well.'

'I owe this to you, princess, since you have laid such a fine hand on me in every way. My riding was thought worthless when I was at home in France.'

Now people arrived from Rome and redeemed both the earl and the other knights who had been captured. Some were redeemed with a hundred marks, and some with fifty or sixty. But Earl Placidus was redeemed with two hundred marks. And everything he took in this payment came to ten thousand marks. Never before, it was said, had more takings been won at the games.

Princess Cecilia now thought it both bad and strange that she did not know who this man was who achieved such great feats. But she felt sure that he was someone other than he claimed.

19. [A GAME OF CHESS]

Now the story goes that on one occasion, the princess visited Justin in his room, and he was playing a game of chess. She now asked who played the best. They said Justin played best, which was true.

'Then we shall play,' she said.

'You must decide that, princess,' he said, 'but I've heard it said that there are not many who can beat you at chess.'

'Visit me,' she said, 'tomorrow at the prime hour.'*

So he did, and now they began playing chess; and so time passed until noon. There was no more hope of finishing then than before.

Then Justin said, 'Isn't it time to go and eat?'

'No,' she said, 'we must keep playing, and try harder.'

And they played chess there until the bell rang for nones.★
Then Justin spoke: 'My lady,' he said, 'don't you want to go to
church?'

'We must keep playing,' she said.

And when they had played for a while, he won a knight from
her. Now she realized she would not win the game of chess. What's
more, she very much wanted to know who he was.

She spoke up like this: 'I think,' she said, 'men in France play chess
well.'

'Some men there play well,' he said.

'Do they indeed?' she said. 'I've heard that the earl played well
who died from the witchcraft his mother prepared for him.'

'I've heard it mentioned,' he said.

'Is it true,' she said, 'that he killed his father?'

'So I've heard,' he said.

She said, 'It's a shame he should have had so much ill luck, such a fine man as he was said to be. Let's play quickly now, for the day is getting on.'

Now he forgot about the chess and brooded on his bad luck. And she mused all the more on that. Then she won a knight from him in his surge of resentment.

He said, 'Now trickery kills the knight, princess, not skill.'

She replied, 'It isn't trickery when people ask for news from other lands.'

And at that moment the bell rang for evensong.

Then she said, 'We shouldn't go on with this game any longer.'

Then they parted. Now she had won by her craft what she could not win in a game of chess. And she now felt she knew for certain who he was. However, she did not mention it in front of other people.

20. [BATTLE WITH KING LUCIDARIUS]

A little later, spies came east from Danubium, and reported that King Lucidarius was on his way with his army and wanted to march against King William. He had seven hundred galliots⋆ and sixty galleons, which carried his horses, and now he was sailing from the west. Northerly winds drove him, and he headed southwards to Sicily and reached a city in Apulia named Otranto.

Justin then went to Princess Cecilia. She asked what he meant to do.

'I mean to oppose this heathen king, your suitor.'

'What do you want to do,' she said, 'when you two meet?'

He replied, 'I'm told he is a good knight and a great dueller. I mean to ride against him on your behalf, and either I shall free you, by the mercy of almighty God and the power of your goodness, or he will overcome me and I shall lose my life.'

She said, 'Why do you want to let yourself risk so much for an unknown woman?'

He replied, 'I was unknown to you when I came to you, but you gave me great help, by the grace of God, with your own hands. And now God may grant you freedom at my hands.'

'You say well,' she said. 'Do as you will, and may God protect you.'

Now they parted, and he went after the king. Lucidarius had pitched camp south of Otranto. And when Justin saw the heathen king's army, he said King William ought to pitch camp, and so it was done.

King Lucidarius saw King William's army. Then he called to the men who were nearest, and said he wanted to speak to King William. They told the king, and he rode to speak to King Lucidarius with eighteen men, and he had the same on the opposite side. Justin also went with the king.

Lucidarius now called to King William and said, 'I know you have heard what my business is here. I want you to grant me your daughter in marriage, or else I will fight for her.'

Then Justin replied, 'To all wise men the circumstances of the case seem unjust, that you, a heathen man, should marry a Christian woman. If you will not give up this foolishness, then she has found a man who wishes to answer for her case and ride against you in single combat as soon as you wish.'

King Lucidarius was glad at these words and asked who that man was.

Justin said it was none of his business – 'but he shall come tomorrow at sunrise.'

Now each rode to his tents. That night went by, and on the next day King William and Justin rose at first light and had three masses read for themselves: one de *Spiritu sancto*, another *de Domina*, and a third de *omnibus sanctis*. After that Mirmann put on his armour, as did all King William's host, and they rode with him to the battlefield.

King Lucidarius had arrived there, and a great army of heathen folk with him.

And as soon as King Lucidarius saw Justin, he asked him, 'What is your name and kin?'

Mirmann replied, 'My name is Justin. And I have kin in England and other places.'

'Long have you searched for a place to lay your bones,' said Lucidarius. 'So what have you heard about this sword named Miral, which my sworn brother Earl Bæring gave me? You shall have full hospitality from it, if Mahomet wishes to help.'

'I think,' declared Justin, 'that Mahomet will help you as he helped your sworn brother Earl Bæring when an eighteen-year-old boy slew him near Gisors in France. And what have you heard said of this sword named Wolfling, which bit both arm and head from your sworn brother Earl Bæring? I expect that with God's power it will do the same for you too.'

Lucidarius said, 'How did you come by that sword?'

'I inherited it from my father,' said Justin.

Lucidarius said, 'I see that fear has come over you. How could you have inherited that from your father? For Earl Mirmann left no son behind him, but King Clovis took the sword. You are talking nonsense, and you are a doomed man.'

'God has power over that, not you. Things will turn out differently for you than if Earl Mirmann had been dead, and this name-dropping will be worth little when we meet.'

Lucidarius now grew angry at his words. He was sitting on the horse which he called Medard, and now he spurred it on. Mirmann was sitting on his horse Marmora, which Earl Bæring had owned; and now they attacked one another. Each laid into the other with his spear, and King Lucidarius's spearshaft broke in two. But Mirmann plunged his spear into his shield, through the shield and mailcoat, and through Lucidarius himself, so that the point came out at the shoulders. But he sat so steadily that he did not even tremble.

Then King Lucidarius spoke, 'Be thankful for it,' he said. 'Now win with gallantry.'

Mirmann then drew Wolfling from its scabbard and hewed at him, and he sliced off a quarter of his shield, and with it his leg from above the knee; and he fell dead to the ground.

Then Mirmann said, 'If you had been a Christian, you would have been a good knight.'

Now the heathen saw their king fall, and they broke into flight. And King William and Justin had their trumpets sounded, and they pursued the fleeing host and killed three hundred heathen before they could reach their galliots.

King William now went home to Sicily with a fair victory and a great deal of booty. The king then asked Justin why he had the sword which had been the bane of Bæring.

Justin replied, 'I had it back then, as always.'

'Indeed,' said the king. 'Long have you hidden yourself from us. We thought you were long dead.'

'My lord,' said Mirmann, 'I thought it shameful to remain in France with the sickness I had, so I left secretly.'

The king said, 'You have given us great help, and we must all do your will.'

21. [MARRIAGE]

King William now set Earl Mirmann in the high-seat beside him and honoured him well.

Then the king spoke to him and said, 'We would like you to stay here in the land with us. I would like to give you a third of my kingdom while I am alive, and arrange the best marriage in this land for you.'

Mirmann thanked him for his words – 'and, my lord, if you are willing to get me the best wife in this land, then I certainly shall stay.'

The king said, 'I think I know that the choicest match would seem to you to be my daughter Cecilia, and I shall not deny you her any more than the others if she will take my advice.'

'You say well, my lord,' said Mirmann, 'and the two of you must discuss this between yourselves.'

Now the king did so, and reported their conversation to his daughter.

And she made this reply: 'I have hardly thought of that up to now. But if I must address myself to such matters, I'll take this man or none at all.'

Now, although more matters were discussed, all the wise men were eager for this, and their conclusion was that Mirmann should pledge himself to Princess Cecilia according to the law and custom of the land. After that, their wedding was arranged with the greatest expense, and then King William gave Mirmann the title of earl.

Afterwards, they came to love each other dearly and enjoyed a happy married life; and everyone in the land, both rich and poor, felt bound to love Earl Mirmann because of the generosity and humility he showed to all people. And some years passed in this way.

22. [MIRMANN VISITS CLOVIS]

One day, Earl Mirmann was talking to Princess Cecilia and spoke as follows: 'My lady,' he said, 'I beg you to give me leave to ride home to France and visit my foster-father King Clovis, because I know that he will experience the greatest joy on earth if he sees me well. And you know how handsomely I have to repay him.'

The princess replied, 'You must determine your travels yourself, but I wish to dissuade you because you have had no luck at all in those lands. Here you are a great man of distinction, and I believe that this is your land of luck – if you know how to look after it. Now, since God has saved you from sickness and given you happiness, then cherish this land and don't risk yourself coming to any harm.'

'I will only be away a short while, and I do want my friends to know I have regained my health.'

She tried to dissuade him, but he wanted to go all the same. And now he prepared his journey with sixty knights, and Godfrey went with him; but Roger stayed behind with the princess.

Now Mirmann rode out from Valerina and did not break his journey until he arrived in France. Then Mirmann sent Godfrey to King Clovis, to tell him about their journey. Godfrey now rode on as fast as possible to Rheims and arrived when the king was sitting at table. He went before the king and greeted him; but he had a large beard, and nobody recognized him.

He then spoke as follows: 'Justin, Earl of Sicily, sends you God's greetings and his own.'

The king sat there and looked at him, then asked who he was.

He said, 'I am Godfrey, who went abroad with your foster-son Earl Mirmann.'

'Is my foster-son well?' asked the king.

'Yes, my lord, he is well and happy, and he has married King William's daughter in Sicily, and he's on his way here now. He will arrive in the city no later than tomorrow evening.'

But the noblemen who were there asked why he was talking nonsense.

'No,' said the king, 'Mirmann was alive when he departed hence, and I think he is telling the truth.'

The next day, as soon as it was light, King Clovis had his horse saddled and rode to meet his foster-son. And on that morning, as soon they met and recognized each other, no knight was so stern that he could hold back tears of joy – neither they themselves, nor the other people. Then they rode to the castle, and there was great joy that the earl had visited his friends. People came to him from all over the land and greeted him with great affection.

Now, it is said that he had not been there long before King Clovis caught a serious and acute illness. It affected his strength in such a way that it looked as though he would soon be unable to stand up – for it sapped his strength and health from one day to the next – and, as it later turned out, he died. Princess Katrin and King Clovis had had a son together: he was no older than three when his father passed away.

It's now mentioned that King Clovis had spoken for a long time with Earl Mirmann and asked him to stay there for twelve months and rule as regent for the boy. And he could not bear to refuse because of his love for the king.

After that King Clovis died, and that seemed a great loss, even though he was old, because he had been a good ruler.

Now Mirmann sent Godfrey with some men south to Sicily to tell the princess about his stay. And while they were away, Queen Katrin turned her thoughts to trickery, and two noblemen plotted with her to delay Earl Mirmann. They hatched a plan to send men on the road to meet Godfrey and his men and give them a message from the queen, that she wanted to see them before they arrived back.

This now went ahead according to plan, and she rode to speak with Godfrey and his men and asked them to go along with her plans.

When they met, she spoke as follows: 'We have been thinking over the needs of the country, now that King Clovis has passed away. And though he has left a son behind him, he is not fit to defend the land, and the land will still be without a leader when the earl is gone. Now, if you are willing to go along with this plan with us, I will pay you as much money as it pleases you to ask for.'

Godfrey asked what the plan was.

The queen said, 'Who is the most celebrated man in Sicily, and nearest to the king?'

Godfrey replied, 'Earl Stephen seems to me to be the most celebrated man there.'

The queen said, 'You must say that this earl has been sleeping with Princess Cecilia, and that Mirmann need not go there except with his war-shield.'

She described it all to them in such a way that they swallowed the bait. And when they returned, the letters which Princess Cecilia had sent to Earl Mirmann were taken and all torn to pieces, and they composed another letter and made it look as if Roger had sent it to Earl Mirmann; and they made its lies as eloquent as possible. Now Godfrey and his men went to the earl and brought him this letter.

When he had read it, he became very upset and said, 'Why did Roger not come here if he knew I'd been dishonoured like this?'

'He didn't come,' they said, 'because the princess had him put in irons as soon as he tried to go away.'

Earl Mirmann replied, 'I don't know what to say about this, except what Solomon the Wise said – that no-one can trust a woman in such matters.'

Now many knights and noblemen came along to console Mirmann, and they said they would go with him as soon as he wanted to avenge his loss. And Queen Katrin didn't hold back her caresses, and it's said that these could hardly fail to bewitch. And with this he began to cheer up, and he forgot that good woman who had given him so much help, and now set his heart on this bad woman who was of no use at all. They now encouraged him to marry Queen Katrin, and that went ahead, though it hardly befitted Earl Mirmann to marry her.

23. [CECILIA SENDS ROGER]

And now Cecilia, queen and king's daughter, heard about this down south in Sicily, and she summoned Roger and asked whether he had heard what Earl Mirmann was up to. He said he had. She asked what such a thing could mean.

'I think,' he said, 'she must have slandered you.'

'I have the same suspicion,' she said, 'and now I want to send you to meet him and find out the reason.'

'I will gladly do that,' said Roger.

Now she prepared his journey and composed a letter for him, using many fair and eloquent words; and then he went on his way with ten knights, and they did not stop until they arrived in France and met Earl Mirmann. He was very appreciative, but Queen Katrin less so. Now Roger showed him the princess's letter.

When he had read it, Mirmann said, 'Did you send me a letter with Godfrey?'

'No,' he said, 'the princess sent you a letter with him.'

'I never saw it. I saw another one, and there was no joy in it for me.'

And now the earl told him all the circumstances of this case.

Roger said, 'Now things have turned out badly. You have abandoned the greatest treasure in the world, by whose means you have been granted the greatest good fortune; and instead you have taken a bad and wicked woman, and you can remember how she drove you away from her table when you were ill. But Princess Cecilia offered up her body to receive that evil creature, and she healed you and made you well. And afterwards she placed herself in your power, and you have rewarded her poorly. Now give up these wicked ways, and come home to your wife and kingdom, which God gave you, and don't cling to what is banned and forbidden to you.'

The earl thanked him for his words and said, 'I don't know whether I could get away now, even if I wanted to, because of the people in the land.'

And as soon as Queen Katrin heard about this message, she did not hold back her spite and hard words against Roger and his men, nor did the other noblemen in the land.

They said there was no point in them trying to tempt the earl into leaving France: 'Since he was brought up here, his kinsmen won't give him up. The people will do you no harm this time, but anyone who returns on this business shall forfeit no less than his life.'

Finally it turned out that they were glad when they got away unharmed. And when they arrived in Sicily, they told Princess Cecilia that she need not expect him back.

'I knew for a long time,' she said, 'that it would turn out like this. It is disastrous for such a valiant man and good knight that this evil woman has managed to deceive him, and that he has broken God's commandment. And a great deal is at stake if he loses his life like this.'

After that, some time passed.

24. [CECILIA'S EXPEDITION]

Now the story goes that on one occasion Princess Cecilia spoke to her father, King William, with these words: 'I beg you, my lord, let me ride north to Otranto or Brindisi to buy myself some Greek brocade or some rare treasures.'

'I would like you,' said the king, 'to decide your travels yourself. But what would you like to have with you for a retinue?'

'I would like to have three hundred knights, whom I shall choose.'

'You shall decide that yourself,' he said.

She now picked all the wisest and most honest men in their kingdom, for everyone was prepared to go with her. Then she told them in confidence all the circumstances of their journey.

And now, when she was ready, she went to meet her father and said, 'You must now say that I have caught a very great sickness, and that nobody is allowed to see me except you. And don't behave strangely, even if I am slow to come home.'

The king agreed to this. She had gathered her retinue in secret, and now she rode away from the city by night with this army. She was wearing men's clothes and a gilded helmet on her head, and she held a shining short-sword. All her knights were wearing mailcoats as for battle. And when they had crossed the sound, they rode west through Apulia, and along the coast from there until they came to Venice. An earl named Hirning ruled there. He was a handsome-looking man, and young; he was a great viking, and renowned for this. They turned on their way north.

When they arrived in Lombardy, they were asked who the leader of this host was, and they said Earl Hirning was.

'Where is he heading?' they said.

They replied, 'He is heading north for Saxony, and we think the earl's chief purpose is to ask for the hand of the King of Saxony's daughter.'

One of them asked, 'Is he a handsome man? Where is he?'

The others replied, 'There he is, riding in front. He's wearing a silken jacket over his mailcoat and a golden fleece on his front and back, and a gilded helmet.'

'Yes,' said he, 'that man certainly is handsome and well-mannered.'

And so it was that wherever they came to stay, no earl's daughters, barons' daughters or other noblewomen cared to do anything but gaze at this beautiful earl. He held back no words or favours from them, and all they wanted to do was to listen to his sagas and beautiful fables – for they were words to which the very grass seemed to grow. But that earl was not quite as manly as they thought he was.

In such honour they rode north to the Trent valley and so into Saxony, and great news spread about their journey. The King of Saxony was in Cologne, and they went that way and arrived there. And when the King of Saxony heard that Hirning had come, he gave him a good welcome and asked him to stay for a long time with him, and to take there whatever supplies seemed fitting to him. The earl told the king that the King of Greece was angry with him because he would not accept Christianity. Now they felt even more joy at his coming, since he wished to follow their faith; and he now stayed there for a while.

The daughter of the King of Saxony admired this beautiful earl so much that it was painful for her; but his courtship later turned out as she thought best.

And when they had stayed there for a month, Earl Hirning spoke to the King of Saxony and said, 'What is Earl Mirmann up to in Saxony?'

The king replied, 'He harries here in our land, but he has not won any victories over us since he married that woman, and he seems to us to be hardly the same man now as he was before.'

The earl replied, 'I think I have heard the same. But why won't you test him out to the full now, since you have hostilities to repay him for?'

The king said, 'Because the man is so valiant that everyone is afraid of him.'

The earl said, 'I suspect he used to draw power and strength from the god he believed in. But I'd guess that they're no longer in agreement, because he has left his wife, the one he had in Sicily, and married another; and I believe that's against his law. Now, my plan is that you gather your army, and we'll put him to the test – for I have dreamt that we shall win a victory over him.'

And the king listened to his words, and he summoned the earls and noblemen to him and asked them to gather his army.

Now the host assembled; but to many people, attacking Earl Justin seemed a bad idea – 'when we know that no-one will have the fortune to prevail against him. And we want to know what Hirning's plans are.'

Then they went to him and asked, 'How confident are you to fight against Justin? Do you want to ride in single combat against him?'

'I won't deny that,' he said.

'Well,' they said, 'you certainly are a handsome-looking man, but we don't expect the two of you to have the same strength in battle.'

'I wish to stipulate that if the earl is captured and does not win, then I want to have power over him and his life; so too if the princess is captured, I want to make the decision on her life, but I shall harm no-one else. Now, so long as you are willing to agree to this by your troth, then I will place myself at the head of the undertaking. We shall only win on condition that you do as I say.'

His words now appeared resolute to them, but a great dread came over them at his speech. Then everyone agreed to what he said.

Justin now heard this news, that an earl had offered himself in single combat against him, that he had come to the King of Saxony, and that they had gathered an invincible army. Now he assembled his army and went to meet the King of Saxony, and pitched camp on the heath which lies north of Avenches.

Earl Hirning said, 'We mustn't hurry on our way, because I know that if Justin has to sit and wait, then he'll send for the princess – and I'd particularly like her to be with him.'

Now it was arranged so that they delayed their journey for some nights. And when it seemed to Justin that their arrival had been held back, he had someone send for the princess. She now came to him. The King of Saxony then went up along the Rhine and so to Avenches, and pitched camp where he could see Justin's camp. And Justin had heard that Earl Hirning had challenged him to single combat.

Justin now rode to the King of Saxony's tents and called out loudly, and asked where this famous Hirning was – 'I want to speak to him.'

The earl was told this, and he rode to speak to him, near enough for them to converse.

And when Justin saw him, he said, 'Are you that famous earl who has come out from Venice and offered himself in single combat against me?'

'I haven't made much of that,' he said.

'If you have said it, you must have the confidence for it, and you must be a man of prowess with a great deal in your power. I don't mind if we try out our skills.'

Then Earl Hirning said, 'We know you are a good knight, and you won great victory and honour when you were a single man. And now you are married to two women: nothing can stand against you now. But even if the god you used to worship when you were good for something wants to give you some protection, I'll take a chance in this case.'

Then Justin replied, 'What need have you to name the god I worship, you heathen?'

'I don't know who can name him more timidly than you. All the same, I shan't make a charge against you for naming God.'

Justin said, 'Come here tomorrow. It may be then that you come up against something other than grand words.'

Then they parted, leaving matters as they stood, and each rode to his camp. And during the night, when Mirmann was asleep, he behaved strangely. When he woke up, he was asked what he had dreamt.

'I dreamt that I seemed to see a host of beasts of prey. And when I tried to go towards them, the nearest lion leapt straight at me, and I thought | it was a female.[4] And a sweet fragrance came from it, so that I knew I did not need to be afraid.'

They asked what he thought it must mean.

Mirmann said, 'I think, if it had been a male, I would be about to suffer some disgrace at the hands of this earl. But that might not be the case now, since it was a female. What's more, no sweet fragrance would come from a heathen man.'

'It may turn out,' they said, 'that we'll come across some good woman on our way.'

'That may be just as well,' said Mirmann.

This subject was now dropped for the time being, and so the night passed. As soon as it was light, Earl Hirning got ready.

Then he spoke to his men and said: 'If Earl Mirmann is unhorsed, then nine of you must follow me and capture him, and a hundred and fifty men must ride to their camp, capture Queen Katrin, and bring her to me.'

25. [THE LAST BATTLE]

On the next morning, after breakfast, each side came to meet the other.

Then Mirmann called out in a loud voice and said: 'Hear this, heathen man. You hold yourself up before a heathen army, and you are waging war on Christendom. Come now. I hold myself up before the holy faith, and I appeal to God.'

Earl Hirning said, 'I have no mind to wage war on your Christianity. I want no more from France than what I own by rights.'

'What you ask for you shall get,' said Mirmann, and spurred his horse on. Earl Hirning rode against him, and he had a lance in his hand with a small iron point on the end of it, so that it would stick in the shield.

Mirmann then sang this verse which David had composed in his psalter: *Adiuva me domine salutare meum*, right up to the end. It is translated as follows: 'Help us, God our Saviour, and for the sake of your name, Lord, redeem us and have mercy on our sins,' and so on.

Then an extraordinary thing happened. Earl Mirmann rode at Earl Hirning and thought he would run him through with his spear, but he lost all his strength so completely that he could hardly hold on to the spear. But the other gained strength with the power of God and thrust his lance into Earl Mirmann's breast, and knocked him off his horse so hard that he landed a long way off; and Earl Hirning's knights captured the earl and his horse and carried him into Earl Hirning's camp.

Earl Mirmann's army was struck by terror at his fall, so that everyone fled and made their escape as best they could. But those knights who had been assigned to capture Queen Katrin did so and brought her to Hirning. Hirning was glad he had caught this woman and thanked God for this fair victory. Afterwards the King of Saxony set off for home; and news now spread of the victory Hirning had won.

Now Earl Mirmann was placed in a carriage with a canopy over him, and Queen Katrin in another carriage, and so they went over along the Rhine with the whole army.

Then Earl Hirning called Roger over to him, and said, 'How do you suppose Earl Mirmann thinks his situation is?'

'Bad, my lady,' said Roger, 'for Mirmann must think he is in the power of heathen men.'

'I think so too,' said Cecilia. 'Ride over there and let Mirmann recognize you, and cheer his heart.'

Roger spoke. 'My lady,' he said, 'that I will gladly do.'

Roger now rode over, lifted up the canopy, and bade Mirmann good day.

He said, 'Is that my friend Roger?'

'Yes, my lord,' said Roger, 'here I am.'

Mirmann said, 'Why are you with heathen men?'

Roger said, 'Necessity determines it, my lord. Be cheerful and glad – you are not with the heathen.'

Now Roger let the canopy fall behind him. Earl Mirmann cheered up at his words, though he did not know what was happening. Then they rode up along the Rhine to Cologne. There Earl Mirmann was found good lodgings, but Queen Katrin was put in a dungeon.

When Earl Hirning had stayed some nights there, he spoke with the King of Saxony and said: 'Now I want to travel home, for now I have defeated Earl Mirmann, and I think it a great honour to take him to my kingdom.'

The King of Saxony replied, 'You must make your own plans, but take care you don't set Earl Mirmann free. Kill him instead.'

The earl said, 'I have no intention of setting him free.'

Now the King of Saxony's men said he should ask for the princess's hand.

Earl Hirning replied, 'I cannot do that, because I've promised myself to the daughter of an earl in Bulgaria, and I mustn't break it off.'

26. [REUNION]

Now Earl Hirning prepared his journey, and when he was ready he went to the dungeon in which Queen Katrin was sitting, and Roger was with him carrying a light.

Then Cecilia spoke up: 'Now she is here, who for a while was called Earl Hirning. But I am Cecilia, the daughter of King William of Sicily. I have come for Earl Mirmann, whom you seduced from me with your wickedness. But now God has ordained it better than you wished, for now you shall go alone to hell, but I will have Earl Mirmann with me in the kingdom of heaven.'

Then Cecilia went up to Katrin and delivered a blow to her neck, which was the custom if someone wanted to disgrace another.

Cecilia said, 'Take that, and wait for worse.'

Now they parted, and with that Queen Katrin died in the dungeon.

Earl Hirning rode out from the city with his retinue. Earl Mirmann was now set on a mule, and each rode in his own party. They travelled like this for some days.

At one point Earl Roger was riding close to Earl Mirmann. The earl cheered up when he saw Roger, and asked, 'Where is Earl Hirning?'

Roger pointed him out to Mirmann.

He said, 'This man is handsome, and his face looks like Queen Cecilia's.'

'Yes,' said Roger, 'I've often said so myself. Now the two of you should talk together.'

'Maybe,' said Mirmann.

And now they arrived at a village in a certain kingdom, and there they alighted from their horses. Roger called both earls.

When they had sat down, Earl Hirning took off his helmet and said, 'Do you know this man at all, Earl Mirmann, who is talking to you?'

And Mirmann sat for a long time and gazed at her.

Then he said, 'I don't know what to say. But it seems to me that you must be Cecilia, the daughter of King William of Sicily, rather than Earl Hirning from Venice.'

'I don't want to hide from you any longer,' said the princess, 'though what has come about may seem somewhat strange to you – that a woman should have unhorsed you, such a champion as you are. But I know you have wisdom enough to understand that

I could not possibly have done this but with the strength of God.'

Mirmann said, 'So too do I know, princess, that God has judged me in secret, and with more mercy than I am worth. To no-one do I owe a greater debt than to you, and I dearly want to stay with you now.'

And there was a very joyful reunion between them all. Then they got on their horses, and nothing is reported about their travels before they arrived in Sicily. A splendid feast was prepared for them, and the feast lasted for six days.

Now not long passed before King William was taken ill and died, and that seemed a great loss to everyone. Mirmann took the realm and kingship after him with the goodwill and support of the whole commons, and with him the celebrated Lady Cecilia; and they governed their realm fairly and well for twelve years. During that time it seemed to them that they enjoyed the very best of earthly delights.

Afterwards they retired into a monastery, at the instigation of Princess Cecilia; and there they spent the rest of their days worshipping God in pure living and obedience as long as they lived. To that one and threefold God, who so fairly defends his dear friends, be glory and honour *per omnia sæcula sæculorum, amen.*

Glossary of Characters
and Terms

Æthelred   *Adalradr*. King of England; Katrin's father (M).

Alfsol   Hring's sister, turned by Luda into a *fingálkn* (H).

An Bow-bender   *Án bogsveigir*. The outlaw hero of his own saga (B).

announcing (a killing)   An essential prerequisite for legal proceedings to
    begin in early Icelandic law. An unannounced killing was tantamount to
    murder (B).

Arngrim the Chieftain   *Arngrímr goði*. According to *Hen-Thorir's Saga*
    (*Hænsa-Þóris saga*), a respectable leader who took part in the disgraceful
    burning of Blund-Ketil (B).

Asmund   Asmund the Berserks' Bane, legendary viking (q.v.) hero and commander of the enormous ship Gnodin. His story is told in *The Saga of Egil and Asmund* (B).

assembly   *þing*. Scandinavian social institution: an official gathering at which free men met and settled business, particularly legal. In early Iceland, each region held its Assembly in the spring, where three chieftains (q.v.) appointed judges to arbitrate local disputes. The national equivalent (*the Alþingi*) took place for a fortnight every summer (S, H, F, B).

Audun Shaft   *Auðun Bjarnarson skökull*, of Vididal. Important original settler (q.v.) of Iceland; Thorstein Shiver's great-grandfather. His sole function in B appears to be to reveal the ogres' fear of certain men: Kolbjorn makes a point of not inviting Audun to the wedding (F, B).

Bag   *Hít*. Bard's friend, a benevolent troll-woman (q.v.) (B).

Bæring   Earl of Spain, Hermann's sworn brother (M).

Bard (the Snowfell God)   *Bárðr Snjófellsáss*. Son of Mist and Mjoll; original settler (q.v.) of Snowfell's Ness in Iceland; later, a kind of god or guardian-wight (qq.v.) living in the Snowfell Glacier. He looks rather like Odin (B).

Bard Hoyanger-Bjarnason   Bard Mist-son's partner who emigrates from Norway and becomes an original settler (q.v.). B's account comes from the *Book of Settlements*.

Beak   *Nefia*. A troll-woman (q.v.) (H).

Bergthor of Black Fell   *Bergþórr Bláfellingr*. A competitor at Eirik's hero-championships (B).

berserk   'Bare-shirt'/'bear-shirt'. A male warrior prone, upon occasion, to a battle frenzy during which his unnatural ferocity renders him almost invulnerable. In sagas, berserks are often associated with Odin (q.v.) and compared to wolves and bears, embodying the evils of heathenism (like *draugar*, q.v.). Pests by definition, they are frequently reduced to a mere plot device for winning the hero fame in Northern areas; but some sagas (*Egil's Saga*, *The Saga of King Hrolf Kraki*) explore their nature more fully (S, H).

black man   *blámaðr*. Another stereotypical adversary for the saga-hero to
eliminate in his quest for fame. The term covers any dark-skinned
person, not only Negroes. Black men form vast armies in Southern areas;
and in North and South alike a single enormous black man will often be
the prized 'secret weapon' of a wily king, who makes visitors wrestle with
him. Like berserks (q.v.), black men are heathen by implication; unlike
berserks, they are insuperably foreign and almost never speak (*H*).

Blund-Ketil   A highly respected chieftain (q.v.) who, according to *Hen-
Thorir's Saga*, was ignominiously burnt in his house by Hen-Thorir,
Arngrim the Chieftain, and Odd of Tongue's son Thorvald (*B*).

Breeze   *Svalr* (literally, 'cold wind'). One of Bard's shipmates (*B*).

Brigida   Hermann's queen and Mirmann's mother (*M*).

Cat's-Eye   *Glyrnna*. A troll-woman (q.v.) (*H*).

Cave-Dwellers   *Hellismenn*. The sons of Smidkel and their friends, who
lived in a stronghold in Surt's Cave at Hellisfitjar (q.v.) before being
killed by their enemies. The giant Surt (q.v.) is said to have helped
them. Their story is told in the post-Reformation *Saga of the Cave-
Dwellers* (*Hellismanna saga*) (*B*).

Cecilia   Sicilian princess, daughter of William (*M*).

Charlemagne   *Karlamagnús*. French king (768-814) and Emperor, later
revered as the ideal Christian monarch, around whom a court of celebrated heroes (e.g. Roland, q.v.) attached itself in mediaeval epic and
romance (*M*).

chickens   The manuscript has 'hawks' at this point in chapter 6 of H,
but 'chickens' a few lines later and in chapter 11 (p.170). Some other
manuscripts show a similar discomfort about the heroes turning into
chickens.

chieftain   *goði*. In early Iceland, a local leader with religious responsibilities
(*B*).

Clement, Pope   *Klemens*. Historically, Bishop of Rome, saint and martyr at
the end of the first century. *M* transplants him to Clovis's time (*M*).

cloaks, newly-made   A newly-made cloak presented by a woman to a man
before a battle conventionally renders him invulnerable. The implica-

tion in *B* (and *The Book of Settlements*) is that Hildigunn has magic
powers.

Clovis   *Hlodvir.* King of France; Mirmann's foster-father. Historically,
a Frankish king (481-511) celebrated for his conversion to Catholic
Christianity, probably via the Arian heresy (*M*).

Clutcher   *Hremsa.* A troll-woman (q.v.) (*H*).

Cow of Turf River   *Torfár-Kolla.* An Icelandic troll-woman (q.v.), also called
Skinhood (*B*).

Crook   *Krekja.* A magician (q.v.) (*B*).

Dagfinn   Court poet to King Geirvid of Gotaland. His name is Icelandic,
standing out from the other Goths' stereotypically 'Gothic' names (all
beginning with G or H) (*S*).

Danubium   A country to the west of Italy under Muslim rule (*M*).

demon   *púki* (as in 'Puck'). In Icelandic folklore, demons/imps, fiends
(*fjándr, dólgar*) and ghosts (*draugar*, q.v.) tend to merge into a single
category. These are not merely disembodied beings, but walking pagan
corpses able to inflict serious physical damage on the living (*F*).

Denys, St   *Dionisius.* Historically, an Italian who preached at Paris and was
martyred *c.*250, becoming the patron saint of France. Later mediaeval
writings conflate him with the neo-Platonist Pseudo-Denys the Areopagite
(allegedly St Paul's disciple) and associate him with Pope Clement's (q.v.)
first-century missionary activity, thus pushing back French Christianity
into apostolic times. *M* follows this account (see p.75).

Diana   A Southern princess (*H*).

Dofri   A Norwegian mountain-dweller and giant (qq.v.), friend of Mist;
foster-father to both Bard and Harald Tanglehair. He also took in Bui,
the hero of *The Saga of the Kjalnesings*, who begot a son upon Dofri's
daughter Frid. Later folklore made Dofri more troll-like, e.g. as the
'Mountain King' in Ibsen's *Peer Gynt.* (*B*).

drápa   Literally, 'a striking' (of a harp?): the most prestigious variety of
courtly praise-poem, popular in Scandinavian courts between the tenth
and thirteenth centuries. Star-Oddi's *drápa* is typical in being skaldic
(see pp.13-14, 84-5) and in having a refrain (*S*).

draugr   A pagan poetic word for 'man' which, in later (i.e. Christian) folk-lore and sagas, came to denote dead pagan men who lived on in their grave-mounds (q.v.). *Draugar* were ghosts, but not disembodied spirits: their undead bodies were often preternaturally strong, and they could emerge when it was dark. A man could be prevented from becoming a *draugr* by being given Christian burial; a time-honoured means of dis-posing of a draugr was to chop off his head and place it by his buttocks, as Gest does in *B*. Demons (q.v.) are often pictured as *draugar*.

dwarf   *dvergr*. Primaeval subterranean beings skilled in craftsmanship and otherworldly wisdom. The earliest sources do not mention their diminutive size: later folklore presumably shrank them as it did elves (q.v.), goblins and Irish/Scottish 'fairy-folk'. While *H* brackets dwarves with trolls (q.v.) as non-human creatures with malevolent magical powers, many other sagas (and European romances) portray dwarfs as otherworldly helpers (*H, B*).

dwarf-talk   *dvergmála*. Echo (*B*).

Eid Skeggjason   Skeggi's fair-minded son, who appears in many other sagas (*B*).

Einar Sigmundarson   Son of Bard's friends Sigmund and Hildigunn. The anecdote about his fight with Lagoon-Einar is taken from the *Book of Settlements*; *B* adds the possibility that Bard helped him. The properties of Einar's grave-mound (q.v.) conventionally signal the uncanny.

Eirik of Skjaldbreid   An otherwise unknown farmer who, according to *B*, hosts superheroes' wrestling matches, presumably because his farm is near Bard's Cave. The younger *Armann's Saga* elaborates on Eirik's games.

Eirik the Red   *Eiríkr rauði Þorvaldsson*. Icelandic original settler (q.v.), then outlaw, who led the settlement of Greenland, traditionally in 985 or 986 (*B*).

elf   *álfr*. An otherworldly being, the same size as a human. The sagas often blend the term with 'wight' (q.v.): in *B*, defecating is described as 'driv-ing the elves away', as if elves were land-wights (q.v.) whose landscape was being desecrated.

Embers   *Íjma*. A troll-woman (q.v.) with nine sisters (*H*).

farmer   *bóndi*. This term carries no country-bumpkin overtones. Free farmers ('householders') were the Icelandic ruling class; some had up to a hundred people in their charge (*F, B, M*).

fetch   *fylgja* (literally, 'one who accompanies'). A personal spirit symbolizing the fate with which people were born: their appearance often portended the death of the person to whom they were attached. Thorhall Prophet's explanation conflates fetches with the family's goddesses (q.v.) (*F*).

fiend   *dólgr*. Loose term for any malevolent being, not necessarily otherworldly: giants, trolls, ghosts, demons (qq.v.) or sorcerers (*F, B*).

Fighter   *Vígi*. Olaf Tryggvason's dog (*B*).

fingálkn   Large big-lipped centaur-like creature, usually hostile to humans (*H*).

Finnmark   Northernmost part of mainland Scandinavia (*B*).

Fitjar   See 'Hellisfitjar'.

Flatey   'Flat Isle'. There are several islands of this name off Iceland (cf. Hebridean islands named Fladda). The one in S is off Temple Head (q.v.); the *Book of Flatey* is named after an isle in Breidafjord to the west (*S, F*).

Flaumgerd   Bard's first wife, Dofri's daughter, by whom Bard has three daughters (*B*).

flokkr   Literally, 'flock': a poem in several verses, distinguished from the drápa (q.v.) by being shorter, less distinguished, and without a refrain (*S*).

Frigg   One of the pagan Norse goddesses, traditionally beloved of Odin (q.v.) whose role has partly been usurped by Thor in *B*.

Fright   *Skrámr*. An ogre (q.v.) from Thambardal, friend of Kolbjorn. The same name is given to Greenland giants in *Jokul Buason's Saga* and *The Saga of Gunnar, the Fool of Keldugnup* (*B*).

galliot   A small Mediterranean warship (*M*).

Gaper   *Gapi*. An ogre (q.v.), friend of Kolbjorn (*B*).

Garp   'Warrior'. One of two robbers camped out in Battlewood (S).

Geirvid   Son of King Hrodbjart and Queen Hildigunn of Gotaland; later
   King (S).

Gest   (1) A common male disguise-name meaning 'guest', assumed by
   many men from Odin downwards. Bard Mist's-son assumes it while
   staying at Skeggi's farm (B).

   (2) Bard's son, whom he fathers on Thordis Skeggjadottir. He is fostered by
   his half-sister Helga (though other accounts say Skeggi himself fostered
   him) (B).

ghost   See *draugr*.

giant   *risi*, *jötunn*. The most ancient race(s) in Norse mythology. The world
   was created from the body of the giant Ymir, and the Æsir sprang from
   giant stock, though many myths represent giants as hostile to both
   gods and humans. The terms *risi* and *jötunn* are often used interchange-
   ably with *þurs* (here 'ogre', q.v.) and even *troll* (q.v.). Modern Icelandic
   folklore sometimes distinguishes *risar*, *jötnar* and *þursar* by their unusual
   height, strength and stupidity, respectively. Mediaeval sagas sometimes
   draw a distinction between the fair-looking, even-tempered *risar* and the
   ugly, surly *þursar*. Giants often have names associated with landscape
   features or weather phenomena (H, B).

Glint   *Glámr*. An ogre (q.v.) from Midfjardarnes, friend of Kolbjorn. He
   shares his name with the nastiest of Grettir's otherworldly opponents
   in *Grettir's Saga*, a herdsman turned *draugr* (q.v.) (B).

Glum Geirason   A poet. B's account is taken from the *Book of Settlements*,
   but adds the detail about the ewe's milk.

Gny   'Clash'. One of two robbers camped out in Battlewood (S).

god, gods   *Áss*, *Æsir*. The Æsir were the major group of pagan Norse deities,
   though the term came to apply to the entire pantheon. The singular
   áss can either refer to a single member of the Æsir, or to a lesser otherworldly being – a local god like Bard the Snowfell God (*Snjófellsáss*) (B).

goddesses   *dísir*. Female otherworldly beings, perhaps similar to fetches
   (q.v.) but more powerful, watching over families and localities rather
   than individuals. Sacrifices were made to them during the Winter
   Nights (q.v.) (F).

Godfrey   *Gudifrey*. One of Mirmann's two trusted retainers (*M*).

gorget   A piece of armour protecting the throat, often made of bone (*M*).

Gotaland   *Gautland* ('Goth-land'). An ancient kingdom in the south of
    Sweden, featuring in several Icelandic sagas as a realm of bygone hero-
    ism and glamour. Possibly the home of the Geats in the Old English
    Beowulf, it should not be confused with the Baltic island of Gotland (*S*).

grave-mound   *haugr*. A powerful physical embodiment of heathenism.
    Historically, nobles and kings throughout Europe were buried in
    mounds from Neolithic times onwards, but Scandinavian examples
    from the late pagan period are particularly common. Individuals of
    particularly high status (e.g. kings) were sometimes buried in a ship
    with their treasure, often with their family and/or slaves. In folklore and
    literature, grave-mounds acquire various otherworldly resonances, the
    commonest being the notion that the dead lived on in their mounds as
    draugar (q.v.). Mound-breaking (entering a grave-mound to steal treas-
    ure and fighting its deceased owner) occurs frequently in sagas set in
    the North. As an Otherworldly location, the interior of a mound often
    functions as a microcosm of Hel (q.v.). Otherworldly encounters also
    occur when someone (e.g. Hjalmther's father) is sitting on top of the
    mound: this pattern is also found in Gaelic folklore (*S*, *H*, *F*, *B*).

Grettir Asmundarson   An ill-starred Icelandic hero, Grettir met several
    of *B*'s giants and other wights (qq.v.) during his many battles against
    otherworldly adversaries and his long outlawry in Iceland's desert wastes.
    Folktales and/or sagas about Grettir were current long before the surviv-
    ing *Grettir's Saga*, a pinnacle of Icelandic literature, was written in the
    fourteenth or fifteenth century.

Grim   'Masked One'. A mysterious fisherman who appears at sea with
    Ingjald of the Hill (*B* is not entirely clear as to whether he appears on
    Ingjald's boat or a different boat). In older texts Grim is a name Odin
    (q.v.) used when in disguise; in *B*, Thor (q.v.) uses this name, showing
    that the two gods have here become partly interchangeable. But the
    combination of a red beard with fishing reveal this Grim as Thor.

Gripper   *Greijp*. A troll-woman (q.v.) (*H*).

Groa   Bard's shipmate; Skjold's wife (*B*).

guardian-wight   *bjargvættr*. A heathen equivalent to a guardian angel. A
    guardian-wight could be called on for help in times of danger (*B*).

Gudrun Gjukadottir   Tragic and formidable heroine of the Elder Edda who loses two husbands, three brothers and several children to violent deaths; hence, a model for the 'lamenting woman' (see especially the *First Lay of Gudrun*) (*B*).

Gulfspear   *Gljúfra-Geir*. An ogre (q.v.), Kolbjorn's best friend (*B*).

Gunnlaug Serpent-tongue   *Gunnlaugr ormstunga Illugason*. Skeggi's grandson; lovelorn poet-hero of his saga (*B*).

Hæng Thorkelsson   Original settler (q.v.) from the Rang River Plains; grandson of Ketil Trout, and sometimes also confusingly known by the same name (*hængr* means 'trout'); grandfather of Orm Storolfsson, whose saga contains much information about Hæng (*B*).

Hakon   *Hákon jarl Sigurðarson*. Earl of Hladir; ruled Norway, *c*.975-995; unregenerate heathen, and arch-enemy of Olaf Tryggvason (*F*).

Hall of Sida   *Síðu-Hallr*. An important Icelander, father of Thidrandi; one of the first Icelanders to be converted to Christianity (*F*).

Hallmund of Ball Glacier   *Hallmundr ór Balljökli*. Much is told of this benevolent *jötunn* ('giant', q.v.) in *Grettir's Saga*, including his friendship with Grettir and his death. In *B* he takes part in Eirik's wrestling matches. In *The Mountain-Dweller's Tale* (*Bergbúa þáttr*), a companion-piece to *S* in *Vatnshyrna*, Hallmund appears in a more threatening guise to two travellers who shelter in his cave, and he recites a long poem about the end of the world.

Halogaland   A district in northern (mainly Arctic) Norway (*B*).

Harald Halfdanarson   See 'Harald Tanglehair'.

Harald Tanglehair/Fairhair   *Haraldr Hálfdanarson lúfa / inn hárfagri*. Traditionally, the first king to bring all Norway under his rule. According to the sagas, several Icelandic settlers left Norway because of Harald's tyranny. He was fostered by the mountain-dweller (q.v.) Dofri (*F*, *B*).

Harald Wartooth   *Haraldr hilditönn*. A legendary Danish heathen king. His story is told in Saxo Grammaticus's *History of the Danes* and the post-Reformation *Harald Wartooth's Saga*. The Battle of Brow Plains, in which Harald fell, is related in the *Saga Fragment about Ancient Kings* (*Sögubrot af fornkongum*) (*F*).

Hard-Worker   *Hardverk*. Arctic ogre (q.v.), enemy of Mist and his kin (*B*).

Hel   The abode of the dead in Norse myth. This word carries no connotations of torment (unlike *helvíti*, 'Hell') but signifies 'the grave' or
'death' like the Hebrew *Sheol* or the Greek *Hades* (*S*, *H*, *B*).

Helga Bardardottir   Bard's unhappy eldest daughter; Skeggi's lover (*B*).

Helgi the Poet   *Skáld-Helgi Þórðarson*. Lover of Thorkatla Halldorsdottir,
as told in the fifteenth-century *Rhymes of Helgi the Poet* and the no-less-
romantic post-Reformation *Saga of Helgi the Poet* (Skáld-Helga saga) (*B*).

Hellisfitjar   An area on the Arnavatn Moors in which there are caves,
including the one named Surt's Cave in which the Cave-Dwellers (q.v.)
lived, as well as the giant (q.v.) himself (see 'Surt of Hellisfitjar') (*B*).

Hermann   Earl in Saxony; Mirmann's father (*M*).

Herraud   Earl in Mannheimar; King Ingi's sworn brother; Olvir's father
(*H*).

Herringsound   *Síldasund*. A sound in Gotaland (see p.50) (*S*)

hersir   A Norwegian local leader (*B*).

Herthrud   Bard's second wife, by whom Bard has six daughters (*B*).

Hervor   King Hunding's daughter; object of Hjalmther's quest; abducted by
Hring, whom she helps to kill her father (*H*).

High-Stepper   *Hástigi*. Extremely nasty counsellor to King Hunding (*H*).

Hildigunn   (1) Wife of King Hrodbjart of Gotaland; later, wife of Hjorvard (*S*).

   (2) Wife of Sigmund at Bard's farm Pool Edge; Einar's mother (see 'Einar' and
'cloaks') (*B*).

Hildisif   Hring's sister; turned into the troll-woman Skinhood by Luda (*H*).

Hirning   Viking (q.v.) and Earl of Venice, whose name Cecilia assumes
(*M*).

Hjalmther   King Ingi's son; Earl Herraud's foster-son; Olvir's sworn
brother (*H*).

Hjaltasons   Thord and Thorvald Hjaltason, who march over to
  Thorskafjord to help their friend Odd of Breidafjord in a lawsuit – as
  related in *The Book of Settlements* (see p.71) (*B*)

Hjalti Thordarson   One of the original settlers (q.v.) of Iceland (*B*).

Hjorgunn   Earl Hjorvard's first wife (*S*).

Hjorvard   Earl over part of Gotaland; father of Hlegunn (*S*).

Hladreid   Daughter of Earl Hjorvard and Queen Hildigunn; Geirvid's
  stepsister (*S*).

Hlegunn   Earl Hjorvard's daughter; later Geirvid's stepsister; shield-
  maiden (q.v.), just like Hrolf's stepsister Skuld in *The Saga of King Hrolf
  Kraki* (*S*).

Hood   Hetta. An Icelandic troll-woman (q.v.) (*B*).

Hook   Krókr. A magician (*B*).

Hord   Apparently Luda's slave; really King Hring of Arabia (*H*).

Hring   Son of King Ptolemy of Arabia; bewitched by his stepmother Luda
  to become Hord the slave (*H*).

Hrodbjart   King of Gotaland (*S*).

Hrollaug Rognvaldsson   The noblest of the original settlers (q.v.) of
  Iceland (*F*).

Hunding   King and wizard; father of Hervor; later a walrus (*H*).

Ingi   King of Mannheimar; Hjalmther's father, later married to Luda (*H*).

Ingjald (of the Hill)   One of Bard's shipmates, whom Bard later saves from
  sorcery at sea. He strongly resembles the sailor Bjorn, who suffers a
  similar accident in the same locality in chapter 12 of *Viglund's Saga*. The
  author of *B* signals this link in Ingjald's initial genealogy.

Jora of Jora's Cliff   According to folktale, a farmer's daughter from Floi who
  turned troll (q.v.) and lived in a cave, ambushing travellers (*B*).

Icelandic Histories & Romances

Jostein   A priest sent by Olaf Tryggvason to accompany Gest Bardarson
   to Raknar's grave-mound. For some reason he is the only one not to be
   given iron shoes by Olaf (*B*).

Justin   *Justinus* ('Righteous'). The name Mirmann assumes when travelling
   to Italy and in battle thereafter (*M*).

Katrin   Daughter of Æthelred; later, Clovis's wife (*M*).

Ketil Trout   *Ketill hœngr*. A member of the legendary heroic dynasty
   from Hrafnista in Halogaland, father of Grim Hairy-Breeches and
   great-grandfather of Arrow-Odd (all saga heroes). The Icelander Orm
   Storolfsson (q.v.), Thorkel Bound-Leg's son-in-law, was Ketil's great-
   grandson (*B*).

Killer-Hord   *Víga-Hörðr*. Ill-starred hero of *Hord's Saga* (*Harðar saga*) and
   leader of the Holm-Dwellers, a band of outlaws with their base on an
   islet called Geirsholm. Hord was killed at the order of his uncle Torfi
   Valbrandsson, a kinsman of Odd of Tongue (*B*).

Kolbjorn   An ogre of Brattagil; host of Thord Thorbjornsson's wedding
   feast (*B*).

Koll   A viking (q.v.), Toki's brother (*H*).

Kvænland   'Woman-land'. A realm in northernmost Finland and Sweden (*B*).

Lagalf Little-Woman's-Son   *Lágálfr lítillardrósarson*. An otherwise unknown
   strong man, whose name suggests elf (q.v.) connections. In walking
   from Siglunes to the wrestling matches at Eirik's farm and back, Lagalf
   covers 250-300 miles in one day, further suggesting that he is not
   entirely human (*B*).

Lagoon-Einar   *Lón-Einar*. A man who accused Hildigunn, Einar
   Sigmundarson's mother, of sorcery (*B*).

land-cleansing   *landshreinsun*. Clearing a district of undesirable characters,
   especially trolls, ogres, giants, berserks, *draugar* (qq.v.) and robbers.
   In the sagas, as in the Old English *Beowulf*, land-cleansing is seen as
   a valuable heroic activity, a prerequisite for the establishment of a
   civilized society; but land-cleansing heroes can end up at odds with that
   society when the need for such primaeval heroism fades – and on occasion a land-cleanser has to withdraw into the wilds, where he becomes
   troll-like (e.g. Grettir) or god-like (e.g. Bard) (*B*).

land-wight *landvættr*. Otherworldly beings – elves, gods, trolls or giants
(qq.v.) – associated with particular landscape features in pagan
Scandinavia, particularly hills and mounds (q.v.), sometimes acting as
the country's guardian-wights (q.v.). See also 'wight'.

Leif the Lucky *Leifr inn heppni*. Son of Eirik the Red, Olaf Tryggvason's
missionary to the new settlement in Greenland, and discoverer
of *Vínland* in North America, as told in *The Greenlanders' Saga*
(*Grænlendinga saga*) (B).

Long Serpent *Ormr inn langi*. Olaf Tryggvason's finest longship, on which
he was killed with his retainers at the Battle of Svold in 1000 (though
some accounts have him escape alive and retire to a monastery) (F).

Lucidarius Saracen king of Danubium; Cecilia's suitor. In the 'C' recension of M, he worships the Norse god Tyr (M).

Luda A troll in disguise (q.v.); stepmother respectively to Hring and
Hjalmther, both of whom she tries to seduce (H).

magician *seiðmaðr*. One who practises seiðr, an art associated with Odin
(q.v.) (B).

Mahomet *Maumet*. Saga Saracens often worship Mahomet as their god (M).

Mannheimar Taken to mean 'Sweden' by seventeenth- and eighteenth-century Swedish editors, but not necessarily by Icelandic saga-authors (H).

Martin Marthinus. A householder in Salerno (M).

Mirmann Son of Hermann and Brigida (M).

Mist *Dumbr* (literally, 'misty'). Part giant, part troll (qq.v.); husband of the
human Mjoll Snow's-daughter; father of Bard the Snowfell God. King
and guardian-wight (q.v.) over the north (B).

Mjoll Daughter of Snow the Old; husband of Mist and mother of Bard;
later, husband of the giant (q.v.) Redcloak and mother of Thorkel
Bound-Leg. She originally lived in Kvænland (q.v.). According to the
genetic system of B, Mjoll counts as human, though her father's name
suggests he is a giant. A different story about how Mjoll left Kvænland
is told in *The Saga of Sturlaug the Busy* (*Sturlaugs saga starfsama*).

monster *flagð*. A colloquial, derogatory term for 'troll' or 'ogre' (qq.v.) (B).

mound   *haugr, hóll.* See also 'grave-mound'. Artificial mounds were raised in
  Scandinavia, as elsewhere in Europe, for ceremonial purposes besides
  burial. Some sagas record instances of women (especially Irish) being
  hidden in mounds or underground hollows from invading armies, along
  with treasure: such women frequently display otherworldly attributes
  (*S, B*).

Mound   *Þúfa.* One of Bard's shipmates, wife of Breeze (*B*).

mount, thieves'   A gallows (*M*).

mountain-dweller   *bergbúi.* Any giant, ogre or troll (qq.v.) who lives in a
  cave in the mountains. In *B* the term carries no pejorative value.

moving-day   *fardagr.* The moving-days were four days in May during which
  householders were allowed to move house. In *Thidrandi's Tale* the
  land-wights (q.v.) prepare to move out of the Icelandic landscape as
  Christianity looms on the horizon (*F*).

Needle   *Nál.* A troll-woman (q.v.) (*H*).

Nicholas Athemas   Early heretic (*M*).

Nipper   *Kneif.* A slave-woman, one of Bard's shipmates (*B*).

nones   3.00 p.m., the fifth canonical hour of prayer (*M*).

Nudus   Saracen prince; Princess Diana's suitor (*H*).

Ocean Gulfs   *Hafsbotnar.* The Misty Ocean (q.v.) (*B*).

Ocean of Mist   *Dumbshaf.* In effect, the Arctic Ocean. *B* describes it as a
  series of 'gulfs' indenting Slabland (q.v.).

Odd of Breidafjord   *Oddr Breiðfirðingr.* An original settler (q.v.), poet,
  and friend of the Hjaltasons, who help him in a lawsuit at which the
  Hjaltasons are compared to the gods (q.v.) in a verse. *B*'s account
  comes from the *Book of Settlements.* He may be identical to Odd the
  Showy (*Skraut-Oddr*), son of King Hlodvir of Gotaland. According to
  Halfdan Eysteinsson's Saga this Odd failed to recover the gold which
  Raknar's brother Val stole from Bard's kinsman Svadi the Giant (q.v.).
  Odd's son Gold-Thorir recovers it in *Gold-Thorir's Saga (Gull-Þóris saga).*

Odd of Tongue   Bard's son-in-law; a farmer, son of Onund Broad-Beard, to whom Bard gives his daughter Thordis. Odd appears in several other sagas (notably *Hen-Thorir's Saga*), but is seldom portrayed as sympathetically as in *B*. *B*'s genealogical information is from the *Book of Settlements*.

Odin   The most important and wisest of the Norse gods (q.v.), Odin is an ambiguous character whose main interests are poetry, occult knowledge, and violent death. He often appears in human form to saga characters ('Red-Moustache' in *B*), and is typically a one-eyed, cloaked wanderer holding a spear. He is particularly associated with ravens and wolves, and his chosen warriors and valkyries (q.v.) sometimes assume these forms. See also 'Thor' (*B*).

ogre   *þurs*. A large troll or giant (qq.v.), usually hostile to humans and strong but stupid. *B*'s ogres are troll-like, inveterate enemies of Bard's kin.

Olaf Haraldsson   Also known as Olaf the Fat and, later, St. Olaf. Missionary king of Norway (1014-1030) who is said to have taken up where Olaf Tryggvason left off and established Christianity in Norway. Several Icelandic sagas were written about him between the twelfth and fourteenth centuries (*B*).

Olaf Tryggvason   Missionary king of Norway (995-1000) (see pp. 59–60) (*F, B*).

Olvir   Hjalmther's sworn brother; Earl Herraud's son (*H*).

Onund Broad-Beard   *Önundr breiðskeggr*. Father of Odd of Tongue (*B*).

original settlers   *landnámsmenn*, 'land-taking people'. Individuals who first claimed land in Iceland during the settlement period (*c.*870-950), moving from Norway and the British Isles, as recorded in the Book of Settlements.

Orm Forest-Nose   *Ormr skógarnefr*. Brother of Gunnar of Hlidarend, the hero of the first part of *The Burning of Njal*. Orm comes into several sagas of Norwegian kings, and (according to one of them) fell on the Long Serpent with Olaf Tryggvason (qq.v.). *B* has him wrestle at Eirik's farm.

Orm Storolfsson   Hæng Thorkelsson's grandson; later Thorkel Bound-Leg's son-in-law. An Icelander whose feats and monster-slayings are told in *Orm Storolfsson's Saga*; allegedly 'the strongest man ever to have lived in Iceland, of those who were not shape-shifters' (q.v.) (*B*).

Orm the Strong   *Ormr sterki*. See 'Orm Storolfsson'.

Placidus   Earl of Rome (*Romania*) and chief of the Roman knights (M).

Prickles   *Skrukka* (literally, 'sea-urchin-like', a common nickname for a rough-skinned crone). Kolbjorn's trollish mother (*B*).

prime hour   6.00 a.m., the second canonical hour of prayer (*M*).

prime-signing   A ritual preliminary to baptism, in which the person is marked on the forehead with the sign of the cross (*B*).

Ptolemy   *Tolomeus*. Hring's father, killed by his wife Luda (*H*).

Raknar   A murderous but long-dead heathen king of Slabland (q.v.), now a *draugr* (q.v.). According to *Halfdan Eysteinsson's Saga* Raknar began his career as a viking and land-cleanser (q.v.), clearing the Slabland wilderness of *jötnar* (giants, q.v.). This would make him a hereditary foe of Bard's kin (see also 'Svadi the Giant'). *Halfdan Eysteinsson's Saga* describes Raknar's burying himself alive in a grave-mound (q.v.) and says he turned troll (q.v.) on his treasure (*B*).

Redcloak   *Rauðfeldr*. (1) Redcloak the Strong, son of Svadi the Giant (q.v.) and second husband of Mjoll; father of Thorkel Bound-Leg (*B*).

   (2) Son of Thorkel Bound-Leg, named after the latter's father (*B*).

Red-Moustache   *Rauðgrani*. A somewhat Thor-like name assumed by Odin (q.v.) in *B*.

Roger   *Rogerus*. One of Mirmann's two trusted retainers (*M*).

Rognvald of More   *Rögnvaldr Mærajarl*. Legendary founder of the earldom of Orkney (*F*).

Roland   Charlemagne's (q.v.) most celebrated retainer and a model of chivalry; hero of the Old French *Song of Roland* (*M*).

Rome   The term used in *M*, chapter 17, is *Romania*, but the area thus referred to is the northern half of Italy, not merely the city of Rome (*Romaborg*).

sacred bull   In *H*, not a potent religious symbol, just a horrible man-eating bull.

Glossary of Characters and Terms

Saxony   *Saxland*. In sagas, the northern half of Germany (*M*).

Sea-Giant   *Margerdur* (*Gerðr* is a giantess-name). A troll-woman (q.v.) (*H*).

Serkland   'Saracen-land', an umbrella term for countries believed by the
saga-authors to have been Muslim (*H*).

settlers   See 'original settlers'.

shape-leaper   *hamhleypa*. A sorcerer who can transform him/herself into the
form of another animal while him/herself lying in a trance. *H* supplies
five examples without actually using the term: Hunding becomes a
walrus, Hord a whale, Hervor a dolphin, and Alfsol and Hildisif vultures. In *B* Hood is said to have been a shape-leaper, but we never see
her at it.

shape-shifter   *hamrammr* (adj.). This term tends to be used of particularly
fierce berserks (q.v.), whose forms alter when in their frenzy. It tends to
imply an access of preternatural strength, especially as evening comes
on, not unlike turning troll (q.v.). It is often blended in the sagas with
shape-leaping (q.v.), particularly into wolf or bear form (*B*).

shield-maiden   *skjáldmær*. A female warrior, like Hlegunn; related to
valkyries (q.v.) and Amazons (*S*).

shieling   A small farm hut built near pasture-land. In Iceland, these out-
posts were (and are) often in relatively wild places. In sagas they provide the scene for encounters with outlaws or the otherworld (*B*).

Sigmund   Friend and shipmate of Bard; married to Hildigunn and father
of Einar; they live with Bard at Pool Edge. Information about Sigmund
and his family is drawn from the *Book of Settlements*, where he (not
Bard) is the original settler (q.v.) of Snowfell's Ness (*B*).

Sigurd the Dragon-slayer   *Sigurðr Fáfnisbani* ('Sigurd, Fafnir's Bane'). The
peerless Volsung hero of several mediaeval German, Norwegian and
Icelandic poems and sagas. A model of heroic courage in the North (*F*).

Simon the Evil   *Simon hinn illi*. The sorcerer Simon Magus. The saga anecdote bears no resemblance to the Biblical account (Acts VIII.9-13), but
stems ultimately from later Latin elaborations of the story (e.g. *The
Passion of Peter and Paul* attributed to Marcellus). Simon later came to
be seen as an originator of the Gnostic heresy (*M*).

Skeggi of Midfjord   *Miðfjarðar-Skeggi*. An important Icelandic chieftain who plays a major role in several Icelandic sagas. He commonly plays the role of the wise adviser, having some occult knowledge – he owned an enchanted sword which he plundered during his viking days from the grave-mound (q.v.) of the legendary Danish king Hrolf Kraki (*B*).

skills, Dagfinn's   Poets in the sagas sometimes have access to supernatural powers. In *S*, Oddi/Dagfinn also benefits from the dreamer's insight into what is happening: he is the 'author' of his own dream.

Skin-Breeches   *Skinnbrók*. A slave-woman, one of Bard's shipmates (*B*).

Skinhood   *Skinnhúfa*. (1) A troll-like creature into which Luda transforms Princess Hildisif, forcing her to live with Luda's ogre-ish brother. Skinhood helps the heroes kill him, and gives Olvir a sword. Once out of her spell (q.v.), she is free to transform herself into a vulture to help kill Hunding (*H*).

(2) Alternative name for the troll-woman (q.v.) Cow of Turf River (*B*).

skin-throwing game   *B*'s explanation of how a 'four-corner' game is played is the most detailed description in the early sources. The game is usually played by giants, and often has otherworldly (or downright hellish) connotations.

Skjold   Bard's unhappily-married shipmate (*B*).

Slabland   *Helluland*. An uninhabited, stony, glaciated land in the North Atlantic, traditionally taken to be Baffin Island or north-east Labrador from descriptions in the *Vínland* sagas. In *B*, this land also extends north of 'Greenland' – in other words, it included northern Greenland as we know it.

Slodinn   Raknar's legendary ship, manned by two hundred men (*B*).

Snout   Trana. A troll-woman (q.v.) (*H*).

Snow the Old   *Snær hinn gamli*. His name suggests he is a giant, but his daughter is the apparently human Mjoll. In the chronicle *How Norway was Settled* (*Hversu Noregr byggðist*) Snow is said to be the son of Glacier (*Jökull*) (*B*).

Snuffler   *Snati*. A dog which Bag gives to Gest Bardarson. B preserves the oldest example of this dog-name, which appears widely in later folklore.

Solrun   Daughter of one Bard in Greenland, held captive by Kolbjorn (B).

Solvi   Thorkel Bound-Leg's son (B).

spell   Ancient swords often come with spells attached, a convention sent up by Wolf-Ember. The spell-and-counter-spell pattern (Hjalmther and Luda) is commonly attested in Icelandic and Irish folklore: the woman causes the man to pine after an unknown princess, and the man condemns the woman to stand on some overhanging piece of rock or building until he comes back, at which point she falls off. The man's utterance acquires supernatural potency at this point, even though he is not otherwise magically gifted (H).

Starkad the Old   *Starkaðr Stórvirksson hinn gamli.* An ill-starred legendary Norse hero, of mixed giant and human stock. He was blessed by his foster-father Odin with unusual longevity, strength and wisdom, but cursed by Thor so that he remains a restless, hated wanderer. His story is told in *Gautrek's Saga* and Saxo Grammaticus's *History of the Danes,* as well as a post-mediaeval *Starkad's Saga* (F).

Star-Oddi   *Stjörnu-Oddi.* A twelfth-century Icelandic scholar and farm worker (S).

Sturlusons   A very powerful group of thirteenth-century Icelandic chieftains, one of whom (Snorri) also wrote and/or collected sagas (F).

Surt of Hellisfitjar   A giant (q.v.) at Bag's feast in B. His name is that of a giant in Norse myth, destined to defeat the gods and bring the world to a fiery end. In *The Saga of the Cave-Dwellers,* Surt is an otherworldly emigrant like Bard, and acts as a guardian-wight (q.v.).

Svadi the Giant   *Svaði jötunn.* Father of Redcloak the Strong; grandfather of Bard's half-brother Thorkel Bound-Leg. According to *Halfdan Eysteinsson's Saga,* Svadi was the son of the god Thor (q.v.) and lived in a mountain north of the Misty Ocean. His gold was stolen by Raknar's (q.v.) brother Val: as told in *Gold-Thorir's Saga* this gold was eventually recovered by Thorir, the Icelandic son of Odd the Showy (q.v.) (B).

Temple Head   *Hofshöfði.* Fictitious headland in Gotaland; real headland in northern Iceland (see pp.49-50) (S).

Thidrandi Sidu-Hallsson   Hall's eldest and favourite son (F).

Thor   Traditionally the strongest of the Norse gods, Thor was particularly celebrated for battling against giants (q.v.) and for the 'fishing
expedition' in which he almost caught the Serpent of Middle Earth
(*Miðgarðsormr*, which encircles the earth), as told in Snorri Sturluson's
Prose Edda. In the sagas Thor often appears in connection with the sea
and stormy weather. As a result of anti-pagan sentiment in the sagas,
Thor and Odin (q.v.) often seem to perform a similar, roughly demonic,
function: thus their distinctive attributes become blended, as in *B* (see
'Frigg', 'Grim' and 'Red-Moustache').

Thoralf Skolmsson   Also known as Thoralf the Strong. A kinsman of Orm
Storolfsson, against whom he engages in trials of strength in *Orm
Storolfsson's Saga* (*B*).

Thorbjorn of Tongue   Son of Grenjud; rich farmer and second husband
of Thordis Skeggjadottir after she has given birth to Gest Bardarson;
father (by her) of Thord and Thorvald. His farm is not the same as
Odd of Tongue's (*B*).

Thorbjorn Oxen-might   *Þorbjörn Arnórsson öxnamegin*. Overbearing farmer
who kills Atli, Grettir Asmundarson's brother, while the latter is
abroad, as told in *Grettir's Saga*. His function in *B* is identical to that of
Audun Shaft (q.v.).

Thorbjornssons   Thord and Thorvald Thorbjornsson, characters possibly invented by the author of *B* and given the same names as the
Hjaltasons (q.v.).

Thord Bellower   *Þórðr Óláfsson gellir*. An important chieftain, who comes into
many sagas. His function in *B* is identical to that of Audun Shaft (q.v.).

Thordis Bardardottir   Bard's second daughter; married to Odd of Tongue
(*B*).

Thordis Skeggjadottir   Skeggi's youngest daughter, seduced by Bard at
twelve (not an unusually young age for childbearing) (*B*).

Thord Thorbjornsson   Thorbjorn of Tongue's eldest son by Thordis
Skeggjadottir, and half-brother to Gest Bardarson; later, husband of
Solrun (*B*).

Thorgils Boomer/the Wise   *Þorgils gjallandi / spaki*. A powerful farmer who
comes into several sagas, included in *B* for the same purpose as Audun
Shaft (q.v.).

Thorhall Prophet *Þórhallr spámaðr*. Second-sighted friend of Hall of Sida (*F*).

Thorir Knarrason One of Bard's shipmates, who looked after Bard's farm at Oxnakelda and killed Cow of Torf River (*B*).

Thorir of Thorisdal An benevolent ogre (q.v.) or half-troll who ruled over an enchanted, fertile valley in Geitland Glacier. Grettir (q.v.) lived with him for a time. Thorir competed at the wrestling matches at Eirik's farm (*B*).

Thorkel the Thin *Þorkell hinn þunni*. Dead retainer of Harald Wartooth; a *draugr* (q.v.) (*F*).

Thorkel Bound-Leg *Þorkell bundinfóti*. Bard's half-brother, son of Redcloak the Strong and Mist; settled first on Snowfell's Ness, then in the south (*B*).

Thorkel Skin-Beak *Þorkell skinnnefja*. Kinsman and friend of Bard. All the other manuscripts give his nickname as *skinnvefja* ('Skin-Swathed'), which makes more sense of the anecdote attached to it; but our first manuscript, AM 158 fol., consistently gives *skinnnefja*, so this form has been used throughout the translation. *Skinnefja* is a troll-name (q.v.): Thorkel's arctic origins do not rule out such a connection.

Thorstein Shiver *Þorsteinn Þorkelsson skelkr*. Icelandic retainer of Olaf Tryggvason (*F*).

Thorvald Thorbjornsson Thorbjorn of Tongue's second son by Thordis Skeggjadottir, and half-brother to Gest Bardarson (*B*).

Toki A viking (q.v.), Koll's brother (*H*).

tongue *tunga*. The (often tongue-shaped) area of land between two converging rivers. One river with several tributaries produces a series of tongues, as in the place-name Tongues of Hvamm River (*B*).

troll, troll-woman A person on the borderline between humanity and monstrosity. Trolls are unnaturally strong and often larger or more thick-set than humans. They are normally hostile to human society and are often credited with supernatural powers: the term 'troll' is often used more loosely of a vicious human skilled in sorcery or shape-changing, or of a *draugr* (qq.v.). In *B* trolls, like ogres (q.v.), are a race distinct from (and more monstrous than) giants (q.v.) and humans. Trolls in the sagas eat horsemeat (forbidden to Christians) and human flesh, and tend to live in northern wildernesses: their names often reflect these harsh natural conditions and landscapes. In the sagas, any human who disappears from society into the wilderness risks 'turning troll' and becoming a menace to society. Later narratives often portray trolls in human disguise, like the beautiful, cannibalistic Luda in *H* (*S*, *H*, *B*).

Trouble   *Raun*. A troll-woman (q.v.) (*H*).

Tub   *Ámr*. An ogre, friend of Kolbjorn (*B*).

Valerina   Sicily's chief city: possibly translates 'Palermo', but not on the coast (*M*).

valkyrie   'Chooser of the slain'. A Northern female otherworldly being who attended battles, sometimes flying above them, to select slain warriors to join Odin (q.v.) in Valhall and train for the apocalyptic final battle at Ragnarok ('the doom/twilight of the gods').

Viglund   Hero of the romantic *Viglund's Saga* who composed elegiac love poems about Ketilrid, a kinswoman of Ingjald of the Hill in *B*. The author of *Viglund's Saga* makes a direct link with *B* in chapter 12, in a fishing episode off Snowfell's Ness (see 'Ingjald').

viking   Earlier usage: a Norse pirate. Later usage (especially ecclesiastical): any robber or outlaw, e.g. the Devil (*S*, *H*, *M*).

Warbattle   *Hergunnur*. A troll-woman (q.v.) (*H*).

Whale   *Skeljungr* (refers to a specific but unknown variety of whale – the same kind which Hord becomes in chapter 11 of *H*). A herdsman and shape-shifter (q.v.) whom Lagalf fights. The killing of Whale is the subject of the seventeenth-century *Saga of Grim Whale-Killer* (*Gríms saga Skeljungsbana*), which seems to be related to *B*.

wight   *vættr* ('being', 'creature'). In sagas the term implies (heathen) otherwordly power and can be translated as 'spirit' – though not usually disembodied. Evil wights (*óvættir* or 'un-wights') tend to be trolls or ogres (qq.v.); other kinds of wight include gods and guardian-wights (qq.v.) (*B*).

William   *Wilhialmur*. King of Sicily; Cecilia's father (*M*).

Winter Nights   *Vetrnœtr*. In pagan Iceland, the first two nights of winter (mid-October) were marked by sacrifices to the family's goddesses (q.v.) (*F*).

Wolf-Ember   *Vargeisa*. A *fingálkn* (q.v.) who gives Hjalmther the sword Snarvendil; really Princess Alfsol (q.v.). Once out of her spell she is free to transform herself into a vulture to help kill Hunding (*H*).

Wolfling   *Ylfingr*. Hermann's sword. Also another name for a Volsung (Sigurd the Dragon Slayer's kin) (*M*).

Zaroes and Arphaxat   Two sorcerers of King Xerxes. They are not found in the New Testament, but are well-known from later apocryphal accounts (e.g. *The Acts of Simon and Jude*) and are often linked with Simon Magus (q.v.) (*M*).

Icelandic Place names

Bag's Valley	*Hítardalr* (also means 'valley of the Hot River') (*B*)
Ball Glacier	*Balljökull* (*B*)
Bard's Cave	*Bárðarhellir* (*B*)
Bard's Pool	*Bárðarlaug* (*B*)
Bard's Road	*Bárðargata* (*B*)
Battlewood	*Jöruskógr* (*S*)
Black Fell	*Bláfell* (*B*)
Breeze Shingle	*Svalsmöl* (*B*)
Children's Rivers	*Barnaár* (*B*)
Cliffs of Midfjord Ness	*Miðfjarðarnessbjörg* (*B*)
Deep Lagoon	*Djúpalón* (*B*)
Fjordfell	*Firðafjall* (now *Kirkjufell*, 'Church Fell') (*B*)
Geitland's Glacier	*Geitlandsjökull* (*B*)
Grim's Bank	*Grímsmið* (*B*)
Groa's Cave	*Gróuhellir* (*B*)
Helgahill	*Helguhóll* (also means 'holy hill') (*B*)
Herringsound	*Síldasund* (*S*)
Hound Cave	*Hundahellir* (now *Kattarhellir*, 'Cat Cave') (*B*)
Hreidar's Enclosure	*Hreiðarsgerði* (*B*)
Hrutafjord Valley	*Hrútafjarðardalr* (*B*)
Ingjald's Hill	*Ingjaldshváll* (*B*)
Jora's Cliff	*Jórukleif* (*B*)
Misty Ocean	*Dumbshaf* (*B*)
Mound Rocks	*Þúfubjörg* (*B*)
Nipperness	*Kneifarnes* (*B*)
North Tongue	*Norðtunga* (*B*)
Ocean Gulfs	*Hafsbotnar* (i.e. *Dumbshaf*) (*B*)

Pool Edge	*Laugarbrekka* (*B*)
Rang River Plains	*Rangárvellir* (*B*)
Redcloak's Ravine	*Rauðfeldsgjá* (*B*)
Rocky Wastes	*Drangahraun* (though *drang* signifies isolated standing rocks rather than a uniform stony landscape) (*B*)
Shit Bay	*Dritvík* (*B*)
Song Cave	*Sönghellir* (*B*)
Skin-Breeches' Brook	*Skinnbrókarlækr* (*B*)
Slabland	*Helluland* (*B*)
Slaves Bay	*Þrælavík* (*B*)
Snowfell	*Snjófell* (now *Snæfell*) (*B*)
Snowfell's Ness	*Snjófellsnes* (now *Snæfellsnes*) (*B*)
Solvi's Cliff	*Sölvahamarr* (*B*)
Temple Head	*Hofshöfði* (*S*)
Tongue	*Tunga* (*B*)
Tongues of Hvamm River	*Hvammsártungur* (*B*)
Trollchurch	*Tröllakirkja* (literally, 'trolls' church') (*B*)

Further Reading

This list is only a starting-point, though it becomes more specialized further down. Items marked with asterisks are particularly recommended for beginners. For further information, see individual entries in *Medieval Scandinavia: An Encyclopedia*, ed. Phillip Pulsiano and Kirsten Wolf (New York, 1993) and *Dictionary of the Middle Ages*, ed. Joseph R. Strayer, 12 vols (New York, 1982-9).

TRANSLATIONS

Many of the sagas mentioned in the Introduction and Glossary have been translated into English. All the (allegedly) mediaeval sagas and tales about 'Viking Age' Icelanders are translated by different scholars (and with differing results) in ★*The Complete Sagas of Icelanders*, ed. Viðar Hreinsson, 5 vols (Reykjavik, 1997). Some are reprinted by Penguin: one very useful collection is in ★*The Sagas of Icelanders*, ed. Örnólfur Thorsson (London, 2000), and the rest are gradually appearing in follow-up volumes, such as Robert Cook's new, revised translation of ★*Njal's Saga* (London, 2001). The old Penguin Classics saga translations by Magnus Magnusson, Hermann Pálsson and Paul Edwards are generally less literal but more engaging, and are to be found in most secondhand bookshops: see especially ★*Njal's Saga* (1960), ★*Laxdaela Saga* (1969) and ★*The Vinland Sagas* (1965). Most of these, with several new translations, have been collected in Magnus Magnusson's two-volume set for the Folio Society, ★*The Icelandic Sagas* (1999, 2002), also strongly recommended. Other sagas mentioned in this book include:

★*The Book of Settlements: Landnámabók*, trans. Hermann Pálsson and Paul
Edwards (Winnipeg, 1972)
Göngu-Hrolf's Saga, trans. Hermann Pálsson and Paul Edwards (Edinburgh,
1980)
★*Grettir's Saga,* trans. Denton Fox and Hermann Pálsson (Toronto, 1974)
Hrolf Gautreksson: A Viking Romance, trans. Hermann Pálsson and Paul
Edwards (Edinburgh, 1972)
★*Icelandic Folktales and Legends*, trans. Jacqueline Simpson, new ed. (Stroud,
2004)
Icelandic Legends, trans. George E.J. Powell and Eiríkur Magnússon (London,
1864; reprinted Felinfach, 1995) [includes *The Saga of Grim Whale-Killer*]
The Poetic Edda, trans. Carolyne Larrington, World's Classics (Oxford, 1996)
★*The Saga of King Hrolf Kraki*, trans. Jesse L. Byock, Penguin Classics (London,
1998)
★*The Saga of the Volsungs: The Norse Epic of Sigurd the Dragon Slayer*, trans. Jesse
L. Byock, Penguin Classics (London, 1999)
★*Seven Viking Romances*, trans. Hermann Pálsson and Paul Edwards, Penguin
Classics (London, 1985) [includes *Halfdan Eysteinsson's Saga*]
★*Vikings in Russia: Yngvar's Saga and Eymund's Saga*, trans. Hermann Pálsson
and Paul Edwards (Edinburgh, 1989)

Detailed English resumés of sagas like *William Purse, Saul and Nikanor and
Sigurd the Silent* may be found in *Late Medieval Icelandic Romances* I-V, ed.
Agnete Loth, 5 vols, Editiones Arnamagnæanæ B 20-4 (Copenhagen, 1962-5).

HISTORY AND MYTHOLOGY

★Byock, Jesse L., *Viking Age Iceland* (London, 2001)
Davidson, H.R. Ellis, *Gods and Myths of Northern Europe* (London, 1964)
★Einar Ólafur Sveinsson, *The Folk-Stories of Iceland*, revised by Einar G.
Pétursson, trans. Benedikt Benedikz, ed. Anthony Faulkes (London,
2003)
Gunnar Karlsson, *Iceland's 1100 Years: The History of a Marginal Society* (London,
2000)
★Haywood, John, *The Penguin Historical Atlas of the Vikings* (London, 1995)
Helle, Knut, ed., *The Cambridge History of Scandinavia Volume I: Prehistory to
1520* (Cambridge, 2003)
Jones, Gwyn, *A History of the Vikings*, 2nd ed. (Oxford, 1984)
★Orchard, Andy, *Dictionary of Norse Myth and Legend* (London, 1997)
Orri Vésteinsson, *The Christianization of Iceland: Priests, Power, and Social Change
1000-1300* (Oxford, 2000)
★Sawyer, Peter, ed., *The Oxford Illustrated History of the Vikings* (Oxford, 1997)

Strömbäck, Dag, *The Conversion of Iceland: A Survey*, trans. Peter Foote
    (London, 1975)
Turville-Petre, E.O.G., *Myth and Religion of the North: The Religion of Ancient
    Scandinavia* (New York, 1964)

LITERARY STUDIES

A good (and inexpensive) general introduction to Icelandic literature for the
beginner is Heather O'Donoghue's *Old Norse-Icelandic Literature: A Short
Introduction* (Oxford, 2004). Other useful books are as follows, with asterisks
marking those books which are written in a more generally accessible style
(though not all are still in print):

Clover, Carol J., and John Lindow, ed., *Old Norse-Icelandic Literature: A Critical
    Guide* (Ithaca, New York, 1985)
Clunies Ross, Margaret, ed., *Old Icelandic Literature and Society* (Cambridge,
    2000)
*Driscoll, Matthew James, *The Unwashed Children of Eve: The Production,
    Dissemination and Reception of Popular Literature in Post-Reformation Iceland*
    (London, 1997)
*Hermann Pálsson and Paul Edwards, *Legendary Fiction in Mediaeval Iceland*
    (Reykjavik, 1971)
*Jónas Kristjánsson, *Eddas and Sagas: Iceland's Medieval Literature*, trans. Peter
    Foote (Reykjavik, 1988)
Kalinke, Marianne E., *Bridal-Quest Romance in Medieval Iceland* (Ithaca, New
    York, 1990)
*Kellogg, Robert, 'Introduction', in *The Sagas of Icelanders*, ed. Örnólfur
    Thorsson (London, 2000)
Lindow, John, *et al.*, ed., *Structure and Meaning in Old Norse Literature: New
    Approaches to Textual Analysis and Literary Criticism* (Odense, 1986)
McTurk, Rory, ed., *A Companion to Old Norse-Icelandic Literature and Culture*
    (Oxford: Blackwell, 2005)
Mitchell, Stephen A., *Heroic Sagas and Ballads* (Ithaca, 1991)
*Schlauch, Margaret, *Romance in Iceland* (Princeton, 1934)
Turville-Petre, E.O.G., *Origins of Icelandic Literature* (Oxford, 1953)
Turville-Petre, E.O.G., *Scaldic Poetry* (Oxford, 1976)
*Vésteinn Ólason, *Dialogues with the Viking Age: Narration and Representation in
    the Sagas of the Icelanders*, trans. Andrew Wawn (Reykjavik, 1998)

THE SAGAS IN THIS BOOK

Hardly any literary analysis of these texts has been published in any language. Full-length articles in English are listed here. Each of the two encyclopaedias mentioned at the beginning also contain brief entries on '*Hjálmþés saga ok Ölvis*', '*Flateyjarbók*', '*Óláfs saga Tryggvasonar*', '*Bárðar saga Snæfellsáss*' and '*Mírmanns saga*'. Richard Harris's unpublished edition of *Hjalmther and Olvir* provides useful commentary, as does Þórhallur Vilmundarson's and Bjarni Vilhjálmsson's (Icelandic) edition of *Star-Oddi's Dream and Bard the Snowfell God*.

Allard, Joe, 'Oral to Literary: *Kvöldvaka*, Textual Instability, and All that Jazz', 2004 conference paper, available online at
    http://w210.ub.uni-tuebingen.de/dbt/volltexte/2004/1073/pdf/19_joe~1.pdf
Ármann Jakobsson, 'History of the Trolls? *Bárðar saga* as an Historical Narrative', Saga-Book of the Viking Society 25/1 (1998), 53-71
Jón Skaptason and Phillip Pulsiano, 'Introduction', in their edition of *Bárðar saga*, Garland Library of Medieval Literature A 8 (New York, 1984), xiii-xxix
Lindow, John, '*Þorsteins þáttr skelks* and the Verisimilitude of Supernatural Experience in Saga Literature', in Lindow *et al.*, *Structure and Meaning* (see above), 264-80
O'Connor, Ralph, '"Stepmother Sagas": An Irish Analogue for *Hjálmþés saga ok Ölvérs*', *Scandinavian Studies* 72 (2000), 1-48
Quinn, Judy, '"Ok verðr henni ljóð á munni" – Eddic Prophecy in the *fornaldarsögur*', *Alvíssmál* 8 (1998), 29-50
Rowe, Elizabeth Ashman, 'Cultural Paternity in the Flateyjarbók *Óláfs saga Tryggvasonar*', *Alvíssmál* 8 (1998), 3-28
Schach, Paul, 'The Theme of the Reluctant Christian in the Icelandic Sagas', *Journal of English and Germanic Philology* 81 (1982), 186-203

Notes

INTRODUCTION

1   On the vikings, see Gwyn Jones, *A History of the Vikings*, 2nd ed. (London, 1984); *The Oxford Illustrated History of the Vikings*, ed. Peter Sawyer (Oxford, 1997).

2   Adam of Bremen, History *of the Archbishops of Hamburg-Bremen*, trans. Francis J. Tschan (New York, 1959), p.217 n.. On the settlement and early history of Iceland see Gunnar Karlsson, *Iceland's 1100 Years: The History of a Marginal Society* (London, 2000), pp.7-86.

3   Alternative translations in *Egil's Saga*, trans. Hermann Pálsson and Paul Edwards (London, 1976), p.75; 'Egil's Saga', trans. Bernard Scudder, in *The Sagas of Icelanders: A Selection*, ed. Örnólfur Thorsson (London, 2000), p.48.

4   See Gwyn Jones, *The Norse Atlantic Saga*, 2nd ed. (Oxford, 1986).

5   On Irish sagas see Pádraig Ó Ríain, 'Early Irish Literature' in *The Celtic Connections*, ed. Glanville Price (Gerrard's Cross, 1992), pp.65-80; Tomás Ó Cathasaigh, 'Pagan Survivals: the Evidence of Early Irish Narrative', in Irland und Europa, *Die Kirche im Frühmittelalter: Ireland and Europe, The Early Church*, ed. Proinséas Ní Chatháin and Michael Richter (Stuttgart, 1984), pp.291-307.

6   See Diana Whaley, 'A Useful Past: Historical Writing in Medieval Iceland', in *Old Icelandic Literature and Society*, ed. Margaret Clunies Ross (Cambridge, 2000), pp.161-202.

7   On verse in general, see Kari Ellen Gade, 'Poetry and its Changing Importance in Medieval Icelandic Culture', in *Old Icelandic Literature and Society*, pp.61-95. On skaldic poetry see Roberta Frank, *Old Norse Court Poetry: The Dróttkvætt Stanza* (Ithaca, New York, 1978).

8 Saxo Grammaticus, *The History of the Danes*, ed. Hilda Ellis Davidson
   and trans. Peter Fisher, 2 vols (Woodbridge, 1979), vol. I, p.5. See also
   Preben Meulengracht Sørensen, 'Social Institutions and Belief Systems
   of Medieval Iceland (c.870-1400) and their Relations to Literary
   Production', trans. Margaret Clunies Ross, in her *Old Icelandic Literature
   and Society*, pp.8-29.

9 Loren Auerbach, 'Female Experience and Authorial Intention in Laxdæla
   saga', *Saga-Book of the Viking Society* 25/1 (1998), 30-52.

10 On the literary dimension see R.N. Swanson, *The Twelfth-Century
   Renaissance* (Manchester, 1999), pp.173-82.

11 See, for example, Roberta L. Krueger, 'Introduction', in *The Cambridge
   Companion to Medieval Romance*, ed. Roberta L. Krueger (Cambridge,
   2000), pp.1-9 (pp.1, 2 and 3). This view of romances was also assumed in
   the Introduction to the first edition of the present book.

12 On the problems associated with applying the concept of 'fiction' to
   mediaeval literature see Ralph O'Connor, 'History or Fiction? Truth-
   Claims and Defensive Narrators in Icelandic Romance-Sagas', forthcoming in *Mediaeval Scandinavia*, 15 (2005). On the broad remit of the
   medieval historian see Ruth Morse, *Truth and Convention in the Middle
   Ages: Rhetoric, Representation, and Reality* (Cambridge, 1991).

13 See Eugène Vinaver, *The Rise of Romance*, 2nd ed. (New York, 1984); *The
   Cambridge Companion to Medieval Romance*, ed. Krueger. On the parodic
   romances see Caroline A. Jewers, *Chivalric Fiction and the Rise of the Novel*
   (Gainesville, 2000).

14 See Geraldine Barnes, 'Authors, Dead and Alive, in Old Norse Fiction',
   Parergon 8/2 (1990), 5-22 (pp.7-10).

15 Alternative translation in *Göngu-Hrolf's Saga*, trans. Hermann Pálsson and
   Paul Edwards (Edinburgh, 1980), p.122.

16 See Marianne E. Kalinke, *King Arthur North-by-Northwest: The matière de
   Bretagne in Old Norse-Icelandic Romances* (Copenhagen, 1981), pp.20-45.

17 See Gerd Wolfgang Weber, 'The Decadence of Feudal Myth: Towards a
   Theory of *riddarasaga* and Romance', in *Structure and Meaning in Old
   Norse Literature: New Approaches to Textual Analysis and Literary Criticism*,
   ed. John Lindow et al. (Odense, 1986), pp.415-54.

18 Matthew J. Driscoll, *The Unwashed Children of Eve: The Production,
   Dissemination and Reception of Popular Literature in Post-Reformation Iceland*
   (Enfield Lock, 1997), p.55; Robert Kellogg, 'Introduction', in *The Sagas
   of Icelanders*, ed. Örnólfur Thorsson (London, 2000), pp.xv-liv (pp.xxiv-
   xxv). For an insightful account of the problems of saga-authorship and
   attribution see Patricia Pires Boulhosa, *Icelanders and the Kings of Norway:
   Mediaeval Sagas and Legal Texts* (Leiden, 2005), pp.5-42.

19 For examples see Matthew J. Driscoll, 'The Oral, the Written, and the
   In-Between: Textual Instability in the Post-Reformation *lygisaga*', in
   *Medieval Insular Literature between the Oral and the Written II: Continuity of

Transmission, ed. Hildegard L.C. Tristram (Tübingen, 1997), pp.193-20. On the relation between script and print, see Jürg Glauser, 'The End of the Saga: Text, Tradition and Transmission in Nineteenth- and Early Twentieth-Century Iceland', in *Northern Antiquity: The Post-Medieval Reception of Edda and Saga*, ed. Andrew Wawn (Enfield Lock, 1994), pp.101-41. The concept of 'scribal performance' can also be applied to certain skaldic poems, despite attributions to named authors: see Christopher Abram, 'Scribal Authority in Skaldic Verse: Þorbjörn horn-klofi's *Glymdrápa*', *Arkiv för nordisk filologi* 116 (2001), 5-19.

20 For example, Jane Smiley's *Preface to The Sagas of Icelanders*, ed. Örnólfur Thorsson, pp.ix-xiv; the Forewords to *The Complete Sagas of Icelanders*, ed. Viðar Hreinsson, 5 vols (Reykjavik, 1997), I, vii-xii.

21 The passages in question may be found in *Njal's Saga*, trans. Magnus Magnusson and Hermann Pálsson (London, 1960), pp.173, 341-52; *Njal's Saga*, trans. Robert Cook (London, 2001), p.130, 296-308.

22 Alternative (highly tendentious) translation in *Sturlunga saga*, trans. Julia H. McGrew and R. George Thomas, 2 vols (New York, 1970-4), vol. I, p.242.

23 See G. T. Shepherd, 'The Emancipation of Story in the Twelfth Century', in *Medieval Narrative: A Symposium*, ed. Hans Bekker-Nielsen et al. (Odense, 1979), pp.44-57.

24 *Tales of the Elders of Ireland: A New Translation of Acallam na Senórach*, trans. Ann Dooley and Harry Roe (Oxford, 1999), p.12.

25 See 'The Saga of the Men of Fljotsdal', trans. John Porter, in *The Complete Sagas of Icelanders,* ed. Viðar Hreinsson, IV, 405. On mediaeval saga-entertainment see Hermann Pálsson, *Sagnaskemmtun Íslendinga* (Reykjavik, 1962).

26 Ebenezer Henderson, *Iceland; or the Journal of a Residence in that Island, during the Years 1814 and 1815* (Edinburgh, 1819), p.284; his account is discussed in Driscoll, *Unwashed Children*, pp.38-46.

27 Alternative translation in *Late Medieval Icelandic Romances*, ed. Agnete Loth, 5 vols (Copenhagen, 1962-5), II, 96.

28 Henderson, *Iceland*, pp.283-4.

29 This translation is an altered version of that in Peter Foote's article 'Sagnaskemtan: Reykjahólar 1119', *Saga-Book of the Viking Society* 14 (1953-7), 226-39, amplified and reprinted in his *Aurvandilstá: Norse Studies*, ed. Michael Barnes, Hans Bekker-Nielsen and Gerd Wolfgang Weber (Odense, 1984), pp.65-83 (p.65). For further discussion of this passage see O'Connor, 'History or Fiction?'.

30 See Morse, *Truth and Convention*. For a tendentious but stimulating account of the 'truth' implicit in Icelandic sagas see M. I. Steblin-Kamenskij, *The Saga Mind*, trans. Kenneth Ober (Odense, 1973), pp.21-48.

31 Alternative translation in *Late Medieval Icelandic Romances*, ed. Loth, IV, 3.

32 Alternative translation in *Göngu-Hrolf's Saga*, trans. Hermann Pálsson and Edwards, pp.28, 125.

33 See Barnes, 'Authors, Dead and Alive'; Barnes, 'Romance in Iceland', in *Old Icelandic Literature and Society*, ed. Clunies Ross, pp.266-86.

34 Alternative translation in *Hrolf Gautreksson*, trans. Hermann Pálsson and Paul Edwards (Edinburgh, 1972), pp.148-9.

35 Alternative translation in *Late Medieval Icelandic Romances*, ed. Loth, IV, 200-1.

36 Alternative translation in *Göngu-Hrolf's Saga*, trans. Hermann Pálsson and Edwards, pp.84-5.

37 The tongue-in-cheek function of these narratorial intrusions has been discussed by Barnes, 'Authors, Dead and Alive'; a different view has been put forward by O'Connor, 'History or Fiction?'.

38 Alternative translation in *Late Medieval Icelandic Romances*, ed. Loth, II, 52-3.

39 Stephen A. Mitchell, *Heroic Sagas and Ballads* (Ithaca, 1991); Driscoll, 'The Oral, the Written, and the In-Between', pp.214-20.

40 On Gudrun see Andy Orchard, *Dictionary of Norse Myth and Legend* (London, 1997), pp.64-5.

41 See Jesse L. Byock, *Viking Age Iceland* (London, 2001), pp.156-8.

42 The best introduction to this 'world' is Vésteinn Ólason, *Dialogues with the Viking Age: Narration and Representation in the Sagas of the Icelanders*, trans. Andrew Wawn (Reykjavik, 1998).

43 Vésteinn Ólason, *Dialogues with the Viking Age*, pp.60-1, 228-37.

44 The most convincing articulation of the traditional classification is Mitchell, *Heroic Sagas and Ballads*, pp.8-42. Definitions of each 'genre' can be found in individual entries in *Medieval Scandinavia: An Encyclopedia*, ed. Phillip Pulsiano (New York, 1993). Philip W. Cardew has provided a cogent critique of the traditional system in his *A Translation of Þorskfirðinga (Gull-Þóris) Saga* (Lampeter, 2000), pp.2-70.

45 See Vésteinn Ólason, *Dialogues with the Viking Age*, pp.211-20.

46 On the earliest Icelandic novels and novelistic sagas, see *Íslensk bókmenntasaga III*, ed. Matthías V. Sæmundsson et al. (Reykjavik, 1996), pp.144-88.

47 Such shifts are discussed in Alaric Hall, 'Changing Style and Changing Meaning: Icelandic Historiography and the Medieval Redactions of Heiðreks saga', *Scandinavian Studies* 77 (2005), 1-30.

48 The concept of geographically-distinct narrative worlds has been analysed (albeit as a generic marker) by Torfi Tulinius: see 'The Matter of the North: Fiction and Uncertain Identities in Thirteenth-Century Iceland', in *Old Icelandic Literature and Society*, pp.242-65 (pp.250-2).

49 Alternative translation in Vikings in Russia: Yngvar's Saga and Eymund's Saga, trans. Hermann Pálsson and Paul Edwards (Edinburgh, 1989), p.63.

50 Alternative translation in *Late Medieval Icelandic Romances*, ed. Loth, IV, 120.

51 *Harðar saga*, ed. Þórhallur Vilmundarson and Bjarni Vilhjálmsson, *Íslenzk fornrit* 13 (Reykjavik, 1991), ccxii-ccxxv.

52 *Harðar saga*, ed. Þórhallur Vilmundarson and Bjarni Vilhjálmsson, pp.ccxiv-ccxxii.

53 Alternative translation in *Late Medieval Icelandic Romances*, ed. Loth, V, 36; see Barnes, 'Romance in Iceland', p.272.

54 On mediaeval dream-theory see Steven F. Kruger, *Dreaming in the Middle Ages* (Cambridge, 1992).

55 On the text's transmission see Richard Harris, 'Hjálmþérs saga: A Scientific Edition', PhD diss., University of Iowa (1970), pp.v–xciv.

56 See Marianne E. Kalinke, *Bridal-Quest Romance in Medieval Iceland* (Ithaca, 1990), p.19, criticizing Jürg Glauser's procedure in *Isländische Märchensagas: Studien zur Prosaliteratur im spätmittelalterlichen Island* (Basel, 1983).

57 On the Luda subplot see Ralph O'Connor, '"Stepmother Sagas": An Irish Analogue for *Hjálmþérs saga ok Ölvérs*', *Scandinavian Studies* 72 (2000), 1–48.

58 Harris, 'Hjálmþérs saga', pp.v–ix; Harris, 'Hjálmþés saga', in *Medieval Scandinavia*, ed. Pulsiano, pp.285–6.

59 On this codex see Elizabeth Ashman Rowe, *The Development of Flateyjarbók: Iceland and the Norwegian Dynastic Crisis of 1389* (Odense, 2005).

60 See Elizabeth Ashman Rowe, 'Cultural Paternity in the Flateyjarbók Óláfs saga Tryggvasonar', *Alvíssmál* 8 (1998), 3–28 (pp.10–13).

61 For this theme in *Beowulf*, see above all J. R. R. Tolkien, 'Beowulf: The Monsters and the Critics', *Proceedings of the British Academy* 22 (1936), 245–95, reprinted in *An Anthology of Beowulf Criticism*, ed. Lewis E. Nicholson (Notre Dame, Indiana, 1963), pp.51–103; for The Burning of Njal, see Lars Lönnroth, *Njáls saga: A Critical Introduction* (Berkeley, California, 1976). I am developing this theme in a forthcoming book on the Irish saga *Togail Bruidne Da Derga*.

62 Dag Strömbäck, 'Tidrande och diserna', reprinted in his *Folklore och Filologi* (Uppsala, 1970), pp.166–91.

63 This view is discussed by Strömbäck, 'Tidrande', pp.171–3.

64 See Ármann Jakobson, 'History of the Trolls? Bárðar saga as an Historical Narrative', *Saga-Book of the Viking Society* 25/1 (1998), 53–71.

65 See *Seven Viking Romances*, trans. Hermann Pálsson and Paul Edwards (London, 1985), p.196.

66 *Harðar saga*, ed. Þórhallur Vilmundarson and Bjarni Vilhjálmsson, pp.lxxix–xcviii.

67 Robert Kellogg, review of *Harðar saga*, *Journal of English and Germanic Philology* 95 (1996), 583.

68 On the manuscripts see *Mírmanns saga*, ed. Desmond Slay (Copenhagen, 1997), xiii–clxvii.

69 O'Connor, 'Stepmother Sagas'.

NOTE ON THE TRANSLATIONS

1 An alternative term is 'cratylic' (after Plato's *Cratylos*): see Anne Barton, *The Names of Comedy* (Oxford, 1990).

STAR-ODDI'S DREAM

1 'Hawk-seat hangings' = bracelets, hanging off the arm (the hawk's seat).

2 'Brine-garth' = sea; 'breeze-steed' = ship.

3 'Wave-steeds' = ships.

4 'Hardeners of Gondul' = warriors (Gondul is a valkyrie*-name); 'sword-trees' = men (holding swords).

5 'Shield-maidens' shimmer' = battle (the glint of valkyries' swords); 'helmsman' = ruler, king.

6 'Ocean-horses' = ships.

7 'Storms of Hogni's sunset' = battle (Hogni is a sea-god, his sunset a shield).

8 'Gondul' = a valkyrie, attendant on battle; 'spear-guardian' = warrior king; 'blood-oar' = sword, spear.

9 'Spear-gape' = jaws full of teeth.

10 'Sea-ski' = ship; 'mare of Gylfi' = ship (Gylfi is a sea-king); 'goddess of Ægir's gleam': woman (Ægir is a sea-god; his gleam is gold; its goddess is woman).

11 'Freya of the wave-star' = woman (the wave's star is gold; its Freya – or goddess – is woman); 'hawk-stem' = shoulders; 'flood-flame's goddess' = woman (the flood's flame is gold); 'sea-beam' = ship.

THE SAGA OF HJAMTHER AND OLVIR

1 'Helmsman' = prince, ruler; 'dwarves'-work' = sword.

2 'Corpse-candle' = sword; 'snake-fleeced wound-flame' = sword in scabbard.

3 'Boar' = warrior.

4 The house was made of the ships' timbers (see Luda's spell on p.138).

5 'Gold-giver' = king.

6 'In a carrion-shroud' = dead.

Notes

EXTRACT FROM THE BOOK OF FLATEY

1 Earl of Orkney.
2 The next tale in the *Book of Flatey* recounts Iceland's (and Hall's) conversion.

THE SAGA OF BARD THE SNOWFELL GOD

1 'Jewel-scarcener' = lord, dispenser of treasure; 'him who clasped treasure' = lord. See p.68.
2 After 'in', we leave AM 158 fol. and take up AM 162h fol..
3 After 'door', we leave AM 162h fol. and take up AM 489 4to.
4 After 'Thorvald', we leave AM 489 4to and resume AM 158 fol. for the rest of the saga.
5 'Men of iron' = warriors; 'skull-prows' = helmets; 'fishes of the sward' = snakes (decorating the helmets); 'Thorskafjord' literally means 'codfish fjord'.

MIRMANN'S SAGA

1 The dots represent illegible letters (or words) which have still not been deciphered.
2 The chief manuscript, Sth. Perg. 4:o nr 6, ends at 'under': here we take up AM 181g fol. for a few lines.
3 After 'ground' we leave AM 181g fol. and take up AM 179 fol.. None of the chapter titles from this point on are original.
4 AM 179 fol. ends at 'thought'. The rest of the saga is taken from JS 634, 4to.